M

Book Two of Millennial Mage
By J.L.Mullins

Copyright © 2023 by J.L.Mullins

All rights reserved.

No part of this publication may be reproduced, distributed, or transmitted in any form or by any means, including photocopying, recording, or other electronic or mechanical methods, without the prior written permission of the author, except as permitted by U.S. copyright law.

The story, all names, characters, and incidents portrayed in this production are fictitious. No identification with actual persons (living or deceased), places, buildings, and products is intended or should be inferred.

Contents

Chapter: 1 - To the Ending Grove 7
Chapter: 2 - Well… That's New 23
Chapter: 3 - Unexpected Results 35
Chapter: 4 - Food and Inquiry 49
Chapter: 5 - So Much More to Learn 63
Chapter: 6 - Bad Birdy? 77
Chapter: 7 - A Day of Departure 91
Chapter: 8 - Potential Conflict 105
Chapter: 9 - Cyclops and Conversation 119
Chapter: 10 - Back on the Road 133
Chapter: 11 - Settling In 145
Chapter: 12 - Through the Pass, Again 159
Chapter: 13 - Worst Proposal Ever 175
Chapter: 14 - Back to Basics 189
Chapter: 15 - Interruptions and Progress 203
Chapter: 16 - A Talented Teacher 215
Chapter: 17 - Right! The Hammer 229
Chapter: 18 - Undiminished Intensity 241
Chapter: 19 - A Cow a Day? 255
Chapter: 20 - Set on Unconventionality 269
Chapter: 21 - It Should Be Fun 283
Chapter: 22 - A Silly Accusation 297
Chapter: 23 - Crush 313
Chapter: 24 - One Thousand Ounces Gold 327
Chapter: 25 - Smell Like Blood and Death 341

Chapter: 26 - A Foolish Form of Immortality 355
Chapter: 27 - I Might Need to Be Attacked More Often 367
Chapter: 28 - More Dangerous Than We Realize 381
Chapter: 29 - Not Nice.. 395
Chapter: 30 - Understatement....................................... 411
Author's Note 427

Chapter: 1
To the Ending Grove

Tala was, by every metric that mattered, a Mage.

Sure, she still lacked some basic knowledge that she would have gained as a mageling, under a master, but she was getting by just fine.

Just fifteen days out from the academy, and she'd reached a level of recognition that would likely take her classmates years to achieve.

She had operated as a Dimensional Mage for the most recent caravan from Bandfast to Alefast, earning quite a bit of gold.

The other Mages she interacted with recognized her prowess and authority.

She had magic inscriptions that left her nearly invulnerable to most threats. *I'll even get the remainder of my inscriptions as soon as I get back to Bandfast.*

And now, she had her own magical items to explore and exploit.

Inside her newly acquired dimensional storage, Tala reached out and placed her right hand back on one wall and pushed power out, directing it straight from her gate into the surface, just as she had with the first cargo wagon she'd tried to empower.

The wall greedily drank in the magic, and there didn't seem to be any resistance due to her lack of a mental construct to shape the power.

Even more interesting. As she continued to feed the wall magic, she watched the hole overhead shift slightly to rest beside one wall and gray ladder rungs sprout from the wall, along with shelving around the opening itself.

"Now, this is amazing." The changes she'd described were complete, so she cut the flow of power and pulled her hand away. As she did so, she felt a staggering, whole-body exhaustion set in. She felt nearly as bad as she had after creating her first Archon Star. *What was that?*

As she thought back, she realized that the lack of resistance had caused her to dramatically underestimate the amount of power she was funneling into the artifact. Instead of just taking power directly from her gate, she'd been pulling from the reserves around her keystone. She was used to draining water from a spout, and this had been like removing the top of the barrel and overturning it.

She groaned. "No fair. I'm trying to work with you, and you drain me?"

There wasn't a response, per se, but the feeling of expectant waiting diminished to almost nothing.

"That's not an apology, but I'll take it." *Tala, you're talking to your pouch...* She groaned, again, and pulled herself up the ladder and out of the hole. With stiff movements, she placed all her carefully arranged piles onto the shelves surrounding the hole and drew the pouch closed, satisfied. She absently patted the side of the bag. "Not too bad." *Not helping. Sanity check, Tala.*

She moved through some brief stretching to relieve the soreness, but she knew that her physical ache was just a manifestation of deep magical exhaustion.

She eyed the two items that she'd left out, aside from her clothing for tomorrow.

The vial containing her blood Archon Star and the artifact knife.

Tala, you're tired. Don't do anything foolish. She picked up the vial and opened the top, looking in on the drop of blood.

She held the knife in her other hand and looked back and forth between the two. *What's the worst that could happen?*

Tala tipped the vial over, dripping the blood onto the pommel of the knife and directly into the small void in its magic.

As she'd hoped, the magic of the knife accepted the Archon Star with ease; the blood vanished as if she were confirming a contract.

She watched in fascination with her magesight as the artifact's magic subtly shifted to incorporate her Archon Star. Physically, the knife darkened in color until the steel was almost black-gray. In the handle, more of the flecks took on a red tint, and those that were already red brightened in color.

Just as with the Archon Star itself, Tala was now aware of exactly where the knife was and its current condition: perfectly fine.

Then, she was struck with a hammer of weariness. She would have said it was soul deep, and that was more accurate than she'd like to admit, even to herself.

She dropped the knife and crawled lethargically to her bed before collapsing into blissful sleep.

* * *

Tala groaned into wakefulness, the room positively glowing around her.

She immediately felt her knife nearby and fumbled around on the bed, trying to find where she'd dropped it. Her hand met the hilt. *There you are.*

Lying there in her comfortable bed, she felt a flickering wave of tiredness threaten to pull her back into slumber, but she resisted. *Nope! Time to get up, Tala.*

She pushed herself upright, looking around the brightly lit room.

The artifact lights were still glowing, but their illumination was pale compared to the outside wall of her room, which positively radiated luminescence under the dawn's light.

East-facing room, indeed. She glanced down at the knife and quirked a smile, setting it on her bedside table. It was good to have a weapon, ready to hand. *If I'd had that under the wagon, I'd not have needed the soldier's sword.*

She hesitated at that. *I had my camp knife. I did need a sword.* Still, she *felt* like her new knife would have fit the bill, somehow. *Strange.*

She stood and arched backward, first working out the kinks of a night spent in an unnatural position. After that, she moved through her morning stretches, looking within herself to verify that each was targeting the correct muscle groups. That done, she moved through her exercises, deciding to add a couple at the end when she noticed several sectors of muscle that weren't worked well enough.

That done, she turned towards the bath but hesitated. After a brief pause, she picked up her belt pouch and her sheathed knife, taking them with her into the bathroom.

After a quick bath—she was running later than usual, after all—she refreshed her salve, guided by the magic detector. Both the salve and detector she pulled from the pouch, and both were returned.

Finally dry and ready, she let out a long sigh. *Last time I have to put these on.* She pulled out her blood-stained clothing and pulled them on.

They weren't precisely filthy, but they were far from clean. *The seamstress should have something better this afternoon.* She needed to move quickly if she was going to get to eat breakfast, swing by the blacksmith, *and* get to the ending grove that Trent had marked for her before noon. *That's what I get for sleeping late, I suppose.*

Dressed, with her knife and pouch at her belt, she surveyed the room. There was nothing of hers remaining. *I'll be back.* Still, it didn't feel like her room, not permanently. *That's good; it isn't.*

She left, heading back to the dining hall, where she was able to grab a quick, hearty, and portable breakfast, foregoing the huge spread in favor of a less awesome but more 'grab-and-go' meal. They would only let her have two cups of coffee, so she guzzled those before departing.

Cloth sack of food safely tucked in her pouch, she strode from the inn and towards the blacksmith.

It was a bright morning, and even after her routine tasks, it was still somewhat early. There were citizens walking about, but not nearly as many as there would be soon enough. She pulled one piece of her breakfast out after another, eating them with gusto to sate her all-too-familiar hunger.

I really need to get better about monitoring my expenditure of power... Using magic didn't directly affect her hunger, but the mental and physical strain of such definitely contributed to her appetite.

The blacksmith was waiting for her when she arrived, and she paid him the additional silver for prompt delivery of her tools.

The pliers easily vanished into the bag, but she had a bit of a comical time maneuvering the fruit picker, on its 10-foot pole, into her pouch. She ended up having to angle it quite extremely to allow it to fit well enough for her to draw the bag closed.

"Thank you, Pedrin." The poor man had watched with obviously subdued mirth at her struggles.

"Our pleasure, Mistress. I hope that you return to us again, for any of your smithing needs."

"I believe I just might. Good day."

"Good day, Mistress."

Without further delay, she strode towards the easternmost gate, as that was the one closest to the grove she sought. The streets were beginning to get busy, and the sky overhead was becoming a true, pale sky-blue as day took firm hold at last.

She grinned to herself, licking the last of her breakfast from her fingers. *Today will be a good day.*

There was a short line to exit the gate, and she waited patiently… for the most part.

It took the better part of a quarter-hour to reach the front of the line.

"Name, reason for departing, and time of expected return?"

"Mage Tala, on a personal errand, and late afternoon."

The guard frowned. "I don't see you on any jobs list for outside the city."

"As I said, I've a personal errand."

The guard's frown deepened. "But… you're not on the lists."

Tala took a deep breath in through her nose before puffing it out in a quick, calming exhale. "Guardsman, are you meaning to imprison me within this city?"

The man blinked. "What? No! Mistress, I would never—"

"Then, note that I have departed, on a personal errand, and will return well before nightfall."

"We can't send anyone out after you if you don't return."

She gave him a flat look. "I didn't ask you to."

He looked more than a little uncomfortable. Thankfully, a man who seemed to be his commanding officer stepped forward. He must have heard the end of the discussion because he bowed to Tala. "Mistress, my apologies. You are, of course, free to leave the city. Thank you for registering your departure with us. We will notify the"—he glanced at the slate the other guard held—"Caravan Guild of your journey, and we will relay any communications from them upon your return, after lunch."

Tala blinked at him. *The Caravan Guild... **Rust**!* "Oh! My... I completely forgot that I didn't pack a lunch. I'll be back, shortly. When I return, do I need to check in with you, or can I simply walk out?"

"You may depart at your leisure."

"Thank you, and thank you for your timely reminder! I'd hate to have gone hungry."

She turned and strode away, as fast as she was able while maintaining a modicum of dignity. It took her another half-hour to reach the workyard near the city's northern gate, where she found twenty cargo-slots awaiting her empowerment.

The foreman appeared to check a watch as she arrived, but he seemed satisfied by what he saw because he smiled and waved. "Mistress! Are these set up to your satisfaction?"

She gave them a quick glance before nodding. "They are indeed. Thank you."

She quickly moved through the now-familiar mental and magical motions of empowering the cargo-slots, though the doubling of their number left her feeling a bit spent by the end. *I could have gone slower, and that would have been easier.* But she needed to go.

She verified that the foreman didn't need anything further from her, and she turned to stride purposefully back towards the eastern gate.

All told, her forgetfulness had cost her more than an hour, but she thanked the heavens that she'd been reminded before departing. *That would have been very bad.*

Millennial Mage, Book 2 - Mage

She waved to the guards as she walked out through the eastern gatehouse and threw her arms wide to bask in the sun streaming down upon her as she stepped free of the city.

The magic in the air hit her like a cool wave, revitalizing her and filling her with energy. She didn't precisely absorb magic from the air, but she did feel it ease the strain on her body, in ways that she didn't quite understand.

Always more to learn.

She also noticed a strange *pulling* that manifested in the magic around her, causing it to distort and seem to flow into her belt pouch. *Recharging, after being in the relatively low magic of the city?* It was an interesting idea, but it was not her current focus.

She pulled out the map as she walked, verifying her memory and checking for landmarks. As the first part of her path mainly took her across land that had been within the city at some point in the past, the ground was incredibly level and smooth, making for an easy, quick pace.

As she walked, she tried to note her balance, posture, and breathing without allowing them to dominate her thoughts. She nudged each of them in the right direction, again without forcing the issue. *Little steps, Tala. Little steps.*

She kept her senses sharp, ready to retreat or fight if any creature approached her, but she didn't see any.

Make no mistake, there was plenty of magic in the region—and even quite a few small, arcanous creatures—but nothing that would be a threat to a child, let alone her. *That's odd. Maybe another group swept through before me?*

She *had* left a bit later than most people she'd seen exiting the eastern gate.

Even so, she didn't allow herself to grow lax. Her eyes were ever-moving, and she tried to be as inconspicuous as possible.

She was just over an hour outside the city, and more than halfway to the grove, when she felt flickers of dimensional magic and turned to find the terror bird regarding her from a dozen paces away.

Lovely, just lovely.

The bird currently stood just shorter than her, its heavily built body likely three or four times her weight.

They stared at each other for a long time. "I wish you could talk."

The bird shook itself like a dog shedding water.

"I suppose that means 'no,' but I already knew you couldn't talk."

The bird didn't react.

"What do you want from me?"

It bent down and mimed tearing a bit of meat from a kill.

"You want meat?"

The bird bobbed its head.

"Can't you kill something yourself?"

It settled down on its haunches, not quite sitting but clearly at its ease.

"You don't want to..." Tala groaned. "I can't possibly feed you enough for you to survive."

It shook again.

"You don't want me to feed you enough to survive?"

Shaking.

She groaned again. "You just like the taste of the jerky..."

Bobbing.

She let out a sigh. "Will you go away if I give you some?"

The bird hesitated, then gave a small bob.

"You just lied to me. You can't even talk, and you lied to me!" She found a grin spreading across her face despite herself.

The bird shook itself, but there wasn't much intensity behind the movement.

"You know, you can't follow me forever."

The bird lifted slightly into what was obviously an aggressive crouch.

"I'm not challenging you, bird. I'm stating a fact. You can't get into cities, and I will be in many cities. You know—" She'd been about to say that she wasn't the only human with jerky, but she realized that telling a dimensional terror bird that it could get tasty treats from humans it considered helpless was *not* the best plan. She scratched her forehead. "Fine. Fine! I'll give you some."

The bird stood upright, clearly perking up at the idea. It shifted back and forth from foot to foot as it waited.

Tala fished out a big chunk of jerky and contemplated for a moment. *I'm not letting it get close to my hand, even if it can't actually bite off my fingers.* On a whim, she pulled back and tossed it off to the side.

A ripple of magic passed over the terror bird, and it shrunk to the size of a large cat. A second pulse caused it to vanish from where it had been and reappear alongside the still-flying jerky, which it snapped from the air. A third pulse of magic took the bird and jerky from her sight altogether.

She didn't feel any other points of dimensional power, so it had moved out of her magesight range. The entire process, shrinking and transporting twice, had taken the bird less than an eyeblink.

That is a terrifying creature... I can't continue to call it 'bird.' It needs a name. Something else to think on.

She sighed and turned to continue her trek through the lush wilds, towards the distant grove.

* * *

Almost an hour later, she had the distinct impression that the bird was back, even though she hadn't sensed any dimensional magic. Following a self-destructive whim, she fished out a second large hunk of jerky and randomly flung it to the side.

Twenty feet from her, the jerky encountered a brief flicker of dimensional power and vanished.

She hadn't seen the bird at all.

"You know," she called out, "I can't just feed you for free. There has to be some give and take, here."

There wasn't a response, and she didn't have any way of knowing if the creature had heard her. *It doesn't really matter. I'm talking to a bird.*

She crested a small rise, small enough to not have been depicted on Trent's map, and she saw the grove of ending trees before her.

They were starkly beautiful in their loneliness. *This used to be part of the farmland around Alefast.*

Unlike in other clusters of trees that she'd passed, no other foliage grew near them, and every tree looked exactly the same. Well, not *exactly* the same. They were clearly all the same species, though.

I wonder why the one we passed on our way here was alone, but these seem to be living in harmony. They were often close enough for the branches to touch, and their unnatural swaying caused the limbs to click or rasp together, creating a constant undercurrent of fairly disturbing sound. *So that's what I was hearing.* The sound had been growing louder on this portion of the trek.

Tala glanced down at herself. She was not fond of the state of her clothing, but she had no interest in having to trudge back to the city naked. *I've still got the shirt the terror bird ripped open and the one with a hole in the chest from where Brand stabbed me.*

Her pants were in a little better state, thankfully. The blood-stained shirt was her most intact shirt, but she could work with the cut and stabbed ones if necessary.

Her belt, however, that she wasn't willing to lose.

Toward that end, she decided to use her iron salve on the belt and belt pouch. She reasoned that the belt pouch's magic, like her own, was below the surface, so it wouldn't be negatively affected by the salve. In addition, the opening would still be free to draw in magic, as it had continued to do throughout her trek.

That decided, she opened the pouch and found two surprises.

First, the fruit picker was clearly standing upright, instead of at the crazed angle she'd finagled it into in order to close it. When she peeked inside, it appeared as if a hole, just bigger than the handle, had opened up, going deep enough for the entire lower portion of the tool to fit in, allowing the basket and hooks at the top to rest comfortably within reach, while still being out of the way. "Huh. That's pretty neat."

Second, the items she'd placed on the upper shelf now each seemed to have somewhat customized resting places, allowing for more secure storage and easier access.

"I think I'm going to like you, bag." She decided that the storage's ability to mold itself was likely directly connected to how much power it could draw in, so her being outside the city had allowed it to shift more easily. "Seems that feeding you magic is going to be a wise decision." *It can't possibly be a bad idea to give power to a semi-sapient, dimension-warping item. Not at all.*

Changes noted, Tala got to work. She pulled out her small glue bottle and painted her palms with the flexible substance. As soon as the paste had dried on her palms and the inside faces of her fingers, Tala pulled out an iron salve bar, working the salve into the leather of her belt and the outside of the dimensional belt pouch. That done, she placed her knife into the pouch and pulled out the fruit picker.

With deliberate care, she worked iron salve into the entirety of the ten-foot wooden handle of the tool. *Patience in the present removes frustration in the future.*

Her work finally complete, she stood, ready to approach the ending grove.

She wore her blood-stained shirt, and she'd changed into the pants that were similarly speckled. Her belt held only the belt pouch, and her hands held only the fruit picker. *Let's do this.*

She walked forward and spotted the first bunch of endingberries on the closest tree.

She carefully maneuvered her fruit picker up and used the hooks to pull the berries free.

As she did so, several of the nearby branches swayed to bump the wooden handle of the tool. Thankfully, the iron salve protected it just fine, and nothing came of the interactions save brief, impotent flashes of magical power.

She moved methodically around the edges of the grove, trying to stay out of reach of the moving branches. She had only gotten the fruit picker's basket about half-full when a tree moved much more than any previously had.

She had no warning as a branch descended and impacted her back.

There wasn't nearly enough force to harm her, or even knock her off balance, but the tree's magic was still imparted.

A ripple of destructive, disintegrating power flowed across her skin but couldn't penetrate her own application of iron salve.

Her shirt did not fare so well, and it puffed to dust, falling to the ground around her.

Tala groaned, looking down at herself. *That's just great.*

She had a decision to make. Was she going to continue harvesting half-naked, or would she risk another shirt?

The one the bird tore up wouldn't be too much of a loss.

She stepped away from the grove and pulled that shirt out, putting it on quickly. *There.*

As she looked back towards the grove, she paused. *Not worth it.* She removed her belt, placing that within her pouch, and then she tucked the pouch beside a very prominent rock. *Much safer to leave it here.*

Moving back to the edge of the tree line, she was even more careful as she continued to fill her basket, dodging the increasingly numerous, wildly moving limbs.

Finally, she'd filled the little basket of her fruit picker, so she withdrew to a nearby boulder, which was poking out of a rather lush field.

She retrieved the dimensional pouch from the base of the rock and fished out one of the jugs, placing it securely between her legs on the rock. Then, with the pole leaning against the rock so the basket was in easy reach, she went to work.

In quick succession, she would take up an endingberry, twist it apart, and drop the two halves into the open jug. The seed would go into her mouth, where she would suck off the juice, enjoying the building buzz of power. Then, she would take the seed and hurtle it back into the ending grove, where it would land among the roots of its ancestral kin.

To her surprise, the seeds of these endingberries did not build towards destruction nearly as quickly as those of the lone tree in the wilds had. As a result, she had almost a minute to work with each berry, if she so chose, leaving it a far less dangerous process.

Maybe this is why there weren't any other trees around that one? None of the seeds could get far enough away for the seedlings to establish... It was an interesting thought. Though, the closeness of the trees in the grove before her made that an unlikely reason.

She'd considered keeping the ending seeds, as she had those from that singular tree, but in the end, she realized that she didn't want to be carrying around what amounted to a massive box of destruction.

Trent would approve of her decision, she assured herself, and that helped make the choice all the firmer.

Many of the endingberries had retained their stems. For those, she used the iron pliers to help remove them before she processed the berries like the others. In the end, the single basket from the fruit picker allowed her to fill the jug somewhere between a quarter and a third full.

Alright. Now, we're getting somewhere. And back to work she went.

Chapter: 2
Well... That's New

Over the next hour, Tala filled the fruit picker seven more times, each time moving back to the rock, or another convenient seat, to process her harvest.

During that time, she lost another shirt and two pairs of pants.

With one of each left, she was forced to continue her work without other covering.

It wasn't unpleasant in the cool weather, but it definitely left her feeling like every tree, rock, or bush held some hidden watcher.

She filled both glass containers completely and ate a picker-basket full of the berries for lunch, supplemented by the travel food she'd purchased in Bandfast. *No need to let this go to waste.*

She drank a *lot* of water, though it did little against her building headache. *Is this from lack of coffee? It's probably from too little coffee.* She grumbled unpleasantly about the stinginess of inns.

Her lunch now finished, she looked down at herself and noted that her fingers were stained a near maroon, and there were some drip stains on her chest as well. She could only imagine what her face looked like if enough had gathered to drip down off her chin. She had tried to be careful, knowing that every drop of juice held power, but there was only so much she could do. She let out a resigned sigh. *Oh well. I suppose I'll bathe when I get back to the city.*

Millennial Mage, Book 2 - Mage

Attempts at rationality aside, she was quite irritated at the waste of power that the juice represented, and she resolved to be even more careful going forward. *Though, I don't really know how I could be...* Such a resolution, without a plan, was probably doomed to failure.

She pulled out the keg she'd purchased and set about emptying the initial containers into it. They filled it quite nicely, just as she'd hoped. She set the keg's lid in place and pulled out a wooden mallet.

She'd purchased the mallet in Bandfast, along with several other random odds and ends, to help round out her options if unexpected things happened. As she'd hoped, it had turned out to be a wise choice.

It was a bit more difficult than she'd expected to properly set the keg's lid, but she got it done, mentally referencing the barrel seller's advice and instructions. *Glad I asked, or this would have gone a* lot *more poorly...*

With *the* full keg again stashed in her belt pouch, she had two empty jugs, ready to fill.

Here we go. Once more, into the grove.

Without clothing to protect, she was a bit less careful in this initial step, favoring speed over safety, and she was brushed, struck, and poked at least half a hundred times over the next hour. They never seemed to reach her skin, so she didn't pay the brushes to much attention.

Her speed paid off, though, as she filled the two jugs and ate her absolute fill of the endingberries.

No wonder no one harvests these. I'd be dead a dozen times over. A hundred, more likely. From her experience, only her iron salve had kept her intact.

She withdrew for the final time, settled down on a comfortably flat boulder, and finished processing the last harvest. Then, she stored the fruit picker in the convenient hole prepared within her belt pouch. *Is hole the right term?*

Carrying case doesn't really work. Mount? Slot? It didn't really matter.

She absently licked her fingers clean, relishing the tiny influx of power added to the storm within her with each drop. It had been a *very* productive outing. Not without its costs, however. She'd lost two shirts, three pairs of pants, and quite a bit of hair. She reached up and felt her patchy scalp with a sigh. She had not come through completely unscathed. *Still, I'm alive, and there is no way I would have been without my peculiarities.*

She had kept her hair growth inscriptions from activating, knowing that she could easily exhaust them if she let them trigger for every disintegrated chunk of hair. *The salve that I worked into my hair helped some, but not as much as I'd hoped.*

That said, she was ready to restore herself to a state that didn't resemble someone newly recovered from a ravaging disease. Tala was about to let the magic loose when she had a realization. *I've no idea if it will grow all my hair the proper length to recover from baldness, or if it will feather the growth so that the result is correct.*

She knew that the inscriptions would restore her hair, but like most acts of magic, she didn't know exactly *how*.

Well, there's no time like the present to learn. So, she allowed power to flow through the activation scripts in her scalp and above her eyes.

Her hair did grow only as much as needed, and she felt the tingling power of one of her eyebrows returning to form. The other was miraculously untouched. *Good to know. It isn't wasteful.* Though, in truth, she had expected nothing less from Holly's work.

She regarded the two jugs alongside the keg, and decided that she wanted to contain and maintain the magic as much as possible.

She'd already worked iron salve into the outside of the keg, so she was able to place that back in her pouch with a happy smile.

The jugs were a different problem, given that they were glass and couldn't really absorb the salve.

In the end, she pulled out two medium cloth sacks, turning them inside out and coating the insides with her salve before inverting them once more and placing a jug within each. *I'll have to buy another keg if I mean to store these longer-term...* She'd been cognizant enough to finish filling her iron flask, and that was comfortably stored alongside the keg, its iron the only containment that vessel needed.

Now, the jugs were bound in iron salve, so the magic in the berries shouldn't fade too quickly—if at all.

She felt positively brimming with power from the berries that she'd eaten. Unlike before, when she'd had her palms uncovered along with her eyes as possible escapes for the power, now only her eyes were open, and her inscriptions were actively working to keep power from flowing through that weak point.

Thankfully, those were gold inscriptions, like those of her passive enhancements, and should easily last until her return to Holly. The idea had been to prevent hostile magic from getting into her through her eyes, not escaping, however, and she could feel, and even see through her magesight, wisps of power slowly leaking from her open eyes.

She blessed the stars that none of the flailing branches had ever caught her in the eye; she wasn't sure her inscriptions would prevent the entry of magic that was physically thrust into her eyeball. *That would have been a disaster.*

Her palms were not open now because she'd left the glue in place after treating the keg and fruit picker handle, earlier, and a healthy coating of iron salve had melded with the paste through the course of her work.

The power had nowhere to go except what little could escape from her eyes, and she felt it settling in within her, strengthening her, and adding weight behind her enhancements.

If she were being honest, she felt as if she could stand before a siege cannon and take the blast. Thankfully, such weapons of war hadn't been seen by humanity in centuries, but they were still a subject of fascination for Tala. The idea that she could withstand one was intoxicating. And she found herself basking in the feeling of power, in the sunlight, in the ambient magic swirling around her, and in the cool breeze playing across her bare skin.

Woah, girl. Focus. You are standing, naked, in the Wilds, acting like some crazed nature sprite. Tala opened her eyes and let her arms fall back to her sides. *Better.*

The sun was past its zenith, and the afternoon was waning around her.

With a sigh of contentment for a job well done, Tala pulled out a pair of almost pristine pants, by her usual standards, and the shirt with the single repaired stab hole over her left breast. It was a much nicer shirt than she'd been wearing, but the stitched hole was obvious. She was not a practiced stitcher. *Seamstress? Tailor?* Probably didn't matter.

She shrugged to herself. *Either the seamstress will come through, or Brand's tailor will make me some new clothing.*

As she turned to go, she felt a twinge, which somehow reminded her of her knife. *Right, I should put that back on my belt, so it's ready to hand.* She stuck her hand into her dimensional storage to search for the knife and found it immediately in her hand. *Huh, I guess I instinctively knew where it was.*

She felt a bit of tiredness wash over her, but it wasn't anything worth considering deeply. She hadn't truly stopped all morning, with even her short breaks filled with work. It made sense that she'd feel some weariness in a moment's pause.

She shrugged as she fastened the blade to hang opposite her belt pouch, balancing out her belt nicely.

Tala turned her steps back towards the city gate but paused when she came to the same rise that had first let her see the grove below. *I didn't take even half a percent of the fruit that's down there...*

It wouldn't be hard to come back tomorrow. She could buy a few more kegs and spend a bit more time collecting. The power thundering within her was a potent argument for such a course of action.

That's a good default plan. I'll keep my options open, though. That decided, she turned her back on the grove and headed back towards the city.

As she walked, she followed her usual routine: reading, taking notes, sketching, and otherwise contemplating the myriad ideas and theories she'd come across.

For one new addition, she added the occasional bit of entertainment; every so often, she would toss a small bit of jerky in a random direction and watch it vanish in a flicker of dimensional energy. *In for a copper.*

As to her musings, she used her note-taking to help herself organize her thoughts and ideas surrounding difficult concepts.

A central figure in her thoughts was her knife.

The connection she felt with it was strong—much stronger than what she'd felt with her Archon Star—but it still felt like a thin thread of what it could and should be. *If I want to strengthen the connection, do I give the knife power, or do I forge more stars and unify them with it?*

More to the point, though, what would that gain her? Why would she want that connection strengthened?

The belt pouch had continued to siphon energy from the countryside as she'd gone about her tasks, showing no signs of slowing, but the knife hadn't shown any signs of such. *Is it storing up for lean times? Making up for time spent in the city?* She had no basis for comparison. *I can ask Artia's husband tonight.*

She hesitated. *And what is the knife doing?* Another question she couldn't answer. *Another thing to investigate, I suppose.*

There was something else that required more immediate attention, however. No matter what she chose to do with another Archon Star, she knew that she needed to make more. Grediv had all but commanded her to make one vastly more powerful than she'd ever managed before.

Towards that end, she began building an Archon Star in her finger, just as she had the second and third times, being sure to hold the mental construct to which she slowly added power. Even so, she still contemplated the knife, occasionally drawing it from its sheath for examination, inspecting its magics more closely.

She was careful, her few experiences of exhausting herself magically lending her caution. She had no desire to lapse into sleep, alone in the Wilds.

Even so, she pushed herself, treating her magic as a muscle and seeking the balance between a comfortable strain and overexertion as she moved the power from her gate, through herself, to concentrate within her finger. It was an *incredibly* difficult balance to maintain.

As she walked, she began to sweat with her internal strain, but it was a good sweat, one that spoke of progress well earned.

It took her two hours to walk back to the city gate, and by the sun in the sky, it was still another couple of hours

Millennial Mage, Book 2 - Mage

before sunset. *I can make it to the gate.* She held her focus as she approached and was greeted by the guard on duty.

"Hello! Can I get your name, please?" He seemed a bit hesitant, and he was staring at her mouth.

What is his issue? "Mistress Tala." She kept herself from panting but only barely. Surprisingly, Adam's breathing pattern was incredibly useful for just that.

"Mistress Tala... Mistress Tala." The man was searching through a list, eyes still occasionally flicking up to glance at her. "Ah! There you are. Welcome back. There are no messages for you." He still seemed a bit hesitant. After a moment, he seemed to come to a decision. "Did you notice any creatures or combat while outside the walls today?"

Tala frowned. *I just want to get through.* "No." She almost stopped there, but her innate curiosity got the better of her. "Why?"

The guard shrugged, marking something down. "Others have reported empty battlefields, places torn up by various types of magic or painted with blood, too dark to be human." He gave her a meaningful look. "In any case, we've not had any reported encounters with beasts, arcane or magical, east of the city today."

Oh! The berry juice stains. I wonder if it looks like I've been eating raw meat... monster meat? She cleared her throat. "Ahh... Thank you."

He gave her another searching look, then shrugged, dismissing her. "Thank you, as well."

I suppose it's no crime to hunt creatures, and even if I was doing it, my reasons are my own. Or some such... With no further comment, Tala walked into the cool shade of the gatehouse. *I can make it a block or two.* She came out the other side, still focused on the Archon Star building in her left ring finger.

Her magesight focus was entirely within herself, homed in on the spell-form steadily growing within her blood. She had set all other thoughts aside, trusting to the general safety of a city in broad daylight.

As she took the final step of those first two blocks within the city, she glanced around. *I can go another two.*

So, she made her way back to the inn; once each goal was reached, she set another just a bit further. She maintained her concentration and continued to funnel as much power as she could without overtaxing herself.

In truth, it felt like carrying the heaviest weight her body could manage without injury as she continued to push for just one more block.

Then, almost unexpectedly, she was in her room. *That's it. I've got to get it out.*

She fumbled at her belt, pulling the knife so that she could prick her finger.

Don't let the inscriptions activate. She diverted a small fraction of her thoughts to her finger's spell-forms, pulling power away from those intended to keep her skin whole, just as she did every time she needed to confirm a contract or transaction. *Done.*

She also needed to tame the power of the endingberries, racing through her system in quantities vastly outstripping those she'd worked with before. She had to draw it away from the site of the cut, or they would prevent her skin from being pierced. *Also done.*

Tala lifted the knife and paused. *I'm an idiot; I'm not thinking clearly.* Her focus was split so many ways, and she knew it was close to breaking. *I've got to move fast.* With careful motions, she sat and pulled out an iron vial. *I almost just let this drop onto the floor. What would that have even done?*

She held her finger over the open vial and carefully slit her skin, allowing the drop of blood to flow out. She maintained full control over the power until it left her body.

As the drop appeared, three things happened in quick succession.

First, her magesight became outward-focused again, and she saw the power within the Archon Star. *Not bad, Tala.* It was at least as potent as the one she'd placed into her knife the night before, and that had been the combination of multiple efforts. *Not bad at all.*

Second, as the drop fell free of her finger, her inscriptions activated behind it to close the small cut flawlessly.

Last, her once again free mind realized something. *Oh... the knife.*

The Archon Star, forged within blood, seemed to sense its like nearby. As it fell, its path changed drastically and instantly.

The drop ticked sideways, briefly stopping against the handle of her knife, which was still held firmly in her grip. Even with that instantaneous pause, there was no time to act, and in less than a blink, the minuscule drop of blood had rolled down the handle and into the pommel, precisely where the other star had gone the night before.

Well, that choice is gone, then.

The knife quivered in her hand, a ripple moving through it from tip to butt, and after the tremor passed, she was a bit surprised by the changes.

The blade's color had returned to a more natural steel gray, though there was depth to the color that reminded her of the difference between red paint and a ruby. The handle's material now resembled nothing so much as a night sky, where every star was the deep, vital red of liquid blood.

Give a knife a blood star, and you get what you gave? She felt *something* deep within her chest like the sadness of missing a friend or the joy of hugging a loved one, and at the same time, she felt a resonance within the weapon she still held. Instinctively, she knew that her bond to the knife had deepened, for better or worse. Thankfully, there was no increase in her exhaustion. Apparently, increasing a bond didn't have the same tiring effects as creating one—well, aside from the strain of creating the star used for such.

Grediv said that the Archon Star would allow me to exert control outside of myself. She could already push magic into something that she was holding, so she took the knife's sheath from her belt, placed the knife in it, and placed both items on the nightstand beside her bed.

How far can it work? She still felt the knife, but not as if it were in her hand. The feeling was more like how she could reliably point at the sun while standing in its light.

She stepped back until a good ten feet of space was between her and the knife. Then, trusting her own instincts, she gathered up a bit of power and pushed it towards the knife.

It was as easy as moving power towards or away from inscriptions within herself. Easier, in fact, if that was possible.

The knife drank in the magic thirstily, and Tala cut off the flow. *Can I draw power back?*

She tried, using the same sort of techniques, but got nothing. *Hmmm... Can I move it?*

She tried to shift the power within the knife, but it was like trying to move a pen by thinking at it: utterly ineffective and headache-inducing.

This is getting nowhere. I can't move power out of it or within it; all I can do is give it power. I don't really see a point to that... She sighed.

But, Tala, you can give it power… at a distance! She snorted a laugh. *That's true, and unique, I suppose.* She smiled. *It's something.*

The seamstress wasn't likely to be by for another hour or so, then she had dinner with Artia, Brand, and Artia's husband. *What was his name?* She hadn't met the man, but Artia had spoken fondly of him, and he seemed like he might have some of the answers she sought. *It was like Adam, but not… Adrill!* That was it. She smiled in satisfaction at remembering.

So, she had a bit of time before the seamstress and dinner with Artia, Adrill, and Brand. *How to spend the time?*

Tala decided that she should go buy one more keg, at the very least, as well as the tools to tap the one she had, for when that time came. *Maybe a larger iron jug or flask?* There were too many things to spend money on. She'd have to consider it on the way. She was almost to the door when the light pressure on her back came to the forefront of her thinking.

Right! The knife. She turned to go back and pick it up, reaching out in preparation, even while still across the room.

In that instant, she felt a tugging, and the knife, sheath and all, zipped through the air to stop lightly in her hand, the handle perfectly situated in her grip for instantaneous use. A pulse of tiredness followed as if she had just sprinted across the room, lifted a heavy crate, and sprinted back, crate in hand.

Tala stared down at the knife, now firmly in her grasp. "Well… that's new."

Chapter: 3
Unexpected Results

After Tala had summoned her knife from across the room, her surprise gave her a moment to pause.

While examining the knife in her hand more closely, she, again, noticed the berry stains, and that had reminded her of the horror her face must be to behold.

She stepped into the bath room, and used the gloriously running hot water to scrub the stains from her face and hands. Thankfully, the inn had provided a bar of soap that seemed to be quite effective against the berry juice, removing it completely from her face.

Her hands, unfortunately, were rendered only mostly clean, even after she'd peeled the glue from her palms and the pads of her fingers.

Good enough. Then, as she looked at herself in the mirror, her eyes went wide. *My iron salve should have helped prevent the juice from staining my skin.*

She frantically pulled out her magic detector and pointed it at her face. A soft glow emanated from the device.

"Rust me to slag." She moved the short stick across herself, finding only a few—but still too many—places where her iron salve had been breached.

It was never a full breach, stars be praised, nor was it more than a small portion of her overall skin, but it was a shocking thing, regardless.

She stripped down, reglued her palms and finger-pads, and worked to re-apply her iron salve, going so far as to thicken it wherever she felt that was reasonable.

I was being careful. I thought I was monitoring my internal magic. Even still, the ending trees would have gotten her if she hadn't already eaten so many of their berries. *They would have at least hit and been a colossal drain on my defenses.* She likely would have noticed that... *Would that have been enough warning?* She didn't know.

Tala sat on the floor, her hands glue-free and fully dressed once more. She panned the magic detector across herself. *Nothing.*

Her hands were shaking as she swept the device about herself once more. *Still nothing.*

She shivered. *I'm pushing my luck too far.* She didn't even know how the ending trees' power had degraded her iron protection, she just knew that it had.

That also explained why she'd earlier felt several hitches in the well of ending power she held within herself. *The trees got through.* She couldn't see any part of her inscriptions activated, nor had she felt any power flow into them. Thus, she concluded that, as she'd hoped, the endingberries within her had shielded her from the tree's magic quite well.

Even so, it had been a bit of a foolish risk. *I should have been monitoring more closely. I should have been more careful.*

She stored the empowered construct and placed her face in her hands, her elbows resting on her knees. *Get it together, Tala. You're alive. You've learned. You can avoid this tomorrow.*

She nodded to herself, slowly regaining control over her nerves. Tomorrow, she would be diligent, using the magic detector and iron salve more than she thought reasonable.

Better to be safe. Better to not risk a breach. She took a deep breath and gave a shaky smile. *Live and learn. Right?*

She shook her head. *Okay. I don't have a lot of time left.*

She stood, letting out a large, puffing exhale.

Tala left her room, examining her sheathed knife to keep her mind focused on the present.

The movement wasn't a function of magic within the knife. I didn't activate some inscribed or empowered ability inherent to the weapon itself.

With her new use of magesight, allowing her to look within and target specific muscles, she was getting used to the feeling of using muscles that were usually ignored.

The mild strain she felt was almost identical to the feeling those neglected parts of her gave when worked. This specific instance, however, didn't seem to have a physical source. What was more, it felt more *real*. It was as if all other movements were through a tool. She'd been picking at the world with pliers, and now, for the first time, she had touched something with her own flesh. It wasn't a perfect analogy, as she was referring to her body both with, and within, the analogy.

She grimaced. Why did her own body feel like a tool in comparison?

Grediv said the star would help me stretch my soul… Am I feeling my soul? It's more real than my body, more me. And it's tired? That had some disturbing implications. Could she strain or tear her own soul? Her mind was at war with itself. One part of her wanted to tuck the knife in her pouch and never touch it again, leaving her soul in its previous, blissful state. The other wanted her to disregard all else and come up with a training regime for this newly accessed part of herself so that it could never be harmed, strained, or torn.

If I could trust in a simple life, I'd go with the first option. Sadly, she knew that wasn't a possibility. *There is only safety in strength—either your own or that of others.* She would prefer to be safe in her own strength.

Soul training it is! Even so, she decided to wait until the current exhausted feeling faded. No need to start on a bad foot. *It should be recovered by tomorrow, right?*

As she'd been musing, she'd returned to the market, where the barrel seller greeted her, inquiring about the items she'd purchased the day before.

She complimented him on them, and they talked briefly about how to tap the keg when the time came, and how to keep it in good function until then. He also informed her that, if she was careful, she could reopen the keg, but probably not without needing a new head. 'Head' was apparently the proper name for the lid. *Who knew?*

Finally, Tala bought four more kegs, along with 'heads' for after they'd been filled, and a tap that could be hammered into any of the kegs to access what was stored within, assuming it was mostly liquid, that was.

As she'd thought about it, she realized that the berries were still mostly intact and likely wouldn't flow smoothly, so she'd bought an additional couple of heads, so if she had to break open the keg as he'd directed, she could at least put a lid back in place after.

She negotiated him to two silver ounces for the lot and completed the transaction on the merchant's slate.

Thankfully, dimensional storage was common enough that he didn't give her pouch more than a passing glance as she slipped each of the items inside. *I'll need to go in and organize, back in my room.*

She bid him farewell and headed back to the inn. As she walked, she felt her lower abdomen gurgling a bit. She wasn't hungry, yet, and the feeling was a bit uncomfortable. *Huh. Did I catch something? Something I ate?* She'd only really eaten the endingberries and a bit of trail food. *Maybe it wasn't the best idea to eat so many...*

Back in her room, she opened the pouch as wide as it could go and took a moment to examine what she saw. *This is a wider opening than last time.* Where, before, she'd had to squeeze her shoulders in, compressing her chest and tucking her elbows to her side to drop through, and then shimmy quite aggressively to get back out, now the pouch seemed to have opened to a size through which she could climb down without scraping the sides, if only just.

Make no mistake, it still wasn't roomy, and a full-grown man would have been hilarious to watch in any attempt to fit, but it would suit her, perfectly. "Thank you, I think?"

The bag did not respond.

She climbed down through the hole, using the rungs of the ladder still in place within the dimensional storage.

The feeling of a comfortable embrace returned as she descended the ladder, stepping down off the last rung with ease. Feet now firmly on the soft-yet-solid floor, she looked around, a frown on her face.

Three things immediately jumped out to her.

Firstly, though there was no obvious source of light, she could easily see. *I wonder if a plant could grow in this space.*

Secondly, there wasn't a pile of kegs, lids, and other items at the base of the ladder as she'd expected. Instead, there was a rack on one wall that appeared to be perfectly sized to hold each of the five kegs individually. A small shelf—made out of the same nondescript, nonspecific material as the walls—also held the extra lids. Her tools, likewise, were hanging on a different wall, each seeming to have a custom place to rest.

Thirdly, the space seemed larger than before.

"There is no way this is standard. Artia would never have sold you if she'd known you could do this."

The comforting feeling of the space didn't alter.

"Or... are all dimensional storage artifacts capable of this? Maybe if they are owned, instead of rented out? Does my knowledge that I'm keeping you influence what happens? Or... maybe they just need to be given sufficient power and interaction?" Tala's frown deepened. "I didn't think I gave you *that* much power, but I suppose a day outside the walls would have helped..." She found herself nodding. "If dimensional storages are mostly used within the city, then most would effectively be magic-starved." She felt a bit of sadness as she looked around herself. "Were you just really hungry?"

The comforting sense *might* have intensified, just slightly. Probably just her imagination, though.

"Not sure if you're actually sapient or just responding to my own emotions..." *And... you're talking to a bag, again.* Tala sighed. "Well, if I'm crazy, at least I'll be true to my insanity."

Her stomach gurgled again, roiling this time.

"Thank you for organizing, I suppose." As she moved back towards the ladder, she noticed that another wall had a shelf with her books on it. *I thought I had those in my satchel...* She grimaced, placing a hand on her stomach against another roil.

She climbed out of the bag and closed it before heading to the latrine, conveniently located off her bath room.

There, she had an... unpleasant few minutes.

Mother always warned me not to eat too much fruit at once. The endingberries had made themselves known, and she'd been punished for overconsumption.

Thankfully, the discomfort had passed in less than half an hour, along with a lot of other things.

Too many berries... Moderation, Tala. She shook her head, now back in her room, lying on her bed. She'd been surprised that the amount of power within her hadn't diminished during the... lesson, but she assumed that her body had simply drawn all the magic out of the berries beforehand.

As she considered that, she realized that the berries' magic should be leaving her in great puffs with each breath. *Why isn't it exiting my lungs?*

She focused inward, sipping a glass of water to continue the calming of her stomach.

Her magesight revealed that while the power from the berries did fill the lungs themselves, it did not distribute into the air within. *Why?*

There was no easy answer. Maybe, like her intestines and kidneys, her lungs didn't see that magic as a toxin, needing to be cleansed from her body, and therefore didn't draw any into what was to leave her? *As good a theory as any, I suppose.*

But her own, internal power seemed to equalize with the air. *Maybe, because the endingberry power is highly specific? Formed in such a way as to not dissipate into the air with much ease?*

It still seemed to leak from her eyes for whatever reason, even if slowly. *Bah! I'll just have to keep note of how it works and try to learn as I go.*

A knock came on the door, and she pushed herself to her feet. She still felt off, but her extended trip to the latrine seemed to have gotten out the worst of it. *Or at least most of it.*

She opened the door to find the diminutive seamstress staring up at her. "You look awful."

Tala sighed. "Yeah, I ate—"

The woman cut her off. "That outfit is the same as before but worse, because it means you have two of them."

Tala actually laughed.

Her laughter seemed to catch the seamstress off guard because the small woman paused, giving her a quizzical look.

"Well, you'll be happy to know that this is now the only one I possess."

The seamstress *harumphed.* "Well, I'm glad of that." She held out a small stack of clothing for Tala. "Put this on."

Tala took the clothing with a smile. "Thank you."

"Put it on, and thank me once you have the information to do it properly."

Tala snorted another laugh. "Very well." She stepped into the bath room and closed the door before stripping.

"Child, you don't have anything I haven't seen before."

"Doesn't mean I want you to see my version of it."

This time Tala heard the seamstress chuckle. "Very well. But be quick about it. Yes?"

Tala simply grunted in reply.

She dropped her old clothes into her pouch, vaguely wondering if the item would add a wardrobe, or something similar, to handle the clothing.

The clothing the seamstress had brought was of a stunningly fine linen. Looking closely, she could see the weave, but just barely, and it felt almost like silk between her fingers.

She pulled on the shirt and pants before examining herself in the mirror.

The pants were a superb fit, molding to her curves perfectly and moving with her smoothly. There wasn't a pinch or pull, no matter how she flexed, bent, or stretched. In addition, the lower leg flared just so, in order to let her bare feet seem an intentional part of the look, rather than a case of forgotten shoes. *Huh. These are amazing.* They were of medium-weight, black linen, of as fine a weave as the shirt.

The shirt was looser on her and hung down almost to her knees. *A tunic, then?*

She'd had to fasten a simple, heavy clasp behind her neck after pulling the garment on, over her head. *Non-metal, nice.* She thought it was a heavy wood but couldn't quite place it.

The collar was snug, against her neck without actually coming up onto it. It rested softly atop her collarbones and left her throat unimpeded. The linen of the shirt was a soft, almost storm-cloud gray, which complemented the mild gray tint of her skin quite nicely.

As she spun to look at herself in the mirror, she noticed that the back of the shirt was still open. The clasp that she'd done up had pulled in the collar, but there was still a circle of flesh exposed on her back: her keystone.

The inscription of her keystone was prominently displayed and highlighted by the shirt. *Interesting choice.*

The shirt's sleeves came down to beyond her wrists, but she noticed simple clasps, similar but smaller than that behind her neck, and once she'd done them up properly, they held the cuffs at her wrists perfectly: Secure without being tight.

"Well? Are you going to spend all afternoon mooning over yourself? Come out and let an old woman see what she's created."

Before complying, Tala put her leather belt back on, situating it to cinch the shirt in a flattering manner. The black leather of the belt complemented the shirt and matched the black pants perfectly.

She pushed open the door, and the seamstress gave her a critical look. "Good, so you do know how to put on clothes properly. I'd been concerned."

"You know, you've never given me your name."

"You've never asked, and it hardly matters."

"What is your name?"

"Call me 'Seamstress.'"

"That's not your name."

"I didn't say it was."

Tala sighed. "Very well. Thank you, Seamstress. These are wonderful."

"Of course, they are. I made them." The seamstress smiled in self-satisfaction.

Tala felt her lips tug up in a half-smile despite herself.

"Now… Now, you look how you should. A woman like you should be naked, but you'd cause a riot."

Tala had been taking a long, slow breath through her nose, but when she heard the seamstress, her breath caught, and she practically choked. "What?"

"You heard me, dear. Don't act daft." The seamstress was walking around her, inspecting the results of her handiwork. "Clothing is like manners—armor for those who couldn't function in society without them."

"Is that why you've no manners? Because you believe that you're good enough to not need them?"

The woman grinned. "And why I wear clothes, my dear. Now. Are you satisfied?"

Tala found herself nodding.

"Good. I'd like you to have ten sets. Two more like this one, for everyday use when you're in a city, but you're a traveler, so five should be a bit more utilitarian, more leather, more durable. I wish I had some arcane skins for that." She clucked her tongue in thought. "I'll make the last two for more formal occasions." She tsked to herself, while cupping her own chin. "Not as form-fitting for those outfits, though. You're not a prostitute."

"You just told me that I should go around naked."

"A cake sitting on a counter is beautiful to behold, and there is no need for every guest in your home to touch it. Put that same cake in a fancy box, and tie a ribbon on it? Then, it's just begging to be unwrapped."

Tala found herself quietly laughing, again. *This woman is crazy.* "So, how much would this cost me?"

"For twenty items of clothing?"

Eighteen... But Tala thought better of interjecting.

"I think a gold ounce will do nicely."

Tala spluttered out. "A gold ounce! That's five silvers a piece! You think each article of clothing is worth the same as a night's stay, here?" She gestured around herself.

The seamstress returned her gaze with a flat calm. "Yes, dear. And so do you." After a brief pause, she made a shooing motion. "Go look in the mirror, again. I'm not going to haggle with you. I'll wait out here for you to come to your senses."

Tala went back into the bath room but didn't close the door. She did take some time examining herself in the mirrors hanging therein. *These do look amazing... Ten full sets of clothing would be nice. If the traveling clothes have a lot of leather, I can work in the iron salve, and that should give them added durability, at least against magic.*

She sighed. *She's right. For ten full outfits of this quality, it's a deal.*

She walked back out to find the seamstress sitting in the reading chair, flipping through what looked like a notebook, occasionally jotting within it. "Well?" The woman didn't look up.

"Two questions."

She sighed, closing her book and tucking it away. "On with it, then."

"If I bought fewer sets, would the price go up for the remaining?"

"Of course it would. What kind of idiot question is that?"

Tala nodded. "And when could you have them done by?"

The seamstress eyed her, seeming to sense a trap. "My underlings could have these done by tomorrow evening, earlier if needed, but the matron told me you're here through the following morning. Do you need one, in particular, earlier?"

Tala shook her head and smiled. "Thank you for the answers. This is the deal: I want twenty outfits, the style and function of them in the ratios you described. I will pay you one and a half gold ounces. I do need the work done by tomorrow evening,"

The old woman stood, opening her mouth to object, but Tala continued.

"And I will know your name." Tala had pulled upon all her memories of haughty Mages for her tone and bearing while speaking her terms, and she realized that, in the outfit, she felt more like an actual Mage. *Rust her, she's good at what she does…*

The seamstress closed her mouth, eyeing Tala for a moment before grinning. "You think yourself quite clever, eh?" She nodded to herself. "Fifteen outfits, one and a half gold, and you may call me Merilin."

"Merilin." Tala nodded. "Fifteen outfits for one and a half gold isn't a better deal."

"I did tell you that I wouldn't haggle. If you want to buy more, though, I won't stop you."

"You said that buying less would cost more per item."

"That's true."

"So, buying more should cost less for each item."

"Except, I'll have to get the work done in the same amount of time. Doing fifteen sets of clothing by morning, day after tomorrow, will be hard enough without taking from my meager profits."

Tala frowned. *I'm not going to move her on this, am I?* She sighed. *And she moved the time of delivery back…* "Very well, Madam Merilin. We are agreed."

Merilin nodded her head in acknowledgment. "I will see you in the morning, the day of your departure. I'll have your clothing, then." She pointed at Tala. "Do try not to destroy that outfit."

Tala quirked a smile. "All fifteen other sets. I'll be ready to pay you, then."

Merilin hesitated, then snorted out a laugh. "As you say, Mistress Tala. Good evening to you."

"And to you, Madam Merilin."

The seamstress left without another word, and Tala slumped down in the reading chair. "By the heavens, I'm glad Artia wasn't so stubborn, or I'd have nothing left to my name."

She supposed that Merilin's age, and obvious familiarity with Mages, had both been advantages that Artia didn't possess.

Tala glanced out of her open windows and saw that it was getting quite late. Her stomach was still a bit off-kilter, but she needed to eat, and she'd promised to join Artia, Adrill, and Brand in Artia's home tonight.

Off to dinner, then.

She checked herself one last time and found that she was pleased. "Merilin was right; this is *much* better."

She verified that she had all her possessions with her. Her knife and pouch were securely in place on her belt, counterbalancing each other. That final check complete, she headed out the door, back towards the marketplace and dinner.

Chapter: 4
Food and Inquiry

The shop was closed and the stall packed up when Tala arrived. She knocked on the side door, and it was a moment or two before she heard movement beyond.

A young man opened the door. *Right! They have a son. I'm pretty sure his name was Brandon.*

"I'm sorry; we're clo—" Brandon's eyes widened as he saw her. "Mistress Tala!" He stepped backward, fumbling to pull the door farther open. "Please, come in! Dinner isn't quite ready, yet, but we're happy to have you."

Tala smiled slightly and gave a small nod. Again, something felt… odd about the boy to her magesight, but she didn't dwell on it. That wasn't why she was here. "Thank you, Brandon. Can you lead the way? I've only ever been in the shop."

"Of course!" He turned and walked back down the small hallway into which the side door opened.

Tala came inside and closed the door behind herself before following him down the hall.

They passed two doors on their way, one into the dark shop and the other would open onto the walled courtyard in back. The passage ended at a T-intersection, with stairs to either side, one set going up, the other down.

Brandon pointed down. "My father's shop is down there."

"I'd be interested in seeing that." *Might be interesting.*

"Really? You know, I help him, sometimes. I'm sure we could show you after dinner, if you'd like."

"I would, if time allows. Thank you."

Brandon smiled to himself as he turned and led her the other way, up the stairs. The murmur of soft conversation, along with the sounds of a kitchen in use, floated down towards them as they ascended.

Tala reached the top of the stairs and turned, finding herself in a spacious dining and sitting room. There were several comfortable couches arranged to one side in a semi-circle to promote conversation. The other side of the room held a large table, easily large enough to seat eight. A door near the couches seemed to lead out onto a balcony, which overlooked the market square below.

The space was clean, well-kept, and tastefully decorated.

Artia came out of another doorway, presumably from the kitchen. "Mistress Tala! Welcome. Brand and I are just finishing up. Adrill should be joining us shortly."

"Thank you, Artia. You have a lovely home."

"Thank you, dear. Can I get you anything while you wait?"

"That isn't necessary, but thank you. Can I help?"

"We've got it sorted."

Tala gave a nod of acknowledgment, then turned to take a seat on one of the couches as Artia went back into the kitchen.

Brandon looked back and forth between his departing mother and Tala, seeming to be debating with himself. Finally, one side must have won out because he turned and took a seat across from Tala. "So... how long have you been a Mage?"

Tala quirked a smile. "Long enough. Have you always helped out here?"

Brandon shrugged. "It's the family business. You know?"

Right, families actually do that... She tried to keep emotion from her face, but she must have failed somehow because Brandon paled, looking away.

"I mean, I like the work, and it's interesting. I think Mom and Dad would have let me go off to become a Mage, but Dad and I have the same... issue."

Tala brought herself back to the moment, dismissing the flood of memories, all centered on a small alchemist shop. "Issue?"

He cleared his throat. "Mom says it's nothing to be embarrassed about, but we don't have a gate." He shrugged. "Can't use magic." He looked back to her, seeming to relax when he noticed her attention. "It hit Dad hardest, but that was before I was born. Before he met Mom, too. The way he tells it, he got the highest score the recruiters had ever seen on the cognitive and mental construction exams, but when they tested him for magic accumulation rate... nothing. No gate at all."

Tala leaned forward. "That's possible?" *Is that what I noticed?* She allowed her magesight to examine the boy as surreptitiously as she could. He still had some power flowing through him, though it was weak, and true to his word, there was no gate to be found. No broken gate, no closed gate, nothing. *Where did the power in his system come from, then? Did he absorb it from ambient power?* Could she ask without being rude?

"Oh, yeah. Apparently, about one percent of people don't have gates within them, so we can't empower inscriptions or constructs or anything, really, let alone be Mages."

"That must have been devastating."

Brandon let out a mirthless laugh. "Yeah. For me, I knew about it from a young age, even though it's supposedly recessive. Dad? His brothers are Mages, his father and mother, too." His smile was sad. "We still see family... sometimes, but we're not really seen as part of it, and no one discusses magic with us. Even if we bring it up." He glanced up at her again and balked. "I'm sorry! You're a guest, here, and I'm telling you sad family stories." He held up both his hands. "I love my life, and I think what Dad does is amazing." He smiled. "He's very excited to meet you and discuss the Order."

Their family are Mages, and they still see them as so prejudiced? She sighed. *Or they see them as so rigid and prejudiced because they have family who are Mages?* "I'm glad that he's excited. I admit I'm hoping to pick his brain about a few things myself."

Brand walked out of the kitchen, wiping his hands on an apron as he took it off. "Mistress Tala! You look amazing, and I see that you no longer need a tailor."

She smiled a bit sheepishly. "I came across someone who seems to do a good job. Have you heard of a seamstress named Merilin?"

"Merilin?" Artia's voice floated from back in the kitchen. "I've heard she's expensive but worth it." She looked Tala up and down, then nodded. "Seems the 'worth it' portion was true enough."

Tala huffed a laugh. "Expensive was true, too, though not overly so." She shrugged. "I just don't like spending money, I suppose."

Artia laughed as well, coming out behind Brand. "Oh, I know that too well."

Tala had the good grace to look a bit sheepish.

"Brandon, go get your father, will you?"

"Yes, Mom."

Brandon moved downstairs quickly, with the comfortable speed and ease of familiarity. Tala stood and moved towards the table. "How can I help, and where should I sit?"

"No help needed, and you can sit here." Artia pointed at a chair beside the head.

Tala simply nodded and took her seat.

Brandon returned a moment later with a man who looked very much like an older version of his son. He was in his middle years but had somehow kept his hair from going gray or white. Instead, it remained a resolutely chestnut brown, though not with the uniformity that would suggest the color was artificial. He was broad-shouldered, and his arms and forearms were corded with trim, strong muscle. He clearly was more used to long work than heavy work, and his figure bore that out.

Tala stood and gave a small nod. "Master Adrill, thank you for having me in your home."

He gave her a small bow. "Mistress Tala, it is our pleasure to have you." He gestured back to the table. "Please, sit, and drop the 'master.' I am no expert in any craft or field." He smiled. "I do hope that the meal will be to your satisfaction."

"Of that, I have little doubt."

He sat beside her, at the head of the table, and Brand and Artia bought out the plates and cups.

The meal was stoved chicken over a mixture of wild rice and several other grains. There was a side of slow-roasted garlic and asparagus, and their mugs were filled with a sweet wine that complemented the flavors of the food superbly.

Needless to say, the meal was delicious.

Talk stalled while they ate—a sure sign that everyone found the food as delectable as Tala did herself. Once the plates were clean and cleared, the cooks had been thoroughly praised, and the mugs were refilled with a bit more wine, Adrill turned to Tala.

"Now, Mage Tala, what do you want with the Order of the Harvest? We have worked very diligently to keep… your kind from taking notice." Everyone else seemed to lean a bit forward, awaiting Tala's answer.

"Well, you seem to have quite extensive research on the potential benefits of consuming arcane and magical creatures. Humanity can use any edge we can get, and on a personal note, *I* can use any edge I can get." She smiled, lifting her mug towards Brand. "Brand has already helped me greatly by providing some of your Order's research notes, and I feel that I can use that to great effect, even if it never goes beyond me. As to the secrecy, I imagine my… odd circumstances caused me to miss many of the standard practices, which would have kept me from coming across what you all were doing."

Adrill glanced to Brand, who nodded, then returned his gaze to Tala. "I see. What do you offer the Order?"

Tala shrugged. "A Mage's perspective? A Mage's hand in harvesting. I imagine few of your people have magesight, making the identification process more difficult. My magesight is actually a bit… Not unique, but more informative than standard, so I can generally get a good guess at what the magic is intended to accomplish."

Adrill's eyebrows rose in surprise. "That is useful." He glanced to Artia, and she smiled.

"So… may I ask my questions now, or do you have more?" Tala inquired.

He quirked a half-smile. "Fair's fair, I suppose. Ask away."

Tala nodded. "The artifact dimensional storage items: they have to be given power, when not within a high-magic area?"

"Yes."

"Is that a constant flow, a top-off every day, or sort of like they are a cistern slowly draining and need to be refilled every once in a while?"

Adrill was nodding along with her question. "It is most like a cistern, though I imagine they'd function best if they received a constant flow, which would best mimic a high-magic zone."

She frowned at that. "But they function in the city just fine?"

"Yes? This is a high-magic area, after all. Even before the waning officially began."

Tala shook her head. "No, it isn't."

The others at the table shared a look, but it was Brand who spoke. "Mistress Tala, you saw the creatures, plants, and… everything outside the walls. How can you doubt that this is a high-magic region?"

She tilted her head, frowning slightly. "This region is, sure, but this city is not. Human cities process all unassociated magic within themselves, drawing in the surrounding power as well. There is almost no ambient magic here."

There were confused noises and murmurings from the others at the table.

Adrill spoke this time. "Then how do artifacts function within the city? They don't seem to degrade, even when they stay within the walls."

Tala sighed. "That was one of my questions for you." She glanced down at her belt pouch. "When I went out of the city today, I could see my pouch actively drawing in power from the surroundings. It wasn't a lot, but in the high density of power, it was an obvious effect to observe."

Again, there were shared looks, and Brandon spoke up. "You went out of the city?"

"Yes."

"Alone?"

She hesitated. "Technically?"

"That's incredibly dangerous."

You're not wrong. Still, she shrugged. "I didn't encounter any…" She trailed off. She was about to say she hadn't encountered anything dangerous, but that was a lie in a dozen different ways. She cleared her throat. "I wasn't in any real danger." She hesitated, again, thinking about her weakened and breached iron salve. "Well"—she cleared her throat—"I was safe, in the end." She smiled weakly.

Maybe, I am a bit insane.

Dying *would* eliminate her debts…

The thought hit her like a slap.

Do I really think that? It was obviously true, trivially so, but did she really have that as a pillar of her actions? *I… I don't know how to feel about that…*

Adrill cocked an eyebrow, seeming unaware of Tala's inner turmoil. "If I didn't see you sitting here and believe you to be truthful, I'd think you were spreading rumors." He shook his head. "What possessed you to go out alone?"

"Endingberries."

Adrill's eyes widened. He looked to Brand. "The two berries you gave us, you said Mistress Tala provided them, yes?"

Brand nodded. "She did. She also conveyed a desire to get more."

"I succeeded, though I'm not certain exactly what I'll do with them." She gave a hesitant laugh. "Besides eat them for safety, of course." Her smile firmed up. "I was also considering going back for more tomorrow." *I am not suicidal. I'm making rational choices, attempting to gather useful resources.*

Adrill leaned back. "You can harvest them safely?"

She hesitated. *Less so than I'd thought, but yes?* "Safe is a relative term, but yes? There are several… oddities about me that allow me to counter their hostile magics."

"That is a bold claim."

She shrugged. "I'm not going to argue. I will not convey how I do what I do. Even if I did, there is a good chance that it still wouldn't be enough." She thought about how the trees had seemed to brush her in different locations every time, testing for any openings in her defenses. There had been times when they had succeeded, and only the endingberries already in her system had saved her. If that had happened earlier in the day, her inscriptions would have kept her alive... probably. But no one else would have that multi-layered defense. She would not send people to their deaths.

Adrill frowned. "I suppose there isn't a reason for me to press then." He sighed. "What other questions do you have?"

Tala smiled, trying to alleviate some of Adrill's disappointment. "In charging the dimensional storage artifacts, and artifacts in general, is raw power required, or should there be a mental construct to funnel the power through?"

The man tilted his head, thinking. "I know of the concept you're referring to; it reduces power requirement for spell-workings or empowering, correct?"

"Close enough, yes."

"Then, no, my understanding is that that doesn't help and can actually be detrimental." He leaned forward, clearly getting a bit excited by the topic. "Artifacts often seem to have a kind of intelligence about them, almost a will of their own. If Mages attempt to force a mental construct on them, if I'm understanding what you're referring to correctly, the item often rebels. It is like someone trying to force you to be something you aren't."

Tala was nodding. "So, they just require power to... what? Grow? Change?"

Adrill shrugged. "To exist. They do seem to change, slowly and subtly, almost like they are trying to incentivize their owner to feed them more." He chuckled at the very idea.

Tala gave a nervous laugh and glanced down at her pouch. *Slow and subtle? Hardly. But, I suppose, most of their experience with artifacts is within the walls.* "And does ownership matter?"

"Strangely, yes. Items that are rented out, like most of our dimensional storage items, tend to stagnate, remaining fixed as they are." He shrugged. "I've attempted to coax some to grow or change, but they always seem to know if I intend to use them myself or grant them to another." He shook his head. "No, saying they 'know' is too far. They aren't alive as we consider it, but they somehow seem to respond to my knowledge of such. It likely colors my will, somehow. The artifacts I've claimed have all slowly grown and changed over time, even without any power coming from me directly." He smiled. "I'm guessing your items have shown minor changes?"

"Something like that... yeah." She took another drink from her mug. "Do you happen to have any notes on artifacts that you'd be willing to share?"

"Do you have any notes on endingberry harvesting?"

Tala frowned. "They would get you killed."

"We could learn so much." He leaned forward, a hunger obvious in his eyes.

"They would get you killed. No." *Even if you wore iron salve and full iron armor, the trees would get through, in the end.* She sighed. "But I could get you some." *I'm already going back. No harm in giving him some of what I get.*

Adrill had looked momentarily disheartened, but then, he perked up. "Oh?"

"How many would you need to be worth a copy of your notes?"

Adrill bit the left side of his lip, eyes ticking back and forth as he looked at the ceiling, contemplating. Finally, he nodded to himself. "Brandon and I could finalize a copy of our notes for you in the next day or so." He glanced at Brand. "She's leaving in your caravan again, yes?"

"That's right."

"Then, they will be done before you leave."

"And the price?"

Again, Adrill hesitated. "You have me at a distinct disadvantage. I don't know how hard they are to harvest for you, nor how many you can harvest in what span of time."

Tala shrugged. "And I don't know how extensive your notes are, or if they will be of use to me."

Adrill glanced to his wife. "I see why you decided on a straight trade."

Artia let out a soft laugh. "She's either clever or just very stubborn."

Tala sighed. "I hear that a lot, actually."

Brand grinned but didn't comment.

After a moment, however, Adrill addressed the head cook. "How much are endingberries really worth?"

Brand shrugged. "A lot, but not very much." He smiled sympathetically. "There is almost no market for them, because they are almost never harvested successfully. Those I have seen were procured on a contract and had a ready buyer at hand. Those that didn't have a ready buyer almost all had their power fade to nothing before being sold, even in an iron box."

"When there was a ready buyer?"

"Close to half their weight in gold."

Tala had been drinking her wine, and thus, she hid her small smile. She had four gallons of compacted endingberries, at close to eight pounds a gallon, that was nearly thirty-two pounds of endingberries. If the price Brand had quoted was accurate—and it was what he had stated before, so he was at least consistent—she had close to two hundred fifty ounces gold worth of berries. *Too bad there isn't a ready market. I'd have most of my debt paid off, now. Maybe, Grediv would want some? He's probably loaded, given how old he claims to be. Only an idiot lives that long without amassing a fortune.*

Brand continued, however. "That said, if you had a purpose for them?" He shrugged. "A temporary invulnerability to injury would be priceless in countless circumstances."

Adrill frowned. "Very well." After a moment, a small, almost mischievous smile crept across his face. "I fear that I am not up to the task of determining a fair trade." He nodded. "I've decided. I will leave it up to you to give me what you believe is a fair quantity, in exchange for my notes. No matter the amount you give, I will consider it fair recompense."

Tala glowered. *He knows exactly what he's doing...* "You, sir, are an evil man."

Adrill simply beamed at her. "I feel that I am in good hands. Do we have a deal?" He held out a hand to her.

Finally, Tala barked a short laugh. "Very well. We have a deal." They clasped hands and smiled. *Well, rust. Now, I have to be the reasonable one.*

The remainder of the evening was filled with polite conversation and little of note. It was getting a bit late when Brand and Tala bid the family good night and departed, walking the same direction for a short way. *I never got to tour Adrill's workshop,* she realized. *Maybe next time.*

When they were about a block away from the home, Tala glanced towards Brand. "If you don't think it to awkward of me to ask: Why did they only have one child?"

Brand smiled, sadly. "They wouldn't mind you knowing. It was a complicated pregnancy. The Mages said it had something to do with the mother having a gate and the child being without. The child's, Brandon's, body was unable to cope with the power flowing into it from Artia, and it caused issues. Remedies were sought, and I was able to find a few rare arcane harvests that were used to keep the baby alive."

"That's why he's 'Brandon?'"

Brand nodded.

"But there were complications."

"But there were complications." Brand sighed. "The process... changed something within Artia, and they were never able to conceive again."

"I'm so sorry to hear that."

"Yeah."

Tala frowned. "Then... how would Adrill's parents not have known he was without a gate?"

Brand shrugged. "I don't know all the details. Apparently, such complications don't always arise."

She grunted an acknowledgment, and they lapsed into silence. Eventually, she broke the silence once more. "Thank you for introducing me to them."

Brand huffed a laugh. "You'd have found them yourself."

"Maybe, but you made everything far smoother. Thank you." She smiled.

"Happy to help."

"You have been. A help, I mean. Ever since you stabbed me, you've been nothing but kind."

He laughed out loud at that. "It's quite the thing to make up for. I still can't believe I did that, no matter how panicked I felt..."

"Well, you've done it." She smiled again, holding out her hand. "Friends?"

He didn't hesitate, taking her hand in his. "Of course, Mistress Tala."

She glanced down a side street and sighed. "This is my turn. Thank you for walking with me."

"It was my pleasure."

She gained a mischievous glint in her eyes. "Are you sure you can get home safely?"

He laughed again. "Oh, to be protected by one such as thee. How will I survive alone in this city of thieves and vagabonds!"

She laughed, too. "Fair enough. Goodnight, Brand."

"Goodnight, Mistress Tala."

They parted ways, each heading towards their respective beds.

Tala had a smile on her face as she walked beneath the stars, under the powerful, magical dome of the waning city of Alefast. *I have a friend.* It had been too long since she'd been sure of that.

Chapter: 5
So Much More to Learn

Tala returned to her room, only to find a note on the slate, which was affixed to her door below the room number.

The note simply read, 'Please see the front desk.'

I suppose they're trying to maintain privacy? She turned and strode to the entrance hall. In order to reach her room, she had gone around the side, choosing to walk through the gardens as much as possible, rather than through the buildings' hallways.

A different older woman was sitting behind a desk, situated in an alcove of the large atrium, at the front of the inn. The matron stood as she saw Tala approach. "Good evening, Mistress. How may I help you?"

"I had a message to come to the front desk?"

"Oh, certainly. Name, please?"

"Tala."

"Oh! Yes." She bent down and lifted a small chest. It was bound in iron and had a solid clasp, though no lock to keep it shut. "This was left for you by Master Grediv. He asked us to convey his apologies for missing you and to ask you to seek him out if you had any questions."

Tala smiled, accepting the box. "Thank you." It wasn't light, but it definitely wasn't too heavy for her. "Goodnight, Matron."

"Goodnight, Mistress."

Tala gave a small nod and returned to her room.

Millennial Mage, Book 2 - Mage

Once in the room, she sat in her chair, the box in her lap, and flipped open the lid. Inside, three thick, leather-bound books rested: 'A Mage's Guide to Their First Mageling: Basics Every Mageling Should be Taught,' 'A Reference for Inscribing Known Materials,' and 'On Determining the Means to Empower Unique or New Materials.' There wasn't a note or anything else in the box.

"Well, thank you, Master Grediv." She smiled. "These will do nicely."

She quickly flipped through the reference book, and just as she'd thought, there were no useful notes on spell-forms for air. To her surprise, though, air was listed. Beside it, there was a simple sentence: 'The creation of spell-forms in the air is the domain of Archons and not within the scope of this work.'

Interesting. She was *definitely* going to pursue this further. She glanced at the box of books, then down at her belt pouch. *I wonder...* She closed the box and opened her bag to slide the box in, letting it go as soon as it was fully inside.

Then, she pulled the belt pouch free, opening it wide and placing it on the floor.

Without delay, she climbed down into it and turned to look at the bookshelf. Sure enough, the three books had been added next to her notebooks. "Well, I suppose this entire space doesn't exist, except under the influence of your power, so why should it be strange that things which enter it can be manipulated by you?"

The pouch did not respond.

"I need someone to talk to..." She sighed. With all the oddities swirling around her, she didn't know exactly who she could trust with all of it—if anyone. *Grediv was too nice... He probably wants something.*

She looked around, then reached her arms out, stretching wide. She couldn't touch the walls. "You've doubled in size..." She turned in a circle. "You also feel low on magic. The ambient power in here is almost as low as in the city." She nodded. "We need to find a way for you to indicate you need more power, without me having to come in... Maybe one of the knots on your tie cord? Not sure how that would work, though... You're connected to my will. Can I 'feel' when you're running low?" *That might be too convenient. Maybe after a few days of consistent refilling?* She sighed, walking to one wall that had a lighter patch in the shape of her right hand. "I assume this is for me." She smiled. *Why not?*

She directed power coming in through her gate in a carefully regulated flow out of her hand and into the inside of the belt pouch. She was mindful of how easily the power flowed and didn't allow the stream to grow too large or to flow for too long.

"There," she said, pulling her hand back. The ambient power in the air of the pouch had now risen to a level near that of the Wilds outside Bandfast. "That should do."

She climbed up out of the hole in her inn-room floor, closed the belt pouch, and set it and her knife on the bedside table.

She stripped out of her clothes and carefully set them out on the chair for the next day. That done, she moved through her nightly stretches and did her hair up so it wouldn't tangle. *No need to get my new clothes all sweaty or covered in wrinkles, after all.* It wasn't like she currently had spares.

She was about to head to bed when her eyes fell on the knife, now across the room from where she'd been working.

She didn't feel the strained exhaustion in her soul anymore, though she did feel a bit of weariness from the same nebulous... sense. *One rep, then.*

She held out her hand and reached for the knife.

Millennial Mage, Book 2 - Mage

Without an instant's hesitation, it zipped across the intervening space, stopping immediately, perfectly aligned and situated in her hand.

The worked soreness returned, and Tala yawned before smiling down at the knife. "That will do nicely."

Without further delay, she climbed into her waiting bed, snapped her fingers to turn off the artifact lights, and promptly fell to sleep.

* * *

She woke at the first hints of light on the horizon, the glowing sky turning the few buildings that poked over the inn's walls into a flat black silhouette of themselves. *Oh, I forgot to draw the curtains.*

She completed her stretching and exercises before she was truly, fully awake. As wakefulness came upon her, she grinned in triumph. Throughout her sets, her sleepy magesight had been focused inward, guiding her movements towards best effect. In addition, she'd maintained balance and proper breathing.

Now awake, she added one more exercise to the regimen. *Soul work.* It was a stupid name, but she couldn't think of a better one.

She stood near the door to her room, knife in hand and in its sheath. With a casual motion, she tossed the knife towards her bed, then *pulled* on the weapon, drawing it back towards her even as it arced away.

Immediately, the knife zipped back to her hand, as easily as her hand might move to rest on her hip.

The strain wasn't as great, today, so she did a second toss and retrieval.

As she caught the knife for the second time, she felt a wave of dizziness and sank to the floor, kneeling and placing her forehead to the soft ground. *Oh my... calm down, Tala. You're alright.*

The dizziness slowly passed, taking with it the slight nausea that had been threatening to rise.

She carefully moved over to her bedside table and reached into her pouch, grabbing a piece of jerky from the shelf just inside the opening and popping it into her mouth.

Chewing on the jerky, she pulled out a brush, undid her hair, and worked out the night's tangles.

That complete, she took her morning bath, careful to keep her hair dry. Then, she refreshed her iron salve, meticulously checking herself over with the magic detector. *Not today, trees. Not today.*

Satisfied, she dressed in her new clothes, strapped on the belt, and added the pouch and knife to it. *Ready to go!*

Again, she took advantage of the to-go breakfast the inn offered, downing the allowed two cups of coffee in quick succession. *Not enough.* But there really wasn't anything she could do about it. She wasn't going to buy more in the city. *I don't have* that *much money.*

The attendant already looked a bit wary of her. *I suppose I shouldn't have drunk it so quickly.*

She thanked the young man, then grabbed some extra bread, cheese, and a couple of pieces of fruit to supplement her lunch. She ate happily as she walked out into the city.

I feel like I'm forgetting something obvious, that would be really useful in my travels. But no matter how she twisted her mind, nothing came to the forefront. *Oh well.*

She made her way to the workyard, much earlier than she'd arrived the day before, and waved to the foreman. The twenty cargo-slots were ready and waiting, a single glowing symbol visible on each.

She moved with calm confidence down the line and finished empowering them all in less than ten minutes. To her great satisfaction, she'd also done so in a manner that she didn't feel any magical or mental strain. Her mental constructs had been quick, efficient, and thorough, and the power requirement for each empowerment had been less than ever. *Repetition breeds precision.* It was too bad that that competence wouldn't translate to empowering anything else, mental models being specific to the working.

The general idea does seem a bit like knowing what my inscriptions will do, as I use them, but that's probably just a coincidence.

"Take care!"

"Thank you. You as well, Mistress."

She walked through the market on the way towards the eastern gate but paused beside the friendly barrel merchant to say good morning.

"I'm afraid I don't have any unspoken-for empty kegs today, Mistress."

Tala laughed and shook her head. "No, no. I think I've enough of those…" She trailed off, looking at the larger barrels. *Water. I would love to have a huge barrel of water available.* She smiled. *A cistern would be perfect…* She shook her head. Now was not the time, she had work to be about. "Thank you, again, for the kegs."

"Thank you for the business, Mistress."

Tala nodded and continued on her way. As she walked, she glanced down at her pouch. "Hey… I hate just calling you pouch, but nothing else really seems appropriate…" *Pouchy? Bag-thing?* She groaned. "I don't even know if you understand me, or if you need words at all, but it would be pretty great if I had a method for storing water in you. If you can make a cistern for me to fill up, that'd be amazing, but if not, can you make an empty rack for the largest barrel that would fit through your opening? I'll just get a barrel if that's the case. No big deal."

The bag did not respond.

Tala cleared her throat as she continued to walk. *I am insane, but the insanity seems to work, so...* She patted the belt pouch. "You'll have most of today to draw in power. Let's see what you can do with it. Thank you for carrying all my stuff." *All my stuff... it's carrying my kit. Kit!* "How about I call you Kit?"

The bag did not respond.

She smiled. "Kit it is, then."

Tala waited in the line at the eastern gate, and once she reached the front of the fast-moving line, the guard waved her through.

She was now, it seemed, on the list.

Tala quirked a smile at that but didn't comment.

She stepped out of the gatehouse and into sunlight and *power*. She stepped aside as a group of people passed, turning north—thankfully the opposite way from her intended heading. She closed her eyes, spread her arms just a bit, and inhaled deeply.

"Wonderful." She wasn't quite sure how she'd like going back to lower magic regions. Maybe, she wouldn't really notice? *Not likely.* The cities would be the same, at the very least.

The moment of reverie passed, and she set out towards the ending grove once more. *Don't eat so many berries today, Tala. And watch your iron salve.*

She still had a comfortable stock of power from the endingberries that she'd consumed the day before, but it had noticeably decreased during the night. As she walked, she took a risk and turned her magesight inward to examine the power. As she did so, she got the impression of streamers of power funneling off the torrent, moving through her and trickling into each of her defensive inscriptions. *Huh... They aren't active...* Even so, the power was flowing through them, and she could almost convince herself that she felt them doing... something.

Millennial Mage, Book 2 - Mage

Maybe, Holly will be able to tell. She shrugged. *Just over a week, and I'll be back.*

She now held about half the amount of endingberry power that she'd taken in the day before. That was still a tremendous amount, likely close to forty berries worth. She'd guessed that she'd eaten close to a pound of endingberries the previous day, but she wasn't at all sure. That didn't factor in how much of the juice she'd gotten by sucking the seeds clean.

Only one cup of berries, or their juice, per day from now on.

That seemed reasonable. That was about a quarter of what she'd eaten the day before, so it *shouldn't* upset her stomach. *As long as I eat other food, too.*

She returned her magesight to focusing outward and continued to scan her surroundings.

Something had stuck in her mind from the previous evening. Everyone had seen her going out as a dangerous prospect. *Was I just lucky, yesterday?* She glanced down at herself, and her new clothing, and sighed. *I should probably change.*

She glanced back at the city, considering the guards she could see up on the walls. Then, she realized that she didn't really need privacy, just to be out of line of sight momentarily.

She stepped behind a group of trees and found a depression among some rocks that was about the right size. She took off her belt pouch and opened it wide before situating it among the rocks on as flat a ground as she could find. Even so, it was at a bit of a tilt. *That shouldn't matter... Right?*

Her magesight showed a small, steady tide of magic moving into the bag. *What do the artifacts do with all the power?*

She really needed Adrill's notes...

Tala climbed down into the pouch and noted that gravity was oriented as usual within the small extra-dimensional space. *So, it's as I figured, the orientation of the bag doesn't affect the environment inside.* That was incredibly good to know as it also implied that no movement was transferred in either. Thus, her items weren't being jostled by her actions throughout the day. *I can do more tests later.*

She quickly stripped down and set her clothes to the side. True to what she'd thought, a small set of shelves had been added beside the one for the books, and on them rested her old shirt and pants.

She slipped into them and replaced her belt overtop. Then, she glanced down at her new clothes, piled on the ground, and sighed. *I'm not going to make bad habits just because I have the option of convenience.* She picked the pieces up, folded them nicely, and placed them on the shelves. "There."

She turned to climb out when she heard voices coming down the ladder.

"There's said to be ruins this way, and you all saw the lady Mage going in this direction. I'd bet she has information we don't."

"So you say, but we're still not equipped to go scouring ruins. We're meant to be felling trees. These axes won't work so well on magical monsters. And Master Sodro's magic isn't good for much beside letting us run away."

Another man made a derisive noise. "That's why we're following the other Mage, idiot. She'll deal with any threats, and we can hunt on her coattails." Sodro either didn't take offense or hadn't heard. *Whoever he is.*

"What if she doesn't like us doing that?"

"There's only one of her. We take what we want. She's out here alone, and accidents happen." There was a chorus of muttered agreements, and she heard no dissent, even hesitantly or quietly uttered.

Tala glanced down at her right hand. *Nineteen rings left. There shouldn't be that many of them...* But she didn't know, and she needed these to last until she got back to Bandfast. *Think, Tala. Don't rush in. You need to think through your options.*

She cursed silently.

She could attack them with her knife; it wasn't like they could hurt her, given her inscriptions and the power flowing through her, but they could catch her. She still didn't really know what she was doing in physical combat, and a dozen men could easily pile on her and pin her down, leaving her helpless.

No, fighting was *not* a good option. *Nice; way to think through that option fully.* She should wait. Hopefully, they would pass her by without even noticing.

There was a pause among the men outside, and she heard them stop walking a throwing distance from where her bag lay, tucked among the rocks. "Where did she go?"

Oh, come on!

"That way? That next rise is close enough that she could be over the ridge."

There was a round of agreement, and Tala counted at least ten voices. *Yeah, way too many...*

One man spoke up. "I don't know. I thought she was heading that way."

There were more mutterings, but Tala couldn't tell if they were agreement or irritation.

"What if she saw us and is trying to hide?"

There was a sound that Tala would bet was a hand slapping the back of a bald head. "Idiot! Why would a Mage hide from us? She shouldn't know us from any other work crew out here."

"Because she's alone? Not every Mage can fight well against people. It's much harder to fight a group of men than a single large wolf... or something. Maybe, she knew we were following her?"

"Oh, and you know that from experience, do you?"

"Don't be daft; it's logical! Would you rather fight one dog or a dozen angry cats?"

There was a round of muttered agreements, and Tala had a sudden, horrifying thought. *What if they find the bag and close it while I'm inside?*

She didn't know if she could force her way out, should they tie it closed. She also didn't know what trying would do to the item, whether she succeeded or not. *Will the space be maintained, or will it close in on me...* Artia's tales of human-eating dimensional storage items came back to the forefront of her thoughts. *Rust shut, stupid mind. Now is not the time.*

"She could be in those trees. There really aren't too many, but it isn't a tiny grove. If she isn't, we could lose her while we try to do a thorough search."

"Fine, then. Let's vote. Who says search the trees?"

Tala heard the rustle of cloth. *The rusting idiots are raising their hands to vote.* She had no way of knowing how the vote was going.

"Who says go for that hill and hope to catch her?" Again, a rustle of cloth.

Come on, come on!

"It's decided, then."

What's decided!?

"You two, search that way, you three go there, and we'll go straight through the middle."

Oh, rust me to slag. Tala cracked her neck. If she could get up the ladder and into a stable position before they were on her, she might have a—

"What's this?" A voice came much louder down the ladder. "Oy! Boys, there's a hole in the ground."

Well... there goes that idea.

She heard the men gathering around the hole. *Why, under the heavens, are you so interested in a hole? You probably can't even fit inside it.*

"That's a small hole. Why are we here?"

Good question. She almost groaned in irritation but realized that any sound would give her away.

"She could be down there."

"We can't fit in that! I can't even see anything in there."

Can't see... Tala looked around, easily able to see her surroundings. Tentatively, she moved over to where she could see up and out of the hole. There was a crowd of faces looking down at it, at her, but none of them seemed to give any indication that they could see her.

"Could be magic."

"If it's magic, we could die trying to get in."

"That's a fair point. Master Sodro, what does your magesight say?"

A rough voice grated a short response. "Dimensional. Magical." The man who spoke wore a deep hood, clearly to hide his face as it was horribly disfigured. *Sometimes better vision isn't a blessing.* Much of his skin appeared to have had rock, earth, or sand laced through it. *Magic poisoning?* If so, it was a fairly advanced case of it. She was actually surprised the man was still functional.

"Not arcane?"

"No." The voice was clipped as if the speaker didn't like talking. *With a voice like that, it's no wonder.* His eyes were glowing with power, no scripts to be seen on the surrounding... stone. *So, his inscriptions have melded with the deformities.* If she remembered correctly, magic-poisoned Mages often had their magic enhanced at the end of their agonizing existence. *Great...*

"Yeah, I don't want to die."

That's right, boys. Go on your way. No need to investigate further. Sodro pulled back, clearly not interested in participating in the discussion.

"So, it's a magic hole. Seems stupid to mess with it. My vote is that we should just search elsewhere."

Yes! Yes, you should.

"Hey, what's this?" One bent closer and pointed to the edge of the hole. "Is that a cord?"

Oh, come on. This was just not her morning. *Maybe, I can throw my knife up, first? Take one out by surprise?* It probably wouldn't help much.

At that moment, she heard a grunt of pain, and some of the men turned to look around.

"Hey, where's Dentric?"

Another grunt came from the other side, and more of the men swiveled.

"Frand?"

This time, there was a short scream of agony before silence returned, and the men began to huddle together—at least, from what Tala could see.

"Who's out there? We're armed!"

One of the men that Tala could see jerked to the side, a spurt of blood painting those around him before he dropped.

The screaming really started, then. And magic began to fly—specifically, earth magic.

Tala was torn between wanting to run up the ladder and see what was going on and staying put where it was safe. *For now.*

Her choice was quickly taken as she heard what sounded like the last man fall, and silence filled the air.

A moment later, a burst of power radiated out, heavily tinged with earth, stone, and sand. *He was further along than I'd have guessed if his death caused that.*

She only hesitated a moment longer. *Well, rust this. I'm not getting stuck in here.*

She surged up the ladder, knife in hand, and leapt up into a grounded stance, straddling the open belt pouch below her.

All around, the rocks and dirt were liberally sprinkled with blood and bodies. Several clustered fields of stone spikes as well as a half-formed wall of earth were the only evidence of meaningful resistance.

Standing proudly over a broken, statue-like form was the terror bird, scratching at its red-painted beak with one of its powerful claws.

Chapter: 6
Bad Birdy?

Tala stood for a moment, regarding the terror bird as it continued to clean its beak.

She looked around at the bodies surrounding them. "Ummm... Bad birdy?"

The bird stopped and looked at her, then at the men surrounding them. It cocked its head and let out a sound that reminded Tala of nothing so much as incredulity.

"Fine, fine. Thank you. You could have driven them off—"

It tilted its head the other way.

She felt a smile tug at her lips. "You're right, that's not really how you work." She bent down and picked up her pouch, fastening it to her belt and pulling out a piece of jerky. "I suppose you want this?"

The head bobbed up and down once.

"Well, what are we going to do about all these bodies?"

The terror bird looked around itself, then started moving, blinking between the various men, pulling off their belts and packs with quick slashing talons and jerks with its beak.

What are you...? It just saw me pull jerky from a belt pouch. She grinned. *It's being extra certain?*

Once all the packs and pouches were separate, the ripple of power washed over the terror bird, and it quadrupled in size.

Tala's eyes widened in alarm for three reasons.

77

The first was that she was afraid the bird might be seen from the city. She glanced back that way but realized that they were well out of sight. *Good, tall trees.*

The second reason was that, in her understanding, terror birds continued to grow until they were killed. *If this is its true size, it must be hundreds upon hundreds of years old.* From her intricate understanding of dimensional magic, it was very easy to shrink something, but enlarging even moderately complex items was not only ludicrously complicated, but it almost always resulted in the destruction of the same. With that in mind, the bird was not likely to be enlarging itself.

The third reason was somewhat more personally practical. The bird now stood more than three times her height and was large enough to easily swallow a person whole.

I do not want to see how I fare in the belly of the creature.

It seemed that her estimates were accurate, because the terror bird began snapping up the bodies and swallowing them whole, one by one.

How can it possibly fit all of them? There were repetitive flickers of dimensional magic emanating from within the creature. *Is it shrinking them? Is its stomach some form of dimensional storage?*

She had no idea, and she silently hoped that she never found out.

In a startlingly short amount of time, the terror bird had finished its work and was standing close, but not too close, now just shorter than Tala, herself. It had left the Mage's body alone. Apparently, it didn't like the magic-tainted flavoring. *Something like that.*

"You are pretty capable."

The bird bobbed its head.

"I need to give you a name." She tossed the chunk of jerky to it, and the bird caught it easily, seeming to savor the flavor, moving the meat across its tongue slowly rather than guzzling it down. "You're a terror bird, that much is obvious. You seem to be fine waiting around for me to come out and give you treats..." She smiled. "You tarry nearby. Terror. Tarry. Terry. I'll call you Terry."

The bird hesitated for a moment, then swallowed before regarding her. After a long moment, it bobbed its head slightly and let out a chirping whistle.

"Very well, Terry, I'll get you a bit more." She pulled free some more jerky and tossed it to the side.

Terry vanished, and the meat did as well, a heartbeat later.

Tala sighed. "And now I've named it." She walked over to the pile of belts and bags, most of which were speckled with drying blood. She groaned. "This is gross..."

Ten minutes later, she had finished processing the items she'd found. The men had each had an ax, though they'd been scattered around the clearing during the... incident. It seemed that there'd been eleven of the men in total, not counting the Mage. Each also had had a simple belt knife—as basically everyone always did. The woodsmen also each had a small, serviceable hatchet.

To her tremendous surprise, one of the men had been carrying a hammer, which turned out to be an artifact. Aside from the same durability inscriptions that her knife bore, the straight-peen hammer's particular magics seemed specifically aimed to redirect force away from the striking surfaces. *Maybe for assisting in the felling of magically dense trees?*

She supposed that the woodsmen had needed the function and hadn't been able to be picky about the form.

The handle of the hammer was a dark gray, almost black metal, where the head had the look of standard steel. Both the handle and head appeared to be made from material which had been twisted into beautiful, regular spirals before being hammered flat and smoothed, leaving only faint inclinations of the work to peek out from the patterns within the material.

Just like in her belt pouch and knife, there was a confluence of power within the head of the hammer that she now knew could accept an Archon Star. *I could sell this… but I'm not going to.* She nodded firmly.

I'm keeping this. I'm not bonding it, though… not yet. One is enough for now. The hatchets, axes, and knives she'd have to sell. *Back in Bandfast…* She felt a momentary flicker of guilt at the deaths of these men, but it passed as she remembered their plans to cause an 'accident' for her. *Too bad you couldn't have just kept at your jobs and left me alone.*

There were some foodstuffs, protected by the men's various pouches and bags from any blood splatter.

She packaged all these together into two groups, perishable and non-perishable. The latter category was, by far, the largest, and she stored those in her pouch, along with the tools she'd already claimed. She ate the perishable foods, which consisted of a large carrot, a hunk of heavy bread, and a handful of radishes.

She threw another piece of jerky to one side, and it vanished in a flicker of dimensional power. "Nicely done, Terry."

If I'm giving him a name, I've got to try to train him. She almost laughed. He was likely older than the waning city to her west. 'Training' sounded a bit insulting. *Maybe… negotiating?* It would be worth a try. *Later.*

She took all of the belts, pouches, and bags as well. They'd each been treated against the coming winter weather, so the blood mostly wiped off on the nearby, clean grass. The remaining flecks came off with some water from her waterskin and easy scrubbing with some rags, which had once been clothing. *That arcanous plant really did a number on these.*

Finally, she looked down on the broken Mage. Terry's attacks had shredded his clothing, skittering across the stone in his flesh until they found his soft spots. He had very few inscriptions as he had very little actual skin left.

It looked... self-done. *Who would do this to themselves?* He had obviously been a Material Creator, and he hadn't properly insulated himself against that power. *I wonder what his story is... well, was.*

She really couldn't just leave his body, but she had no idea what to do with it. Finally, she took off his belt, pouches and all, opened Kit wide, and maneuvered his body inside, dropping the belt in after.

I'll look through his pouches later. It's time to be moving. I've delayed too long as it is.

With a sigh, she set off, leaving the red-splattered clearing behind.

Thanks to her care, she'd avoided getting almost any blood on herself, and what little had gotten on her hands, she scraped off on some rocks and trees as she passed. She had to use some more water and judicious scrubbing as she walked to get the last bits. She was grateful that she'd kept as clean as she had because while the iron salve helped, blood was notoriously hard to remove.

Thankfully, the few spots that just wouldn't respond to her ministrations blended with the berry stains already on her palms and finger-pads. *Good enough, I suppose.*

Just like the previous day's walk, there was no snow, even in the deepest dells or in the shade of trees. The mountains to the north bore snow, but that was likely to be a year-round state for this region. The verdant fields hid many arcane and a few magical creatures from her normal vision if not her magesight. Still, none were large or aggressive enough to do her harm.

She did note the distinct lack of larger threats, and she pondered, not for the first time, if Terry was keeping the way clear for her. At the thought, she decided to toss another bit of jerky.

It promptly vanished.

Should I be worried that I'm becoming used to that? It was a concern for another day.

She easily reached the grove of endingberry trees well before noon and looked about, feeling a bit nervous, given her recent encounter. "Terry?"

The bird popped into existence ten feet in front of her. At the moment, he was just larger than a house cat and was looking at her questioningly.

"Are there any humans about?"

He vanished in a flick of dimensional power, and Tala felt a cascade of dimensional blips all across the range of her senses.

Less than thirty seconds later, Terry was standing before her once more.

He shook himself, indicating a negative.

Tala grinned. "Thank you, Terry." She tossed him another hunk of jerky, which he happily caught.

With as much solemn reverence as she could muster, Tala upended Kit, dumping the Mage's body out onto the ground. *I suppose I'm glad that Kit can understand what I want?* She didn't quite know how the body had come out, especially since gravity in the pouch was seemingly unrelated to its orientation, but she wasn't going to complain. *I'd have hated to drag him up the ladder...*

She glanced at the body and had a *moment's* hesitation. His eyes resembled huge gemstones, after all. She turned away in disgust. *I am NOT prying his eyes out. That is a horrific idea.*

Without pausing further, lest she somehow change her mind, she rolled him down the hill.

Tala stripped out of her clothes, placing them into her belt pouch. Then, she went down and dragged the body the last stretch to the base of the closest ending tree.

Several branches, which had been well above her head moments before, brushed against her and her burden.

A fraction later, the body *puffed* into dust. Tala staggered back, doing her best to not inhale any of the fine powder. *There. That's done.*

She trekked back up to her pouch, removed her fruit picker, and went to work.

Noon came and went, and while she paused for lunch, she was diligent in her work.

Late afternoon arrived, and she was pushing against the edge of her time if she wanted to get back into the city before dark. She smiled as she arched back, stretching aching muscles.

She had just finished refilling the second jug for the last time.

She'd filled all but one keg, and those, along with the two jugs, meant that she had a total of ten gallons of endingberries. She couldn't have asked for a better haul.

In order to speed up her work, and get access to berries after she'd done her best to pick the outside of the grove clean of easy-to-reach fruit, she'd had to delve deeper in.

She had lost count of how many branches, leaves, and twigs had come in contact with her, even before the first hour had passed. The trees still seemed to favor contacting new locations, if at all possible, and that had worked in her favor.

Today, she had been far, far more careful. After each basket full of berries had been gathered, she'd swept herself with the magic detector and re-applied iron salve on any portion of her that even *might* have registered to the construct. She also added more to any place she could remember the tree touching. A few times, when she felt a particularly potent spike of power from a nearby tree, she had retreated with a partially full basket and reinforced her protection. *I will not be complacent.*

She pulled out the remnants of her shredded clothes, those that the arcanous plant had torn to ribbons, along with a water skin. She wetted the rags and used them to clean herself of the dirt, dust, and sweat that she'd gathered through the day.

All clean, or at least as clean as she was likely to get before returning to the inn, Tala dressed in the fading light of an autumn afternoon.

She didn't climb down into the bag, as she was still feeling a bit of trepidation after her near miss earlier that day. *I really need some way of securing this, while I'm inside it…*

Another project to add to her list.

Dressed and packed to go, she set out, back towards the city, taking a bit of a different route so as to avoid the site of the earlier massacre.

She did toss bits of jerky every so often, confirming Terry's continued proximity. *And protection.*

When she knew that the city was just over the next rise, she found a sheltered place, among a striking rock formation, and changed back into her nicer clothing. Once again, she did not change within the pouch's dimensional space.

Shortly thereafter, she arrived at the eastern gates, the sun just touching the horizon on the far side of the city.

"State your name!"

The now-familiar 'greeting' caused Tala to smile, and she complied.

There was a bit of a pause before she was acknowledged and let inside.

"Any problems, guardsmen?"

"No, Mistress."

Tala shrugged and smiled. "Very well. Have a good night!"

"Thank you, Mistress. Goodnight to you, as well."

Without looking back, she strode out of the gatehouse and into the city proper.

* * *

Tala walked up to Artia's stall as the woman was finishing closing up for the night.

"Mistress Tala! Welcome. I assume you're here to see Adrill?"

Tala smiled, nodding. "I am. Thank you."

"Brandon! Get your father, please."

Brandon's voice floated back from within the shop. "Yes, Mom."

While she waited, Tala helped Artia pack up the last pieces of the stall and bring them inside. "I don't suppose you've gotten any other items you might want to part with?"

Artia laughed. "Nothing unique if that's what you're asking. A few new dimensional storage bags, another knife, and a few more odds and ends." She shrugged. "From what you conveyed, nothing seems to fall in line with what you'd be seeking."

"Fair enough. Thank you."

Adrill came in through the door in the back, a small book in his hand, Brandon right behind him. "Did I hear Mistress Tala?" He smiled when he saw her. "Welcome back! I assume you're here for this?" He held up what was obviously a notebook full of his research into artifacts.

"I am." Tala had given a lot of thought to the price she should pay for those notes and had decided that generosity would serve her best in the long run. From what she knew, this city was likely the best, if not only, source of artifacts that she could get to, and Artia and Adrill were the best source within the city—at least now that they didn't consider her a hostile Mage to be avoided if at all possible.

Therefore, she pulled out one of the gallon jugs, wrapped in iron-salve-treated cloth. "This is for you." She set the heavy jug on the table. "I believe this is just under eight pounds of endingberries, de-seeded."

Everyone stopped and stared in stunned silence.

After a long moment, Brandon cleared his throat. "Mistress Tala?"

"Hmm?"

"I believe I misheard you—likely my parents did, too—but I thought I heard you say eight *pounds*. That can't be right, because that would be worth nearly sixty-four ounces gold."

Quick with numbers, I see. Tala shrugged with a nonchalance she didn't feel. "If there was a market, I'd sell them. Without a steady supply, their uses are limited and uncertain. If there were a steady supply, they wouldn't be worth nearly so much." After a moment, she realized that she hadn't actually answered him. "But, no, you didn't mishear."

Adrill came forward and set the book on the counter. "You have overvalued these notes, Mistress Tala, even though what you say is true. I will be able to take much greater risks in my research with those available to me."

Tala smiled. "I'd hoped that would be the case. The bag is… something that will help contain the magic, but an iron box or iron jug will function better, I think. Please be careful not to let the berries rust it out." She grinned.

"Mistress… Tala, I don't know what to say. This is too much. What else can we give you in exchange?"

She was about to say, 'Nothing' when she remembered two things. "Well... the comb would actually be pretty helpful."

"Comb?" Adrill looked confused, but Artia laughed, stepping over to a display table to pick up the simple, but magic-filled, comb. Adrill nodded. "Ahh! Yes. It is a simple thing, but consider it yours."

Tala smiled, nodding her thanks as she slipped the comb into her belt pouch. "Do you happen to have something that can create water?"

As it turned out, they did, in fact, have a small bronze ring that accomplished what she wanted.

The ring was just large enough for her two thumbs to go through, together, and when a Mage funneled power into it, water would flow out the other side. It was actually an example of a class of magical item that Tala hadn't encountered before called a lensing item or an 'incorporator,' which simply took raw magic power and output a single, predefined substance. They weren't rare, but they were fairly expensive.

To Artia's understanding, they weren't widely used because of two things. First, they were quite power intensive. A Material Creator could magic-up close to ten times the volume of material for the same amount of power. Second, incorporators only created substances temporarily.

In the case of water, or anything else ingestible, it functioned as expected. It would hydrate the consumer and pass through without harm, ill effect, or oddity. However, if left in the open, the water or other substance would begin to evaporate back into intangible power within an hour, give or take. The greater the quantity exposed together, the faster it would begin to vanish.

Thus, incorporators were very niche in their usefulness, and Artia and Adrill parted with the one for water incorporation happily. They only had this one because it was the cheapest type of incorporator available. They explained that Adrill had purchased it for study ages ago, but that research hadn't gone anywhere because a Mage was absolutely required to use it. It had been gathering dust in his shop ever since.

Tala bid the family goodnight and headed back towards the inn, Adrill's notes in hand, feeling content with her decision to bias towards generosity. The endingberries still had a theoretical value much greater than what she'd received, but she had no doubt that she'd gotten the better end of the bargain, in the long run at the very least.

* * *

Tala giggled with joy as she pointed the water incorporator towards the bathtub within her room in the Wandering Magician.

With an effort of will, she pushed a trickle of power into the ring clutched in her hand. She used only a tenth of the flowrate that she'd utilized the day before, during the process of creating her latest Archon Star. The result was a thin stream of water fountaining out of the very center of the ring, seeming to originate from thin air before arching far away from her to land in the tub.

She'd soaked a towel or two in the beginning as she'd gotten her aim down, but they were all dry now; she'd been playing for well more than an hour, after all.

"This is amazing!" She giggled again. "I'm so glad that I'm not a Material Creator, or I'd never do anything else." She shot another spurt of water, sweeping the thin stream back and forth.

She had her magesight focused on the ring as it worked, and was fascinated at what she saw. The ring acted as a sort of lens, but where an optical lens bent light, often revealing the multitudes of colors within, this ring bent magic, revealing the water within… or something like that. She didn't really have a good grasp on what was happening, but it was still fascinating… and fun.

I need more of these. I need every kind of incorporator there is!

Finally, she was able to rein in her inner child, and she got ready for bed.

She stripped down, stretched, lightly exercised the muscles the day's activities hadn't worked, and tossed her knife, drawing it back to her.

She was able to draw it back three times that night, though the final one had her groaning on the floor with a splitting headache right afterward.

Slower, Tala. Keep your soul intact, please?

To her great relief, the headache passed fairly quickly.

She indulged in a bit more play while she bathed, removing the day's grime, but after that, she resolutely placed the bronze ring away.

She braided her hair and climbed into bed, content.

Today was a good day.

Chapter: 7
A Day of Departure

Tala woke even earlier than usual, the sky still dark outside. *Back on the road today.*

She moved through her stretches and exercises with determined efficiency, smiling as she noticed the improvements her micromanagement was bringing about. *It's amazing what you can do when you can see every individual muscle fiber.* She couldn't control her muscles that finely, yet, but it let her subtly modify every stretch and exercise towards better results.

She was able to toss and retrieve the knife three times without obvious ill effect, though it left her very being aching, much like her muscles. *Not ready for a fourth rep.*

Tala combed out her hair, which consisted of a single stroke through each portion, due to the artifact comb. *This is going to save me hours, all told, over the coming months!* She smiled happily, climbing into her bath.

She allowed herself an extra minute or two in the comfortably hot water before she dried herself off and went to work with the iron salve. Even though she'd been meticulous the day before, she wasn't going to let it fall by the wayside again, at least not anytime soon.

She still had the pleasant buzz of endingberry power within her, though it had settled into feeling similar to a comfortably warm mug of coffee, instead of the raging, industrial crucible of the first day. *It's probably healthier for me to keep the power at about this level.* She'd need to have Holly give her a good, deep examination to determine if her fervor had made any permanent changes. *Hopefully, only good ones…*

She was wrapped in a towel, back in her room, when a knock came on her door.

She glanced to the still-dark windows in her outer wall before calling out. "Who is it?"

"Merilin, with your clothing."

Tala opened the door with a smile before freezing in place. Merilin was, indeed, standing out in the hallway… along with a male servant.

Tala and the servant both immediately blushed, the servant looking away, Tala pulling the door partially closed once more. Even with the towel, she did *not* like that type of surprise.

"Merilin?"

"Yes, child?"

"Why is he here?"

"Did you want an old woman to carry all your clothes herself?"

Tala paused for a moment before grumbling a negative. "I'm going to go into the bath room. Please place the clothing on the bed and ask him to leave. I'll come out and pay you, then."

Merilin nodded.

Tala tried to be dignified as she scampered to the bath room and closed the door.

She heard movement outside, rustling near the bed, then a single set of footfalls retreated back out the door, and it closed behind them.

Tala came back out to find Merilin sitting in her reading chair.

"You're perfectly covered."

"I'm in a towel."

Merilin shrugged. "Young people these days. What does it matter what you're wearing? It should only matter what you show."

Tala gave her a flat look. "You're a seamstress. You really don't think it matters what people are wearing?"

Merilin paused at that. "You know what I meant." She gestured at the bed. "You're leaving today, yes?"

Tala nodded.

"Then, I recommend the far stack."

As Tala turned her attention fully to the bed, she noticed three things. First, there were three piles of varying sizes. Second, there were far fewer items than she'd been expecting. Third, there was magic coming from the pile that Merilin indicated. "What did you do?"

"I made an executive decision. Take a look."

Tala opened the brown paper encasing the single outfit in the final stack. Inside, on top, was a leather jerkin that had powerful reconstitution magic woven through it; there were no inscriptions, the power was a natural property of the material.

"That is leather from an immortal elk." The woman scoffed. "Obviously, it's not immortal, but the name comes from how devilish they are to kill. They can heal from nearly any wound, so they are almost never able to be harvested." She sighed. "To kill them usually requires such overwhelming destruction that nothing is left."

Tala looked down at the item. "So…?"

"So, unless you get these utterly obliterated, they will reconstitute." She waggled a finger. "That doesn't give you the excuse to be careless. They are no more durable than any high-quality leather, initially, so take good care of them. You're a Mage; you can give them power as you wear through its natural stores."

Tala was frowning. "How can the clothes rebuild themselves? Why wouldn't they return to the form of the elk's hide?" She looked down. "Why don't they have hair if they regenerate?"

Merilin muttered under her breath, so low that Tala hardly heard it. "Mages always want to know 'How? How? How?' It's never 'Thank you, Merilin. You're amazing, Merilin.'" She huffed, then spoke more loudly. "Their power is suspended by a proprietary, secret method while the clothing is made. When the power is returned, the garment's state at that time becomes the default to which the magic returns."

Tala nodded. That made some sense. "Well, let's try these on, then."

She took the package and returned to the bath room, closing the door before dropping her towel. She set the package down and pulled out the tunic. It was beautifully composed, looking almost like fabric in its working. She wiggled into the garment and found it soft, smooth, and silky, inside and out. *This won't chafe at all!* That was a boon—leather could easily cause rubbing and soreness if not properly treated or sized.

There were ties up each side, starting at her armpit and going down to her waist. The ties were of leather as well. The sleeves were loose without being billowy, and there were several minimal, stiff, segmented ridges that ran down the arms to hold them in place. Somehow, the stays didn't inhibit movement at all. The ridges were evenly spaced around each sleeve, creating a subtly beautiful pattern, mirrored by similarly flexible, yet ridged, features on the torso. *How did she insert boning that holds the shape without inhibiting movement?* It was a masterpiece.

She expected to immediately feel warm within the leather top, but to her surprise, it seemed to breathe like linen. "How is this so breathable?"

Merilin's voice came through the door. "Immortal elk are massive creatures, and their hides are breathable to keep them from overheating during the summer. Their fur thickens in the winters to compensate, but that is no longer an issue."

Tala nodded, doing up the ties easily. She had to reach down through the collar to arrange herself properly within the garment, but after she did so, it fit splendidly.

The leather of the tunic was a light gray, nearly white, while the ties were marginally darker, offering a nice hint of contrast. Below the ties, the tunic continued down to just above her knees, providing some modesty and adding to the look. She smiled, then turned to the second item in the parcel: pants.

The pants fit exactly as well as the linen version had the day before. They were a dark enough gray to evoke thoughts of thunder, storms, and torrents of driving rain. They moved with her, once she was properly situated within them, and the flare towards her feet was as subtle as it was functional. She strapped on her belt, her knife and pouch balancing each other nicely.

She strode out of the bath room, grinning happily. "These are amazing."

Merilin stood, examining her. "Of course they are; I made them." She walked around Tala. "I'm glad you're flexible enough to do up the ties. Did you notice the boning?"

Tala nodded, feeling along several portions in the tunic and sleeves. "It's highly segmented. It adds stiffness and structure without impairing movement. I can't even conceive of how you made it work, but it does."

"You need to be able to move properly to survive, and you can't have it pinching, pulling, or impinging on you. I'm not going to let you die in my garment, at least not because of my work." She huffed. "That would be unprofessional."

Tala glanced at the remaining bundles on the bed. "Two formal outfits, and three everyday, correct?"

Merilin nodded.

"That isn't what we agreed." Even as she spoke, Tala was running her hands over the leather on her abdomen.

Merilin barked a laugh. "Do you want me to take that back?"

She hesitated. "Well… no…"

"I thought not. It should serve you better in the long run, so long as you keep it empowered."

Tala was frowning, again. "I'd thought that harvests had to be fed, and inscriptions inlaid, to make a magic item work."

Merilin sat back down with a self-satisfied smile. "If it were a magic item, yes."

Tala glanced down, then back up. "It is an item, that is magic."

The seamstress waved a hand dismissively. "For all it knows, it's just a part of some magical creature. So long as you feed it power, it will do what it does." She hesitated. "Don't try to give it power from more than one source. It'll latch onto the next source that feeds it power, and it will… be angry if other power tries to force its way in."

Tala frowned, then shrugged. "You're the seamstress." She placed a hand on her side. "Does it need any special mental model or…"

"No idea what that means, so probably not. Give it a trickle of power and see. Come on, girl. You're supposed to be the Mage."

That sounds suspiciously like an artifact… Tala hesitantly gathered up a small portion of the power flowing out of her gate and fed it through her hand into the tunic. Unlike Kit, the belt pouch, the tunic was not receptive to her influx at first. Even so, the leather seemed starved for power, and after a brief resistance, the power moved through it in a rush.

A pulse radiated out from her hand, and the leather shifted subtly. There was no visible change, but as she moved and twisted, Tala found that it somehow fit even better than before. Minute portions that hadn't been *quite* right were now snugged into place, and it shifted with her like a flexible, stylish, second skin.

I suppose it basically is a second skin... That was a somewhat disturbing thought. Before she could talk herself out of it, she repeated the process on the pants and felt the same perfecting of the garment.

Merilin smiled, self-satisfied. "Good. That worked."

Tala slowly turned to stare wide-eyed at the seamstress. "What do you mean, 'good?'"

"I've never done this before."

Tala gaped at the older woman. "What."

"My mother left extensive notes, and I followed them to the letter, but there were always dangers." She shrugged. "Immortal elk don't die every day, child."

Tala narrowed her eyes. "This sounds much more expensive than I agreed to."

"I was contacted last night to alter the order. Your benefactor asked to remain anonymous. My mother was known to have worked with this material, and so they were content for me to do the work." She nodded, smiling, then pulled out a tablet. "Your balance stands, though. One and one-half ounces gold."

Tala sighed, then examined the tablet before pricking her finger and confirming the purchase. It was becoming very easy for her to withdraw both power from her scripts and the power of the endingberries to enable the confirmation of contracts and purchases—trivially so.

Merilin pushed herself back to her feet. "Well, child, I hope to see you again. Do be sure to tell others where you got your clothing, yes?" She cackled a laugh as she left the room, not waiting for Tala to respond.

Tala stared after the woman for a long moment before shaking her head and quickly pushing the clothing into her belt pouch. "Thanks, Kit. I'll organize later if you're not up for it."

The pouch did not respond.

Light was just beginning to build in the east as she left the room for the last time. It had been quite a comfortable place to stay, and she was a bit sad to leave it behind. *A bit expensive, though.* Lyn's house would be a better long-term residence.

She smiled at that. *It will be good to go home.*

Tala walked into the dining hall and immediately saw Renix stand and wave to her. "Mistress Tala!"

She smiled and waved, then pointed to the buffet laid out, laden with breakfast foods. He nodded and sat back down.

She loaded a platter high, downed one mug of coffee and got her allowed refill, and then walked over to join Renix and Trent. "Where's Mistress Atrexia?" *It would be wonderful to get back on the road, back to coffee.*

"She's taken on another assignment."

Tala frowned. "I'd thought she was contracted for the return trip." *Am I remembering right? No, she said she wasn't coming on the trip back.*

"She was pulled away." Trent shrugged. "Happens sometimes when someone's specialty comes into play. I suspect that was actually one reason she came here, the hope that that would happen." He held up one hand. "Before you ask, no, I don't know what's happening or precisely what her specialty is that got her called off."

She shrugged. "Fair enough." Tala dug into the food. It was good, just as it had been the previous days, but there was something about it that just wasn't great. It was filling, fairly tasty, and at least somewhat nutritious. *I'm getting spoiled.*

Trent glanced at Renix, but the younger man was eating with gusto. Smiling slightly, Trent glanced back at her. "The new outfit looks nice."

Tala glanced down at herself and smiled. "Thank you. Should work better on the road as well."

Trent touched his own side. "Won't the leather chafe?"

"A bit of a personal question, but no. This is… uniquely done. One side effect is that it won't rub or pinch or pull."

He shook his head. "Another benefit from your hand-based expressions. I'd never be able to wear something like that. At least a portion would be torn to shreds the first time I cast."

That actually makes sense, now that I think about it. Most of those who can afford outfits like this almost universally don't want them. Tala shrugged. "There are some advantages." She smiled slightly and took another bite.

Renix swallowed, glancing her way. "You really do look nice."

"Thank you, Renix." She glanced back to Trent. "Will you two be alone on the trip back?"

Trent shook his head. "No, we've another Mage joining us. He was actually a mageling under Master Grediv, though he's carving his own path now. I think there will be a fourth, too, but I'll know soon enough."

Tala waved a sausage on the end of her fork. "What's your deal with Master Grediv? You two seemed to know each other."

He smiled slightly. "He's been mentoring me on my path towards Archon. He actually wants me to begin attempting a star soon."

Renix turned to his master, grinning widely. "Master Trent is amazing!"

Trent patted the young man on his shoulder. "And you should be a Mage in your own right." He glanced to Tala. "Renix doesn't like me to say, but he refuses to buy his own inscriptions and graduate from my tutelage. He says he still has too much to learn."

Renix gave a frustrated look to Trent, then turned to Tala. "And he retaliated by starting with the basics, again and again." He rolled his eyes. "I *am* picking up some new insights from the review, though." He smiled. "Thank you, again, for the overview that you gave. Master Trent is right that new perspectives can shine fresh light on old ideas. Especially since the education for each of the four quadrants seems to be so varied."

Tala nodded. "Happy to have helped." *Well, that explains a lot. I was a bit confused why my take was new to him. I wonder how much they didn't teach me because I'm an Immaterial Guide?*

They finished eating, exchanging small talk, and discussing the journey ahead. Trent and Renix each offered her their allowed coffee refill, and she thanked them profusely, draining the extra cups with gusto.

When they'd all finished, they cleared their table and gathered up their things.

Most of Trent and Renix's belongings were in their wagon, with the caravan, but they'd each brought a bag to the inn.

Trent glanced around for Tala's pack, then his eyes fell on the pouch. "Right, your dimensional storage."

She smiled and patted the bag. "Yup! Kit's the best."

Trent frowned. "Kit? You... named it?"

She stopped, feeling suddenly self-conscious. "Yeah, well... It seemed appropriate. She's been really helpful."

He opened his mouth to say something more, but Renix spoke overtop his master. "The drivers name their wagons sometimes. I think it's nice to appreciate when an item works well for you."

Trent rolled his eyes. "Yeah, yeah. I don't see any inscriptions. Are they internal, or is it an artifact?"

"Artifact."

He nodded. "That won't be an issue to keep charged, will it? Along with the extra cargo-slots?"

She shook her head. There were going to be twenty cargo-slots, in two cargo wagons, on the way back. "Shouldn't be an issue in the least."

He shrugged. "Never liked artifacts myself, but Master Grediv seems to think they're fine."

"Why is that?"

Trent hesitated, then shrugged. "Always seemed too intelligent. It's probably foolish, but I don't really feel like items should be more than items."

"Can't say I agree, but fair enough." She smiled to negate any implications in her response.

They walked from the dining hall together, towards the workyard beside the northern gate. "So, who is the new Mage?"

"Never met him, myself, but I've heard good things." Trent smiled. "He has to be something special to have been picked as a mageling beneath any Archon, let alone one of Master Grediv's standing."

"But you don't know his quadrant or anything like that?"

Trent shook his head. "All I know is that he's considered very good." He hesitated, then sighed. "He's also considered a little strange."

Tala grinned. "I'm a bit strange myself. Maybe we'll get along."

Trent laughed. "Maybe you will, at that."

They entered the workyard, and Tala broke away from the others and went to the cargo-slots for their final empowerment before departure. True to form, the cargo-slots were now loaded onto two wagons, ten slots each. Den was already working over the front wagon, and he greeted her.

"Mistress Tala! I trust you had a relaxing couple of days?"

"Thank you, Den. More productive than relaxing, but I like it that way. How about yourself?"

He smiled. "It was nice, yes. Glad to be getting back on the road, though. I miss the wife and kids."

She nodded. "I can understand that. It'll be nice to get home."

She began empowering the cargo-slots, and Den went back to his work, not wanting to interrupt her. When she finished those in his wagon a few minutes later, he noticed and turned back to her. "Do you need the box again?" He patted the large wooden container.

"I don't think so, but I might take you up on it later. Mind if I ride on the roof again?"

"Of course not! You're welcome whenever you like."

Tala smiled and gave a slight bow. "Thank you." She glanced towards the other wagon. "I should get those, too."

"You do your work, Mistress. I've enough of my own to be about. We can chat on the road if it works out."

She nodded. "I'd like that."

Without further conversation, Tala walked over to the other cargo wagon and moved through the empowerment process. She was halfway through the third cargo-slot when she heard someone yelling, nearby.

"What are you doing? Get away from there!"

She didn't think anything of it and simply finished empowering that cargo-slot, but as she moved to the fourth, someone placed a hand on her shoulder and spun her around.

"I said, 'What are you doing?'"

Tala felt her eyes widen and her face color at the forceful contact, and she looked up at the man, towering over her in chainmail armor and heavy gambeson, noting the armaments hung about him. He had a master sergeant's badge on each arm, and he was furious.

And, in truth, so was she.

Chapter: 8
Potential Conflict

Tala stared up at the master sergeant as he loomed over her, irritation clear in his bearing as well as his tone. "Are you daft, girl!? These are magical and highly sensitive. You could kill us all by messing with them."

Tala cocked one eyebrow. *Careful now, Tala. No need to be rash.* "I am well aware, master sergeant. I am left baffled as to why you thought it wise to interrupt me." She saw Trent near the far side of the workyard, eyes wide, jogging their direction, but he was still quite a ways away.

"You're aware? If you know, you shouldn't be touching them, girl. Of course, I'm going to stop you from disturbing these infernal things! What if the Dimensional Mage had seen you touching her stuff? I've heard this one is crazy, child. Don't go playing with things you don't understand."

Tala was now quite confused, and that dampened her fury, if only slightly. She knew that the inscriptions on her face and hands had to be visible to this man, and if he'd been watching her at all, he would have seen her empower Den's wagon full of cargo-slots, as well as the three now charged on this wagon. "What do you think is happening, here, sergeant?"

The man's face lost the little bit of the outward concern it had shown, and his voice hardened. "I think a child is poking her nose somewhere it's going to be cut off."

Tala closed her eyes and took a deep breath, attempting to calm herself. *Breathe, Tala. Don't lash out at the frustrating man.*

"Don't get huffy with me, girly. I don't care if you are rich enough for inscribed enhancements. You're not allowed to mess with my caravan."

Her eyes snapped open, and she felt the rage boiling inside herself threaten to break free. *Tala. Calm down. He's made assumptions and is acting the fool. Don't prove his assessment of your maturity correct.* She took another deep breath, grateful that he hadn't kept a hold of her. "Sir, you have grossly misinterpreted the situation. I—"

"Don't you talk down to me, you little spit of slag. You shut your mouth this instant, or I'll throw you and your family from the roster. I won't have a stuck-up brat as a passenger in my caravan."

She opened her mouth, again, but he thrust his finger towards her with such violent intent that she took a step back.

"That's what I thought. Now, get to the passenger wagons!"

Tala had had enough. She closed her mouth and began lifting her right hand. *Yeah, rust restraint.* In that moment, Trent arrived. "Master Sergeant Furgel, what seems to be the problem?"

The sergeant's entire demeanor shifted. "No problem, Master Trent, sir. I was just dealing with a wayward child."

Tala could practically feel the heat of her own fury, irritation, and embarrassment rolling off of her in waves, but Trent gave her a small shake of his head.

"Master Sergeant, there seems to be a misunderstanding." Trent cleared his throat, obviously feeling a bit awkward, or at least projecting such to ease tensions. "This is *Mage* Tala. She is the dimensional expert contracted for this caravan."

Furgel looked to the cargo wagons, seeming to notice for the first time that most of the cargo-slots were charged. He then looked at Tala, then back to Trent. "I'm confused. This is a child. She can't be more than twenty."

Tala closed her eyes again and carefully counted to ten, while Trent cleared his throat and continued. "Ummm... No. This is Mage Tala; I assure you. I was in the caravan with her on the trip here, and she performed this same duty for that venture."

Tala opened her eyes and met Furgel's stare. She was able to see the dawning horror in those eyes, even as they flicked to her half-raised hand.

He swallowed involuntarily, then looked back to Master Trent, if only briefly.

"I... I'm sorry for the misunderstanding, Mistress. I'll be about my work to get us on the road." Without a backward glance, he scurried away.

Tala took several more deep breaths, noticing that there were many, many eyes on her and Master Trent.

Trent, for his part, seemed one-part horrified, and the other part was fighting to keep from laughing.

Tala saw the fight and felt something within her break. She barked a laugh, her anger gone in an instant as she turned back to the cargo-slots, beginning the empowering of the fourth on this wagon.

Trent took her laughter as a cue and burst out himself. After a moment, he was shaking his head. "You were about to kill him."

She didn't take her eyes off her work. "I seriously considered it."

"I'm glad you didn't. The paperwork for a justified killing around these parts is a *pain*."

Tala flicked her gaze his way for a brief moment. *Justified killing?* "Oh?"

"Yeah, it takes testimonies and truth detection and all sorts of bureaucratic nonsense." He hesitated, then clarified. "I'm not saying it would have been justified, by the way."

She huffed a laugh, again. "Yeah... sure. I know that. I wouldn't have actually killed him... probably." *No wonder people are so hesitant around Mages.* After a moment's thought, she nodded to herself. *Yeah, I have no complaints about them not explaining that at the academy.*

Trent patted her shoulder. "He did have a good guess on your age, though."

"You're kind of a jerk, too." She gave him a fake glare.

Trent laughed, again. "I'll leave you to it."

She grunted, then as Trent turned to walk away, she let out a breath. "Thank you, Master Trent. That was kind of you to intervene."

He didn't stop but spoke over his shoulder. "Always happy to help if I can. I expect to hear how you used that map, by the way. I heard some interesting rumors from the eastern gate, and I'd love to test the truth of them."

Tala grunted. *Great.* "Maybe tonight." She finished empowering the remaining seven cargo-slots and walked over to climb up on Den's wagon.

She saw Furgel casting furtive glances her way and decided not to judge the man too harshly. He'd been a bit of a jerk, but he'd been well-intentioned. *And you were going to what? Restrain him?* Yeah, that was what she had been planning. Just restraining.

She began thinking about their journey and the city defenses they were leaving behind and had a thought. *If I'm actually going to be engaging with Terry, I'll need a way to get him into Bandfast.* She needed a collar for an arcane pet. *Well, rust.* "Den?"

"Mistress?"

"How soon do we leave?"

"Less than an hour, why?"

Tala thought for a long moment, then nodded. "I'll be right back." She took off—not quite jogging, but nearly—heading for Artia's shop.

Less than half an hour later, she was back at Den's wagon and very frustrated. Apparently, somehow, all the ready-to-hand collars had been purchased. Artia only knew that because a buyer had contacted her as their 'last check,' and she'd sold the only two she had to the messenger.

On the bright side, apparently the messenger had implied that the buyer was leaving this morning, so in all likelihood, he was in her caravan. *I'll have to hunt him down... or try. Maybe Trent knows something?* It was a topic for later.

Now that she was back, and clearly in an irritated mood, Den asked after her even as she climbed up. "I'll be fine. Let's just get on the road. Yeah?" After a moment, she sighed. "But thank you for asking."

"Of course, Mistress." He smiled. "We're just about ready."

"Let me know before we go. I'm going to lie down for a bit to clear my head." She pulled out her wide-brimmed hat and placed it over her face as she lay down on the roof to do just that.

A commotion drew Tala out of her rest almost as soon as she'd lain down. *What in zeme?* She sat up and looked over to see a man had set up a table on the far side of the workyard. He was calling out. "Change your copper, change your silver, change your gold! Don't leave without making a profit on your metals."

Right! Tala had completely forgotten that. *Come on, Tala. That would have been colossally foolish.*

She rolled, vaulting off the side of the wagon and dropping to land in a crouch. She felt the endingberry power within her dwindle a fractional amount. *Huh. I'd have broken a leg… or something.* She stood and walked over to the man. Thankfully, it didn't look like anyone had seen her land.

She pushed her hat into Kit and snagged her coin purse. She wasn't the first in line, but those before her moved quickly. When she came to the front, she handed over every coin she had.

"Total worth is five gold, seventy-five silver."

The man opened the pouch and quickly counted it before nodding. "Seven gold, eighteen silver, and seventy-five copper. Acceptable?"

Tala nodded. She'd done the math while waiting in line. "Agreed."

She pricked her finger to confirm, and the amount was added to her account. *Maybe, I should just come straight back, with all the coinage I can find…* Probably wouldn't be a time-effective way to make money, though. At least, it wouldn't be until she had enough money that such things weren't effective uses of her time. *Probably why the rate stays so high. If everyone was able to easily bring their coinage, the percentage would drop dramatically.*

She walked away, feeling happy. *Easiest money I've ever made.* No obligation, no work, just a short walk.

As she was moving back towards the cargo wagon, she heard a group arrive behind her and turned to look.

Grediv was riding a horse, followed by two men. One man was obviously a servant, and the other was just as obviously a Mage.

Tala almost gaped. The Mage following Grediv was at least six and a half feet tall, and the poor horse he was riding was clearly straining under the broad load. Given that he *was* a Mage, it almost went without saying that he wasn't overweight, but he was clearly muscular, and that combined with this build was enough to irritate the normal-sized horse.

Grediv saw her and turned her way. "Mistress Tala!" He waved.

Is he growing out his beard? It did look like the Archon had about two days of growth across his face. She pulled on her gloves and returned the gesture, greeting him as he drew near. "Master Grediv. Good to see you again."

The two Mages swung down off their horses, handed the reins to the servant, and approached Tala on foot. "Mistress Tala, this is Rane. He will be joining you on this trip." Grediv turned to Rane. "Rane, this is Mistress Tala. I've told you about her, and you are to treat her with the utmost respect, yes?"

Rane, for his part, seemed embarrassed by the command. "What do you expect me to do normally?" He stuck out his massive hand towards Tala.

Tala shook the offered hand, noting several oddities about the man. He was likely even taller than she'd first thought, and he was easily as broad as the horse he'd been riding. He was an Immaterial Creator, and he seemed to specialize in kinetic energy, or the energy of movement. His power density was almost as high as Trent's, though he was closer to Renix in age. He was handsome in an awkward sort of way, even accounting for a faded series of scars that speckled his entire face. Tala might have mistaken them for pox scars, except that she'd seen those before. These looked more like someone who had grown up in a smithy without practicing proper safety.

"Well, aren't you just travel-sized." Rane shook her hand gently. "You could just fit in my pocket."

Grediv grabbed his own face with both hands as he turned away in obvious consternation. Tala looked up at the big man and sighed. *I kind of hate you.* "I wouldn't try it, big guy. One of us is likely to get hurt."

Rane was smiling, opening his mouth again, when Grediv turned back around. "Enough, Rane. That. That was what I was expecting you to do."

Rane closed his mouth, coloring with embarrassment. "But... Oh."

Grediv sighed. "Mistress Tala, I apologize. Please don't judge him by—" His eyes flicked to her side, looking at the belt pouch, then they moved over to the knife. He closed his mouth and looked at her from head to toe. "Mistress Tala. Do you remember our conversation about taking care with certain... items? I believe the *soul* of the matter was that you'd wait a while. Yes?"

Tala quirked a smile. "It just sort of happened."

"That's a lie, Mistress Tala. You can't—" He glanced around, then lowered his voice to a volume that even Rane couldn't have easily heard, standing right next to the man. "You can't bond something to your soul accidentally, it requires your permission. What were you thinking?"

She didn't lower her voice. "I was thinking that I need to get stronger."

Grediv opened his mouth, then closed it. Then, he scratched his forehead, frowning in irritation. "Mistress Tala, I was going to ask for your assistance with something, but I'm not sure I can trust your judgment at the moment."

Tala cocked an eyebrow. "Oh?"

Grediv nodded. "I have a short job outside the city to the north. The caravan will be heading the same way, and it will have to delay until I'm done anyways. I'm going to clear your path. Are you willing to come along?"

Tala gave him a flat look. "I'll pass."

Both Rane and Grediv turned to her, seeming incredulous. Grediv was the one who spoke. "Why?"

"Because that sounds likely to get me killed. I like you well enough—you've been kind to me—but something they send an Archon to deal with? Pass."

"You shouldn't be in real danger." He glanced at her. "Certainly not with that power still in your system. I need a distraction so I can perform the proper invocations."

And I didn't even feel his magesight pushing against the iron salve this time... Did he just see it through my palms or eyes? "So, you need someone for a magical beast to play target practice with. Do you realize how unappealing that sounds?" *Hey! I'm getting smarter every day.*

"It's not target practice. The mountain cyclops uses a club, not anything ranged."

Tala was flabbergasted. "You want me to fight a mountain cyclops. Are you out of your mind?" She'd had to fight to keep from raising her voice. "If it was anything less than an adult, you wouldn't ask for an assist. An adult could pulp that ox with a casual kick." She pointed at one of the oxen hooked to a wagon. *I think I have that right...* She didn't have *that* extensive a knowledge base to draw on. *Another thing a master would have corrected, I suppose...* "How am I supposed to distract it?"

Grediv shrugged. "Seems like a good idea to get you some field experience."

She gave him a deeply skeptical look. "You're insane. No."

"I'll pay you eight gold ounces."

Tala hesitated. *That's a lot, Tala. You got barely more than that after you took out a thunder bull... This can't be as dangerous as that, can it?* "Ten, right now." She held up a finger. "And you best have the means to get rid of that thing because if you get me killed, I will find a way to come back and haunt you, Archon Grediv."

Grediv grinned. "Ten, then." He pulled out a tablet, holding it out to her.

Tala looked down and saw that it was already set up to transfer ten gold ounces to her account from his. *Well, rust. I was played.*

* * *

Tala and Grediv were walking at a brisk pace, north of the city, heading almost directly back towards the pass.

"Is the caravan really going to go back through the pass?"

"It's dangerous because it can be anticipated, but the drop in magical density is so much faster that it makes the trip, overall, much safer than if they went around the mountains to the west. The next caravan will have to use that route, though."

Tala grunted.

He glanced her way, then back towards the wall already fading into the distance behind them. "You know, bonding an item is serious business."

"That's why I've only done the one."

He shook his head. "You've only used an Archon Star on one. You've only bound your soul to one, but all four of those items are bound to you."

"Four?"

"Pants, tunic, pouch, and knife. The knife has the strongest connection to you, by far, but the other three are tilted towards your magic and away from anything else."

"Why are bonds dangerous?"

"Because they influence both parties."

Tala almost stopped walking at that. *The cargo-slots... I'm bound to twenty of them... What does that even mean?*

"True, you have more of a sense of self, so you won't be pulled as far from your original as they will, but you will still be altered. It will be in little ways. You likely won't even notice them."

Tala grunted. "Nebulous danger weighed against tangible gain. I know which wins out in my books. It can't be too dangerous, else we couldn't use cargo wagons and such."

"Fair point, but you should still be careful." There seemed to be something he wasn't saying. Knowing him, it was something he couldn't say. He didn't seem like one to hold back.

"I'll keep that in mind."

There was another long pause as they trudged up the road at a fast walk. Finally, Grediv broke the silence again. "Why the knife?"

"Hmm?"

"Why use the Archon Star on the knife?"

Tala shrugged. "It felt right. When I was looking through artifacts, the knife seemed to call to me like it belonged with me, and I saw where I could insert the Archon Star on it first." She shrugged again. "As I said, just felt right."

He regarded her as they walked before finally sighing. "Well, what's done is done. You don't need to put any more stars into the knife, by the way."

She looked at him. "Oh?"

"I imagine you've thought of doing it. It wouldn't change anything, given the nature of your stars. For others, they couldn't even attempt it. The star established your bond, you just need power to strengthen it. Even with that, you can only go so far as you are, but that's approaching knowledge you aren't ready for."

Tala grunted. "So, just feed it power? What about calling it?"

He frowned, and she briefly explained about her soul exercises. Her explanation left him shaking his head. "You are going to kill yourself, Mistress Tala."

She swallowed. "So…"

"Oh, you're fine, but I would have bet good money that you'd tear your soul in half without it doing a thing." He grunted. "I suppose you've some strength to you." He laughed. "No surprise there, I guess."

"So...?"

"You can continue those exercises. Shouldn't hurt you the way you're doing it."

She let out a relieved breath. "Good to hear."

"With enough power, the knife will grow and develop. Eventually, it will be ready to change, becoming more of what you need, when you need it."

"What does that even mean?"

He shrugged. "It's different for every item and for every Mage. You'll have to wait and see."

"So... I shouldn't bond other artifacts? Other items?"

He gave her a flat look. "If I say 'no,' will you listen?"

"If you give good reasons."

He groaned. "You really should strengthen your soul more before you spread it out to multiple bonds... Can you at least give it a month before you bond anything else?"

"I'd do better with a strength requirement, rather than an arbitrary timeline."

He regarded her, then let out a small laugh. "Fair enough. When you can do that exercise with your knife a dozen times without feeling strained, I'd bet you're ready for another bond."

"A dozen? I can wait for that."

"Somehow, I doubt you will, but we can hope, right?"

Tala grinned. "Glad to set proper expectations."

"You know, it would be better if you made a real Archon Star and were elevated first."

"I'll consider it."

They crested a rise, and Tala stopped, looking down at what lay in the valley below.

A giant, at least thirty feet tall, stood in the center of the wide, long valley laid out before them. It was wider in proportions than a man, and the eye in the center of its forehead was an obvious indicator of its nature. A club almost as long as the humanoid was tall was braced on its shoulder as it waited.

To Tala's magesight, the beastly humanoid radiated power like the sun. To her surprise, aside from being able to see the nature of the various aspects of magic within the creature, there seemed to be an underlying hue to the power. "Why does it have a strange color to the magic?"

Grediv looked at her in surprise. "Those are impressive inscriptions. That is an easy way to identify power level. I, myself, don't see it as a color, but from what others have told me, who have similar spell-forms, it follows the standard rainbow scale in that manner of seeing it."

"It's orange."

"Yup, it is more powerful than some, but still near the bottom of the scale."

"Why have I never seen this before?" *Or, wait… Is that what I saw around Holly? Master Himmal? And the midnight fox?*

"Because below red is infrared, and I'd bet that nearly everyone and everything you've beheld was in that range or kept you from seeing entirely."

That was an interesting prospect. "So, this is more magically powerful than anything I've ever seen?" *Yeah, the midnight fox had a red aura to it.*

"Most likely."

Tala sighed. "I asked for too little, didn't I…?"

Chapter: 9
Cyclops and Conversation

Tala glanced towards Grediv as he pulled something out of a dimensional storage, which she couldn't see. She looked closer, curious about what weapon he would choose over his magics in the coming fight.

It was a staff of what appeared to be pure sapphire, and it radiated something that blocked her magesight as effectively as Grediv himself did. *Soul-bound?*

"You are a sapphire Archon?"

He laughed. "By that titling, yes. I still find it easiest to make Archon Stars in that gem, though I don't have much need to do so anymore."

That brought up so, so many questions, but now was hardly the time.

"So… what are you going to do, and what do you need from me?"

"I am going to pull together an act of obliteration, but that creature will recognize the danger of my working and seek to stop me. I don't wish the time or collateral damage that that fight would bring, so I need you to engage the cyclops, and then, I will begin."

"How long will you need?"

"Thirty seconds?"

She frowned. "It couldn't cover this distance that fast." She gestured to the cyclops, easily a quarter-mile away.

"You'd be surprised what a fused is capable of."

"Fused?"

"Orange, by your magesight's scale. Its body and soul are fused, magically."

Tala frowned. "What would you be?"

He smiled, slightly. "I stopped climbing the ladder long ago. If I were to loosen my control, you would easily see me as green. Most know my ranking as Paragon."

I thought I'd seen green around him, before! She hesitated. *Wasn't that the level of beast that obliterated the inter-city road?* "I don't know what that means."

He shrugged. "You don't really need to know, not yet." He turned to regard the cyclops, still waiting for them. "So? Are you ready?"

Tala let out a breath, examined her endingberry power reserves, and nodded. "As ready as I'm likely to be today."

Grediv laughed. "Excellent."

Tala started forward, limbering her arms as she walked.

He called out to her, even as she continued to walk. "Don't use your combat magic on him. It would take more power than you possess to harm him or even properly restrain him. Leave that to me."

She didn't understand how that was possible but decided he probably knew best. She waved without looking back. "Sure thing." *I'm still trying if I need to.*

She covered the distance to the cyclops at a steady pace, the monster regarding her calmly.

Its eye looked from her to Grediv up on the hill, then back to her. A voice issued forth from the beast, its mouth moving awkwardly. "It sends a snack before my main meal? How considerate."

Tala didn't slow, but she felt suddenly a bit more uncertain. *Great, it's intelligent…*

She closed the distance, moving to a jog for the last hundred feet. As she entered into the area of its orange aura, she felt an oppressive weight—not on her body, that was moving just fine— on the magic of her being. It was as if the power used to keep her body functional was being pulled, her ownership of it being contested. *Even through the iron? No.* She could feel the foreign influence coming through her palms and eyes, straining against the defenses she had there.

She hated it. She had no idea what would happen if her defenses failed or if she lost that internal contest, but she wasn't going to find out. She clamped down on her internal power, refusing to let it *shift* into another's control, and that seemed to bolster her defense.

The cyclops shook its great head in what seemed to be mild irritation, lifting its club off of its shoulder.

She was almost in range of the brute's club, so she pulled her knife and flung it at the creature's eye.

The cyclops, for its part, seemed so bemused that it didn't even dodge. Tala's aim was true, and the blade struck the massive eye point first. *Ha! First try!* Maybe she didn't need as much practice as she'd thought she would.

Behind her, Tala felt Grediv begin building towards his working.

The knife fell away as the cyclops swiped at its face, acting like it had an itch.

Tala called the knife back to her, catching it as she stared up at the massive humanoid. *Oh… well, that's—*

She saw the club twitch, then blur; then, *pain* blossomed across her entire right side.

She was airborne and unable to get her bearings. The instant of flight lengthened as she examined herself. More than half the remaining power from the endingberries had been drained away in that instant. Her clothing had been obliterated at the point of impact, leaving her right shoulder, upper arm, and hip suddenly bare.

The berries' power had done their work, however, and she was intact.

She then hit the ground, skipping across the bolder-strewn landscape like a rock across still water. She was thrown into a spin that, again, disoriented her.

As she rolled to a stop, she felt the last of the endingberries' power as it was expended. Her clothes were ragged, but already, the leather was regrowing over the holes, and even the scuffed portions were rapidly returning to an undamaged state, boning reformed in the appropriate places. *Ha! That's fantastic.*

It was a bright spot in an otherwise disastrous moment.

As she pushed herself up, she retched, spilling the remains of her breakfast across the ground. Though, she couldn't have said if it was from dizziness or something more dire.

Large impacts were approaching quickly. She looked up to see the cyclops already before her, club raised, ready to bring down.

She moved on instinct, lunging to the side before he moved. Even so, it was almost too slow.

Impossibly, the club traveled in its massive arc faster than she could move a half-dozen feet. Thankfully, the club was only four feet wide.

The ground exploded beside Tala, even as she moved away, stone shards peppering her from head to toe, activating the defensive scripts across the majority of her skin on that side. Her clothing had a host of new holes, which immediately began to pull closed.

How long has it been? "Archon!" Tala yelled, putting all the volume she could into it, trying to keep the desperation at bay.

The cyclops definitely heard her because it paused, eye going wide. Spinning, it turned back towards where Grediv was raising his staff, a smile painted across the Archon's features.

Despite her horrifying position, Tala found herself frozen in awe. In front of the tip of his staff was the most complex working of magic she'd ever seen. It put the city defenses to shame, and she couldn't begin to understand it. True to what he'd said, the underlying hue behind the working was a deep, vibrant green, not a hint of blue in evidence.

His spell-lines were blazing with light, but she still couldn't see magic coming from them. His control was as awe-inspiring as his power.

The cyclops roared and moved to hurl his club at Grediv.

And you said it had no ranged attack.

Grediv closed his hand, and the light shot forward, faster than a blink, striking the cyclops in the center of its chest.

The cyclops ceased to exist.

The massive humanoid—club, clothes, everything—was simply gone, along with the working. A resounding silence fell over the Wilds around them, and Tala pushed herself to her feet, pulling out a rag to wipe her mouth.

Somehow, the utter silence was more terrifying than an explosion would have been.

She tossed aside the small strip of cloth, which had once been a part of one of her pairs of pants if she wasn't mistaken. Her water incorporator was retrieved, and she used a pulse of power to shoot a bit of water into her open mouth.

She underestimated the amount, and the force, that would be produced and almost puked again as she began hacking and gagging. *Nicely done, Tala.*

She aimed for the inside of her cheek, instead of straight down her throat, and used a bit less power. A large mouthful of water blossomed into being, and she swished and spat. *Better.*

That done, she walked back towards Grediv.

She reached her senses into her clothing, even as it fully returned to form. She could tell it was strained. *I'm amazed it remade itself that quickly, twice in a row.* She moved the incorporator to her left hand and placed her right palm on her side, beginning to funnel power into the tunic in a steady stream. When she felt like she was pressing up against the leather's capacity, she moved to the pants, shifting her hand to her hip, under the tunic.

She finished topping off the clothing's reserves just as she reached easy speaking range of Grediv. "You didn't pay me enough."

He snorted. "No, I didn't." He smiled. "But you should never pay someone more than you have to, right?"

She gave him a flat look.

He laughed. "Fine, fine. I'll think of some way to repay you. Come on. The caravan will have left already. They're heading this way. We can meet them back towards the city."

Tala sighed. "Why don't we just wait here?"

He thought for a moment, then shrugged. "Fine by me. We can wait at least a little while." He pulled a folding chair seemingly out of nowhere and sat.

Tala looked at him, then the chair, then back at him.

"What? I don't carry extra chairs."

She sighed, again, and sat on a nearby rock.

There was a prolonged silence, in which Grediv pulled out some sort of sandwich and began to eat.

"You know, you almost got me killed."

He shrugged, speaking around a bit of food. "You should have dodged better." He swallowed. "You did well enough, though. You served as a nice distraction. I'm glad that immortal elk leather regenerates so quickly, or you would have a real wardrobe problem, given how you fight."

She glared. "You promised I'd be fine." *Wait, immortal elk leather? Does he know the material on sight?*

"And you are."

She opened her mouth to continue, but he held up his hand. "Listen, Mistress Tala. You are going down a dangerous road. If you can't survive a little danger at this point, you are going to meet an unpleasant end." He leaned back, taking another bite. "If this is too much for you"—he swallowed—"you should quit now. Do caravan routes, get married, settle down, have happy babies, live your life."

"Are you saying I can't do that if I continue to pursue growing stronger?"

"It'll be harder." He gestured towards where the cyclops had been. "That will not be the strongest creature you have to fight. Not by a foot or a mile."

"But I'll get stronger, right? I'll be able to face something like that easily?"

"Eventually, yeah." He shrugged. "Or you'll die. Those are the only results of the road you're on right now: death or improvement. As I said, if that's too much, choose another road."

"You aren't improving any more. You said so."

He took another bite, continuing to speak around the food. "I left that road behind. The next steps would have been… even more unpleasant than those previous, and I'm happy with my life. As long as nothing insane comes in the next couple decades, I'll keep it." He frowned. "Though, a fused this early in the waning…" He shook his head. "It'll be fine."

Tala didn't know how to process all the implications of what he was saying. "What color would I show?"

He snorted. "You're barely more than non-magical, though your power density is impressive. You wouldn't register to your magesight's scale in that sense. As I said, you haven't really begun, yet."

Tala was nodding. "So, an Archon would be red?"

"A newly raised, full Archon would be red, yes."

She frowned, again. "What changed? Why are you willing to tell me so much more, today?"

He gestured. "You fought a fused." He shrugged. "Rules are laxer for those who have faced greater powers."

She blinked at him. "That's why you invited me…"

He smiled. "That, and the power in you meant you were probably pretty safe." He shrugged. "If you'd died, I'd've had a large penalty from the Caravan Guild, and I'd have known you weren't what I thought."

"And what did you think I was?"

"Worth my time."

The supreme arrogance of the statement was held in contrast with the man's obvious power. "I think… Thank you?"

"You're welcome. Seems you're worth my time, so thank you for not wasting it. I'd have been cross if you died."

"So… worth your time for what?"

"You'll likely make something of yourself someday. You're worth the effort to help because we'll likely know each other for a *very* long time."

"So… relational capital?"

"Something like that."

Tala snorted. "Not a great way to get it."

"Oh? Do you feel particularly angry at me?"

She opened her mouth to say yes, then stopped, realizing that it wasn't true. "I'm a bit irritated, but not really angry." She narrowed her eyes. "Though, I should be."

He nodded, grinning. "Irritation will pass, and the lessons you gained today will help you for a long time. Every time they do, the irritation will diminish until one day, you'll just be grateful." He smiled. "It's only up from there."

She grunted. "Fine, then. We've a bit of time. Tell me more about soul-bonds and bonds in general. Can I use an Archon Star only on artifacts?"

"You can use them on things other than artifacts, but the results will be mixed."

"Okay… What about standard magical items?"

"Don't, don't do that. You don't want to bind your soul to something so temporary. You would *not* like what happened when its spell-lines ran dry. If it's your vessel… Well, we can't discuss that now." He made a disgusted sound.

She frowned. "Couldn't I just have it re-inscribed and give it more power?"

He shook his head, laughing. "Oh, rust no."

"But, I get inscribed, why is it…?" She connected a few things, nodding slowly. "My body is inscribed, not my soul."

He pointed at her, clicking his tongue in acknowledgment. "Got it in one."

She glanced at her knife. "So, this is a part of my soul, now?" That was a bit of a horrifying thought.

He shrugged. "Yes and no. Your soul has become invested in it. The weapon can be broken without killing you or permanently harming your soul, but not easily, and you wouldn't be the same after." He thought for a moment. "It might actually shatter your gate if you're particularly unlucky."

"Because my gate is a part of my soul."

He gave her a funny look. "Child, your gate *is* your soul."

She frowned. "But what about people without gates?"

"Malformed souls, for a—" He cut himself off, sighed, and shrugged. "Don't mistake me, most are still perfectly fine people, but it's like being born with a crippled or malformed body. The body is still there—they are still people—it just doesn't work normally."

She nodded, though she still didn't particularly like the implications. She was getting off-topic, however. "What about harvests like these clothes, can I bind them?"

"You can. It would likely have some fun side-effects, too." He grinned.

"Like?"

He shrugged. "Nothing harmful. I think that's a lesson you should learn for yourself. It's not like I'd actually be able to dissuade you from trying."

She narrowed her eyes at him. *That actually makes me not want to do it. He's manipulating me, still.* "Is the bonding process the same?"

"Close enough. You'll figure it out, or you won't." He smiled.

"Not really helpful, but fine. What about people, or arcanous or magical animals?"

"Don't. Don't *ever* put an Archon Star into another person." He sat up straighter, his last bit of sandwich vanishing.

"Why not?"

"Because a human body can only have one soul."

"So, what does—" Her eyes widened. "I'd be kicking them out?"

"You'd be starting a fight, yeah. Human souls are surprisingly ferocious in defending their home turf, though. As you are, now? You'd lose, and your soul would be damaged for that. Even if you greatly outpowered the subject of the attempt, you'd be forever changed. Don't do it." He leaned forward, locking gazes with her. "I cannot stress this enough, Mistress Tala. If you even attempt this, any Archon that sees you will know, and the first one will strike you down without a second's hesitation. Trying to enslave another in that way is one of the most heinous things any Mage can do." Grediv leaned back. "Don't do it to a dead body, either. Souls aren't meant to be connected to the dead, and forcing it is necromantic slag."

She swallowed. "Okay, then... I won't... Is it the same with arcanous or magical entities?"

"No. Animals don't have souls in the same way humans do." He seemed to be relaxed, again.

She gave him a skeptical look.

He laughed. "They have *something* spiritual, don't mistake me, but it isn't anything like a human soul. I'd recommend against it, though." He sighed. "Many of my peers disagree with me, however. A lot of them take on familiars."

She frowned. "Like in the children's stories? Arcanes, deep caverns, hags, and black cats?"

"Something like that. The entity or animal gains far more than the Mage. Usually, their minds are opened, and they can truly move beyond instinct. The most intelligent animals or entities gain more. Their natural abilities increase, their lives are extended, and they gain access to your gate." He gave her a meaningful look. "And *that* is the downside. They are bound to you, they can pull power through your soul, and you don't control them."

Tala's eyes widened.

"Good, you understand. Some of the most evil things I've had to fight were beings who tricked their way into being familiars, then rendered their Mage little more than a power source. If you don't care about the long-term consequences to your soul, and if you can endure unimaginable pain, there are easy ways to become more powerful. Now, if you can put those consequences and pain on another?" He shrugged. "It's not great."

"Yeah... I'm getting that."

"You don't actually need Archon Stars to make a soul-bond, but it is the safest, most reliable way." He gave her a look. "At your level, you'd kill yourself." After a breath, he spoke again. "Let me be utterly clear. Not 'you might kill yourself.' Not 'I don't think you're up for it.' You would die. Full stop. If you are going to bond anything, which I highly recommend against as we've already discussed, use a star. There are no downsides, especially with how easily you can create them."

She hesitated, then nodded. "Fair enough." She shifted, getting a bit more comfortable on her rock. *I should find a comfortable folding chair to keep in Kit.* "What benefit is there from feeding power to a bonded item?"

"Good question. Aside from keeping it functional in the case of magic-bound items, it gives the item power to become *more*."

"More?"

"More of itself." He shrugged. "All items have limits, so you can't expect eternal growth, though soul-bound items will be able to grow more as you progress."

"Because as my soul grows in power, the things it's bound to can as well?"

"Precisely."

"So... why don't you have an arsenal? You could have a host of powerful items to aid you." She laughed. "You could probably organize it so you don't even need inscriptions anymore, except maybe your keystone."

He quirked a smile but shook his head slightly. "Some people do *try* that, but I'd recommend against that path unless you're planning on staying in cities your whole life. Placing all your power into external objects *radically* stunts your growth and power. It might even stop it completely. There's also the fact that as you and your bound items grow in power, they need more power at an ever-increasing rate. The accepted number is eight. Virtually every Archon worth their power will recommend that you have less than eight soul-bonds of any kind." He hesitated, then sighed, adding, "Your clothes, as I imagine you're considering them, can be bound as a single item. I *strongly* recommend that you figure out how before attempting to bond either. You'll be very happy, in the long run, that you took that extra time."

She grunted. "Seems fair. Thank you for the advice."

He stood, folding the chair and tucking it away… somewhere. "We're getting close to things that I really should leave until you attain Archon. Work hard, and our next conversation can cover more." He smiled. "Come on, let's get you to the caravan."

She almost argued but thought better of it. "Very well. Thank you."

"My pleasure."

Chapter: 10
Back on the Road

Tala and Grediv walked back south, down the slope and towards the city. An amiable silence fell between them as they walked, and Tala found herself going over what he'd said, taking notes on the soul-bond, as well as implications of other bonds, which he'd mentioned.

Grediv occasionally glanced over at her as they walked but didn't interrupt her work.

Finally, when she'd paused for a long moment, he cleared his throat. "You have another question?"

She started briefly, coming back from far-flung thoughts. "Hmm? Oh, yes. If I soul-bond with multiple items, won't they, in some senses, be bound to each other?"

He grinned widely. "Very good. Yes. The nature of our bound items will not only affect you but each other as well."

"What does that mean?"

"The combinations are too numerous to have any meaningful research done, but a common occurrence is the binding both of a weapon and a dimensional storage item."

"And that does…?"

He gave her a flat look. "Come now, Mistress Tala."

She rolled her eyes. "Let me guess, then. The storage can defend itself?"

He barked a laugh. "Well, in some cases yes, but not really, and never very effectively, even when it does occur. Some will hurt anything that tries to damage them, but that is usually the extent of it. No, the most common result is a weapon that can be summoned directly into your hand and dismissed just as easily."

"And it would go into the dimensional storage?"

"Sometimes. Other times, it seems to create its own storage, bound to the wielder's hand, which can only hold the weapon itself."

She frowned. "That's... handy?"

He groaned. "No. Bad pun, Mistress Tala."

She quirked a smile. "Fine, fine. But I can basically do that now?"

"Oh? You think it's the same?"

She hesitated. "Well, obviously not the same..." She thought about it. "I suppose there are different applications."

He shrugged. "It doesn't always happen, in any case."

"So, what about combining items? You implied that I could bind my tunic and pants as one item."

"Those are two different things, and I said you'd have to figure out the latter on your own." He seemed to consider for a moment, then shrugged. "Artifacts, bound or not, can be coaxed into combining, with mixed results. If one of the items is bound, the outcome is more likely to be beneficial, more so for soul-bound than just magic-bound, but I've seen some horrible items come from the process. Don't forget, it's bound to you, so even if it's a dud in some way, you're stuck with it." After a moment, he added, "Well, unless you're willing to break off that part of your soul, but the folly of that should be obvious."

"What if they're both bound to you?"

"Then, you can't combine them. For items to be combined, they must be compatible and not overly independent. Two bound items are each too set in their identity, as part of you, to be combined. Two unbound items will fight it out, as it were, and the winning item sets most of the parameters of the combination."

"You make it sound like a negotiation."

"In some ways, it is." He glanced over, noticing her writing down bits of their conversation as they spoke. He shook his head, smiling. "Artifacts aren't sapient, but they do have instincts of a sort. Their nature dictates how they act, and that nature fights to be supreme." He scratched his head. "Again, I'm not a great teacher, but I think you can understand."

She was nodding. "So, if one item is bound, it has the upper hand in the negotiations."

"That's right, but be aware, if the item being combined with your bonded one is new, things can go wrong much more often."

"Why?"

"Because you're forcing it to join with your soul. If it doesn't know you, if its instincts aren't aligned towards seeing you as an ally? That's just begging for a crack in your soul."

"Which you won't explain to me."

"Which I won't explain to you."

She sighed. "So, only combine items with a similar purpose, and use any artifacts I'm considering combining for a while before attempting even that."

"Correct."

"I still say that you're treating them like they're intelligent."

He shrugged. "Then, that's my poor teaching showing through. Harvests are a different conversation, though. And, no, I won't go into that, either." He smiled widely.

Tala rolled her eyes, adding a few more notes to her notebook. "Your staff looks like sapphire."

He nodded. "Bound items often take on aspects of the Archon Star used to bind them."

They both looked at her knife. "I'm glad it didn't turn to blood…"

Grediv snorted a laugh. "That would have been less than ideal. It probably took on some other property than appearance. My staff isn't actually sapphire, as that would be too brittle to be useful."

She grunted. "Fair…" She frowned. "So… I only get, at maximum, eight items, and one of mine is a knife? That seems wasteful." She glanced down. "Don't get me wrong, I'll use this thing forever, if I can, but it isn't exactly a great fighting weapon."

"Yeah… I was a bit surprised at that. It is actually why I didn't notice it at first." He frowned. "Most artifact weapons, almost no matter the form, will shift into a more useful shape when bound." He shrugged, yet again. "I suppose it thought you needed a knife more than anything else? You'll have to tell me if you're satisfied with it in the coming years. There is also the fact that you used a drastically underpowered star. No one knows how that could be affecting the results, because it shouldn't be possible."

"Fair enough." She heard something and looked up, seeing Den's wagon cresting a hill close to a mile away. "There's my ride."

"So, it is."

She turned to him, expectantly.

"What?"

"You said you'd think of some way to repay me."

"I answered all your questions, didn't I?"

She gave him a flat look.

Grediv chuckled to himself. "Fine, fine." He thought for a moment. "Master Trent said that you borrowed some of his basic volumes to reference on the trip down. Did you get your own in Alefast?"

Tala blinked several times. *Oh... rust it all.* "No... I forgot." She let out an irritated sigh. *That's what happens when you try to do too much, Tala.*

He shrugged. "Then, here. I can get myself another set." He proceeded to pull a pile of books out of nowhere, one after another. Tala took each and pushed them into her pouch as quickly as possible, but he was already ready with each before she was ready to take it. She lost count, but there were at least two dozen volumes of various thicknesses, clearly a matched set of magical reference books. *This is a way larger set than Trent has.*

When the transfer was complete, Tala looked at Grediv critically. "Thank you. That was strangely kind of you."

He shrugged. "You could have gotten something similar in town for less than half a gold. Most of the value is in giving it to you a week before you'd have a chance to pick up your own, again." He smiled. "I'm pretty sure I didn't give you anything that you shouldn't have yet, but we did the exchange so quickly that I didn't really have a chance to check." He winked at her. "Oh well."

Tala glanced at her pouch, then back to him, then back to her pouch. She wanted to dive in and search through the books he'd given her immediately but knew that it wasn't the time. As she looked at her pouch, she noticed the vortex of magic being pulled in, as usual. "Oh! Is that standard?"

"Is what standard?"

She pointed at the pouch. "It's pulling in power from the surrounding area."

Grediv looked intently at the pouch, and once again Tala felt a bit disconcerted, knowing that he was using magic that she couldn't feel; his current use was so subtle she couldn't feel it either. "Huh. Well, yes, but no. It seems like that little bag has developed a larger appetite than usual for artifacts at their level." He frowned. "Shouldn't be an issue. It likely just means that they have more latent power and will grow with you more easily." He paused, giving her a hard look. "Don't bond with the pouch, yet. Remember?"

She laughed. "I remember. Twelve repetitions without exhaustion."

"*At least* twelve. I'd prefer you got to fifteen or twenty, but you *will* damage yourself, likely permanently, if you try another bond before twelve. And you *should* be driving towards a full-powered star, so you can be evaluated as an Archon."

"I already agreed." She meant it, too. "I will probably take a shot at Archon before I bond anything else. I understand that is the wiser course." And that was true, as much as she *really* wanted to bond Kit. *Patience, Tala.*

"Fine. I'll leave that matter be then." As the wagons were not closing the distance fast enough for his liking, Grediv began walking once more.

Tala walked beside him in silence but spoke when they were about halfway to the front of the caravan. "Master Grediv?"

"Hm?"

"Thank you."

He glanced her way, not responding for a long moment. Eventually, he nodded. "You're welcome, Mistress Tala. Don't get yourself killed, yeah? I think you will be interesting to watch in the coming decades."

She huffed a laugh. "I'll do my best." Then, she had a thought. "Do you have any use for endingberries?"

Grediv gave her an arch look. "My good Mistress, if I had use for them, I would get them."

She frowned. "Why don't you have use for them? They're dead useful."

He sighed. "You think so because their power is nearly identical to your inscriptions' base structure. There's no interference. I'm guessing that isn't a coincidence?"

She shrugged. "It is and it isn't. I was inspired to seek out these inscriptions because of stories, which I now suspect originated about people eating these, so... not a coincidence?"

"There you are, then."

"So... what would happen if you ate one?"

"Best case, my body would reject the power, and the berries would pass through me without effect. Worst, there would be a clashing of powers, and the endingberries would succeed in subverting some of my body's natural magical pathways, weakening me for months or years."

That's... pretty bad. She frowned. "Could something similar happen with arcanous meat?"

He hesitated. After a moment, he shrugged. "Probably not? Magic that enhances natural processes can be integrated much more easily. After all, I still have natural muscles, so power that helps muscles work better shouldn't override anything else. I also don't have inscriptions in my muscles because that could easily lead to magic poisoning, so there isn't really anything for them to interfere with." He hesitated. "But I don't know. It really isn't done, but that might be an interesting line of research." He was frowning in consideration. "Why?" After a moment, he sighed. "That's a foolish question. It's you—Master Trent told me of your... adventures."

She cleared her throat, deciding to ignore the last comment. "Well, with the kills we make, it seems like the meat shouldn't just be left there." She shrugged. "We use other parts of the animal."

Grediv grunted. "True enough." After a moment to consider, he shrugged. "I do believe that the cooks sometimes supplement their supplies with arcanous meat. From what little I know, they seem to be wise about what they select. At least, I've never heard of a magic-poisoning incident because of the food, so it doesn't bear comment or interference. I'd recommend talking to them if you're truly interested in this line of research." He clicked his tongue. "Maybe I should, as well. It has merit..." After a long moment, he shook his head. "No. I've too much in process already. Maybe in a decade or two." He gave her a half-smile. "I'll be sure to remember your curiosity, should I ever choose to take up that research."

"Uh, thank you." She smiled in return. *That makes quite a bit of sense. I suppose the cooks never give healing harvests to Mages because they get priority treatment from the Mage healer of the caravan.*

Den hailed them happily as they walked up beside the wagon, and Tala swung onto the ladder climbing up to sit on the roof. She turned back around to wave goodbye to Master Grediv, but he was already gone.

She searched up and down the wagon train, but she couldn't see any sign of him. *Gone, again.* She frowned. *Does he go invisible? Or does he move so fast I can't track him?* There were likely other possibilities, but it seemed that the realms of magic, about which she knew nothing, were much more expansive than she'd ever realized. *The more I learn, the more I realize that I don't know...* It was a daunting prospect.

She pulled out her wide-brimmed hat and settled it back atop her head, feeling the coolness of shade wash over her. She let out a long, contented sigh. *Things are looking up.*

"How was it getting out of the city, Den?"

The driver turned to her with a smile. "No difficulty, Mistress. It's good to have you back with us." His grin shifted, picking up what seemed to be a bit of mischief. "It would have been frustrating to wait for another Dimensional Mage if you didn't return."

Tala snorted a laugh, moving to sit beside him. "I knew you loved me." She settled in and sighed. "Did you have a good stay in Alefast?"

Den shrugged. "I've some cousins in the city, and it was good to see them and their families." He leaned back, turning his eyes back to the landscape ahead. "My family has been in the driver business for generations. We're spread out throughout the cities." He chuckled to himself. "It's probably one reason we stay in the business. It's really the only way for us to stay in touch with each other without breaking the bank."

They chatted for a while about his family and how much the kids had grown since he'd last seen them. They discussed quite a few little things, and Tala kept Den from ever turning the questions about family to her. She felt a pull of sadness but had decided that her own family history shouldn't drag Den down. "I'm glad you got some good time with them."

"Thank you, Mistress." He eyed her, without turning. "I noticed earlier; you did some shopping?"

She glanced down. "A bit, yeah. I was quite tired of..." She sighed. "Wearing rags?"

"You mean you were tired of making rags."

She huffed a soft laugh. "True enough."

"Those do look a bit sturdier." He seemed to hesitate, then continued. "I don't really see how they'll fare better, though. You seem to have a knack for destructive encounters."

"Isn't that the truth." She shook her head, smiling slightly. "These are a bit special, though, so I'm hoping they'll hold up better."

"As you say, Mistress." He seemed *very* hesitant but resolute as he continued. "If I may be so bold, most Dimensional Mages tend to refrain from... violence. At least while they have that duty in a caravan."

She sighed. "Too true, Den. I have a habit of... well, of being a bit reckless."

"People are counting on you now, Mistress." His tone was not *quite* paternal.

"I know... I truly do, but I'm not used to that." She sighed. "I will try to be better, this leg of the trip."

He smiled at her. "That would be much appreciated." He glanced back at her, returning the conversation to her wardrobe. "I assume that little bag's your new storage?"

She gave him a critical look. "What makes you say that?"

"I'm not blind. You near filled one of these storage boxes on the way out." He kicked the wooden box beneath his seat with his heel. "The way I figure it, you should have more, now, than when we headed the other way, but you've no luggage at all."

She frowned. *I am advertising myself a bit...* Was it worth obfuscating the truth? "Den, could you try something for me?"

He glanced her way, then sighed. "Just don't get me killed. My wife would be a bit cross with me if I died."

I really hope he's joking. Does he really think I'd endanger him? Tala laughed a bit nervously. "It shouldn't be dangerous." She pulled off her belt pouch. "Can you open this?"

He looked at the pouch, then hooked his reins on an anchor built into the seat for the purpose. He reached out. His fingers closed on empty air, the bag seeming to have moved just enough that his fingers slid off of it. Den frowned. "That's odd."

Tala set the bag on the bench, and Den very slowly moved his hands from both sides. She saw the area warp slightly as his hands approached, but he was focused now and was able to get a grip on the little belt pouch.

"Slippery little thing." He glanced at her. "It doesn't feel slick, now, but it was kinda hard to grab."

She nodded. *Without magesight, it makes sense that that is how it would appear.*

He tried to open the bag, but it remained cinched tight. After a moment, he handed it back. "I could try cutting the ties, but that seems like it wouldn't be a good idea, and I don't want to hurt your item."

"Thank you. That actually was quite informative." No one else could easily grab or open her pouch. *Fantastic.* She was sure that a concerted effort on the part of someone who didn't care if they hurt the pouch would probably succeed, but whether that would gain them access, or simply destroy the dimensional storage, she didn't know. *And I hope I never learn.*

Den nodded. "Happy to help. You have some reading to do?"

"That obvious?"

"You do seem to like your books. Go on. Thank you for stopping to talk for a bit."

"Are you sure?"

"I'm not a driver because I like to be around people all day, Mistress. I enjoy time to myself." He winked. "But feel free to stop by for short visits whenever you like." He patted the seat between them. "My bench has plenty of space."

"Will do." She grinned, climbing backward, returning to the wagon's roof.

Standing atop the roof, she looked back on the receding city of Alefast. She'd only been there two days. It had felt like months.

What do I do now? Now, she should at least itemize what Grediv had given her. After that, she should probably begin prepping for her full inscriptions. *I have a lot of biology to brush up on.*

But that was for later. Now was a time for new books. *How can I get into Kit without risking any number of catastrophes?* She contemplated. She could ask Den to watch it, but she didn't want to impose upon him. She searched her mind, letting her eyes move without really thinking about where they were looking. Eventually, her gaze fell on the swivel ring mounted into the roof of the wagon and moved to inspect the locking mechanisms more closely. There were catches used to lock the huge tower shields into place. *Yeah, that should do.*

She opened the pouch, hooking the cord in two places on the locking mechanisms on the swivel ring. *That should hold it open.* Now, to hide it.

The answer to that was quite simple. As she climbed down in, her hat settled into place, the brim wider than the hole. She took the chin loop and lightly secured it to an anchor that was, suspiciously, already in place. "Thank you?"

The comforting feeling that she always felt within the pouch almost seemed to briefly intensify. *Or you're imagining things, Tala.* Either was equally likely.

She climbed the rest of the way down the ladder and looked about.

What do you have for me today, Kit?

Chapter: 11
Settling In

Tala grinned as she stood on solid footing, looking around the inside of Kit, her dimensionally enhanced belt pouch.

The space was just a *bit* bigger than before, and something seemed to give her the impression that it was as large as it could get for the moment. It was roughly six feet in every dimension, though several things pushed into the walls.

With her back to the ladder, the rack for her kegs and jug was embedded into the wall to her right, along with a shelf for the extra lids, tapping tools, and other miscellaneous items relating to endingberries. That wall also had homes for her water skin and other liquid containers.

To her left, the wall was bristling with tools, including eleven axes, eleven hatchets, and eleven belt knives, each perfectly situated for maximum space efficiency. The fruit-picker was still tucked into its place alongside the ladder.

She really did have quite the collection of odds and ends, mostly picked up in Bandfast in preparation for the unknowns of her first mission. *Most of this is useless to me, now.* Well, that wasn't fair. It wasn't burdening her, and it might come in handy one day. The artifact hammer was there, too. *I really need to study that some more...*

Connected to that same wall was a small worksurface, which hadn't been there before. Below it rested the leather which she'd taken from the fallen men, in the form of pouches, belts, and packs. *Huh, it will be nice to have a place to work with this stuff.* "Thank you, again."

Directly opposite the ladder, the wall was divided in two, split from top to bottom. The right side held a sort of closet within the wall, though there was no means of closing it off. Several of her items hung from a short rod, and the rest were folded neatly on various shelves. Her bedroll and accompanying items were stored under the lowest shelf, resting on the ground. "Thanks, Kit. This looks really nice."

The pouch did not respond.

To the left of the closet stood a mostly empty bookcase, set back into the wall. Quite a few of the books glowed with power, but she put that aside for the moment. She wanted to see what they were, first, then examine whatever magic they contained.

Along with her five notebooks and Adrill's notes on artifacts, a middle shelf held the now heavily annotated 'Why Organize When You Can Expand?'

The shelf below that held 'A Mage's Guide to Their First Mageling: Basics Every Mageling Should be Taught,' 'A Reference for Inscribing Known Materials,' and 'On Determining the Means to Empower Unique or New Materials.' And beside those three books rested the collection that Grediv had just given her.

Each volume in the collection had a dark leather cover, almost black in truth, though the specific color varied on that theme. The lettering inlaid in the hard covers was not quite silver but was much brighter than steel. *What material is that?* To her surprise, she realized that the three books Grediv had given her earlier looked to be a part of this larger set. *Was this his plan from the beginning? Or does he just like this style, and he gets all his books bound in this manner...?* Either way seemed equally likely.

The new collection contained the four basic texts, describing the four quadrants. The volume on basic magic item theory was there, as well, but the books continued after those most basic books. There were two successively thicker tomes on each of the quadrants, as well as magic item theory—clearly the second and third volumes in each series. There were also three books on 'Bound Magic Items.' Though these were much smaller than those on other topics.

Nine books remained: one set and one individual book.

The set was labeled: 'A Brief Overview of Entities.' The eight books were sub-headed 'Arcane,' 'Bound,' 'Fused,' 'Refined,' 'Paragon,' 'Reforged,' 'Ascending,' and 'Transcendent.' *Grediv had called the cyclops a fused.* If these were what she assumed, they covered, at least in brief, every known category of magical entity in the world. She shivered as she looked at the last sub-heading. *I don't know that I want to mess with anything truly transcendent.*

Her eyes moved to the final, slim volume, which was labeled simply: 'Soul Work.'

Tala gaped at the books. *Twenty-seven books.* It was a treasure trove of information. Master Trent's set only had two volumes on each of the quadrants and only one on item theory. *This is… amazing.*

She reached for the book titled 'Soul Work' first. She opened the cover and frowned. She could read the words, but they made no sense. They didn't form coherent sentences, and the longer she stared, the more her head began to ache. As she focused, her magesight triggered, and she saw power swirling around the little book. She looked up and again saw it encompassing quite a few of the collection. The third volume of each set was empowered, along with all but the first three volumes of 'A Brief Overview of Entities.'

She pushed through the growing pain and nausea to determine the purpose of the magic, though she thought she already knew.

They are warded against me, at least until I achieve Archon. Well, they're warded against anyone below Archon. She knew that with certainty, though she didn't understand either how she knew, exactly, or how the books would determine she met the criteria.

She growled. *Grediv, you evil slag, why would you give me something I can't use yet?* Was he protecting himself against punishment? Were these really books she shouldn't have, yet? *Then, why give them to me?*

Then, she had a thought and grinned. She pulled out her knife and examined it. Her magesight could still see her Archon Star, embedded into the pommel, though it was quite thoroughly integrated. *That should do it.* She pushed the pommel against the book in her hands, and the magic shifted.

Victory!

A single section became understandable to her, within the book.

> 'This is a restricted text, bound to those above your current level. Please return when your soul is of sufficient strength to warrant access to the information within. Thank you.'

"You're a snarky book, aren't you…?"

For good measure, she tested the knife pommel against the other magic-bound books, to similar results. The wording varied, but the message was the same. 'You aren't worthy of this information.'

She sighed but felt a smile tugging at her lips. "Strengthen my soul, eh? I can work with that."

Tala had taken enough time looking about inside of Kit, so she climbed back out the pouch, unhooking and taking her hat with her. She hadn't been down in the dimensional storage for too long, but it had been enough to cover most of the distance that she and Grediv had walked.

Den glanced back at her. "Do you know anything about that?"

They were heading down into the valley where she'd been the cyclops' practice dummy. She could see an almost perfectly straight line of sporadic furrows carved into the earth where she'd been sent skipping. The end was punctuated with a massive crater from the beast's downward strike. She grunted. "Yeah. Cyclops."

Den let out a low whistle. "Those are nasty. I've only ever seen a valley cyclops at a distance, and it took two Mages and their magelings to bring it down."

Valley cyclops? "It wasn't a pleasant creature."

"I'll bet. Are you sure you want to be a Dimensional Mage?"

Tala sighed. "It makes good money. I promise, I'll try to keep out of trouble on this journey back."

He glanced back at her, shrugged, and didn't press. "Guardsman Adam stopped by. He asked me to relay a message."

"Oh?"

"'Please come see me, when you have a free moment.'"

"Thank you, Den. I didn't mean for you to be my message service."

He laughed. "Not like it took any effort." He gave her a bit of a searching look. "You're about my daughter's age. She has the same effect on boys that you seem to. They always come calling."

Tala blushed deeply, caught completely by surprise, trying to formulate a response.

"I'll tell you the same thing I told her. It may seem fun to get all the attention, but the love of one man, if he's the right one, is better than the fleeting affection, lust, and passion of thousands."

She cleared her throat, very much embarrassed. "I'll... uh... keep that in mind. But it isn't like that. Adam is teaching me how to fight..."

He cocked an eyebrow at her. "Mmhm."

She cleared her throat again, scratching the back of her neck. "Anyways, thank you for the message... and the advice. I'll try to keep it in mind."

He nodded once, then returned to his duties.

Well, I suppose I should go find him.

* * *

Adam was easy to find as he was currently riding atop one of the wagons, eyes unceasingly scanning their surroundings.

"Adam!" she called to him as she began climbing the ladder.

"Mistress Tala. Good to see you alive and well." He did, in fact, spare her a glance and a smile.

She quirked a smile in return. *Yeah... I deserved that.* "Den said you came looking for me?"

"Yes, from what I've seen, you have progressed well in balance, breathing, and posture."

"Thank you? What, have you been stalking me or something?"

He snorted a laugh. "Hardly. You are simply moving more easily and seem to be shifting your movements towards that of a fighter."

"So, just staring at me, then."

He sighed. "Do you wish to learn, or do you wish to poke and prod?"

It was a fair question. *Den's comment set me a bit on edge, I guess...* "Learn, of course."

"Good." He was still moving his gaze across the surrounding trees. "Core."

"Hmmm?"

"The next step is core. I want you to strive to keep your core engaged as much as possible. This means keeping your abdomen tensed, and your body stabilized. This is an extension of all three previous tasks. In addition, we are going to start hand-to-hand sparring each morning, after your duties are complete and before mine begin."

"I'm going to fight you?"

He shrugged, not looking at her. "I will be your opponent some of the time, but I'll enlist others as well, where appropriate." He did glance her way, then. "Based on your miraculous survivals, I assume that you have either a means of avoiding damage or healing. Is that correct?"

"Yes? What are you planning?"

He shrugged, again. "It will be better for you if your opponents don't have to hold back. It will feel worse, but you will learn faster. That said, I have no wish to harm you or reduce your ability to work during this trip."

"Fair enough, I suppose." She was beginning to feel a bit nervous. Even so, she took a moment to do as he asked, tensing her core. She didn't clamp down, instead simply ensuring that there was tension throughout the stabilization muscles in her torso. "Is that it? Keep my core taut?"

He smiled, eyes continuing to move. "It's enough."

"Alright."

"Come find me before you've eaten tomorrow morning, but after your duties and other regular morning tasks are complete." After a moment, he met her gaze, lowering his voice to just above a whisper. "I'd advise against seeking out Master Sergeant Furgel. He's pretty embarrassed, and while I don't think he will be so unprofessional again, sometimes men like that prefer to double down on their foolishness, no matter how otherwise competent."

"Will do, and I will keep that in mind. Thank you." With no further comment forthcoming, she climbed back down the ladder. *Today's been odd enough, I suppose, and tomorrow will at least have an interesting start. I've never done hand-to-hand sparring before.*

* * *

Tala returned to the front wagon, having walked just faster than the rumbling caravan.

I need to run some tests. If she was going to get her soul stronger, she needed to go about it in a logical way. As she began figuring out how to test what she needed to, she made sure to keep her core tense. It was already becoming difficult. She was used to exercising her stabilization muscles, but she was not used to extended engagement of her core at large.

This is what he meant... She sighed. *More to work on.* She quickly realized that she couldn't keep the muscles engaged constantly, and not just because she wasn't used to it. Keeping any muscle engaged constantly was not feasible. *Like with the breathing pattern, he is trying to shift my natural patterns by having me aim for extremes to begin with.* She'd had teachers use the method before. Even so, she decided to follow his instruction.

As she made her way back onto the roof of her wagon, she noticed that she was feeling a little bit anxious and took a moment to analyze her own feelings in an attempt to figure out why.

There was a feeling of absence within her, and she quickly realized that it seemed to stem from the fact that she had no endingberry power within her at the moment. *The cyclops well and truly drained that.*

That realization in mind, she reached into her pouch and pulled out her iron flask. She took a few quick drinks, downing half of the thick, pulpy mixture. *There. About one cup of berries.*

The texture wasn't that pleasant, but she didn't mind, given the results.

She sighed, feeling content at the returned sense of thrumming power within her. *One cup a day. That's a good limit.* Tala glanced at the flask as she closed it and before she stored it. *I wonder if the power is in the juice alone or if it's in the meat of the berry...* She should borrow a cider press and see if she could render this down to an easier to consume liquid without losing too much of the power. *I could probably dry out the remainder, after the press, and get a nice fruit leather...* She might need to mix it with something else to keep the taste from becoming monotonous. *Worth considering, but I won't have the ability to do anything about it until we reach Bandfast.*

It was possible that Brand had a press in the chuckwagon, but she had enough on her plate that she didn't want to pursue that, at least not yet. *If the opportunity presents itself, I'll ask.*

But that was for later.

She took her knife from her belt and sat down, leaving it in its sheath.

First, she placed the knife at arm's length, where she could just reach it by bending forwards. She flexed, drawing the knife back to her hand.

It was much easier at this distance, and she grinned broadly. *Oh, that's fantastic.*

She'd suspected that distance would affect difficulty, as the implications otherwise would have been staggering, but she hadn't *known*. Now, she did. She jotted that down, along with some other thoughts.

Okay. She stood, setting the knife up near the front of the wagon, then walked carefully to the back, keeping her core engaged as much as she was able.

One. She pulled it to her. It was exponentially harder to pull it to her across twenty feet than it had been to pull it the four feet or so.

She walked back and replaced it at the front of the wagon, returning to the rear before repeating the exercise.

Two. This was close to double the distance she'd ever pulled the knife to her before, excepting during the fight with the cyclops. For some reason, that had felt easier, though all the aches, pains, and exhaustion that had come upon her after the brief scuffle made it difficult to determine. *Maybe if the knife is already moving towards me, it's easier? It takes less energy?* That made a sort of sense. It worked that way with her physical muscles, so why not her spiritual ones?

Three.

She did not feel up to a fourth, especially in light of her earlier exertion, so she placed the knife at the three-quarters point.

One. It was easier than pulling the item the full length of the wagon, but only just.

Two. She found herself sweating, even within the shade of her wide-brimmed hat.

Three. That was all she felt capable of at this distance.

Halfway, now. *One.*

Two.

Three. She was gasping, and she took a moment to pull her breathing back into proper pattern. Long inhale through the nose, quick exhale through the mouth.

Only five feet from her, now. *One.*

Two. She found that if she exhaled, while pulling the knife to her, it felt a bit easier, as if she was able to exert herself with less strain. *Good to know.*

Three. She was breathing regularly, now, but it was an effort. She pulled out her water incorporator and carefully shot water into her dry mouth at an angle, allowing her to drink with relative ease. She splashed herself with water through the process, but she didn't care much. It would evaporate, either naturally or magically, soon enough.

She looked down at the incorporator again. *Can I use this as a magical exercise?* She pointed the device off to the side and threw power into it, directing the flow straight from her gate to the item. She gathered up what she could from her reserves along the way.

A stream of water as thick as her thumb shot outward, arcing to the ground. She was pushing more power than she could sustain through the device, and she quickly came to the end of her reserves, allowing the flow, both of magic and water, to come to an end.

Interesting. She examined herself critically, turning her magesight upon her power. *If making an Archon Star is like carefully loading heavy cargo, powering this is like picking up and hurling heavy rocks randomly.* In short, it was a similar process but would likely work her power in different ways. *Nice.* Her goal, when she used this, would be to express as much power as quickly as possible and sustain it until it tapered off. Today, that had been about a second and a half. *I have to start somewhere.*

There was an oddity, however. Just like when her first Archon Star had drawn power out of her, there were vestiges that seemed to cling more tightly to her physical form. The only part that she was able to redirect into the incorporator was the nebulous power that seemed to settle around her gate and keystone, rather than being spread through her body. *I wonder why that is...*

She noticed Den glancing back at her, and she waved.

He turned a bit more. "What are you up to, Mistress?"

She smiled. "Just exercising my magic."

He opened his mouth, then thought for a moment, closing it.

Tala cocked her head, waiting.

"You know, I've no meaningful comment. It's not dangerous, right?"

"No. It's safe." *It also shouldn't be a beacon like my magic-popping-breath last time.*

"Fair enough. Enjoy."

Tala laughed a bit self-consciously. "Thank you, Den."

He waved over his shoulder as he turned to face forward once more.

Hmmm... Den mentioned a valley cyclops. She sat down, reaching into her pouch and pulling out the book 'A Brief Overview of Entities: Fused.'

She flipped through the index and found cyclops, but a valley cyclops wasn't listed. *Huh.* She placed the book back in and drew out 'A Brief Overview of Entities: Bound.' After finding the right page in the index, she again opened to the cyclops entry. There it was.

> 'Cyclops, Valley – Valley cyclops stand between eight and fifteen feet tall and have the attributes of any cyclops. See *Cyclops.*'

She looked up to the start of the cyclops section.

> 'Cyclops are as resistant to direct magical manipulation as a foe in full armor: they are not impossible to affect, but it takes a great deal more power and/or precision. In addition, their physical strength greatly exceeds what would be expected, given their size and level of advancement. Expect any Bound cyclops to be as strong, physically, as the average Fused of most other entity types. Cyclops, unlike their giant kin, continue to grow as they age

> until they become too big for their body to survive, or they find a method of advancement to a higher class of entity. Cyclops tend to use clubs, or other close-range weapons, and think poorly of those who attack from a distance.'

There were a few other general facts but nothing of significance in the moment. *Den saw Mages guarding a caravan fighting one of these... a Bound entity.* She felt her thoughts racing. *Grediv obliterated an entity a full order more powerful than this with ease.* Thinking back on his words, that did make sense. *He claimed to be a Paragon, which is two orders higher still.* She shivered. How powerful did that make him? She couldn't look at the book on entities of that order, so she couldn't even get a general idea.

She had myriad things running through her head that she wanted to look into, or do, or practice, or contemplate, or... *Too many...* She sighed, leaning back and allowing her eyes to take in the countryside around her.

It was beautiful.

Dark green trees that were ripe with magic grew in clusters, groves, and whole forests easily within sight as the caravan was currently on a rise. Trees with less magic were easily visible as their leaves had changed in the autumn weather, more subject to the seasons than their magic-full cousins.

Tall, thick grass swayed in the breeze, looking like rippling waves moving across the surrounding treeless land. What had been a worn path, leaving Alefast, had quickly faded away as traffic patterns dispersed enough to make the wearing of a road unlikely. Even so, there was a road of sorts since they were headed for the pass—as many caravans did. Really, it was mostly a strip of land, cleared of trees and undergrowth. The grass was too full of life to be easily killed by wagon traffic, and even if it died, it would be back so quickly that it hardly mattered.

Ahead, the pass loomed large, the magnificent mountain cleft in two in time before memory. Snow covered the separated peaks, as well as the other peaks visible in the range. The mountain range was a stark thing from this side.

There were some foothills, leading up to the mountains, but they were dwarfed by the peaks that they heralded. On the northern side, the progression was far more gradual.

I prefer this. The clear, definitive majesty of the mountains were on easy display from the south, and she loved the harsh beauty before her.

As the wind changed direction, a cold breeze swept down from those mountains and tousled her hair, causing some stray strands to sway across her vision.

The air wasn't frozen, but it was close. It smelled crisp and clean and *perfect.* She let out a contented sigh, closing her eyes and letting her arms spread wide in a subconscious attempt to catch more of that wonderful wind.

She wished that Merilin's travel clothes were lighter so that she could feel more of the breeze, even though they were already semi-permeable. She would have loved for the garments to allow the air to play pleasantly across her skin.

As if in response to her thoughts, the garments almost seemed to relax, just slightly, and suddenly the wind felt like it was striking her bare skin. She glanced down, startled, but she was still fully clothed, and the clothing was still solid, though it did seem a bit looser on her than before.

She grinned, closing her eyes once more and basking in the wind until it passed a couple of minutes later. For those few minutes, there were no experiments to be run, no skills or muscles to train, and no looming debt to dig free of. For that time, she was simply Tala, free in the autumn breeze.

Chapter: 12
Through the Pass, Again

Tala sighed, feeling a fleeting disappointment.

As suddenly as it had come, the cool breeze departed, the wind switching to come up from the plains behind them. It was not a warm wind, but it was warmer than that from the mountains.

Tala sighed, letting her arms fall back to her lap. She felt her clothing shift back into form, tightening the fit once more. *Merilin did say that the immortal elk had a few ways of keeping cool. I suppose this is one of them?*

As she reached for the book most likely to contain information on that entity, she froze, hand in the pouch, book in hand. *Wait... I know these books were on the shelf, within the space.* She looked down, into the bag, trying to see past the book, and her hand. It was only darkness. She couldn't see the ladder; she couldn't see the little room. Nothing.

Okay, Tala. Calm down.

She pulled her hand out and closed the bag, leaving the book inside. She spoke softly, so that Den was unlikely to hear. "How are you doing that?"

Kit did not respond.

Tala stared at the bag, focusing until her magesight began to highlight the power flowing through the bag. She was hampered in that because of the iron salve she'd worked into the outside, but she could still see through the top, closed though it was.

She saw what she'd seen before, dimensional power, twisted and harnessed towards the pouch's functions. "How do you know what I am reaching for?"

The pouch did not respond.

She frowned. "I'm reaching for a pencil." She stuck her hand in, thinking about reaching for a notebook, specifically without a pencil.

Her hand instantly found a notebook.

It's bound to me, to my magic. After a moment, she reached in and took out a pencil as well and began writing notes, thoughts, theories. Finally, she realized that she had a resource ready to hand.

She pulled out the first volume on bound items, skipping the introduction for the moment and looking in the index.

Behavior… behavior, behavior… There!

She flipped to the corresponding page.

> 'Bound magic items often seem to act with what is misdiagnosed as intuition, on the part of their wielder. The truth of the matter is that because the item is bound to a Mage's magic, they are bound to the Mage's will. Therefore, if a Mage takes an action, and it is within the item's ability to act to aid that action, the Mage's will often intuitively manipulates the item to bring it about.'

"Huh, that is a disappointingly sensible answer…" She looked down at Kit. "Oh well. And here I thought you might be reading my mind and trying to be helpful." She smiled. "Thank you, anyways, Kit." She patted the bag.

The pouch did not respond.

She regarded the volume in her hand. "I already have this out. Might as well learn what I can." With that, she flipped to the beginning of the book and began to read.

* * *

Tala was enjoying the book on bound items, and she felt like she was learning a lot.

The first and most important thing she'd learned was that *any* item that she empowered was bound to her. Thankfully, it was bound to her magic, not her soul, but it was still a surprising revelation. This bond was actually the chief reason that cargo-slots, like those riding in the wagons both beneath and behind her, couldn't have another Mage give them power. That was not the only reason to be sure, but it was a core one.

It was a much more thorough explanation than she'd been given previously, and she was grateful for it. As it turned out, the cargo-slots would remain bonded to her until they fully drained of power, at which point, they could be reinscribed, and a different Mage could bond them for the course of a different journey.

Did Grediv mention something about this? If he did, she'd lost it in the outpouring of information. *And here I thought I had perfect memory...* She *thought* she could likely delve back into the conversation with Grediv and find out if he'd told her this tidbit, but in the end, it didn't really matter. *I suppose perfect memory doesn't mean perfect ability to access it.* It seemed like a rusting stupid limitation to her.

She returned her thoughts to the magic-bound items. Apparently, there was a pervasive theory, which the book's author thought of as nonsense, which held that the magic items were alive in a rudimentary sense, and that it wasn't until the item died that another could be brought into being, within the same shell, ready to bond some other Mage.

The idea made Tala vaguely uncomfortable as it seemed akin to creating a slave solely for your own purposes, then letting them die when you were through with them.

Thankfully, it seemed that even the most ardent supporters of this theory hypothesized that the intelligence of inscribed items wasn't even equivalent to an insect. They did seem to claim that artifacts were closer to mammals in intellect, though.

"Kit, are you alive?"

Kit did not respond.

Oh, well. She really hadn't expected anything else.

Tala looked to her right, hearing a horse drawing near, and sighed. A man, dressed in heavy chainmail and armed with the standard guard weaponry, was approaching. The insignia of a master sergeant was highly visible on his near shoulder. *Great.*

He glanced her way and saw her regarding him. He lifted his hand and called out, "Mistress Tala, may I come up to speak with you for a moment?"

Why not. "Sure." *Maybe Adam misjudged him?*

Furgel was surprisingly lithe, slipping off his horse and tying the reins to the ladder as he swung up onto it. He climbed quickly and easily despite the weight of his armor and weapons. When he achieved the roof, he hesitated, glancing down at himself. "My apologies." He patted his armor. "I can doff my iron and leave it aside if you wish. I apologize for not thinking of it earlier."

She waved that aside. "No need, Master Sergeant, you're on duty, and I don't mind." After a moment, she sighed and added, "But I do appreciate the consideration in asking." *Or... were you trying to throw me off by wearing the armor to begin with?* That seemed a bit uncharitable for her to assume, so she set that aside.

Furgel nodded, taking a seat between her and Den, facing her from about five feet away.

There was an uncomfortable silence, during which Tala placed her book, notebook, and pencil into her belt pouch.

He cleared his throat. "I... I owe you an apology, Mistress Tala."

She didn't react, simply watching him, impassively.

He looked off to one side. "I behaved poorly and disrespected you greatly. I was attempting to perform my duties and thought I was in the right, but that is no excuse for how I acted. I apologize. Will you forgive my blunder?"

That was surprisingly eloquent. She took a slow breath in, then nodded. "Yes, thank you, Master Sergeant. I am aware how I appear to others, and while I do not appreciate being treated as you did, I understand that you did not have malicious intent."

He seemed to relax slightly, several worry lines fading from his face.

However, before he spoke, Tala continued, "That said, I would recommend not treating anyone that way, ever. Even if I was whom you assumed, that would have been an inappropriate means of handling the situation."

He reddened but not with embarrassment, and he opened his mouth to retort.

Tala held up a hand, forestalling him. "Every person in a caravan is here by right. Either they earned that right through competence and contract, or they purchased that right as a passenger. This is not your kingdom, and you are not a god. Respect and patient listening will go a long way, Sergeant."

He was so red as to almost appear purple, but he seemed to maintain enough control not to utter his clear objections. "Mistress." He stood, turning to the ladder and dropping out of sight. Tala shortly saw him on his horse, riding quickly back down the wagon train.

Den turned to regard her. "While you weren't wrong, it probably wasn't wise to give unsolicited advice."

Tala grunted. "Probably true. I wonder why he came at all? I'd have thought someone like that would want an audience for his 'act of humility.'"

Den laughed, turning back around. "Oh, he did. I'm head driver, and I'd have taken news to the others." He snorted. "I still will." He glanced back, grinning.

Tala laughed. "Remind me to stay in your good graces."

"Oh, Mistress, you're fine. Especially now that you're being more cautious." He lapsed back into silence, his hatted head barely visible above the edge of the wagon.

Tala stood, looking back down the wagon train. Unlike the trip to Alefast, during which the caravan had been composed of eight wagons, this trip was *much* larger. There were the two cargo wagons, three Mages' wagons, and the chuckwagon. Three bunk wagons had been brought along for a tripled contingent of guardsmen. One of those wagons trundled along directly behind the second cargo wagon and another was at the back of the wagon train. Each had a guard posted on top.

Adam was the frontmost of those guards, and he waved as he noticed her before continuing his vigilance.

Her mind took a step back. *Wait, three Mages' wagons?* She hadn't met the third Mage Protector of this caravan. *It'll be interesting to see who it is.*

The passenger wagons were still the most numerous, but now it was by an even greater margin. If she was guessing correctly, there were four for more wealthy passengers and three for poorer, though that was relative for anyone wealthy enough to travel between cities in a trade caravan.

Sixteen wagons. Between ninety and one hundred guards, likely between twenty-three and twenty-seven passengers, plus servants, drivers, and the cooks. That was approaching a hundred-sixty people. *I wonder if Brand has more than two assistants this trip.* She'd find out soon enough.

Nearly three times as many people on this trip, but she supposed that made sense. Every caravan leaving a waning city *should* take more away than it brought. *Thus continues the cycle of civilization.*

She saw a huge shape on horseback, riding near the middle of the caravan. *Rane...* That was a strange man, from what little she'd seen. *Did he get a bigger horse?* She grinned at that thought.

I don't see Ashin. She allowed her gaze to move over the guardsmen and women out on duty but didn't spot him. She shrugged. *Might have a different duty shift.* He might be out and about after lunch or whenever they switched shifts.

They were nearing the entrance to the pass, even as the sun neared its zenith.

I wonder... Tala fished into her pouch and pulled out a bit of jerky. She flicked it out to the side, without fanfare or warning.

A blip of dimensional energy heralded its vanishing.

So, Terry is along for the trip, then. She wasn't really surprised.

She stretched backward, feeling the tightness in her muscles. She froze.

Well, rust me to slag... She groaned, settling down into a seated position. *I forgot to get a massage...* That was irritating, and now that she was taking the time to sit, again, her tight muscles were beginning to nag her.

Well, nothing for it, now. She began to stretch, using her magesight, internally focused, to pinpoint the trigger-points that were giving her the most issue. Funnily enough, the process allowed her to discover some strangely relaxing positions, which slowly helped her body unwind itself.

In addition, she pulled out her last blank notebook and put it to use, whenever her hands and eyes were free, which, admittedly, wasn't that often. Her self-appointed task was to do a detailed overview of her knowledge of biology. Thankfully, she wasn't seeking to write a reference book, she simply built out a list of which specifics she remembered and those she didn't feel confident in, without detailing what those actually were. *I'm making an index of my knowledge.* She found that helped her decide what was too much detail to include.

As she began to stretch, the caravan entered the pass.

As they continued, her muscles loosened, and she steadily filled the blank pages, using any and all blank space she could, while still making the things she needed to brush up on all too clear. *I'll need all this at least well understood before I can properly use the full inscriptions from Holly.*

The caravan was well inside the shadowed pass when she heard someone begin to climb the ladder.

"Mistress Tala?"

She straightened out of a particularly deep stretch, turned towards the ladder but remaining seated. "Brand?"

"Yes, Mistress."

"Come on up."

He pulled himself up, bearing a tray laden with food.

"Good to see you, Brand. What's on the menu today?"

He held out the large wooden bowl, showing her the content. "A large salad, while we're still close to some gardens that can grow it for us." He smiled. "Bought out half the stalls in the fresh food market this morning."

Tala grinned, taking the offered bowl and fork. "Thank you. Dressing?"

"A garlic herb vinaigrette."

"You know how to spoil me." She set the bowl down. "What can I do for you?"

He waved the question away. "I have to get back to work."

"Very well." She picked up the bowl as he moved back towards the ladder. However, he hesitated with his head still poking up.

"Mistress Tala?"

"Hmmm?"

"Thank you."

"What for?"

He quirked a smile. "I think you know."

Before she could respond, he sank out of sight. "Huh…" She looked down at the salad, then back up to where Brand had disappeared. She smiled to herself as she dug into the delicious salad.

* * *

Her lunch complete, she took time to slowly restart her stretching and note taking as she digested, continuing to work through her sore muscles. In her deep, internal looks, she also noticed some areas in which the muscles were still much weaker than those surrounding them, and so she also began to work on rounding out her fitness. *And here I thought I found all those slackers.*

A couple of slow, satisfying hours passed before she was fully done, and she was able to turn her attention to another task.

Her soul felt mostly recovered. *That still feels odd to think…* She did another group of progressively easier sets with her knife, thoroughly working her spiritual muscles without approaching overexertion. *I hope.*

Again, she pulled out 'Soul Work' and attempted to decipher anything meaningful from the warded book.

She did not succeed.

Disgruntled, she put the book back in the pouch. "Thanks anyway, Kit."

The pouch did not respond.

She pulled out the water incorporator, drank a little, then sent a large stream shooting out to the side to exercise her power once more.

Tala lay back, twiddling her thumbs. *I've so much to do, but I don't know what to do first.*

Just do the next thing, Tala.

Well, what thing's next?

What comes to mind? Brand. *I didn't ask him about the press.* She groaned, sitting up. *Might as well.*

She climbed down, dropping from the moving wagon, and walked back towards the chuckwagon. It felt really nice to be using her legs, and she reminded herself that she'd enjoyed walking beside the caravan on the previous trip.

She gave a short knock on the chuckwagon's back door, and it swung open, revealing an assistant cook, whom she'd not seen before.

"Mistress? Can I help you?"

She smiled in what she hoped was a reassuring manner. "Yes. Is Brand free for a moment? I have a quick question."

The older man looked surprised. "Yes, of course, Mistress." He disappeared inside, and she could hear him calling out to Brand and discussing with other cooks. She tried not to listen. After all, she didn't need to know what they were saying. *It would be rude... right?*

A minute later, Brand came out, wiping his hands free of flour on his apron. "Mistress Tala? Is everything alright?"

"Yes, yes. Everything's fine." She smiled. "I just have a strange question."

"Sure."

"Do you happen to have a cider press or something like it?"

He hesitated, then started nodding. "For the... berries. Am I right?"

She smiled. "Correct."

He smiled in turn. "I do, yes. I'll even let you use it if you don't clean it after."

She laughed. "Hoping to get some juice out after?"

"One can hope."

"Sounds fair. I'll try to be quick, as well." Thinking of a part of her discussion with Grediv, she frowned. "Anything you use it for shouldn't go to other Mages. It could interfere with their power. Not violently, but it would be inconvenient to weaken our protectors."

Brand gave her a surprised look. "Really? Of course, then."

She shrugged. "I know it does for an Archon, so I'd assume so for any Mage or inscribed."

He clicked his tongue. "Fascinating. I knew that some Mages could eat that which us mundanes could not, but I had not truly considered the reverse." He smiled. "I will keep that in mind. Thank you." He went back inside and quickly returned with a metal-bound, wooden device. There was a spout out the bottom and a wheel-like handle on top.

"Thank you, Brand." She slipped it into Kit. It was *just* small enough to go in.

Brand regarded her belt pouch. "You know, I'm sure that opens wider than it used to."

"Could be."

He smiled again. "I'm glad that your purchase is working out."

"Thank you for introducing me to Artia." She waved. "I'll try to get this back to you by dinner."

He nodded, turning back and closing the door.

Tala returned to her wagon, affixing her bag open as before and slipping inside, leaving her hat to act as a hatch, of sorts.

The cider press was already sitting on the worktable, spout pointed out, an empty keg waiting below.

Tala laughed. "Thanks, Kit. Let's do this."

The warm comfort was ever-present as she worked, processing all the berries she'd harvested, which she hadn't consumed or traded away.

As it turned out, the meat of the berries had virtually no power in and of itself. Thus, she was actually able to increase the concentration of power by removing that mostly neutral material. *I suppose that part is needed for the natural processes of the fruit?*

In the end, she took the roughly nine gallons of crushed berries and turned it into five gallons of berry juice, storing it in two kegs and her one jug. There was a bit extra, which fit into her flask rather perfectly. She ensured the keg and jug were properly sealed, then checked them over with her magic detector. The iron salve barrier was intact and effective, the jug resting inside its salved sack.

She finished clean-up, leaving the press dirty, and climbed back out of Kit.

It was pushing towards evening, and they were almost through the pass. She stood and stretched. *An afternoon well spent.*

She took a few minutes to return the press to Brand, offering him the pressed berry remains, which he happily accepted, explaining that he could still boil them down to make a wonderful dessert, even if it wouldn't be quite as flavorful without the majority of the juices. He also assured her that he would make up something extra special for the Mages, to keep them from the berry dish.

That accomplished, she decided to walk up and down the much longer caravan, continuing her review of human biology.

She thought she saw the other Mage on the far side of the caravan, but it was only a flash. If she was right, he was a much older man, maybe in his fifties. *I was beginning to wonder if caravanning was a young person's game.* It seemed that that wasn't the case.

The mountain pass was stunning in the late afternoon light, though most of that was reflected off the eastern slope. She breathed in the cool, crisp air and smiled. *I've nothing but time.*

"Ho! Mistress Tala!"

She opened her eyes, turning to regard the man riding up to her. *Rane.* "Hello. Master Rane, right?"

The massive man swung down off of his horse, and Tala got another good look at him.

He wore standard Mage's robes, by their cut, at least. They had quick releases and were excellently crafted.

I could have gone that route, to avoid always losing clothes. She was still mildly uncomfortable at the prospect, however. Even though she kept ending up naked, she generally preferred to be as covered as possible. Merilin's elk leather clothing facilitated that nicely.

Aside from the Mage's robes, he wore sturdy sandals, the straps and his inscriptions seemingly designed to avoid each other—for the most part. He also wore an odd wooden handle on his belt. It almost looked like a slim, two-handed sword hilt, but there wasn't a visible blade; instead, the object ended in a small, oblong ring affixed to Rane's belt. Her magesight showed dimensional distortions around the ring, however. *A dimensional storage, specifically for that weapon?*

"Yes, Mistress. Glad you remembered; I was afraid you wouldn't bother."

What's that supposed to mean? She smiled sweetly. "Well, you made quite the impression. It's hard for a girl to forget something like that."

He grimaced. "I… I do apologize for that, Mistress. I'm not good at realizing how my words will sound to others.

Master Grediv always called it a soon-to-be-fatal flaw." He smiled with the last, trying to lighten the mood.

Tala laughed. "I kind of like that."

His smile turned sheepish. "Yeah, it always struck me as pretty funny." His smile faded a bit. "I'm pretty sure he was never joking, though…"

There was a momentary pause as Tala waited for him to say something more.

Instead, the big man shifted his grip on the horse's reins and fell into step beside her.

"So, Master Rane, how can I help you?"

"Hmmm? Oh, I thought it would be nice to walk for a bit, and you were walking."

When he didn't elaborate, she prompted, again. "So, you want to walk? Talk? What, exactly?"

He shrugged, looking obviously awkward. "Master Grediv said that you were someone worth knowing. So, I guess I'd like to get to know you?"

Tala blinked in surprise at that. *He said that?* It did seem in line with other things he'd told her. "Huh… imagine that."

"Yeah." Rane laughed. "Most of the time he tells me to avoid this person or not to speak to that person more than necessary. There have been a few that he's pointed out, like Master Trent, but I've not heard him give the sort of recommendation he gave for you before." After a deep breath, he continued, "Also, he said I'm to keep you from endangering yourself if I can."

She actually felt herself flush a little. "I… don't know what to say to that."

He shrugged, again. "I guess there isn't a need for direct response. I am at least partially responsible for the safety of every member of the caravan anyways, as one of the Mage Protectors." He cleared his throat, changing the subject. "So, Bandfast. Are you from there?"

Her expression stiffened, and she turned her attention back to the way ahead. "That is my home. It will be good to be back, I think. I've some work to do before I can go out again." She sighed. *Not his fault. He's just trying to be inquisitive.* "What about you? Are you from Alefast?"

"Oh, yeah. My family's been there for generations. Our house's founder helped build the city, and he likes to keep us close, whenever possible."

"Keep... present tense?"

"Yeah. He has quite the active hand, though he does so behind the scenes mostly."

"Master Grediv is your ancestor," she said, flatly.

Rane glanced at her with slight surprise. "It's that obvious?"

"You said your founder was still involved. I know Master Grediv is at least that old, and he is involved with you. It wasn't a large leap."

"Oh... I guess so." He shrugged. "He doesn't like us referencing our familial relationship. Apparently, it's caused him issues in the past." He laughed half-heartedly, then did a passible impression of the much older Mage. "'I'm not leveling another arcane city for one of you idiots. Stop flaunting my name.'"

Tala's eyes widened. "Arcane city?"

"Oh, yeah, Master Grediv says there are a whole bunch of them beyond the wilds. He says society at large has just forgotten about them, and it's best not to remind them. Causes too many questions."

She hesitated for a moment. "Like you just did?"

He glanced her way, frowning, then his eyes widened. "Oh! Oh my... I... Forget I said that. I..." He lapsed into silence.

"You don't get out much, do you."

He shook his head, lips firmly sealed.

"First mission alone as a full Mage?"

He nodded.

"Well, I'd recommend thinking through your words before you utter them. Might help you out."

Rane gave her an almost pitiable look, then turned to look ahead.

She shrugged. "Well, I'm not just going to babble. We can walk in silence if you want, but if you want conversation, you've got to talk."

He nodded, again, and didn't speak further.

What, under heaven, am I going to do with this one?

Chapter: 13
Worst Proposal Ever

The caravan made it through the pass without violent incident. Though, Tala thought she'd seen some guards conversing every so often, looking at some things in the surrounding terrain. She almost went to see what they were looking at, at several points, but decided against it each time. *No need to stick my nose into their jobs.*

By the end of the day, the caravan had even returned to what seemed to be the same campsite that they'd used before going through the pass last time.

Was that only four days ago? It depended on how she reckoned it, but yeah, pretty close. *It really does feel like months.* She *might* be overloading her time and mind. *No help for it...*

The use of the same campsite was a bit odd to her because it hadn't taken a full day to get from this campsite to the city on the last trip. As she considered, she realized that they had not started quite as early on this outbound trip, and the oxen had been moving a bit slower than before. *Will our pace be that much slower the whole time, or was it just to make today an easy start to the journey?* She'd have to ask Den if she remembered.

The wagon train, being much larger this time around, didn't simply circle up. Instead, the wagons were positioned into a rounded, hourglass shape. The cargo and bunk wagons made a smaller circle, with the passenger and

Mage wagons in a larger ring. The chuckwagon was positioned in the choke point.

This formation allowed all the oxen to be left free to roam within the smaller ring, while the people of the caravan were able to still have the shelter and perceived safety of the bigger circle.

Cleverly done.

Rane had stayed with Tala for the rest of the afternoon, walking beside her the last three hours or so.

They hadn't really talked aside from the occasional, not-quite-awkward small exchanges of words.

She'd considered climbing back up on Den's wagon, but she'd slightly feared that he would have followed, and something about him made her feel like sending him away would be akin to kicking a puppy.

How do I get myself into these things? If she was rude, once, she'd have her peace and quiet for the remainder of the trip, but she couldn't bring herself to do it, at least not to him. *I could kick a barking, aggressive dog, just not a puppy...*

Even so, she'd used the time to good effect, making great progress on her review of biology, physiology, and organic chemistry, all while practicing all parts of what Adam had assigned her.

While the wagons were getting into formation for the evening, however, Rane had been required to move out and scout the perimeter. *Thankfully.*

In that time, she'd moved through her new exercises, both for her soul and her magic. *I really need to be making Archon Stars.* But her mind was already split too many ways. *Tomorrow. I'll make one, tomorrow.*

She was surprised at how quickly her spiritual muscles were recovering and strengthening. It was already a much easier task to pull the knife towards herself, regardless of the distance, but it still seemed to exhaust her fairly quickly. *Nowhere near a dozen pulls from ten feet.* She almost laughed at herself, then. *Did I expect to meet Grediv's requirements in a day?*

The larger circle within the wagons was surprisingly full, as people milled around, without being crowded. Many were doing light exercises or stretching, clearly trying to work out some stiffness from a day within a passenger wagon.

I'm glad that I don't have to deal with that.

Several of the passengers gave her slight bows and greetings in the vein of, "Good evening, Mistress."

The sky overhead was trending through the fiery hues, blushing towards twilight and the dark of night. She took a moment to smile upward, her eyes flicking towards the few stars already visible through the remaining light.

Tala felt a previously unnoticed tension release when no web of magic came into view. The feeling made her introspective, and she took several slow breaths to consider what she was feeling. *I hate being constrained, and seeing the web of power over Alefast really did make me a bit claustrophobic.* It hadn't helped that her view of that constraint had come into prominence whenever she allowed her gaze to focus, thus inspiring her to keep her eyes moving. *That* did not promote relaxed regard for the beauty of the sky above.

I suppose I could have pulled power away from my magesight inscriptions. She hadn't thought of that earlier, but even now, she felt like it would be a bad idea. *Holly's recommendation to have them active at all times was wise, and I really shouldn't countermand the design without reason.*

About half the larger circle had been designated for eating with tables set out and the side of the chuckwagon open to serve dinner. The scents wafting from the mobile kitchen smelled amazing—as usual.

It was deep-fried steak, asparagus, and potatoes with a thick brown gravy. A slightly magical berry crisp was beautifully presented to the side for dessert. Brand had individualized, chocolate-lava cakes just for the Mages.

Tala grinned openly at Brand when he'd handed her tray to her, and he'd rolled his eyes, a smile tugging at his lips as well. "Yours has a berry-flavored chocolate."

She nodded, having already seen the vestiges of power in the center of the creation. "Looks great, Brand. Thank you."

"Happy to oblige, Mistress."

"Thank your cooks for me too, please?"

He smiled widely at that. "I will. Thank you."

She carried her tray off to one side and set it down to fill a wooden cup with water before picking the tray back up and moving around the outside of the assembled tables. Those eating were in various clusters, spread throughout the tables, and Tala was on the hunt for something in particular.

Finally, she spotted what she'd been looking for and smiled. *An entirely empty table.*

She was the first person at the table she chose, and she took the moment of solitude to dig in. It was wonderous to not have anyone directly around her. *I'm falling back into old habits…*

She had done her best to avoid connections while at the academy. She'd hated that she was there, and even though she'd decided to make the best of it, she had *not* wanted to have a pleasant time. She'd been there for one purpose: to improve herself. When she got out, she would not let anyone tie her down again. At least that had been the plan. *Amazing how little fun you can have when you put your mind to it.*

She had known that she would have to sign a contract of indenture to get work, to pay off the debt, and while that necessity had galled her, she'd done it anyway. *Just one more hard thing to be free.* But then, she'd started encountering people who seemed to genuinely care. Oh, they had their own motivations, their own agendas, but that almost made it better. They weren't being altruistic, so she didn't feel obligated to be so, either.

Now, she was falling back into her habits from the academy. Training, striving, improving. Alone.

And now I'm eating alone. She sighed irritably.

Come on, Tala. It isn't a binary. You are allowed to enjoy some solitude every once in a while and still allow yourself to enjoy being around people. You are not withdrawing again.

She smiled, nodding to herself. *Yeah, I can enjoy a bit of time alone.*

Of course, once she decided that, it didn't last.

An older man sat down across from her and smiled.

Tala glanced up. *Mage, Material Creator with a focus on...* She frowned. *Breathable air?* She realized that she was frowning and forced her face to shift into a smile. "Hello. I'm Tala."

"Greetings, Mistress Tala. My name is Tang." He had a cleanly shaved head and no beard—as was common among Mages without access to Holly or inscribers who purchased her special needles. *Or those unwilling to pay for the use of such needles on themselves.*

Apparently, many Mages had Holly's needles used on their scalp or face so that they could keep their hair, but that method was too expensive to use elsewhere, for most.

"Good to meet you, Master Tang." She nodded politely in greeting before taking another bite of her dinner.

He paused for a moment, then seemed to shrug before digging into his own meal. "Pleasant evening, tonight. I love the slight breeze."

She frowned, not feeling the breeze, then she nodded. *Right! His magic, reflected off my iron, might feel like a breeze.* "It is, isn't it." She returned to her food. *I hope he doesn't notice the 'wind' isn't affecting anything besides himself.*

Trent and Renix joined them shortly thereafter. "Master Tang."

"Master Trent, mageling Renix."

"Master Tang." Renix's greeting came across somehow stiffly formal, as well as being more monotone than Trent's had been.

Trent smiled. "Tala. How are you?"

Tang's eyebrows rose, likely at the lack of the honorific.

Tala smiled in return. "I'm doing well, Trent. Thank you. Quiet day."

Trent's eyes were twinkling. He knew she'd left off his honorific to mirror him, even if she didn't really know why. "About that. If I hadn't known for a fact that you'd stayed near the caravan, I'd have thought you were out harvesting."

Master Tang harumphed. "Of course, she wouldn't do that. A Dimensional Mage's place is safe, with the other valuable cargo and important passengers."

Tala gave Trent an innocent look. "Master Tang has the right of it. I do my best to stay where it's safe." She held back a snicker. "Why, though?"

Trent just rolled his eyes at her antics, simply choosing to respond to her question. "We found a few arcanous bodies along the route before the pass, and a couple since then, usually dragged off the route."

She perked up at that. "Anything worth harvesting?" Then, she deflated. "No… you'd have told me earlier if they were."

Trent grinned. "Right you are. No, nothing worth salvaging. They were ravaged, actually, mostly eaten whenever we found them, and if the one who found them so much as took their eyes off the body, the carcasses vanished." He gave her a questioning look. "I'd bet there were more that we never found." He huffed a laugh. "We found several places where the earth was wet with blood too, but no bodies. I know of five such places, confirmed."

Tala had a suspicion that Terry was responsible, but she didn't say so. "Interesting. So, we've some sort of guardian out there, then?"

Renix snorted. "Hardly. None of the creatures that we found would have been likely to confront a group this large." He gestured around himself. "We probably wouldn't have had any issues, regardless."

Tang cleaned his mouth with a napkin and cleared his throat. "I think that might be a bit hasty, mageling. We only saw a few, and they seemed to have been positioned for us to find. It is possible that something is tailing us and might want us to fall into a false sense of security." He took on a slight tone of lecture. "As a caravan grows, it dissuades smaller threats, while attracting larger."

Renix deflated a bit, turning to his food.

"Or." A voice came from behind Tala, just before Rane set his tray down beside her. "Or, something is trailing us, using the draw of our caravan as a lure to aid it in hunting. In that case, we would be secure, if only because it wants its bait intact."

Trent nodded towards Rane. "Assuming the hunter doesn't want to chum the waters."

Renix frowned, looking to his master.

"Fishing metaphor."

"Ah." Renix turned back to the food.

"Mistress Tala, Master Trent, Master Tang, Renix. Good evening to you all." He snorted. "Our names are all of a theme, it seems. Tala, Tang, Trent, Renix, and Rane."

He said the last with a bit of a sing-song, under his breath. Tala didn't think anyone but she had heard.

A chorus of greetings came back to him, and Rane smiled.

Belatedly, he glanced at Tala. "Uh… mind if I sit here?"

He took up nearly half the bench with his broad build; though, he had sat far enough away to avoid brushing her or impinging on her mobility. "I suppose not. Seat was open."

Renix opened his mouth, seeming about to say something, but his eyes flicked to Tang, and he put a bite in instead.

Tang shifted a bit, using the movement to draw attention. "So, Master Rane, you are from the Gredial family, yes?"

"That's right. Have we met before this morning?"

"Not that I'm aware of. So, I've heard that Archon Grediv is actually the founder of your family, the namesake even. Is that true?"

Rane seemed at a loss.

Really? She sighed, internally. *Shouldn't let someone else kick a puppy either.* "Master Tang, is this conjecture, or were you told that?"

Seeming puzzled, Master Tang turned slightly to face her. "Merely conjecture. The origins of the Gredial family are quite shrouded in mystery, and I've always thought that an Archon with such a similar name *had* to be connected."

She smiled sweetly. "If it's a family secret, it sounds like a question that Master Rane might not appreciate too much."

Tang opened his mouth to respond, but Trent spoke first. "Oh, come on, Master Tang. Everyone's guessed Grediv at one point or another. The old goat even encourages it occasionally. You know how he likes making people look the fool." Trent huffed a laugh. "I halfway figure that he steps in on their behalf occasionally just because so many people *think* there's a connection. He can't let bad come their way because it would look bad for him, even though they're unrelated."

Tang closed his mouth, thinking for a moment. "You do know the Archon fairly well, Master Trent." He drummed his fingers on the table, then sighed. "Ah, well. It would be nice to put an old mystery to rest, but you're right, that would be a bit too convenient."

Tala glanced at Rane, while Tang's attention was on Trent, and she found him looking at her with gratitude radiating from his all-too-easy-to-read features.

They returned to eating, and soon, Tang was pushing back his tray. "Fantastic, and that lava cake had a nice richness to it." Tang patted his belly, then stood. "I suppose I should do a check of the perimeter. This close to the pass, we need to maintain vigilance." He glanced at each of them with a smile. "Good night to you."

A smattering of "Goodnight" echoed back, and he departed.

Renix looked back to Tala. "Why didn't the cooks want us to eat the magic berry dessert?"

Rane, who had just put a spoonful of the cake into his mouth, almost choked. "What?!" He'd spoken around the food.

Tala sighed. "Because some things aren't good for Mages, even if they help mundanes, Renix. You know, most people aren't aware of magical foods." She gave him a meaningful look. "And it's best to keep that number small. Yes?"

Renix looked at Rane, then seem to shrink a bit. "Oh... right."

Tala rubbed her face with both hands. "There are two of them. Heavens help me."

Trent laughed. "Most everything has a bit of magic in it, Renix. We don't need to point out every trace when we find it." He gave his mageling a meaningful look as well.

"Right, yes. I'm sorry, Master Trent."

"It's fine." He turned to look at Rane. "Renix has especially acute senses, and he's been refining his use of magesight and can sometimes sense magic in food." He shrugged. "I never really notice myself, and it seems that Master Tang might not either." Trent grinned mischievously. "It'd be a shame if he never learned."

Rane frowned. "Yeah... Should I go tell him?"

Trent hesitated, his smile slipping just slightly. "No... I was being..." He sighed. "No. He's better off not knowing. His type are very 'by the book,' and we don't want to make trouble for our well-meaning cooks." He gave Tala a meaningful look as he said that.

Well, rust. "Am I going to have an issue with him?"

"Knowing you? Yes. But I hope not. If he presses you on any of your... oddities, feel free to simply, *politely* decline to answer."

I can do that. "I'll keep it civil."

"No, Mistress Tala, not civil, polite. He is senior to you, and he has enough connections to be a pain if he thinks you're disrespecting him. You're already likely to have some difficulty, regardless."

She sighed. *Great...* "Okay. I'll aim for polite."

Trent grunted. "It's something."

Renix was seeming to open up, now that the older Mage had departed. "So, Master Rane, Master Grediv was your master through your time as a mageling?"

"That's right."

"What was it like?"

Rane seemed to chew on the idea, even while finishing the bite that had still been in his mouth. After he swallowed, he nodded amiably. "Oh, it was a rusting party.

He took me out into the Wilds, only bringing me back to civilization to get reinscribed."

Renix opened his mouth in shock. "Wait, what?"

"Yeah, we left at midnight on my twelfth birthday."

"So, you didn't go to the academy?"

"Nope."

Well, that explains a lot. Socially isolated since he was twelve? Tala actually felt bad for the guy. *I was never that isolated.*

"How long have you been a Mage?"

Rane shrugged. "Two years? Though he's still kept me close. This is my first venture 'away.'"

Renix gaped. "Two years?!"

Rane shrugged self-consciously. "Yeah. I've been running around Alefast's countryside, protecting various work details. Not much time to do anything but fight." His eyes flicked briefly to Tala, then back to Renix. "Master Grediv thought I could use a change of pace, so he recommended I take a caravan contract. The benefits will be many. At least that's what he says." He shrugged. "It is a bit better money, and slower pace, for the day's work." He sighed, pushing his plate back. "I haven't gotten to *just* walk through the countryside in…" He hesitated, seeming to be thinking back. "A decade?" He nodded. "Yeah, about then."

Tala didn't know how to react to that. It sounded like Grediv had been pushing Rane harder than Tala was pushing herself. *Huh.*

Still, the boy wasn't an Archon, and if Tala had understood Grediv correctly, she could be one pretty soon, if she dedicated herself to the process. *So, driven, resourceful, and well trained, but not really a prodigy?* That was likely unfair, but she found herself resenting all the special treatment the young man had likely gotten. Though, if she'd thought about it, she would have conceded that most people, other than her, would not consider a decade of rigorous, likely-brutal training to be a positive thing.

"Wow." Renix was still in awe. "You must be all kinds of powerful."

"Well, not really..." Rane frowned. "Master Grediv helped me choose a rather obscure power set, with regard to kinetic energy..." He sighed. "But that's probably something else that I shouldn't discuss." He looked apologetic as he said that.

Trent interrupted. "You boys will have plenty of time to talk later. Master Tang was right about one thing. We do need to be extra vigilant tonight." He picked up his own tray, along with Tang's, to carry back to the chuckwagon.

Tala cleared her throat, and the Mage paused. "So, Tala and Trent?"

Trent grinned at her. "Master Tang is a stickler for edict and tradition."

She cocked an eyebrow. "Oh? And what did we just signify by the lack of honorifics?"

He actually hesitated. "Well, it could really mean anything from a rock-solid alliance to..." He cleared his throat.

"Yes?"

"Well, it could mean that we were engaged."

She snorted. "Worst proposal ever."

Trent laughed, seeming to relax a bit. "I suppose so."

"Oh! I think one of our fellows in this caravan bought up a ton of arcanous collars. Do you mind keeping an ear out?"

Trent gave her an odd look. "You want one?"

"At least to examine, but yeah, I think I might have a use."

He shook his head. "I feel like I'll regret it, but sure. I'll keep my eyes and ears out." After a moment, he cleared his throat. "Can I ask for something in return?"

She shrugged. "Sure."

"Please try to stay out of danger? I'd really love a less eventful trip back."

She looked away, feeling a bit embarrassed. "Yeah. I'll do my best."

"Thank you. Goodnight, Mistress Tala."

She smiled, looking back towards him. "Goodnight, Master Trent."

Renix and Rane followed Trent's lead and stood to go.

Tala, who had finished her meal before the others, likewise stood. They dealt with their dishes and said goodnight.

Now, I need to find a guard who will part with his mountable shield.

Chapter: 14
Back to Basics

Tala woke bright and early to an overwhelming feeling of hunger, accompanied by a sense burgeoning on panic. Well, that wasn't quite right, but it was as close as her magesight could get to conveying the reality of the situation. In any case, both sensations were coming from her side.

She sat up, hoisting up the shield, which had been resting over her, to a steep angle and locking it there. That done, she turned to find Kit.

The belt pouch's magic was dim, and it was radiating a feeling akin to desperation. *I'm anthropomorphizing.* Even so, it was clear the pouch was low on power.

Still groggy, Tala stuck her right hand into the pouch and felt the palm-shaped panel within. *Kit helping, again.*

She pulled together power that was flowing through her gate, ensured her gate was wide open, and began to feed the magic into the pouch.

Instantly, there was a feeling of relief and… attachment? The image the sense called to mind was a baby nursing from its mother. The concept made Tala feel more than a little uncomfortable.

Not sure what to do with that… She continued to feed Kit until she sensed a feeling of fullness, and the magic was moving out of her more slowly, indicating that that pouch was coming to a state of equilibrium.

Her eyes snapped open, and she looked down at the pouch. *I guess I'm not fully awake.*

With Kit refilled, Tala decided to quickly check her other items.

True to Artia's word, the comb didn't need any magic and seemed to be quite stable. Since the comb was already in hand, she undid her hair from the night, quickly ran the comb through it, and re-braided it for the day. *This really is a remarkable item.* It was incredibly practical in its simplicity.

Her travel clothes, while not dry of magic, were not as full as they had been the day before. That intrigued her because she couldn't think of anything that would have used the missing power, unlike Kit, which was using power constantly to maintain dimensional space for her things.

As she examined the traveling clothes, she noticed that they were perfectly clean. *Is that it, then? Self-cleaning?* No, that wasn't the right paradigm. They were maintaining their original state, and any dirt that wasn't embedded or attached somehow would obviously fall off, while any that *was* embedded or otherwise attached would be pushed out and dislodged. The cleaning was a side effect, not a core function. *Fascinating.*

She checked her knife and found it full. She also realized that it was full to the maximum level that she'd pushed it to, at the most extreme. She blinked rapidly, trying to clear her eyes of sleep, and she fully focused on her weapon. It was sitting beside where she'd been lying, not in her hand.

I can check its levels and capacity without touching it. Well, she supposed that her soul was always touching it, so that wasn't quite accurate. *Still neat.* She smiled a bit to herself. *Not sure what it means, though...*

That chore done, she stood and began to roll up her bedding. As she did so, there was a muted *thump* from near where she'd left Kit.

Tala glanced that way and saw a dark-handled hammer laying, propped against the belt pouch.

Oh! I completely forgot about the hammer. She finished folding and rolling up her travel bed and stuck it into Kit before picking up the hammer.

The metal of the handle was cool in her hand, and it seemed to fit comfortably within her grasp. *I need to experiment with you soon.* She was looking into the hammer with her magesight and saw that it was very low on power, like Kit had been, though not to the same extent.

Apparently, its functions are more complicated than simply staying functional and intact like an artifact knife. She hesitated. *If I give it power, I'm bonding it to my magic, and I can't sell it...* She sighed. *And if I don't give it power, most likely it will be a mundane hammer before we reach Bandfast.*

She gathered her power flow once more and fed the hammer.

Because her magesight was focused on the tool, she was able to see the ripple of magic wash over its surface before a strange echo seemed to sound from within it, sending a flick of power back to her. *Bonded. So, that's what it looks like.* She smiled, again.

She topped off the hammer, then stood, tucking it back into Kit. "Thanks, Kit. I'd forgotten the hammer. I didn't intend to let it starve."

The pouch did not respond.

Tala unhooked the shield and climbed down the ladder with it held in one arm. It was harder to stay balanced with such a burden, but she still did her best to follow the dictates that Guardsman Adam had set for her. As the oxen were sleeping inside this smaller portion of the caravan formation, Den had oriented the ladder towards the outside. There was a bit of a different sense to climbing down on the outside of the caravan, and it left her feeling strangely exposed.

Almost as a ward against that sense of exposure, she reached in and grabbed a bit of jerky, flicking it out, away from the wagon and into the early light.

It arched for quite a ways before it disappeared in a flicker of dimensional power. *Weren't watching closely, eh, Terry?*

"Morning, Terry." She spoke softly, and she knew it was unlikely that the bird heard her, but it still seemed polite.

The sky was just lightening towards dawn, and she was finally wide awake. So, she decided she might as well start her day.

She charged the twenty cargo-slots, taking less than ten minutes to complete the task, even walking between the two wagons.

She stretched her body, then exercised her magic, muscles, and soul.

Feeling both deeply worked and invigorated, she took a good look around, verifying that no one was near and that Den was still asleep. She was getting practiced enough with her magesight that she could tell if someone was sleeping heavily or lightly when she focused on them, and Den was sleeping deeply. The flow of innate power was more subdued in those who weren't conscious. *Good.*

She stripped out of the clothes she'd worn for the night and for her exercises.

Naked in the cool morning air, she undid her braid once more, pulled out the water incorporator, and quickly ran it over herself. She used a minor torrent of power to create a mild flow of water. She rinsed off the sweat gathered through the night and her morning exertions.

The water was *cold*, but she didn't really mind. Her muscles were warm, and the cool water felt good along with the slight mountain breeze. *Amazing acquisition. Well done, Tala.* She immediately felt a bit guilty. *Thank you, Adrill and Artia.* They had given her the device, after all. She should find a way to thank them when next she was in Alefast. *Hopefully, the endingberries will be useful to them.*

That complete, she ran the comb back through her hair, dried herself, and found a pleasant surprise. A secondary effect of the comb's magical untangling was that it stripped all the water from around her hair, thus almost completely drying it with a single stroke. *That is dead useful.*

Mostly dry and thoroughly enjoying the feel of the wind on her skin, she tamed her hair once more.

She spot-checked and refreshed her iron salve, then begrudgingly pulled on her travel leathers. *Modesty, Tala. You are naked too often as it is…*

She shifted and stretched to settle into the garments, then sighed, content. *Okay. Time for breakfast!* That thought keyed off a memory, and she realized that she likely shouldn't have gotten clean yet. *Rust. I forgot. I'm supposed to spar with Adam this morning.*

* * *

She found Adam stretching inside the larger caravan ring. It was still too early for most of the passengers to be up and about, and most of the people who would likely bear witness were the guards, still on duty, and the servants or drivers who were early risers.

"Good morning, Mistress Tala. I trust you slept well?"

She smiled, setting her borrowed shield off to one side. "Good morning, Adam. I did, thank you." She gestured towards the shield. "And thank you, again, for letting me borrow that each night."

He nodded. "Happy to oblige. It is certainly better than you sleeping exposed, under the stars."

"Did you sleep well?"

"As well as I ever do." He smiled brightly.

"Glad to hear that?"

He laughed. "I did sleep well, yes."

"Good." She looked around and didn't see any practice weapons, padding, or anything else that had been standard for the academy combat arenas. "So... how are we going to do this?"

"Are you prepped to take damage?"

Right! She pulled out her iron flask and drank her daily cup of endingberry juice, topping off her reserves of that power within herself. "Yup."

He gave her an odd look but didn't comment. "So, then you attack me."

"I just... attack you."

He nodded.

"No advice, no training, no tactics, just me attacking you."

"That's right." He held up his hand. "No magic, no weapons though. I need to see what we're working with. I'll give advice, suggestions, tactics, and training after each engagement, assuming we need multiple. Please tell me if we are taxing your defenses as I'd hate to actually damage you."

She snorted a laugh. "I'll keep that in mind."

He gave a half-smile. "See that you do."

She lunged at him, not really expecting to catch him off guard. She didn't.

She had her arms wide, going for a tackle.

He punched her in the nose. Hard.

There wasn't pain, precisely, just a fractional drop in her reserves of endingberry power and a sure knowledge that her nose *should* be broken.

The blow rocked her head backward, even as her body continued forward. The new opposing movement caused her feet to come out from under her, flipping her up and off of the ground, arms flailing wildly.

She struck the earth flat on her back, and the wind was driven from her.

"Ow…" It didn't actually hurt, but it really, really felt like it should have, and there was another accompanying downward tick in her reserves. Her vision was a bit fuzzy, though. *From the hit to the nose? Or my head smacking the ground?* She didn't know; she hadn't been focusing on her vision between the two impacts.

Adam stepped forward to stand over her, holding out his hand.

She accepted with a sigh, and he pulled her to her feet. "Okay. This time, keep your guard up." He showed her how, placing his fists in front of his face, with his elbows tucked tightly against his own ribs.

She mimicked the stance. It felt a bit awkward. She had never actually physically attacked someone. *Roughhousing with the littles doesn't count.* She shoved that thought aside; she was not going to think about her siblings.

"Ready?" He smiled encouragingly.

She nodded, clearing her mind. "Ready."

He hit her in the side of the head, staggering her towards her right. Then, as she stumbled in that direction, he kicked her in that hip, driving her backward and stealing what little balance she'd managed to retain. She dropped back to the ground.

This time she landed hard on her backside before her momentum carried her backward onto her back. She did manage to tuck her head, so it was just her back that struck the earth.

She stared up at the sky once more. *He is* fast. *I'm barely seeing him move...* It wasn't inscriptions—she was pretty sure that she'd have noticed anything like that. He was just *very* well practiced and trained. She could focus on him and allow her magesight to give her greater perception and insight, but she felt like that might be cheating. *He said no magic...*

He helped her to her feet, again. "So, do you know how to block?"

She glanced at the ground, then back up at him. "Evidence suggests no." *Never really had to.*

He laughed, and she found herself smiling along with him. "Fair enough. Let's begin at the very beginning, then."

He began helping her move through basic attacks and defenses, showing her how to position herself, and explaining what parts of herself to engage at which point during the movement. It was a *lot* of information. Near the end of their short half-hour, she realized that if she focused on Adam with her magesight, while he was demonstrating a technique or movement, she could easily see exactly how he was accomplishing it, what muscles were being engaged, and even how his bones were moving.

It wasn't like looking at a biology reference guide. She couldn't see the muscles or other parts like a cadaver open on the table before her. It was more that she could see the way energy and power moved through the guardsman, and it gave hints and insights into how he was doing what he was doing.

It helped a little.

Finally, Adam gave her a small bow. "I need to eat and take my post, my shift starts soon."

She nodded in return. "Thank you. Could we do another session after your shift?"

He thought for a moment, then nodded. "I can do another half-hour or so, then I have some other tasks."

"That sounds wonderful. Thank you, Guardsman Adam."

He smiled. "I am happy to assist, Mistress Tala. I will see you this afternoon."

He moved towards the chuckwagon, which had just opened its side wall in preparation for breakfast. The man wasn't even breathing hard, let alone sweating.

Tala had considered herself in good shape, and truthfully, she was, but the new movements and large number of repetitions left her feeling deeply sore. *Fine, a massage in Bandfast is a one-hundred percent, definite must.*

She stepped between a pair of wagons, getting outside the formation as she moved back around towards Den's wagon. As she moved, she tried to stretch her worked muscles, hoping to find enough privacy for another quick rinse before seeking out her own breakfast.

It was not to be. *Improvise, then.* She took her water incorporator and soaked her hair once again, letting it hang free. She wasn't out of everyone's view, but there were few enough people around, moving about their tasks, that she didn't feel too 'on display.'

She then dumped water from the magical device through each of the seven openings in her shirt and pants, sweeping the stream around herself the best she could. It was clumsy at best.

That done, she used the comb to detangle and dry her hair, then took a moment to focus. She strove to find the mental state that she'd had yesterday, when enjoying the cool mountain breeze, and she willed herself to be dry.

Now, she could not actually make herself dry any more than she could make herself cool, but the immortal elk leather of her clothing responded to her will, becoming incredibly permeable to the nigh omnipresent wind.

Tala held her arms out wide, and the sun, combined with the wind, quickly evaporated the water that had clung to her.

The process was incredibly sped up because of two factors. One, her hair was already dry. Two, the leather of her outfit, in keeping to its steady state, did not absorb any water or allow any water to cling to it.

Thus, it was as if she were only drying her skin.

In five minutes, she was sufficiently waterless to seek breakfast. *That was not very efficient... I need to find a better means of cleaning up, privately.*

Her clothing shifted back to its standard fit, and she was acutely aware of the few places that had not dried quite as well. She sighed. *Half-formed ideas get half-formed results.*

She did her best to ignore the mild irritants, knowing they would dry in time; the magical clothing practically guaranteed it.

Speaking of magical clothing. She directed power from her gate into her outfit as she walked, topping off both the tunic and pants.

She was not the last to get her breakfast, but she was close.

"Good morning, Mistress Tala."

"Good morning, Brand."

"Did I see you fighting with Guardsman Adam?"

A few nearby people turned their way, clearly interested in what they thought they'd heard. "No, Brand. We weren't fighting." She leaned closer, speaking much more softly. "He's just showing me how to fight without magic."

"Ahh, I see, my mistake." He spoke at a normal volume, and their audience mostly turned their attention away, disappointed. "Sorry about that. I didn't actually think about how it would sound." He grinned widely, speaking as quietly as she had.

"It's fine. That looks fantastic."

He gave her a searching look. "You seemed to have an odd love of food... for a Mage."

"And you have an odd love of stabbing people... for a cook."

He stiffened, responding in a stiff whisper, "It was one time, and I was panicking. It was clearly an idiotic thing, even if I'd succeeded." He closed his eyes, shaking his head. "Even if I'd gotten away with it, it would have been horribly foolish."

Tala groaned, rubbing her forehead. "I'm sorry, Brand. That was silly of me to bring up. I know you didn't really mean anything. You were just teasing."

He snorted at that, the tension shattering. "I *am* glad I failed—to stab you, I mean."

You did succeed in that... But she knew what he meant.

He smiled, changing the subject quite obviously. "So? Why are you so food focused?"

"Why can't a Mage enjoy the taste of good food?"

He cocked an eyebrow. "Because if any of you put on weight, you could kill us all? Or am I misunderstanding?"

She laughed. "It's not quite that bad or dangerous. Besides, I use a *lot* of energy with my particular inscriptions."

"Really? I'd thought that most of it came from your gate." He frowned, contemplating.

She shrugged. "For many Mages, it does. And truthfully, most comes from mine as well, but my spell-lines are much more..." She hesitated, trying to think of the right word. "Natural? Yeah, my spell-work integrates with my natural state much more than most Mages'."

"I see; so that uses energy from the food you eat, then?"

"Usually." She smiled. "No need to risk it, right? I'm not a Material Creator, after all."

He laughed and gave her another helping of bacon beside her sausage, creamed grains, and pieces of fruit. "Too true, Mistress. Enjoy!"

She paused, giving him an expectant look.

Brand, for his part, pretended not to notice her and began bustling around the chuckwagon.

Tala rolled her eyes and cleared her throat.

"Oh! You're still here?" His mirthful smile highlighted his words as false.

"Come on, Brand. The fate of the caravan is in your hands."

He snorted a chuckle and pulled out an earthenware jug, stoppered for easy transport. "One ludicrous amount of coffee, ready and waiting."

She grinned, catching up the jug. "Thank you, Brand."

"Any time. Now, shoo! I've work to be about."

She waved awkwardly around her load of food and set off back to her wagon. She really wasn't interested in repeating the political awkwardness of the day before.

She was about to squeeze between two wagons to get outside the larger circle when she realized she was being foolish. She maneuvered just a bit and went to stick the jug of coffee into Kit.

To her surprise, Kit was already open just the right amount to receive the jug. "Well… fancy that." It made sense. She knew that Kit could manipulate dimensionality around itself as a defensive mechanism, and that wasn't even considering how it could maneuver the items and space within itself. *Why shouldn't it be able to open on its own?* Well, not entirely on its own. It was acting at her will. She'd wanted to put the jug away, and it had responded.

But what of the hammer...? She frowned.

Now, with only her breakfast tray in hand, she continued moving out of the encircling wagons. *Kit maneuvered the hammer and disgorged it all on its own...* She had been thinking of charging all her magic items. Was that enough for the pouch to work with? *Just like I wanted my items organized, but Kit seemed to arrange itself towards the best effect.*

It was something further to research. Thankfully, it was quite well in line with many other topics she wanted more information on, so it wasn't really an added task. *Thank heavens for that.*

She cleared the wagons and walked around the formation, seeking her cargo wagon and a comfortable place to sit and eat as the caravan got underway.

The sun was bright, now that it peeked over the horizon, and she pulled out her wide-brimmed hat, placing it atop her head at an extreme angle to give her some respite from the early-morning glare.

All she wanted was a quiet breakfast, by herself, to sit and think and decide how to spend the day. *Alone at last.*

"Mistress Tala!" a familiar voice called to her.

Or not.

Chapter: 15
Interruptions and Progress

Tala turned, breakfast in hand, sweet solitude awaiting her atop Den's cargo wagon, behind. "Ashin. It's been too long."

The young man smiled as he jogged up to stop beside her. "Good morning, Mistress Tala."

"Good morning." She waited for a moment, but when he didn't say anything further, she smiled. "What can I do for you?" *So... hungry...*

"Did I see you sparring with Guardsman Adam earlier?"

She shrugged. "Sort of. It seemed more like him throwing me to the ground and then telling me how I should have avoided it." She smiled weakly.

"Oh... okay." He glanced over his shoulder, then back. "So, if you need another sparring partner, I have a different shift than Adam, and I'd be happy to help."

Oh! That's actually a kind offer. "Thank you, Ashin, that's kind of you." She hesitated. "Do you know the methods that Adam uses? It might slow down my progress if I get differing information."

He waved that away. "In a sparring partner, differing styles can actually be really helpful, past a certain point. But that's not what you're asking. Adam was actually one of my teachers before he started taking breaks from his role as a trainer to pull caravan duty. I've not seen him in a few years." A happy smile settled onto his face. "I'm glad to have had this journey to catch up, actually."

"I'm glad to hear it." She glanced down at her food, then back to Ashin. *It could be really nice to keep progressing…*

"Yes."

"Yes?"

"Yes. Not now, obviously." She slightly lifted her tray to indicate that she was about to eat. "Are you free in… an hour?"

"Definitely! Yeah. I'll come to the wagon? It would probably be interesting, fighting on a moving surface."

"Yeah." She was suddenly a bit uncertain. "I'll see you then."

He nodded, waved, and went on his way.

"Huh. That might work out well." She turned and finished the trek to her wagon. She climbed just enough that she was able to slip the tray onto the roof above her when another voice called out to her.

"Mistress Tala!"

You have to be rusting kidding me. She sighed, making sure the tray was secure on top of the wagon before climbing back down to face her new accoster. "Master Rane?"

Rane stopped just out of arm's reach and gave a shallow bow. "Good morning, Mistress Tala."

"Good morning, Master Rane."

They stood for a moment in frustrated and awkward silence.

Finally, Tala cleared her throat. "Can I help you with something?"

"Oh! Right. Yes. Did I see a guardsman throwing you around earlier?"

Was the whole caravan watching? She sighed, again. "I've no way of knowing what you saw or didn't see, but I am learning to fight, yes."

"Why?"

"Because if one is bad at something, one very rarely succeeds. If I fight, I want to win." She took a deep breath, closing her eyes for a moment. *Tala, you've no idea why he's here. Give the man a moment.* "Why do you ask?"

He was frowning. "Most active magic is focused on ranged engagement. Why do you want to fight anything up close?"

"I don't want to." She purposely did *not* recall the instance of slapping a thunder bull upside the head with an ending stick. "I am learning so that if it happens, I'm not an open extract over the fire."

"A what?"

She shook her head. "A fish out of water?"

"Ahh."

They stood for another long moment, Tala thinking about her cooling breakfast. "So…?"

"Oh! So, if you are learning close-up fighting, I'd love to spar sometimes. I'd be a terrible teacher, but it would be fun to test each other at some point."

"Well, I'm very much just starting, so you'd likely destroy me, but maybe?"

"Master Grediv always says that attrition is the best teacher."

"He sounds lovely." *Maybe, I don't want to maintain contact with that man. He sounds like kind of a jerk.* She almost snorted a laugh. *He* was *kind of a jerk.*

"Oh, he's alright. After I got used to being thrown into combat, it was actually kind of fun." He smiled, but there was a hint of sadness there. "Oh! I forgot. Did I hear you mention to Master Trent that you are interested in harvests?"

She perked up. "Yes. Why?"

"Well, to tell the truth, I've been missing combat… Is there anything, in particular, you'd like?"

She thought of Terry and grinned. "Yes, actually. I'd love all the thunder bull meat you could help me acquire."

"Thunder bull... that's an arcanous beast, right? Sounds like it would be fun." He grinned in turn. "If I see one, I'll take it down for you. I'll have to look it up, to make sure I don't endanger the caravan or myself, but when I can, I'll see what's possible."

"Thank you!" She felt giddy at that. She wasn't burning through her jerky stores *too* fast, but she still saw the end of that road as all too close, and she did *not* want to find out what would happen if Terry no longer received jerky bribes. *I need to verify with Brand that he'll jerk more meat for me...* "Truly, thank you."

He gave a short laugh. "I haven't done it yet, but you're welcome. You'll let me know if you want to spar?"

"I will." She thought for a second, then clarified. "Let you know, that is. I'll let you know if I want to. Thank you."

He smiled, ignoring, or not noticing, her awkwardness. "Sounds like a plan. I'll leave you to it. We'll be rolling out soon, and I'm rear-guard today. Ride safe!"

She waved as he turned to go. "You too, I suppose."

She was up the ladder quickly, and she only waited long enough to get comfortably seated before she began devouring her breakfast. She was so hungry her head hurt, and to her irritation, the headache remained, even after she ate the provided food, washing it down with water from her incorporator.

Despite the pain in her head, she wanted to be productive. *Another set!*

She moved through her spiritual exercises, pulling the knife to herself from twenty, fifteen, ten, and five feet. She was able to do four repetitions from both twenty and fifteen feet, but she wore out on the third at ten and five feet. *Progress is progress.*

Her head hurt worse, so she drank some more water. *What now, what now. Hmmmm...*

She stood and moved through the techniques that Adam had shown her, allowing her magesight to guide her into as perfect a replication of his movements as possible. *He said repetition was key. I need to have these movements be my default.*

As she was working, Den hooked up the oxen, climbed up, gave her a happy wave, and started them on their way for the day.

For each technique, she performed the movement a hundred times on one side, slow enough to ensure she was doing it right. Then, she did it a hundred more as quickly as she could, focusing on speed over perfect technique. Then she switched sides. *Just as Adam suggested.*

That was not quite accurate. Adam had suggested that she do each movement three times fast and then three times slow, to each side. *A hundred is better.*

After she'd done all the basic techniques in the same manner, she was feeling *very* worked and quite warm.

Her outfit had relaxed, allowing the cool air to flow around her more easily, and that helped. Her wide-brimmed hat helped, too.

She sat, drinking deeply via the incorporator and breathing as evenly and deeply as she could manage, ensuring that she kept with a quick exhale. *Very nice, Tala. You can do this!*

Now what?

Archon Star. She decided that the creation of the star in her finger was the most pleasant way she knew of, for the moment, so she began moving her power in that direction.

She opened her gate wide and began guiding all her incoming power into her finger, forming the spell-shape within a bit of blood, right near the skin of her left ring finger.

She pulled against her gate, not allowing the extra power she wanted to come from her reserves around her keystone. *That's likely what's been exhausting me.* Instead, she moved the power directly from her gate to the star, doing her utmost to pull as much as possible.

It was mentally exhausting, taking much more of her concentration than when she allowed some of the power to come from her reserves. When she did that, she'd let her gate refill those reserves even as she pulled the power free.

Her flowrate was... lacking. That said, it felt like her gate was a muscle, and her efforts were forcing it further open. *I'm relating many things back to muscular exercise... It's like studying? No. That's idiotic. Muscular exercise is a perfectly fine way to conceive of this.*

To her surprise, she was making monumental progress. As if she'd never really tried to force it open before. *That's not true. I've forced it open lots of times...* She hesitated, trying to search back through her memory with the little bit of mental space not otherwise engaged. *A few times?*

She thought further. *A couple of times, and never for more than a moment...* It was no wonder that her gate was responsive. It had basically been a passive part of her magical ability that she simply allowed to refill the vast reserves within her. *That was foolish of me...*

As a result, even though her gate began with little more than a stream, she quickly got it much closer to a healthy flow, and she was building the Archon Star at a rate slightly faster than the last one she'd done, without exhausting her reserves. *This is* so *much better!*

Now that the spell-form was established, and her gate was thrown wide, the power was almost moving on its own, requiring very little of her will, and therefore mental power, to continue.

She let out a long, slow, contented breath. "There we go." She took a moment of that freedom to delve into herself, feeling out her gate with her magesight.

To her surprise, it actually seemed like the gate itself naturally wanted to be open. Just as muscles usually wanted to relax. To open it, she was fighting years of something akin to cramping, due to lack of use. Additionally, she was working against her own keystone, which was designed to prevent her gate from tearing open irreparably. *That would be bad...*

Without that restriction, it was technically possible for a Mage to turn their entire being into an open gate, thus obliterating themselves and leaving behind a hurricane of power without end. It was a major task to shut those down when they were found. At least that was Tala's understanding.

Thankfully, as far as Tala knew, no Mage had succumbed to that sort of accident since the invention of modern keystones, some five hundred years ago. *Score another one for research and rigor.*

With the keystone in place, she did have to fight against it, mentally, but it also meant that anything she accomplished would be safe. It was a tradeoff, but extra effort was well worth the removal of that risk.

At her current rate, she would need to keep this up for one hundred hours to make an Archon Star powerful enough to meet Grediv's expectations. *Not likely...* Still, she determined that she'd keep it up for as long as possible, keeping her efforts on increasing her rate of flow through her gate.

She found that she had enough mental space to continue some light reading and note-taking. So, she forwent her biology review for the time being.

She considered throwing some meat for Terry but didn't want to draw attention to him. *I'll give you a treat tonight, buddy.* Thus, she passed the morning.

*   *   *

Noon was fast approaching, and she was at her limit, even with the easier method.

Throughout the morning, her gate had continued to open wider, though at an ever-slower rate. If she had to guess, she was drawing through at close to double the rate that she'd funneled into the most recent Archon Star. *And nearly four hours to boot.* She was hoping for a star that was at least three times as potent as her last attempt.

She carefully removed an iron vial and a non-magical knife from Kit. Maintaining her concentration, she withdrew her myriad defensive and regenerative abilities from her finger before pricking the surface and letting the drop fall free.

As it was breaking free, she relaxed, happy to have completed the effort, and she felt a *tearing* sensation. It felt like someone had filled her body with spiders' webs and then pulled them all out at once, through her left ring finger.

Virtually all of her reserves were gone in an instant, though the endingberry power remained untouched.

Weariness slapped her upside the head, and she was barely able to stay conscious enough to catch the drop in the vial, cap it, and return the vial and knife to her pouch.

Well done, Tala, way to lose focus in the eleventh hour.

She groaned, curling up in a ball and succumbing to sleep.

*   *   *

Tala awoke, sitting up with a groan.

Her eyes were stuck shut with sleep, and she rubbed them to clear the crustiness.

She blinked into full wakefulness, looking out at a late afternoon sky. *Well, rust.*

Den turned to look at her, and he smiled. "Hello! Guardsmen Adam and Ashin each stopped by, separately, and asked me to let you know such. Brand left you that." He nodded towards a new tray of food, though it was cold now. "And he took away your breakfast tray. He also said that he'd have refilled your coffee jug if he could find it." He smiled back at her.

"Oh, no! Do you know where the guardsmen are now?"

Den shrugged. "On duty or asleep, I'd wager."

Tala sighed, feeling quite guilty. *I can't believe I missed our sparring and training times...* "Thank you, Den." *And thank you, Brand.* She yawned. "I didn't mean to sleep."

He laughed, turning forward. "You're doing something wrong then, Mistress."

She grinned ruefully, even though she knew he couldn't see. "You're not wrong."

She pulled the food towards herself and ate without really noticing what it was. She had a vague sense that it was good, but that was really all. *Coffee...* She was irritated that he hadn't brought more. *Why didn't he...?* Her eyes widened. *Well... I forgot.*

She reached into Kit and pulled out the full jug of coffee that Brand had given her that morning. To her surprise, it was hot. *How is that possible?* She looked down at Kit. "Are you a perfect insulator?" On some level, that made sense. The pouch could nearly perfectly isolate items, thus preserving them in an almost steady state.

The pouch did not respond.

Oh, well. The earthenware was actually quite hot to the touch, likely fully equalized with the coffee it contained. She bore through the discomfort and drank deeply, washing her late lunch down with gusto. *That's so much better.*

"Thank you, Kit."

Kit did not respond.

Tala stood and stretched. *Right, so don't lose focus at the end, or the stupid Archon Star will take everything it can on the way out.* She pulled out the iron vial and opened it, looking in with enough focus to key off her magesight.

The star was radiating at least four times the power of any of her previous stars, and she felt ecstatic at the discovery. True, a chunk of that had been because of her mistake at the end, and she was *not* going to replicate that, but it still meant that she was improving, quickly.

That verified, she stored the vial and went through her exercises: muscular, spiritual, magical, and martial. It was becoming a lengthy regimen.

Now done, and feeling very content in her efforts, she sat down to empower her items. She fed Kit up to nearly bursting, topped off her clothing and the hammer, and finally, she decided to increase the knife's capacity. *I need to find a name for you at some point.* Perhaps, it would be wisest to wait until the knife demonstrated what it could really do. *Yeah, you should earn a name.* She smiled at that.

In a very similar process to creating the Archon Star, Tala opened her gate wide and channeled the power directly into the knife, though she didn't form the power or otherwise attempt to influence it beyond that. She didn't have to be touching the weapon, so she left it sitting a few feet from her.

It didn't feel any different or harder than giving the knife power when it was in her hand, but she thought it couldn't hurt. *Best case, this is a bit harder, and it's good exercise.*

The knife had started with a relatively weak Archon Star, mainly because the stars she was creating were incredibly weak. Thankfully, as Grediv had assured her, she found that she could increase the power of the connection, and thus the power residing within the knife, simply by giving the tool an influx of magic.

The power she gave was more effective than when she built it into an Archon Star. Thus, over the next hour she pushed the knife's capacity to almost double its previous capacity. *Not sure why that's useful, but yeah! Progress.*

As she was finishing up, she let out a contented sigh and got Den's attention. "Anything else eventful happen?"

Den glanced back at her, then hesitated. "You did have one other visitor, but he asked me not to tell you... a few things." He took a deep breath and let it out. "Mistress, I understand that, because I'm here it makes sense for me to pass along messages as such, but it really isn't my job." He gave a sympathetic look. "I'm not cut out to be a footman or servant or anyone who has to make potentially political decisions." He frowned.

"Den! I'm so sorry. I never meant for you to be a message service or anything like that."

He waved her away. "Oh, I know. That's not what I meant. I mean that, I've information that I would normally simply tell you, but I've been asked to not do so by someone I don't really know."

It was Tala's turn to frown. "Is someone ordering you about, Den?"

"Not really." He let out an exasperated sigh. "Please just... take your dishes to Brand. Yes? He'll handle it better than I will..."

Tala smiled and patted him on the shoulder before climbing down the ladder. "I will, Den. Thank you, and I'm sorry."

"It's fine, it's fine. Just... stop having so many suitors, maybe?"

She colored. "Den. It isn't like that. Brand and Adam are both married!"

He shook his head. "But the other two gentlemen don't seem to be. Though, if their actions are any indication, they're open to the idea."

Blushing further, Tala cleared her throat. "I'm not addressing that…" She glanced back towards Den, seeing laughter dancing in his eyes, though he had the good grace to not give voice to it. *I guess I shouldn't hold his good humor against him…* "If there is ever anything I can do for you, please let me know?"

"I will. Thank you, Mistress."

Chapter: 16
A Talented Teacher

Tala smiled and nodded to Den, before dropping down without another word and walking back down the moving caravan, to the chuckwagon.

She knocked on the door and almost immediately Brand ripped it open, eye twitching just slightly. "Yes?"

Tala almost jumped back but prevented herself from doing so. She glanced at the oxen, somewhat close behind her. *That would have been unfortunate.* "Brand? What's going on?"

He let out an irritated breath. "Oh, Mistress Tala. Good, you're here. Please…please step up."

She stepped up, onto the wagon's back stair, and looked inside. Within the wagon, Tala saw several other cooks all working feverishly. *So, there are more than three cooks this trip.* "You look busy."

He gave her a flat look. "Your suitor has put demands on our time."

Tala looked at Brand in confusion. "Say again?"

"Your suitor. The boy interested in you. The man who is making my life irritatingly complex with too-reasonable-to-refuse requests."

She continued to give him a look of non-comprehension.

Brand groaned. "Master Rane, Mistress."

Tala reddened, though she couldn't have said if it was with embarrassment or irritation. "He's not my suitor!"

"Oh? Well, you might want to clarify that then. Most men don't do this for someone they aren't interested in."

She felt herself coloring, again. "What happened?"

"Well, apparently Master Rane got the idea that you were interested in thunder bulls."

Her eyes widened. "Oh, no..." *What did he do?*

"Oh, yes." He cocked an eyebrow at her.

She swallowed. "Go on."

"Well, he took it upon himself to cleanly decapitate a small herd of the bovine: Six, in all."

"Did we harvest them?" Tala looked around in confusion, seeing if the carcasses might still be within range.

"Oh, don't you worry, Mistress. He has a dimensional bag sized for, and I quote: 'Large things I might find useful, later.' He stuffed them all in that sack and brought them along." Brand pointed at a clearly inscribed leather duffel bag, resting on one counter within the chuckwagon.

"Why is it here, then?"

"Well." He gave her an exasperated look. "You were apparently napping and missed his heroics. So, he consulted with Master Trent, and the good Master Trent let the indomitable Master Rane know that you had worked with us to process your previous acquisitions. He came here right away and enlisted us to process the meat: 'As Mistress Tala has requested in the past.' "

"Brand, I'm so sorry. I can pay for the processing..." *How much is that going to cost?* A moment later, another thought came to her. *How much jerky is that going to produce?*

Brand waved her away. "He granted us all non-meat parts of the beast as payment."

She hesitated. Oh...wow. That's a lot of money... "That sounds wonderful for you. Why are you irritated?" *What's the catch? I should have told him I was interested in all of the bull, not just the meat...* But she didn't really want hand-outs...did she?

He threw up his hands. "Do you know how to process close to five thousand pounds of meat? I can't let it rot; I can't turn him down, because you're right, this is a treasure trove! And there is no way I'm alienating someone so willing to give us harvests." He gave her a look. "But teach that boy some moderation."

She cleared her throat. "He said he missed combat and would be happy to get some harvests, if it was convenient."

"Well, it seems to have rusting been convenient." He leaned back against the doorframe and sighed wearily. "I'm a miner complaining that the gold seam is too large."

Tala smiled consolingly, patting him on the arm. "At least we both get a lot from this, yes?"

He eyed her warily. "Why do you think we can process all of this?"

"Aside from your implications?" She gave him a knowing smile. "Because you clearly have some magic augmentations you don't want to admit to." She gave a mischievous grin. "I can come into the chuckwagon and–"

"Nope!" He blocked her. "You're fine out there."

"You know, I was in there on the trip up, when my arm was broken."

"And did you think to look around?" He gave her a sly grin.

She hesitated. *No, I didn't...why was that?* "Why didn't I feel any desire to look around the inside of your wagon, Brand?"

"We all have our secrets."

She pulled out the token for the order of the harvest, but Brand just snorted. "Put that away. I'm under a contract of indenture that bars me from sharing. Take it up with the Culinary Guild."

"Are they involved in the Order?"

"I cannot discuss that." But he gave her a rather patronizing look, which made the answer obvious.

"Fair enough. So, when can I expect my jerky?"

He eyed her. "You know, you're lucky we carry spices in bulk."

"That doesn't sound like a timeline." She spoke with a bit of sing-song playfulness.

He laughed. "It'll be done by the time we reach Bandfast." He held up a finger. "Don't let him bring us anymore. I'd kill myself before turning him down, and it would likely kill *us* to try to process it all before it goes bad."

She grinned. "Fair. I'll let him know."

She turned to go, but Brand touched her shoulder. "Mistress?"

"Yeah?"

"In all seriousness, talk to the boy. This is no small thing he's just done for you, and I don't want you to be maneuvered into something, because you didn't consider what was happening."

She slowly nodded. "I'll see what I can do."

That burden added, Brand smiled, waved, and closed the door.

Feeling both elated and deeply uncertain, Tala turned back towards the front of the caravan. *Great...More to figure out.*

* * *

Tala absently flicked a bit of jerky out, away from the caravan, noting how quickly it flickered from existence. *I wonder how he does that. Does he transport in and out so quickly? He can't move things other than himself, else he'd be behaving differently. Can he open portals?* That was a bit of a disturbing thought, though she didn't really know all the ramifications. *And, I doubt he can, anyways.*

She sighed, shaking her head. *No, I watched him flicker away and back to avoid a crossbow bolt. He's just that fast.*

Tala grinned at a sudden realization. *My role here is as a dimensional Mage, and I've been doing strange exercises and workings all over the place. No one is going to bat an eye, if they notice the dimensional flickers of power.*

She tossed another chunk. Interestingly, it arced for longer before vanishing. *Didn't think I'd send another so soon, eh?* She felt her burdens lighten, just a bit, as her smile settled in, and she exhaled a quick, relaxing breath. *Things are looking up, Tala. Don't focus on the negative.*

That, of course, caused her mind to shift towards the tasks before her, when she got home.

I have to make my first payment towards my debt. They'd let her delay, if she wanted, but it would invoke interest. Thankfully, her debts were such that interest was only added if she skipped a payment. *Yup, if I can't pay my debt, I now owe more!* Even so, she was grateful. She knew that many loans accrued interest regardless.

So, the first payment is two gold, and I have another week and a half, give or take, before it is due, or I gain interest. She could pay it now, well, as soon as she got to Bandfast. That would set the start date for her repayment. A minimum of two gold per month for just over twenty years. *I'll be paying it off faster than that.*

She owed Holly at least eight ounces, gold, so she'd finish Tala's inscriptions. With the other items she'd asked Holly to investigate and possibly add on top, not to mention her use of her active magics, she'd be surprised if she didn't owe at least another three. *Probably more...*

So, twelve ounces to Holly. I have almost twenty-two ounces, now, and I'll get another five and a half when we reach Bandfast. Almost twenty-eight ounces, gold. That was a ridiculous amount of wealth, if the world had been as she'd seen it, while still a child.

Not enough. It wasn't even a tenth of her debt. *Come on, Tala. You're only on your second contract, and you've gathered this much? If you keep on at this rate, you'll have your debts paid off in a year.*

That was likely a bit too optimistic, especially with the time she'd need for her body to adjust to the deeper layers of inscriptions. Plus, winter was just around the corner, and that would make contracts take longer, but not really pay more. *Plus, the inscriptions themselves need to be refreshed...*

Even so, somehow, it almost looked like she might be able to do this in just more than a year. *Unbelievable.*

Her smile returned. *See that, stupid self? Try to depress me, and I find the way through.*

She was walking alongside the caravan and almost back to the front wagon. "You're talking to yourself again, Tala." She shook her head. "You desperately need some closer traveling companions."

That brought Rane to mind. *Both Brand and Den seem to think he's trying to court me, or something...*

As she neared her wagon, she saw someone standing on top of it. Their eyes met, and Adam waved.

She picked up the pace and caught up *quickly*, pulling herself up to stand beside him.

"Hello, Mistress Tala. I was afraid that I'd missed you."

She shook her head. "No, I apologize, Adam. I didn't know when you'd be free, and I had business to attend to. Ready?"

"Are you sufficiently stretched?"

She sighed. "No, not really..."

"Good enough." He punched at her.

Surprised, she didn't have time to think. Even so, the motions that she'd practiced more than four hundred times that day came quickly, though they still felt a bit awkward and her arms were *tired*.

She blocked, stepping back and to her right, moving herself out of the line of attack even while she moved the line of attack the opposite direction.

Adam's eyes widened, but he didn't stop. He swept at her feet.

She stepped back, resisting the urge to attempt hopping over, Adam's words echoing in her mind. *'Don't jump if you don't have to. Once you go ballistic, you are incredibly easy to predict and attack.'* Adam, apparently, defined going ballistic as any time she was completely airborne.

What followed was a series of attacks that Tala did her best to avoid or block. To her surprise, she succeeded. As it continued, however, she realized that Adam was not going at full speed. Instead, he was moving just fast enough to force *her* to react as quickly as she was able.

She focused, calling on her magesight to give her an edge. *He didn't say no magic, this time.*

Immediately, she was able to better anticipate his attacks and tell which of them were feints.

Adam clearly noticed her improvement, because he picked up the pace, though his relaxed demeanor indicated that he was still holding back considerably. Finally, he moved to full speed, or near enough, and quickly overwhelmed her attempts to deflect him, and he drove her to the wagon's roof with a punishing kick to the inside of her right knee.

As she dropped, he struck her across the left cheek, spinning her away to land, sprawling, on her stomach.

"Good. Great even!"

She could hear the smile in his voice as she spun back around, trying to recover her feet to attack, but the world was *not* cooperating, and she was having a hard time focusing on him.

"Hold, Mistress."

She paused, her gaze finally locking onto her target and the world steadying. She was crouched and ready to spring. She fully processed his words, relaxed, and stood.

He was nodding. "You have improved remarkably. I'd not be surprised if you told me you'd been training for a month, if not a little more." He smiled. "You'd still lose most fights against an untrained man, but we're working on it. Strength and reach disparities are hard to overcome."

She grunted. "Both Guardsman Ashin and Mage Rane have offered to spar with me. Do you think that would help?"

Adam seemed to consider. "Ashin, yes. He's a good lad. Top of his class." He grinned. "Which is why he's allowed to be a caravan guard." The smile faded just a bit. "Rane? I don't know... I think there's a good chance of him killing you outright."

She blinked. "In a sparring match?"

"You missed his little encounter with the thunder bulls." He shook his head. "I genuinely don't know which hurt them more, when they managed to strike him, or when he struck back. His magic seems aimed at close-quarters combat, and his sword is perfect for it."

Sword? I haven't seen him with a sword. "Is that handle on his belt the sword?"

Adam nodded. "The blade seems to be in a dimensional storage space of some kind. The entire weapon is wooden, but whatever magics it has don't seem to rely on the material's properties." He shrugged. "I'm probably being too paranoid. If he offered to spar with you, he likely has a method of doing so non-lethally. I'll leave it up to you. Even so, I'd recommend against it, until you have the fundamentals down, else he might influence you in dangerous ways."

"Would it help?"

"If you aren't injured or killed, yes. But again, only once you have a solid basis."

Okay, then. It would be nice to have more ways to improve. "Alright then."

Adam nodded once. "Let's review. I want to tweak your techniques a bit. It looks like you're trying to move like…" He hesitated, frowning. "You are trying to move exactly like me. How are you even doing that?"

She shrugged. "Is 'how' really important? Yes, though. I am trying to move like you showed me."

He shook his head. "No, no, that isn't right. I think I see the issue, then. Though again, I've no idea how you got there. Your body is different, so the techniques need to be altered to accommodate the differences between our shapes, our physiology."

She nodded, understanding. "Like spell-lines. To get the same result, we need slightly different forms, because of our differing structure."

"I suppose?" He shrugged. "I'm no Mage."

"Alright, then. Let's get to work."

* * *

Adam stayed past the half hour he'd promised, but not by much. He made sure to go back through each of the techniques he'd taught her and shift them to take advantage of her own shape, her own body, while negating the difficulties of the same.

They said goodbye, and he departed, leaving her to practice, which she did.

She again went through every movement on each side, but now, she did two hundred slow repetitions and only one hundred fast, always in groups of three. Two slow, one fast.

Slow. Slow. Fast.

In that manner, she was able to draw her use of the techniques to match what Adam had changed. She was surprised at how much of a difference it made. The movements quickly went from awkward, hitching movements, to the kinesthetics feeling incredibly natural. *He is a talented teacher.*

It also thoroughly and utterly exhausted her.

In the end, she lay panting on the roof of the wagon, limbs spread wide, incorporator clutched in her right hand.

She drank whenever she could calm her breathing enough to allow it.

Her clothes had accommodated her elevated activity and temperature by allowing the cool breeze to reach her. It helped.

"Good clothes." She was *not* going to name an outfit. *That way lies pretension and pomposity.*

She was splayed out, head towards the front of the wagon and the ladder, when she heard someone clear their throat.

She moved her hat off of her face and looked up to see Ashin peaking over the edge.

"Mistress Tala?"

She did her best to spin around, coming up into a seated position facing him. She mostly succeeded. "Guardsman Ashin!"

"May I…come up?"

Den huffed a laugh, but Tala ignored him, and hoped that it had been quiet enough that Ashin hadn't heard. "Of course. What can I do for you?" Her breathing was basically back to normal.

Ashin came up and sat. "Well, I came by to spar earlier, and you were so focused that you didn't notice, so I assumed that I shouldn't disturb you." He glanced away, seeming a bit embarrassed. "When I came back after that, you were sleeping."

Tala colored. "Oh! I'm so sorry, Ashin. You were kind enough to offer me help, then I left you unable to give it."

He smiled hesitantly. "I understand. You've a lot going on. Do you still need a sparring partner?"

She opened her mouth to say no, given how worn she felt, but then hesitated. *I'll have to fight tired sometimes...* It was possible she was pushing too hard, but she didn't allow herself to consider that. "Sure!" She stood, only swaying a little with the motion of the wagon.

Ashin gave her a skeptical look. "Are you...sure?"

She nodded, giving him a 'come at me' motion with her hands, now raised in a fighting guard. *Hey! I didn't have to remember to do that. They did it on their own. Good hands!* She was feeling a bit lightheaded, but it seemed to be passing. "You won't be able to hurt me, so let me see what you can do."

Ashin seemed a bit hesitant but shrugged. "If you insist."

Tala saw his next movements as if in slow motion. He tucked his front leg up and into his own chest, then drove his heel outward. *Oh! That's a sidekick.*

To her great surprise, Tala was able to sweep his kick to the side, intercepting and redirecting it. Unfortunately, she wasn't quite fast or strong enough. His heel struck her in the chest, up near her left shoulder and knocked her backwards...off of the roof.

She squeaked in surprise, even as his eyes went wide in horror.

Ashin lunged forward and caught her flailing hand, arresting her fall. Her heels were still on the roof, though much of her was out over the edge.

How did he move from kicking me to catching me? Despite the question, she didn't argue, clinging to his hand as he pulled her back.

"Sorry about that. I wasn't thinking about what might be behind you." He looked down and away. "That was foolish of me."

Tala let go of his hand, turning to look at the edge of the roof. She then looked back, meeting the eyes of the driver behind Den's wagon. He had a look of utter bafflement. *He's had quite the show, today. I'm basically on a stage, in front of him...* She hadn't really considered that either. "Well...Good kick?"

Ashin laughed self-consciously. "That was a pretty good block. If you had allowed your shoulder to move more freely, it would have been perfect."

"Move my shoulder?"

He nodded. "It's a hard subtlety to practice, alone. You know how you twist your torso with the block?"

"Yeah, it gives power and strength to it."

"Well, your torso can be loose before you turn, only tightening for that movement. If you hadn't been tensing, you'd have just been pushed into a twist, moving out of the way when I hit you. It might have hurt, but it wouldn't have unbalanced you very much."

"Huh." She thought back to how she'd been moving, considering. "I'm holding in the transition positions very stiffly..." It seemed that just knowing how to position herself wasn't enough. *I need all the right muscles tense or relaxed in the right sequence to properly execute the movement.* It was a bit daunting.

Ashin smiled. "Honestly, though, that one movement seemed well done."

She gave him a flat look. "Now, you're just patronizing me."

He held up his hands. "Maybe, but I don't think so."

She growled irritably. "Fine. Again." She glanced over the edge. "Maybe no high kicks?"

He laughed. "I did that because it's slower and easier to block. *Never* kick above the waist in a real fight." He hesitated. "Well, unless you have a really, *really* good reason."

She shrugged. "Seems fair." Her guard came up, and she advanced.

Chapter: 17
Right! The Hammer

More than an hour later, Tala felt like she couldn't lift her head, let alone her arms, and she lay sprawled on the roof of the wagon once more.

This was not her first break.

While she recovered, Ashin stretched and drank from a waterskin that he'd brought. "You're improving, but I think you might be overdoing it."

She groaned. The endingberries, it seemed, did not prevent her from working the muscles. *That would have been a disaster. 'No, you can't get stronger while we're here!'* Though, the muscles did seem to be prevented from tearing. *That's useful. I can't overwork them… at least not in that way.*

To her surprise, the endingberries' power had been draining away at a steady, if minuscule, rate over the past hour, and when she investigated, during one of her gasping respites, she'd found that the power was being funneled through her regenerative spell-forms and reflected away from her skin, into her muscles, causing them to recover in minutes from what should have taken days.

And that's a secondary effect. I can't wait until the muscles are inscribed and powered properly.

Even so, she was at her limit. *One more.* She tried to sit up. She failed.

Den called back. "We're about to make camp, so expect a bit more side-to-side movement from the wagon pretty soon."

Tala waved his way, or at least she tried. Her hand mainly just flopped a bit at her side. "Thank you, Den. I guess we have to call it a day, eh?"

Ashin snorted a laugh. "Honestly, I expected us to be done... nearly an hour ago?"

She glared at him. "You think so little of me?"

He held up his hands placatingly. "Not at all. Sparring is really taxing. And what we're doing is closer to full-on fighting. You can take hits; I'll give you that. I'd say it was your magic, but I don't see any spell-forms active." He genuinely sounded impressed. "They would be glowing right? Like when that plant attacked you? Or the thunder bull?"

"You are quite right. No glowing, no magic... for the most part." She pulled out her flask and took a drink. *An extra cup, today, won't kill me.* "Liquid courage."

He gave her a flat look. "There is no way you're drunk." He sniffed the air. "There's no alcohol in that at all."

"What are you, some sort of bloodhound?"

He grunted, standing from where he'd been stretching. "Want help up?"

"Don't you dare."

He grinned down at her. "I'm going to go get cleaned up. My shift starts after dinner."

She groaned, rolling over and pushing herself up into a seated position. "How are you not exhausted?"

"Well, I wasn't just kicked, punched, thrown, and placed into innumerable locks and holds." He shook his head. "You *really* should have at least a few bruises. I was trying to pull my hits, but I'm not perfect at that."

She shrugged. "I'll be fine. That doesn't answer my question, though; you were moving at least as much as I was." *Slippery rust bucket.* "I didn't even get a single solid hit on you."

He grinned at that. "You landed a few glancing blows. You are improving much faster than normal." He gave her a questioning look, but when she didn't respond, he shrugged. "As to my weariness? Training. Lots and lots of training. I ran twenty miles each day that we were in Alefast as a warm-up. This is my job, Mistress Tala. I have to be able to fight for as long as it takes to keep this caravan safe." He hesitated. "What did you do while we were in Alefast?"

She sighed, thinking of the endingberry grove. "Mostly hunted up tasty food."

He snorted another laugh. "There you go." He shrugged. "This is known as a safer route, and we still had fighting almost every day. You might be aware, but some arcanous creatures can take hours to bring down. They aren't tough enough to warrant the expense of Mage involvement, so we have to be able to go toe-to-toe with them and bring victory. They aren't very common, but we have to be ready."

That sounds horrible. "Well, you seem well suited to it."

He smiled gratefully, seeming to stand a bit straighter. "I've really got to go."

She waved goodbye. "Thank you, Ashin."

He simply nodded, climbing down the ladder.

A minute or so after Ashin had departed, Den turned to glance her way. "So… not a suitor?"

She glowered. "No, Den."

A small smile was evident across his features. "You spend more than an hour getting sweaty with a man, and you want me to believe there's nothing there."

"You're making it weird, Den."

He shrugged. "Fine, fine. But if you were my daughter, I'd be giving that young man a stern talking to. Because, in all likelihood, *he's* thinking along those lines." His voice lost some of its mirth. "Also, he was far too ready to hit you."

She sighed. "He asked to *spar,* Den. That's where his mind was." *I hope.* "As to hitting me, I asked him to. Besides, I'm fine." She gestured to herself, but he wasn't looking. "Thank you for the concern, though."

He grunted. "I don't want to see you get hurt, and I don't just mean physically." After a moment, he added, "And you are making my trip *much* more complicated. You know, I come on these for some time away." He gave her a mock-stern look over his shoulder.

She held up her hands. "Fair, fair. If you ever want me to go elsewhere, just say so."

He smiled at that. "Probably won't, but I'll keep that in mind. Thank you."

Satisfied, she moved a bit of power through the incorporator and took a long drink, then flopped back down on the roof to rest and wait for them to make camp.

* * *

Light was beginning to color the sky into a stunning sunset when Tala finally sat back up.

The wagons were back in their dual circle formation, the oxen unhitched, and from the sound coming from the larger circle, dinner was well underway. *Food.* Her stomach practically roared at her, though it didn't make an audible sound. *Yeah... I really need to eat.*

She stood, feeling *much* better after the extended rest. The endingberries' power was not intended as a regenerative aid, so it was *not* efficient at such. Only her own spell-forms and will, driven by her subconscious and conscious desires to improve and recover, made it possible at all.

The result was that she'd burned through half of the power granted by the two cups of the juice. *I could have taken a death blow from that cyclops with the same amount of power.* That was not quite true, but even so…

It was not efficient at all. *I really need to get back to Holly and finish getting my inscriptions.*

She climbed down the ladder with ease, feeling a spring in her step due to the added strength in her muscles, small though it was. She'd cheated, and the result was akin to a week's worth of dedicated, carefully directed training, gained over the course of a day.

Heavens help me if I had to do this as a mundane. That thought brought both Adam and Ashin to mind. Their drive, determination, and strength of character was cast in a new light. She huffed a laugh. *All the guards, really.* What Adam had said implied that the two she'd worked with were standard specimens among the caravan guard.

She passed sentries on patrol on her way towards dinner and gave them deeper nods of acknowledgment than she had in the past. *These men and women deserve respect for what they have done, and what they do.*

The guards showed mild surprise but nodded back in turn.

She began sorting through her upcoming tasks, trying to decide what she should do next, after dinner. *Trent wanted to hear about the endingberry harvest. I'll have to discuss it with him, at some point, but not tonight. I don't particularly want to have another conversation right now.*

So, she would take the food back to her wagon… *Or…* The terrain around the caravan was a bit rocky, and she'd been needing to test out her hammer. *I could go up on that rise and eat, then test the hammer?* The guards might not like that, though.

She sighed. *Eat at my wagon, then find a rock nearby to test, first.* It was the safer, wiser course.

That settled, she slipped into the back of the line for food, taking her hat from her head and tucking it into Kit.

She got her dinner without difficulty or incident, exchanging a few words with the cook serving the food that evening.

Meal in hand, she returned to the cargo wagon and ate under the sunset-painted sky.

Her mind was elsewhere as she ate, and she took the time to feed her items as well. Her clothes had actually done a lot of work that day, shifting to keep her cooler, as well as keeping themselves clean. As a result, she had to give them significantly more power than she ever had before, discounting the recharge after the cyclops, that was. Still, it wasn't that much.

She hadn't had as much time to read as she'd have liked, given both her success with the Archon Star and her focus on physical training, so she pulled out the first two volumes on bonded items, as well as those on magic item theory. *I can take a break from my review, for a little while.*

She cross-referenced as she ate, hunting for something that Grediv had mentioned. *Combining items… combining items… Oh!*

She was almost done with her dinner when she finally came across what she was looking for. *Bonding items to each other.* That was why it hadn't been an easy index search.

There was a lot of information, now that she knew what to look for, though it was spread throughout the four tomes.

Huh… you basically force the items to soul-bond each other… items have souls? That started a whole other line of research, which was easily brought to a close. *While artifacts seem to act as if they have a rudimentary form of spirit, other magic items do not seem to, though they can utilize methodologies intended for entities which do.* It was clunky and pulled from a dozen scattered sentences, but it seemed sound.

Fair enough.

"So, Kit, you've got a bit of a spirit, eh?"

The pouch did not respond.

She patted the knife. "That means you do, too… and the hammer… huh." But she was getting off-track.

She wanted to combine the two parts of her wardrobe into a single item. The books hinted that there were numerous benefits from shared pools of power, to increased capacity for the same. Other benefits depended on the item, though there seemed to be implications that she could also bond non-magic items to magical ones, thereby adding to or altering them in various ways. It also spoke of the foolishness of attempting to combine items with different core functions. *Never bind a weapon to a dimensional storage directly. Noted.*

The example of a tried-and-true bonding that was given was the binding of a dimensional storage to a different container, thereby changing its exterior shape and altering the inside somewhat.

Apparently, there had been a length of time where many dimensional storage artifacts had manifested as barrels, which were highly inconvenient to transport. She found it interesting that such seemed to correspond to the waning of a city that had been known for its wine.

She'd like to have claimed credit for making that connection, but the books, themselves, pointed out that there seemed to be connections between what form artifacts took and the places they manifested.

Yet more mysteries.

But back to the matter at hand. The process was supposedly incredibly simple when both items were magical.

Following the instructions that she'd pieced together and written out in her notes, she placed her hand on her own thigh, touching both her tunic and her pants.

Then, she began funneling a trickle of power into both at once.

The two items seemed to begin straining, trying to pull the power towards themselves, alone. To her magesight, that looked like power was flowing out of the items, back up the insubstantial stream she was sending out.

When the two searching tendrils met, Tala seized the power. This was only possible because the tendrils from the tunic and pants had reached up into her hand of their own accord, trying to get an advantage on the other item in acquiring power.

Thus, with the power now within herself, she had mastery over it. In an effort of will, she flipped the tendrils together, turning them back on themselves and forming a very rudimentary facsimile of a now-familiar shape: an Archon Star. The book had called it a binding knot, only describing it in how it differed from an Archon Star. *This would be useless to me if I didn't know that spell-form... Is that why it isn't restricted knowledge?* The result *was* much simpler than the Archon Stars she'd made.

Aside from her familiarity with a very similar spell-form, she somehow felt that the process was made almost trivially easy because the two garments *had* been one, previously, when they were still a part of the immortal elk. *Got it. Don't expect such an easy time in the future.*

The spell-form complete, three things happened.

First, a knot-shaped, bright brand seemed to blossom into existence on each garment simultaneously before fading once more from normal sight. To her magesight, they seemed to have but one brand, spread across both pieces, and that didn't fade.

Second, what had been two shallow puddles of power splashed together, clashing and swirling into a single, much deeper basin. It didn't quite seem to reside in either part while, at the same time, it was clearly within both. It was like looking at a fountain cross-eyed. She saw two, while knowing they were one and the same.

Third, the clothing moved around her, seeming almost to flow over her for a brief instant as the magical and physical manifestations of the two items became briefly malleable.

It was a surprisingly intimate experience, like witnessing a baby being born or attending a wedding. *And two have become one, and out of the two come a new creation.* She smiled. *This, this is real magic.*

She laughed out loud at that. *Sure, manipulating fundamental forces of the universe is a neat trick, but I've made my clothing harmonize!*

She laughed again, with a snort.

Still, the working felt like something deeper than manipulating gravity. Something more potent. She couldn't explain it, even to herself.

She closed her books and her notes, the task complete, and stored them in Kit.

That done, she placed her right hand back where it had been, intuitively knowing that that was the right place, and pushed power into the leather.

It drank in the power, taking at least four times more than the two pieces had before, combined. *That should give it more staying power...* She grinned. *And, so long as a scrap survives of either, both should be able to regrow with the application of enough power.* That was a relief. She'd been mildly concerned that something would wholly eliminate just one piece, leaving her in a state of perpetual half-nakedness whenever she went through damaging experiences. *Never again!*

Her dinner done and the binding of the items complete, she leaned back, satisfied. *I'd been planning on doing something after dinner... What was it...?* She couldn't remember.

She took her dishes back to the chuckwagon and dealt with them there, quickly returning to her wagon to avoid interacting with anyone.

She was about to climb back up when her eye caught sight of a particularly interesting rock formation, and that tickled something in the back of her mind.

It was something to do with rocks...?

"Right! The hammer." She pulled out the hammer and examined it. She'd already topped off its power, though she really wasn't sure why it needed it. *Not like I've used you...*

From examining the portions of its magic, which she could see, it appeared that it would take most of any force exerted on its striking surfaces and send it back, so long as someone wielded it with intention.

For every action, there is an equal and opposite reaction. If she understood it correctly, that should mean that any blow would have nearly double the force that would have been delivered by a normal hammer, used with the same strength.

Huh. Why would the hammer stop moving, then? If the hammer didn't have full force exerted against it, it should continue, barely slowed. *Would that mean it would continue to exert nearly the same force, which would again have a reactionary force applied against it? The magic would then turn most of that around, with the hammer still barely being slowed...*

It was a dizzying concept, one that she couldn't quite fathom, but if she was understanding it correctly, it would make any simple strike into an almost infinite string of hits, possibly repeating endlessly, forever, until the wielder pulled the hammer back or the object struck moved or was destroyed. *Or until the iterating force diminished so much that it was virtually meaningless.* After all, all objects resting on the ground were constantly exerting downward force, and that didn't crack the world.

Even so, how can that be correct? Only one way to find out.

She walked over to a small, plain-looking rock and started by striking it with the butt of the hammer's handle. There was a soft, but not quiet, ring of metal on stone, just as expected. The rock, which was barely bigger than her head, was virtually undamaged, though there was a small speck of lighter rock where the metal handle had made contact.

Okay. That's the baseline, I guess? She then moved with the same gentle motion to tap with the hammer's face.

The sound of a thousand small raps—no, a million. *More?*—rang out in a single long peal as the rock seemed to vibrate, skittering across the ground out of the way as the hammer continued, virtually unimpeded, into the dirt.

When it hit the dirt, there was a burst of wet earth, and the hammer came to rest, head completely buried.

She pulled back, and the earth vibrated around the metal, allowing the hammer to come free easily.

She examined the rock, finding a line of lightened material where the hammer had skittered down the surface. *Fascinating.*

She clicked her tongue, considering. *So, that was a soft tap. What does a normal strike do?*

She pulled her arm back and struck a true blow against the rock.

There was a *crack* like thunder, which her enhanced mind was able to distinguish as more than a dozen overlapping hits coming nearly simultaneously.

The rock exploded, and the world went black.

Pain.

Pain filled her dark world, and she was greeted with the crystal-clear memory of rock shards zipping outwards in all directions, including straight into her eyes.

Chapter: 18
Undiminished Intensity

Tala's eyes were pulped.

Stone shards had been driven deeply into them, bouncing around within her ocular orbits and rendering the soft organs to little more than bloody jelly.

She had not allowed Holly to inscribe her eyes with the same defensive enchantments that covered the rest of her exposed flesh. The very idea had given her shivers.

She was paying for that, now.

In abject agony, she dropped the hammer, reaching up to feel at her face.

Her cheeks were slick to her touch.

She could vaguely hear people calling out and what was likely the sound of running boots drawing near.

It was hard to hear over all that screaming. *Who is screaming at a time like this?*

Her fingers searched upward until she found the mush-filled cavities of her eye sockets.

Her inscriptions still worked perfectly, and her magesight brought her an all-too-detailed look at the devastation. Her thoughts were full of curses as she tried to override the pain, letting her magesight guide her fingers to the fragments of stone in her eye-sockets. Thankfully, it looked like most of what was there was in large pieces, which she quickly pulled free despite the nauseating agony and general revulsion that the action brought forth within her.

She closed her mouth, and the screaming came to an abrupt end. *Oh… it was me.* That was a bit embarrassing.

The inscriptions around the ocular orbits in her skull had activated and were in process of attempting to repair her eyes, but she didn't want to chance the big chunks. What remained amounted to sand, and she'd have to flush that out later if the scripts didn't take care of it.

Hands fell on her shoulders, and she realized that people had been calling to her.

"Mistress Tala! What happened? Are you alright? What do we need to do?"

It was… she couldn't place the voice, and the pressure and itching in her eyes as making it hard to focus. "No danger." She managed to get out. "Mistake. Don't touch the hammer." *What idiot thought that was a useful tool?*

The itching turned to an irritating burning sensation as the hands left her shoulders, and she heard other people begin to arrive.

The guard who had spoken to her, at least she assumed he was a guard, relayed her words to the others as they came up, and they sent runners back to the caravan with word that they were not, in fact, under attack.

Finally, light began to return to the world, and she began blinking rapidly.

She heard the one who'd spoken to her speaking to someone else and was able to focus enough to hear. "Her eyes are gone, turned to pulp. I…" The guard paused, seeming to gather himself. "I've not seen the like. How was no other part of her touched?"

Trent's voice came back. "Do you see the glowing lines, guardsman?" *I knew it was a guard.*

"Yes, Master Trent."

"Her magic protected her from whatever happened. Apparently, it didn't extend to her eyes." *Because, idiot that I am, I didn't think to protect my eyes from physical damage... Wait a moment. Why didn't the endingberries stop this?*

She thought back, even as she bent over, blinking furiously over her refilling sockets.

The shards were incoming, I couldn't blink fast enough so I tried to pull back... She groaned. And she heard Trent moved up beside her. *I'm an idiot. I somehow pulled the endingberries' protective power back without realizing it. That was a stupid reaction. I suppose we can't expect our subconscious to behave rationally.* Still, it had kept the damage confined to her eyes, themselves. *There is that...*

"Tala. I'm here."

No 'Mistress,' eh? She supposed he saw this as a dire situation. "Hi, Master Trent. Good of you to come."

He seemed a bit stymied by her reaction but pressed on. "We can get you healed up right quick. I'll send for Master Tang. He has some inscriptions for healing, which should help, but we likely won't be able to restore your sight fully, or maybe at all, until we return to Bandfast. You won't bleed out, though." He hesitated. "Are you okay?"

She kept blinking until, finally, a clump of goopy sand fell from each eye, and she could see. "Ow..." She sat back, looking over at him.

He made a face and shifted back. "You... do not look great."

"Just what every woman wants to hear."

He snorted. "Your eyes look fine, though... How? I mean, they're a bit blood-shot, but the guards said they were pulped..."

"Oh, he was right. That *really* hurt."

Trent frowned. "Mistress Tala..." Then, he made a silent 'Oh...' "You have self-healing inscriptions."

She nodded, noting the return of the honorific. *No longer as concerned it seems.* "Yup, at least around my head... They rusting *hurt*, though." *And I'm starving...* She pulled out a small bag of dried fruit and began scarfing it down.

"Better than being blind."

"Too true." She reached down and picked up the offending hammer with her offhand. *What a moronic bit of magic.* "This. This is a..." She trailed off as she saw the rock or, more accurately, as she saw the remains of the rock. It had been turned entirely into gravel, which had been scattered out to nearly a dozen yards. She could tell because there were still tendrils of kinetic magic steaming off of the bigger chunks. She felt a smile tug at her lips. "This is dangerous."

Trent regarded the hammer skeptically. "You do have a tendency to pick up dangerous items... May I?" He held out his hand.

Tala placed the hammer's handle into his awaiting palm and watched as his magesight scripts activated. "Huh, a repeating hammer. An efficient one, too. Most don't have this kind of scope." He glanced at her. "The best I've seen only takes about half the force acting on the striking surface and redirects it. This is much better than that." He glanced at the destruction, then at her face, which still felt slick. "Well, better in most circumstances." He sighed. "I could have warned you to wear protective gear. You're lucky it didn't shred your clothes..." He looked at her pristine clothing, magesight still active. "Ah... you picked up all sorts of items, didn't you."

She smiled. "I tried to make it a profitable trip."

He sighed, handing the hammer back, handle first. "Be careful, Mistress. Artifacts aren't toys."

She grunted. "I'm beginning to realize that."

"About time." He smiled humorously, seeming to be trying to take some bite from the rebuke. It didn't work.

"Fair enough, I suppose." She pulled out her incorporator and sprayed her face clean with a minimal amount of water, generated by a large amount of power. "I know I promised to be more careful; I apologize. I really did try to take this slow and carefully."

"Thank you for the apology and for recognizing the slip." Trent sighed and handed her a small towel, pulled from his own dimensional storage. She accepted it gratefully, drying her face and chest where the water had dripped.

I never noticed his storage before. She handed the damp towel back. "Is that new?" She gestured to the sack, nearly the size of a backpack, once again slung over one of Trent's shoulders.

He glanced at it, then shrugged. "Yeah, I figured it was time. I'm going to be taking some different types of contracts going forward, so I can't count on the wagon for Renix and my things." He patted the bag. "Seemed worth the expense."

She nodded. "Artifact, right? Bound to you?" *That wasn't one I saw in Artia's shop.* Then again, Artia would likely have sent Trent to the Constructionists, or elsewhere, if he'd stopped through.

"Yup. I've had constructed dimensional storage in the past." He shook his head. "Just not worth it in the long run. Too costly to maintain for personal use."

"Too true."

"And with the… advice Master Grediv gave me, empowering it myself isn't an issue like it might once have been." Trent stood before she could question him about that.

The guardsman who had gotten to her first was waiting nearby, and she walked over and thanked him.

He was understandably surprised to see her eyes had healed, but he seemed happy for her. "I'm so glad that your injury didn't last. That looked quite agonizing."

She gave a pained smile. "Oh, it was. Thank you, again."

He gave a shallow bow. "My pleasure, Mistress."

Tala bid Trent goodnight, and Trent promised to inform the other Mages, as tactfully as possible, that there had been no threat, just a simple, minor accident.

"Thank you, Master Trent."

He nodded acknowledgment, waved goodbye, and headed back for the main circle of wagons.

Well, all things considered, that went pretty well.

She snorted a derisive laugh. *All in favor of sleep?*

Eye, eye! She laughed again, feeling a bit of mild hysteria at what she'd lost, even if just temporarily.

Don't think about it, Tala. You'll feel better in the morning.

With that thought, she climbed the ladder in search of rest.

* * *

Tala awoke, blinking up at the stars.

It was somewhere near midnight, and a cool wind played across her, pulling at the strands of her hair that hadn't made it into her hastily done braid.

Under the shining jewels, she was brought into awareness of two things.

First, something soft, warm, and feathered was tucked under her left arm, a portion of it laying across her diaphragm as a comfortable weight.

Second, magic, more powerful than she had ever felt, was thrumming an irregular cadence to the north, deep within the mountains of that region.

It was power that had woken her, managing to drive through the gap between her eyelids to trigger her magesight.

She sat up, eliciting a grumbling, soft squawk from Terry, the small, warm weight that had been curled up with her.

She fished out a bit of jerky and fed it to the still half-asleep bird.

He snapped it up before settling down, his head in her lap.

Tala stared to the north, willing her magesight to inform her what she was seeing.

Somewhere, likely at least a couple of hundred miles away, there was a battle raging.

There were at least five sources of power, and her magesight overlaid them in various hues. She couldn't see any details; they were simply too far away. In fact, their distance was so great, only their overwhelming power allowed her to see anything at all.

As she watched, she was able to put together a picture, if a vague one.

A being with a blue hue was fighting four others: two seemed green-ish but closer to yellow than blue, and two were a yellow-orange.

At this distance, she couldn't tell what they were doing, or how they were fighting, but it was spectacular. Each engagement held more power than all that she had wielded in her entire life, and she could somehow feel that they were merely testing blows, searching for weaknesses to exploit.

Grediv is green. But the greens she felt didn't feel like him—whatever that meant.

At a deep level, she knew something else: *They are fighting over the fate of humanity, or at least the fate of some of humanity.* Though, she couldn't tell who was on which side.

The pulses of power grew in intensity as the engagement moved into full conflict. Birds and other wildlife in the surrounding foothills seemed to stir, and soft cries rose in the night.

The oxen, enshrouded within the smaller circle of the caravan, shuffled nervously, a few even letting out low, deep bellows that sounded almost like pleas for help, though they weren't truly panicked. *Thankfully.*

Terry stirred fitfully, and she rested her hand on his head, stroking him and muttering reassurances, all without taking her eyes off the dark horizon and occasional peaks silhouetted before her magesight.

She had never felt so small.

She knew, without a doubt, that any one of the myriad strikes thrown in those great heights would erase her in an instant. She almost laughed; even the backlash of power would annihilate her.

She could drink every drop of endingberry juice in her possession, and it *might* give her another second of life before such a collective onslaught.

She was *nothing*.

She shivered, and Terry crooned softly beneath her hand.

They were both nothing, naked before the awesome power of the universe, wielded by who-knew-what entities.

She found herself clutching her knife, handle in hand, blade bare. At other times, she would have been clutching her arms across her chest, hugging herself tightly.

She almost laughed at that thought. The knife *was* herself, now.

She began feeding a trickle of power into the weapon, a pitiful bulwark against the stark reality of her own powerlessness.

As she did so, she felt a strange duality. As if there was another way she could give the knife power. It distracted her enough that she was able to think back, considering.

I've never given the knife power while I held it, drawn and ready for use. Is that the difference?

In a desperate attempt to distract herself from the battle playing out both before her sight and at an impossible distance from her, she pushed power down the secondary channel. It was like attempting to grind herbs with a feather.

Blinking in surprise, she turned her full attention to the knife, held in her right hand.

Her left hand still stroked Terry, absently.

She pushed again on this new, secondary path, and she felt the power flex, just slightly. To her normal sight, the blade of her knife seemed to shift, becoming more liquid and elongating just slightly. She stopped pushing power through, and the metal snapped back to its previous shape. *What under the sky?*

Magic blazed, causing her head to snap up and her focus to return to the battle.

The creatures that had been restless or roused by the distant conflict went instantly still—even Terry stiffened—prey, hoping beyond reason that the predator it sensed would pass by.

The sky flared with light to her normal vision, temporarily putting out the stars and causing her to raise a hand to block the light, lest she be blinded.

Not again. Please, not again... She shuddered at remembered blackness.

The power, the light, had a decidedly blue hue, but it was somehow twisted or wounded.

She felt each of the four lesser beings flicker before the onslaught, but still, they held.

Candles before a hurricane, but they held.

Then, impossibly, the blue power began to retreat, not truly defeated but driven back.

As the blue moved beyond her perception, traveling unbelievably fast, she felt one of the yellow-orange entity's power waning. It dimmed, sputtered, and died.

One candle, snuffed out by the retreating storm.

In that moment, Tala knew, beyond the shadow of a doubt, that it had been four humans, Archons, fighting some creature. She knew that they had faced it on behalf of humanity and had scraped together a marginal victory.

She also knew that one of the brave warriors had fallen as a result of the battle. She did not know if they would rise again.

The other powers faded and vanished as if falling under veils. *Like what Grediv was doing?*

The night was dark once more to eyes and sight alike.

Tala sat for a long time without moving, riveted by the realities laid bare in what she'd witnessed.

I can't fight that. I can't even resist the least of those involved. More than that, she had to admit to herself that she'd likely seen a minor skirmish, not a true battle.

What if whatever-that-was decided to fight to the death? She shuddered. The world was a much wider, scarier place than she had let herself admit.

No. She straightened her back. *I will not be cowed. Grediv was green, from what I could tell, from what he said. If he can gain that strength, so can I.* She would need vastly more power if she was going to be safe before creatures like the one that had been driven off.

She felt fear, the likes of which she had never known, at the idea of facing such a thing. *And I don't know anything about it, save its power.* She didn't let the fear bow her, though she felt tears in her eyes.

Deep within her, she felt a yearning rise up in opposition to the fear, and in her current state, she couldn't help but voice it.

"I want my dad."

That utterance broke loose something within her, and she curled up on the roof and wept, Terry wedging himself within the circle of her huddled form.

*   *   *

Dawn came early, to Tala's reckoning. The first tendrils of light were turning the sky gray, and Terry was gone.

She sat up, wiping her sleep- and tear-encrusted eyes.

The weight of the previous night was still pressing down on her, and she needed a distraction. She pulled out a bit of jerky, but instead of tossing it, she set it on the rooftop in front of her.

It sat there for a good minute, her staring at it, before Terry popped into being with a slight flick of power.

He bent down and snapped up the meat before looking up at her as if asking, "You called?"

She felt herself smile. "So, Terry. What are we going to do?"

He tilted his head to the side.

"What do I mean? Well, I think you're good to have around, and you seem to like staying around. Is that true?"

He bobbed his head.

"Is it just for the jerky?"

He tilted his head to one side, then shook slightly.

"Not really?"

He bobbed his head.

"Why else then?"

He gave her a flat look.

"Right, right, you can't talk… Can you show me?"

After a moment's hesitation, he bobbed his head slightly. Then, he moved forward.

Tala reached forward, not sure what to expect.

Terry flicked his head forward and bit her, not too hard, but it would have broken skin, except a small bit of the remaining endingberry power kept her whole. *Didn't even activate my scripts.*

Terry looked a bit amused, somehow, but flicked his head at where he'd bitten.

"Because you can't hurt me?"

He tilted his head, then shook.

Not quite right... "Because I'm hard to hurt?"

He nodded to that.

"And I feed you."

He nodded.

Her eyes widened, several things clicking into place. "Like a pack-mate."

Terry nodded once, decisively.

"You don't have a pack... a kettle?" She seemed to remember a teacher calling a group of predatory birds a kettle.

Terry gave her an odd look, then nodded.

"You're alone."

He stepped forward tentatively.

She smiled. "You don't have to be alone. You can stay with me."

He straightened, shimmying slightly and settling back, almost sitting like a duck settling down atop its eggs.

"A few rules."

Terry cocked his head but didn't rise. Instead, he opened his mouth.

She let out a little laugh, and heard Den shift, groaning in his sleep. Tala lowered her voice. "Fine, fine." She tossed him another bit of meat, which he caught easily. "So, first rule: no killing humans, except at my say so."

He finished the bit of meat, then dropped his beak, giving her a skeptical look.

She lowered her voice a bit further. "Yes, yes, I know you helped me with those brutes in Alefast, but I don't want that to become a habit. I'll ask for your help if I need it, okay?"

He shimmied slightly, settling down to listen.

"Okay. No killing animals or creatures that belong to humans, again, unless I say so."

Terry let out a little huff, then bobbed affirmatively.

"And whenever any other human is around, you need to stay this size." She gestured to his current shape, roughly the size of a raven, if an entirely different shape. "We might make exceptions in the future, but not now. Again, unless I say so."

He seemed to consider for a moment, then gave a bit of a shrug. It looked almost comical from his avian body.

"So, do you have any requests?"

He opened his mouth.

She smiled. "More food?"

He opened his mouth wider.

"A lot more? You can still hunt when we're in the Wilds." She hesitated. "I'll need to get you a collar if you want to come into the city." *Right, there should be someone with a ton of them in this caravan.*

Terry leapt to his feet, head low, eyes angry, hissing.

She held up her hands, glancing towards Den, but she didn't see any other movement. "It's up to you, but the collar protects you from the city's wardings, its defenses. It isn't because you're a pet."

He hesitated at that, then tilted his head as if in thought. Finally, he nodded and settled back down.

She gave him a narrow-eyed look. "I'm going to make sure it only functions when I'm around. You can't just use me to get a collar and go on a killing spree in any city you like."

He settled down further and let out a disgruntled huff.

Glad I thought of that... She had to remind herself that this creature had tried to kill her. It was likely older than any currently occupied human city, and it was *not* a pet. "We might have to imply you're a pet, and a hatchling, to keep people from being suspicious."

He rolled over onto his back, feigning sleep.

"Alright, alright. You don't really care, so long as *I* don't think of you as a pet."

He cracked one eye, then opened his mouth.

She snorted a chuckle and tossed him another bit of jerky. He snapped it up happily. "Okay. I've things to be about."

This was a *perfect* distraction from the traumas of the previous night. She had put them from her mind completely. They weren't affecting her, not one bit.

She didn't even notice that she had to wipe a few stray tears from her cheeks. *Nope, not thinking about it at all.*

Chapter: 19
A Cow a Day?

Tala stood, stretching. Terry settled down into a ready crouch, seeming ready to spring away, but did not leave.

She moved through her morning routine, progressing her abilities—physical, spiritual, and magical—and not allowing her mind to return to the night before.

This morning, she added a new task. After feeding Kit, her clothing, and the hammer their morning dose of power, Tala took out her knife and held it ready.

Terry eyed her, a hint of suspicion in his gaze, but he still didn't depart.

She *pushed* against the second path within the knife, causing the blade to seemingly liquify and elongate.

She strained, her gate thrown wide and the entirety of her power flowing straight into the weapon. It wasn't enough.

I want to know what this does! She grabbed some of her power, just drawing the barest amount from her reserve, so as to not exhaust herself. She pushed it into the new path all at once.

That flow of power was enough.

The blade of the knife flowed outward, forming into a hair-thin outline of a sweeping sword blade. It had a subtle curve, almost like a falchion but not as broad. *If I'm remembering the name right.* She had never really made a study of specific weaponry.

This was no mundane weapon, however. There was, after all, no blade, just the outline of one.

At the same time, a flare of heat began to radiate from the gap within that outline, and she *knew* that this would cut better than any sword forged by the hand of man.

Then, the end of her pulse of power came. The blade contracted back to its former shape, and she was left gasping and swaying from the expenditure of power. *So much for not exhausting myself.*

She shook her head to clear it. *Well, that's one more thing to aim for, I suppose. When I'm stronger, I can actually use this as a true weapon.*

She felt an odd satisfaction, much like the way her body felt when she moved just right. There was a correctness to what she'd done with the knife, and it was pleasing to have accomplished it. *Huh. Good to know, my soul has kinesthetic sense of spiritual rightness of action.* Now that she thought of it that way, she realized that the sensation had been akin to the warmth she felt after doing a good deed. *The more you know...*

That done, it was time to empower the cargo-slots. *I'll do the martial training later.* That would have taken more time than she had before the wagons departed, even though she suspected most people had yet to eat breakfast.

When she climbed down the ladder to empower the cargo-slots for the day, Terry flickered, disappearing and reappearing perched on her shoulder.

Tala grunted at the change in weight but didn't slip. "That will take a bit of getting used to." She didn't trust the bird, not really, but she thought she might understand some small part of it. Right now, it was motivated by loneliness and a lack of true companionship. That left the potential to actually create a bond of comradery if such a creature was capable of long-term bonds with a human. *I hope he is... I'd hate to have to kill him some day.* Worse, if she somehow allowed him to hurt others… She shook her head. *I'll be as careful as I can be. He could kill either way, but in this case, I might be close enough to notice.* She nodded to herself at that. At the very least, she would be a limiting factor for the bird.

She hopped off the ladder, Terry shifting to stay in place.

Tala quickly empowered the twenty cargo-slots, the mental model coming easier than ever, and the task taking less power than any time before. *I'm really getting the hang of this.*

It was time for breakfast.

She walked towards the main circle, Terry comfortably switching shoulders with a silent pop of power. *That's odd. He must be doing something more than just shortening the distance between things, else he would have just gone straight through my head. My iron should have prevented that, even if it wouldn't have hurt me… which I'm not sure about.* She considered but came to the conclusion that until she had an intelligent guess, she wasn't likely to find out.

Terry's certainly not talking. She grinned at that.

"Gah!" The startled exclamation brought Tala up short.

She turned to find Trent staring, wide-eyed, at Terry. "Good morning, Master Trent. Are you alright?"

"Mistress Tala." He seemed to master himself, not taking his gaze from the bird. "Why do you have a terror hatchling on your shoulder?"

"Oh, Terry?" She reached over and scratched the bird under the chin. Terry leaned into her hand. "I came across him, and he seems to like me."

"Mistress Tala." Trent seemed at a loss for words. "That creature will grow very quickly. It will be as tall as you within a year if it eats enough."

She frowned. "Do they continue to grow at that rate?" *Maybe, Terry is much younger than I thought.*

"No... from my understanding, they slow to growing about an inch a year after the initial spurt, but that is hardly the point."

An inch... a year? She looked at Terry, who was crooning contentedly. *How old are you?* She did her best to keep her thoughts from showing. "Yes, but I think he and I have an understanding. He's..." She had been going to say 'safe' but that was an outright lie. "He's not going to hurt people or human-owned animals."

Trent gave her a deeply skeptical look. "Mistress Tala, research shows that they don't approach human level intelligence until they are close to three decades old, and even then, that doesn't mean they think or reason the way we do. At that size?" He gestured. "You're lucky it likes you enough not to bite out your throat the first chance it has."

Tala sighed. *How am I going to—*

There was a startled gasp from off to the other side, and she turned to see Tang staring, open-mouthed. It was an almost comical mirroring of Trent's reaction.

Oh, no...

"You have a hatchling!" The man rushed forward but pulled to a stop two paces away. "That's incredible! Terror birds are amazing creatures." He turned his eyes to her. "Did you find it with others of its kind or alone?"

Trent looked confused, and Tala felt bewildered, but she responded. "Alone, why?"

"Well, they have a *very* strong maternal bond. There have been documented cases of humans and terror birds forming long-term partnerships, when the hatchling forms such an attachment to the human." He leaned in just slightly, eagerly studying Terry. "Has it taken food from you? Has it shown any aggression?"

She cleared her throat, trying to stall for time to think. *He clearly has some knowledge... Honesty might be best?*

At least a little honesty. "When I found him, he did try to attack me, but when he was unable to hurt me, it seemed to puzzle him." She glanced at Terry. He was staring at her, and she could see what she would swear was a mischievous glint in his eyes. "After that, he did take food from me."

"Oh!" Tang clasped his hands together. "That's wonderful! Better to get that out of the way." He became suddenly serious. "He'll try again, at least a couple of times. You did say 'he,' right? How can you tell? He should be too small to sex properly."

She shrugged and answered truthfully. "He just seems like a he?"

Tang shrugged. "Good enough for now. You will have to watch yourself. If he does manage to hurt you, you will have to strike back immediately to restore the balance." He met her gaze. "This is critical. He'll test you again, and he cannot see you as a target, or he will become fixated on hunting humans."

She nodded, a bit startled. "Yes, of course. I'm well protected. My magic is actually bent that way." Tala pulled out a notebook and wrote down a few thoughts, both from what Tang had said and from what his words had sparked in her own mind. She was still reeling a bit from the Mage's seeming change in attitude. *Maybe he just really likes animals?*

He was nodding, a smile on his face. "Oh! I'm so glad. Good, yes, take lots of notes! I can't believe I get to see a hatchling up close." He turned his gaze to Trent. "Now, Master Trent, we need to reassure the guard and others that the bird is safe but should not, under any circumstances, be approached. They look cute but can be vicious."

Trent was frowning, clearly recovering from his confusion. "You really think this is wise, Master Tang?"

"Wise?" He made a dismissive noise. "It's *necessary.* We know so much about arcane animals, but also so little.

Such chances are rare and must be seized upon." He paused for a moment. "If it works out, and the little one stays around until we reach Bandfast, we'll need a collar."

"That's foolish, Master Tang." Trent hesitated. Then, his eyes widened slightly, and he looked to Tala, his eyes narrowing again. *Right... I asked him about a collar yesterday...* Tala smiled as innocently as she could.

"Not a domestic collar, Master Trent. We'll need to get an escort style. Keyed to you, of course, Mistress Tala." He nodded her way.

She returned her attention to Tang, feeling a bit overwhelmed by the flood of information.

"There are quite a few arcane specimens in Bandfast under observation at the moment, but I don't think any are terror birds. Ah!" He clasped his hands together again. "This is *exciting!*" He turned and walked away quickly, calling over his shoulder as he went. "I'll see if I have a schema for such a collar. I might even have one in my storage, but it will be buried if so. Ha! Wouldn't that be perfect!" He disappeared from sight, still happily talking to himself.

Tala turned to look at the bemused Trent. "Well, that was unexpected." *Is he going to make an issue of it?*

Trent sighed. "And here I thought he might be a voice of reason." He gave her a searching look. "Are you sure, Mistress? I seem to remember you asking for a collar before having that terror bird…" He left the question unasked.

She hesitated for a moment, looking down at Terry as the bird regarded her closely. "Yes, I think it is worth an attempt." She decided some honesty would go a long way. "I did come across him before today. That's why I asked about a collar in case he did end up following me." She smiled as that seemed to mollify the Mage. "If he is willing, I don't see why he and I can't be great partners."

Terry nuzzled the side of her face, the same mischievous glint shining in his eyes with undiminished intensity.

*   *   *

Tala had almost gotten breakfast before she'd seen Adam and remembered her morning martial training. *I keep forgetting that.*

The guardsman had been a bit hesitant after seeing the little arcanous creature on her shoulder, but when she'd taken a moment to explain to Terry that Adam attacking her, this morning, was fine, and she'd stood still for him to punch her with no reaction from Terry, Adam had seemed mollified.

Terry sat on a nearby wagon-step as Adam alternated between instructing Tala, attacking her, and easily avoiding her attacks.

She was improving rapidly, but she still couldn't consistently defend against his strikes, let alone mount any sort of counter.

He assured her that that would come in time. "You are progressing vastly faster than most recruits do."

She'd grunted at that, but not because she didn't have a response. At the time, her face had been pressing into the dirt, with her arm twisted painfully behind her.

They continued until they noticed the chuckwagon beginning to close up, and they called it a morning so they could get breakfast.

Apparently, Tang had spoken to the kitchen about Terry. So, when Tala approached, Terry on her shoulder, the cooks didn't react, save to give the bird wary looks and her a second plate, piled high with meat scraps. Terry perked up when he saw that and squawked happily, bobbing up and down and shuffle-stepping on Tala's shoulder. "Please wait, Terry. We'll eat soon."

The bird shifted unhappily but settled back down.

The cook gave a nervous chuckle. "I can't even get my kid to listen that well, Mistress. He must really like you…"

Tala thanked the cook and took the tray of food, along with a jug of coffee.

The jug went into Kit, and she balanced the tray precariously as Terry continued to shift in anticipation.

"Remarkable." Tang was walking towards them. "Truly remarkable that he is following your cues already."

Terry gave a deep rumble that was, quite honestly, lower than a creature his current size should be able to make, and Tang stopped his approach. "Thank you, Master Tang, for talking with the cooks."

He waved the notion away. "Nonsense. We have to make sure the hatchling gets fed. A growing terror bird can eat their weight in food every day. Something about their arcane digestion allows for faster processing." He frowned. "Has he shown any magical tendencies? I've seen flame, lightning, and even ice abilities from terror birds I've faced in the wilds."

Tala glanced to Terry, and the diminutive bird gave a small bob. She shrugged. "I get the sense of dimensional power from him."

Tang's eyes widened. "Amazing! Dimensional arcane creatures aren't rare, but most are of the smaller species. I've not encountered anything larger than a sheep with power in that vein." He was nodding happily. "What a rare chance, indeed!"

Tala cleared her throat, gesturing with her tray. "Well, we were going to go eat…"

"Oh! Of course, by all means. Please let me know if anything unusual happens, or if there is anything I can do?"

"Sure," she responded hesitantly.

"Good, good. I'll keep on the quest for the collar." He pumped his fist excitedly. "We don't want our little friend obliterated by Bandfast's defenses now, do we?" With that happy proclamation, he turned and strode away, seemingly heading back towards his own wagon.

"What a strange man." Tala spoke very quietly, trusting to Terry's nearness to allow the bird to hear her.

The bird bobbed in acknowledgment.

Tala sighed and returned to her wagon-top perch. Den was already back at the wagon after his own breakfast, beginning to prepare the harnesses for his oxen. "Mistress Tala!"

"Good morning, Den."

"Good morning. And who do we have here?" Den stopped well more than an arm's length away.

Terry, for his part, perked up a bit, seeming to focus in on Den for some reason that Tala couldn't determine. "This is Terry, Den. Terry, this is Den. Play nice?"

Terry bobbed but ended the motion in a low crouch, his head moving side to side inquisitively.

Den laughed, pulling something out of his pocket. "The little guy has a good nose. May I?"

Tala couldn't see what he held, but Terry was bobbing up and down enthusiastically. "Sure? Be careful, please?"

Den nodded, approaching the last few feet carefully.

Tala whispered. "Be gentle, Terry. If you hurt him, he isn't likely to give you more of whatever he has for you."

Terry seemed to hesitate, his focus momentarily breaking, then he bobbed a nod as Den got within reach.

Den, for his part, took the treat, which turned out to be several chunks of roasted pork-belly, and set them on the back of his closed right hand. He extended it tentatively towards Terry.

Terry carefully reached forward and snapped up the meat, happily gulping it down before presenting the top of his head towards Den.

Den laughed and reached out, slowly, to scratch the bird on the head. "He's a good boy!"

Tala gave Terry a suspicious look. "Yeah…"

"Well, I have to get back to work. Good to meet you, Terry." He patted the bird one last time before moving back to his task.

Tala climbed up with Terry and their tray, sitting in the center of the roof, on the padded square. As she and the bird ate from their respective plates piled with food, she eyed Terry. "You've observed humans quite extensively, haven't you?"

The bird paused, glancing her way, then bobbed a nod.

"And you haven't approached any before?"

It made a clawing motion towards her, while gulping down another bit of food.

"You attacked them."

Another bob.

"They didn't put up enough resistance, so they weren't worth your time?"

Another bob.

"Terry, how many have you killed?"

The bird paused, giving her a side-eyed look.

She huffed, taking another bite. "You're right, I probably don't want to know…"

They both went back to eating, silence falling comfortably over the rooftop meal.

*   *   *

An hour later, the caravan was underway, and Tala was sweating profusely, sprawled upon the roof. She had just finished her high-repetition, martial training, trying to cement what Adam was teaching her more firmly.

She drank deeply, whenever she could, and allowed herself to regain some semblance of physical energy.

After another five minutes, she sat up and pulled out her flask, taking a deep swig... or she tried to. *I forgot to refill it.*

She pulled out the jug of berry juice and carefully poured some into the flask before returning the jug to her pouch.

"Thank you, Kit."

The pouch did not respond.

She drank her daily cup of juice and reveled in the feeling of endingberry power flowing through her. "Alright!"

She stood and stretched, loosening the muscles she'd so recently worked.

"Time for the next thing." She flipped a piece of meat to Terry, who lazily caught it. "Feeding you. Or the logistics of such."

At the first, Terry had perked up, but he'd lain his head back down as she continued.

She was speaking quietly, so Den, at the front of the wagon, couldn't overhear. "Am I going to need to bring you like... a cow a day?"

Terry seemed hesitant, but eventually shook himself.

"So, does your manifested size determine how much you need to eat?"

He shook himself in the negative.

She blinked, a bit confused, trying to understand. "Well, I don't really understand, but I suppose I don't need to." Even so, she let out a grateful breath. "I was realizing that I could go broke trying to feed you... well, more broke."

Terry gave her a quizzical look.

"You probably have no concept of money, do you. It's not like you've seen humans anywhere outside the Wilds." She sighed. "I'm not going to explain basic economics to a terror bird. You can watch, listen, and pick up the basics."

He closed his eyes and stretched out in the warm sun.

She quirked a smile. That out of the way, she went about her day as usual.

She exercised her spirit by calling the knife to her at various distances. She was steadily improving.

She strove to expand her power accumulation rate, using the knife and the new path for power she'd discovered within it. It turned out to be a better exercise than making an Archon Star for two reasons.

First, it became dynamically harder the more power she poured into the knife. The closer she came to the threshold of transforming it into a sword, the more power it took to progress. That made it much more engaging to practice with than with the comparably static formation of an Archon Star.

Second, there was no danger of the knife suddenly sucking most of the magic from her body, leaving her exhausted. *No, if I'm exhausted after, I've only myself to blame.*

She would get back to making Archon Stars soon enough, but the knife seemed a better training tool for the moment.

The magic pouring into the knife, when not enough to key off the transformation, didn't simply vanish. Instead of building up to reach a level high enough to bring out the sword, the power was shunted into the other path. That way, she was actually doing two things at once. First, she was stretching her gate wider, to increase the rate of flow, and second, she was deepening the capacity of the knife itself. *Still not sure how that will help, but I'm sure it will.*

Thus, she spent the day in training and review for her upcoming, full-bodied inscription. If she was honest, she felt a bit nervous. She'd never actually had all the inscriptions before, though she'd done her best to properly prepare. Where most who took the physiology and other healing-related courses did so for just that purpose, to learn to heal, Tala had taken them to learn how to have her entire body inscribed effectively. *And I'm almost there.*

Though, to get all the inscribing she expected, it was going to be a *long* few days with Holly.

Adam and Ashin were both reluctant to spar with Terry watching, despite the former's experience that morning, but they warmed to the idea and soon forgot the bird for the time each worked with Tala.

Between those stints of combat training, she continued to push in other areas. Aside from adding to her ever-growing list of biological nuances to brush up on when she got to Bandfast, she took breaks by reading the books that were not warded against her, seeking all the knowledge she could grasp. To her surprise, there was quite a large entry on terror birds in 'A Brief Overview of Entities: Arcane.'

"Huh, Master Tang knows his stuff." Everything he'd said was backed up by the book, and he'd even conveyed a few subtleties that the book didn't. True, the entry covered much that the man hadn't mentioned, but he hadn't been attempting to recite a research paper to her. *I may have judged you too harshly, old man.* That, of course, was quite unfair given he was likely less than thrice her age, putting him firmly on the young side of mid-life, especially for a Mage.

She frowned at that thought. *Where are all the older Mages?* She'd seen a couple, but there should be more relatively old Mages than young, shouldn't there? Yet almost every one that she'd met had been relatively close to her own age. *That is strange...*

True, many of her teachers had been older, but they'd also been teachers for decades, centuries in a few cases.

I'll have to ask Lyn about it... Maybe Trent, too? It was something to investigate. *I'll add it to the list.*

Also, throughout the day, she had asked leading questions of those around her, only to discover that no one else had noticed the magical display the night before, not even the other Mages.

Rane was mysteriously absent, so she hadn't been able to prod him, but she hadn't actually tried to search him out. He was likely just acting as rearguard again or something similar. *I suppose I'll have to find him around dinner.* She sighed. It made the most sense.

Brand had brought lunch for both herself and Terry, though Terry hadn't acknowledged the head chef, only feasting once the man had departed.

As evening was approaching and the caravan was once again formed up for the night, Tala finally put aside her new notebook, now more filled with notes than blank pages, and yawned dramatically. "Well, Terry. What do you say, time for food?"

The bird flickered to her shoulder, perching happily.

She smiled. "I thought so."

Chapter: 20
Set on Unconventionality

Dinner in hand, Terry on her left shoulder, Tala walked towards a table near the edge of the larger wagon circle.

Rane sat, alone, eating his own meal.

"Master Rane?"

His head snapped up, the young man seeming startled. "Mistress Tala. I'm sorry, I didn't see you there."

"May I join you?"

He looked perplexed. "Of course, you may… Is there something I can do for you?"

Tala hid a wince as she sat down. *I haven't been very kind to him, have I?* "Nothing comes to mind, but I haven't seen you today, and I haven't thanked you for the thunder bulls, yet."

He smiled a bit at that. "It was a quick fight but good exercise."

"Well, thank you. It was overly generous of you to give all the carcasses to the cooks."

He shrugged. "I'm not on contract for the money. Others can make better use of the materials than I."

Tala cocked her head, even as Terry hopped from her shoulder and dug into his awaiting plate. "Then, why are you with us, Master Rane?"

He smiled. "Quite a few reasons, actually. To see the wider world, to work with others, to visit an uncle in Bandfast, and to establish a connection with you."

She blinked back at him. "Oh?"

He shrugged. "I've said it already. Master Grediv suggested that I'd be wise to work with you and at least become friends." He smiled ruefully. "I'm not too good at it, though. I killed things, I offered to hit you, and that was about all I've got."

She snorted a laugh. "Hardly. I'd love to pick your brain on some things, if you're willing."

He straightened a bit, swallowing his current bite. "Oh? What do you wish to discuss?"

She waved her hand. "In a minute. I want to discuss sparring; I'd like to, but I'm not sure I'm ready to fight someone with your skill and abilities."

He gave a half-smile. "Shouldn't be a problem, especially since it would have to be a magicless fight. No offensive magics, and no retributive defenses."

She frowned.

"Retributive, meaning magic that harms those who harm you."

"Oh!" *That's clever. I wonder if I could auto target anything that hit me... It wouldn't be power or metal efficient, but it might save me in a pinch, or when I can't figure out exactly what is attacking me or where from.* It might help in crowds, too... "That's an interesting idea."

He gave her a puzzled look. "You've not come across that concept before?"

She shrugged. "It's probably been mentioned, but I've a whole new set of experiences since my last formal lesson. I'm seeing things in a new light."

He quirked an eyebrow. "That makes sense. The type of light *would* affect how you see."

She grunted irritably. "You know what I mean."

He smiled. "Yeah, I think I do. Once you fight your first monsters, it changes your perspective."

Terry paused, glancing up at Rane with a searching look. The Mage seemed to notice because he held up his hands placatingly, addressing the little terror bird.

"Not all arcane creatures are monsters, but many are. Magical creatures more so, but again, there are some that description doesn't fit."

Terry seemed mollified as he returned to gobbling down his food. Tala moved the plate to the bench, forcing the diminutive avian to hop down, giving her an irritated glance. That left the tabletop in a more ordered state and seemed to allow them both to think more clearly.

"So, yes. Sparring. I'd like that." He smiled, and it seemed genuine.

Well, I didn't really agree... However, seeing his expression brought a smile to her face as well. *It'll probably be fine.* She nodded her thanks, taking another bite.

"So... what is it you wanted to talk about? Some esoteric magical entity?"

"I wanted to ask you about familiars."

As it turned out, Rane didn't know much more about familiars than the books that Tala had been reading. His knowledge was more holistic because he'd had more time to read, study, and absorb the information. Grediv had apparently given him a set of tomes similar to Tala's. He was just as irritated as she was by the warded books in the collection. Even so, they both agreed that they'd rather have the books, solely for use later, than not have them at all.

They chatted amiably through dinner, eating slowly as the other members of the caravan came and went, consuming their own evening meals.

It was getting late when Tala bid Rane a good night and headed for her starlit bed atop the caravan.

She hummed softly to herself as she re-braided her hair and stretched, making sure not to disturb Den, who seemed close to sleep, tucked under an enclosure drawn around his driver's seat for the night.

She did a final set of spiritual exercises, tossing her knife out and drawing it back to herself six times in quick succession. A proud grin stretched across her features at the sixth pull. *Halfway there!* While not *quite* true, she still reveled in the accomplishment.

That done, she pulled out her bedroll and laid it out beneath the starry sky.

Her eyes traced the familiar shapes above her as she let her mind wander over the last few weeks.

She had left a place of lonely learning for the wider world. *And I promptly continued to seek learning, alone.* The conversation over dinner, with Rane, had been enlightening. Not so much because he'd said things she'd never heard, but because the act of speaking about the myriad topics had settled the information deeper into her own mind. *Perhaps the others who formed study groups had had the right idea...* It was another reminder of her previous isolation.

She'd had similar discussions with Trent or Renix, but it hadn't been the same. Rane seemed to be invested in growing stronger as quickly as he could, just as she was, and he'd had years longer to comb through Grediv's books.

I'll have to find more time to talk with him, to bounce ideas and see what sticks. She smiled at that.

Terry blipped back onto the roof. Where he'd been off to, she didn't really know, but she'd been sure he'd return.

He padded over to her with heavy, yet soft and nearly soundless, steps, lying down to curl up beside her on the bedroll.

With Terry next to her, a warm pressure in pleasantly cool night, she drifted off to sleep, feeling less burdened, and less alone, than she had in a long, long time.

*   *   *

Tala woke in the middle of the night, mind racing. She stared up at the stars and tried to quiet her mind but couldn't.

She'd had nightmares, again.

That wasn't fair. It had been nearly three weeks since her last one, before she'd left the academy, but they were back. She cursed, sitting up and rubbing at her eyes.

Terry was curled up beside her but hadn't stirred as she'd sat upright. *Good bird. Sleep.* From long experience, she knew that she needed to move, let her mind reattach to the real world, and then she could get back to sleep.

The night was dead quiet through the caravan, the oxen were deeply asleep, and she couldn't hear the guards patrolling. *That's either really good or really bad.*

She shivered. *No, Tala, focus on reality, not on the horrors your mind can conjure.*

She didn't want to exercise, or even stretch, as she feared it would wake her body too much, so she slowly climbed down the wagon, saw to the call of nature, and returned.

She was still under the sway of the nightmare and was starting at every movement, shadow, or stray thought. *Not ready yet.* If she fell asleep, now, she'd fall straight back into the horror.

Grumbling to herself, she looked over the wagons, the cargo wagons. *It isn't too long 'til morning.* She decided to charge the cargo-slots a bit early. Her studies had revealed that even with only the one symbol alight, the wagons could remain stable for close to a full day, so her being a few hours early wouldn't hurt anything.

She moved through the now rote motions and soon had all twenty charged. *Well done.* She smiled. It had been enough, and her mind was now free of the clawing dragging fear and back in reality.

Somewhat settled, she climbed back up the ladder, lay down beside Terry, and drifted back into a deep, and now thankfully dreamless, sleep.

* * *

Tala woke early and moved through her routine. She didn't need to charge the wagons this morning, due to her mid-night restlessness, so after her stretching and workouts, targeting physical, spiritual, and magical muscles, she sought out Adam for the morning sparring and martial lessons.

To her surprise, Rane was there. She smiled a greeting and waved to return his gesture.

"Good morning, Mistress Tala."

"Good morning, Master Rane."

"Did I see you working magic last night?"

She shrugged. "You were on duty?"

He nodded. "I'd just taken over." He yawned a bit. "I'm going to take a bit of a nap after this." He gestured towards Adam. "So…?"

She reluctantly nodded. "I needed to recenter my mind, so I charged the cargo-slots."

"Reasonable." He waited, a questioning look on his face, but he didn't ask.

She felt another smile tug at her lips, this one of gratitude. *I'm not up for talking about it, now.* "So… Adam? What's going on here?"

The two Mages turned to the guardsman as he stepped forward. "I want to observe you two fight. Just to the first solid hit. I'll instruct Tala based on each result."

Rane nodded. "Unarmed, no offensive magic, yes?"

Adam nodded.

Tala grinned. "Should be fun. Are you safe?" She'd drunk her cup of endingberry juice just after waking up.

He shrugged. "Any hit you land, I'll deserve."

Arrogant, but true? She raised her hands in a guard, and Rane quirked a smile.

He moved unbelievably fast. If Tala had fought him a week earlier, his stomping kick to her gut would have driven her to the ground in vomiting humiliation.

But it wasn't a week ago, and Adam had been a faster opponent. Tala had been training against one of the most skilled fighters in the caravan and taking his feedback to heart.

As Rane's kick came in, she clapped one hand above, and one below, twisting the driving foot, even as she stepped back, to move her stomach out of the line of attack.

The result was a torsion on Rane's hip, which spun him on his planted foot to face away from her.

The last she saw of his features was a look of surprise.

Grinning in exaltation, she shot out her closer hand to snag Rane's belt and launched her back knee upward, contracting her whole body to drive the attack up between Rane's legs.

If she'd taken a moment to think, she would have realized that not only was it a *very* cheap shot, but it was also, quite literally, a low blow. That said, if she'd taken a moment to think, he'd have stomp-kicked her into the dirt, so it evened out.

As her knee impacted, she saw magic explode outward. All the force she'd imparted was redirected back into her as a direct application of power. It seemed to be intended to spread the energy in an even distribution across her body.

Now, if Rane's magic had acted like Tala's hammer and simply taken the incoming force and redirected it, she would have felt as if she'd kneed a stone wall. Instead, Rane's defense had attempted to affect all of her, directly.

The iron across her skin made Tala almost impervious to direct magical affects, at least any that she was likely to encounter. Thus, the magic literally *tinged* off of her iron salve.

There were two other results.

First, the force had to go somewhere, so, denied Tala, the magic exploded outward in a ring, shredding the knee of her pants, and tearing at the inside of Rane's legs. Because the magic was his, it mostly bypassed the flesh, instead cleanly tearing through the mid-thigh of his pants leg, and blasting outward to create an expanding pressure wave that kicked up dust and rattled the closest wagon.

Second, all inertia was stolen from her, and Tala was left balancing on one foot, her knee jammed into a rather uncomfortable position, her left hand still locked onto Rane's belt.

Rane looked shocked to still have an opponent so close after his defenses had activated.

Tala was surprised to be in such an awkward position, without her opponent writhing in agony.

Adam seemed confused that they weren't continuing.

Rane recovered a blink faster, sweeping his already extended leg up and back at Tala's head in a surprisingly flexible maneuver.

Tala rolled with the motion, bending to allow the kick to deflect off of her rising arm.

He spun with the kick, using the inertia to pull him around again as he drove his fist for her chest.

Why do you people always aim for my chest! Trusting the endingberry power within her, she did something colossally stupid.

She struck, punching the much bigger, oncoming fist with her own.

She felt an ache radiate from her knuckles through every bone, joint, and connection down her arm, through her shoulder, and into her back at the moment of impact. Her form had been perfect, but fists weren't meant to hit one another.

She was driven backward, feet skidding cross the dirt, but she maintained her balance, and her stance, arm extended. An alarming amount of endingberry power was consumed in that instant as nearly half of her body was put under destructive strain. Most of that energy was consumed in keeping her hand from splitting as his knuckles had impacted between hers, driving with enough force that her hand *should* have been divided into bloody sections. Her own knuckles had similarly impacted on him, but her hand was much smaller, and his much stronger. Even so…

Rane, for his part, held perfect form after his own punch for a heartbeat before loosing a string of nonsense words, clutching his fist in his offhand and dancing in a circle, trying to bear through the pain.

Despite Rane's frantic movements, Tala was able to see that the hand didn't look quite right.

Adam was stunned, and he spoke to himself, with Tala barely able to catch the words. "She punched… his punch. Did I not teach her how to block? What madness…?" Then, his eyes snapped to Rane, and he sprang into action. "Healer! Someone call Master Tang, and if the chuckwagon has ice, we could use it."

Some of the random people, who'd been about, turned and ran in various directions, seeking to obey his instructions.

Rane stopped his dancing about and took deep, gulping breaths, staring at his hand in horrified fascination. The knuckles were spread just further apart than they should be, and the entire limb was beginning to swell.

Tala gaped, eyes going wide. "Oh, Master Rane! I'm so, so sorry."

She almost offered him some of her endingberry juice, but that was a protective, not a healing, magic. It wouldn't help him. *He doesn't have healing scripts to cheat with, either.*

He gave her a wonder-filled look. "Are your bones hardened steel?"

She cringed guiltily. "I'm protected from physical damage of all kinds. I'm just glad you drove me backward. I can't even imagine what would have happened if I'd been properly braced and hadn't moved."

Rane looked down at his hand, still clearly in agony, and simply nodded, closing his eyes against the pain.

He sank to the ground, settling into place, cradling his hand.

One of the cooks ran up with a bowl of ice, towel draped over the top, just as Master Tang arrived.

Terry, for his part, was eyeing Tala suspiciously.

She glared at the bird, walking over to him, and whispering for him alone, "I didn't mean to hurt him. He is not an exception to the 'no hurting humans' part of our agreement."

Terry gave a reluctant bob.

"Good."

Terry flicked up onto her shoulder, and she returned to Rane's side, looking to Master Tang. "What can I do?"

The Mage glanced at Terry and frowned. "The terror bird should be taking advantage of Master Rane's weakness and attacking, especially because you damaged the good Master." Tang looked puzzled.

"About Master Rane… Master Tang?"

The Mage seemed to return to himself. "Right! Right, apologies." He moved his focus back to Rane, and at the same time, Tala allowed herself to truly focus on the injured hand.

What she saw caused her to go pale. Her magesight brought her a cacophony of information, but if she was interpreting it right, there were small tears all through the big man's hand, along with small fractures evident in the small bones therein. She swallowed involuntarily.

Master Tang closed his eyes, and Tala watched as the older Mage activated a careful series of inscriptions, focusing on Rane's injury. Power flowed forth, and Tala was able to watch as the energy of the healing was consumed, pulling the hand back into correct shape and almost stitching the tears back together. The only way that metaphor fell short was that they were left utterly restored, rather than with sutures or scars.

It was awe-inspiring.

The swelling didn't diminish, precisely, but as the hand contracted, the blood that had been rushing to begin work on the injury was squeezed out, leaving behind a slightly misshapen, but fully healed, appendage.

Master Tang settled backward, smiling. "There, good as new, or as good as can be done, I'd say. It will be swollen for a day or two, and I'd recommend keeping it cool." He pointed to the waiting bowl. "The ice is a wonderful idea." He gave Adam an approving nod. "There is no damage, but the swelling will be uncomfortable, and I'd recommend taking it easy until we reach Bandfast, just to be safe."

Rane was breathing easier, now, and he nodded. "Thank you, Master Tang."

"Now"—the older man slapped his knees and stood, looking from Adam to Rane, to Tala—"what exactly happened?"

Tala opened her mouth, then closed it, unsure of exactly what to say.

Adam stepped forward. "A sparring accident. Mistress Tala seems set on unconventionality, and while it worked out for her, this time, it injured Master Rane."

Tang clucked his tongue. "I can't say I approve of Mages brawling like animals, but I'm glad they had a master of the craft to observe, even if only to have a coherent account of what the idiocy caused."

Adam seemed perplexed by the mix of insult and compliment in one, but he also seemed unwilling to make an issue of it with the Mage. He simply nodded in acknowledgment. "Thank you, Master Tang, for your assistance. I know that Master Rane is grateful for it, even if he is still in a bit of shock."

Tala stepped forward. "Yes. Thank you, Master Tang. We appreciate your healing."

He glanced her way, then smiled and nodded. "Now, I need to finish my breakfast. Good morning to you all." Without a backward glance, he departed.

The other onlookers began to disperse as Rane placed his hand on the towel and into the bowl of ice. He let out a sigh of contentment, though it was obvious that he was still uncomfortable.

Tala turned towards Adam, her face clearly conveying that she expected a reprimand.

Adam opened his mouth, seeming about to deliver just that, but then he stopped himself. Finally, he sighed and shook his head. "Well, Mistress Tala, it seems that I've done you a disservice. I've been training you like a mundane guard, and you are anything but mundane. That little maneuver would likely have cost you a hand if you were." He took another deep breath and let it out slowly. "Two things." He gave her a questioning look.

She nodded once, doing everything she could to indicate attentiveness. "Yes?"

"First, never do that again, especially not with a sparring partner who isn't protected against the damage."

She nodded vigorously. "Of course."

"Second, what I've been teaching you is a good foundation, but we're going to need to build a fighting style that fits your particular talents. Once we're back in Bandfast, I'm off for the winter and in need of a project for one of the classes I am assisting: 'Fighting Opponents who Defy Physics.' You are going to be a subject for my students, and we are going to craft you a means of fighting that will take full advantage of who and what you are."

Rane raised his hand. He *raised his hand.* Tala felt a smile tug at her lips.

"Yes, Master Rane?" Adam turned to regard the Mage.

"Can I join in that project? Master Grediv helped me a bit, but he's never been the most talented up-close combatant."

Adam hesitated, then glanced to Tala. She gave a shrug, then a small nod.

"Sure. It will be a good object lesson, when your two fighting styles diverge. It will keep in the forefront the idea that no two magical beings will be the same." He nodded as if to himself. "Yeah, that will be perfect."

Adam gave Tala a few more comments, then he sent Rane away to get some breakfast, and Adam and Tala spent a few more minutes finishing up their morning sparring and lesson.

Chapter: 21
It Should Be Fun

Tala was uncomfortably sweaty when she and Terry picked up their tray of food and bid a good morning to the cooks.

Back at the wagon, she again did her best to clean herself but was quite unhappy with the result.

She groaned in irritation. "Kit. Can you alter your interior so I can get clean easier?"

The pouch did not respond.

In the hopes of a miracle, Tala secured the pouch and climbed down in.

As soon as she was in, she looked around hopefully.

The inside of the pouch was vastly changed, with almost all of Tala's possessions crammed in barely organized shelving, right up around the entrance. The ladder went lower, into a circular empty space not quite wide enough for Tala to stretch her elbows fully out.

If anything, there was a smaller volume of space, but it was mostly vertical, keeping her belongings up high. To aid in the process to come, the small circular space around the ladder flared outward, and all her belongings were tucked back, just a bit, on their respective shelves.

Honestly, it seemed like it could have been the inside of a massive vase.

"This will work, Kit. Thank you."

The feeling of warm contentment, ever present within the pouch, was the only response. Though, Tala did feel the deficit of magic caused by such a radical rearrangement, even as she reached the bottom and saw the hand-shaped different-colored patch of wall.

"Ahh, you're hungry." She placed her hand on the offered location and refilled Kit's reserves.

Then, without delaying, she stripped, tossing the clothes upwards. They didn't come back down, so it must have worked.

Then, standing naked at the bottom of a hole dug into nowhere, she found the water incorporator and a small box of powdered soap on little bump-outs. "You think of everything, Kit."

Kit did not respond.

She took a luxuriant shower only shortened by the deeply cold temperature of the water and the knowledge that breakfast lay above.

She brushed her hair dry and free of tangles before braiding it and briefly verified her layer of iron salve was still intact and refreshing where it was lacking. She then dressed in the already clean travel clothes and climbed back out. She wasn't fully dry, but the magically incorporated water would fade soon enough.

When she reached topside once more, she returned the pouch to her belt and gave a generous dose of power to Kit once more.

That done, she fed her outfit, which was markedly low on power. *Likely drained from removing the grime, sweat, and dirt from itself and repairing the obliterated knee on the right leg earlier this morning.*

She shivered slightly even as the sun warmed her. Terry had finished his plate, and hers was suspiciously low on meat-stuff, though the predator had left her one sausage and one piece of bacon. She gave Terry a mock glare. "I'll need more than this." The other food—fruit and a surprisingly tasty oat pancake—weren't enough to fill her.

Sighing, she ate what had been left for her, then climbed down, bearing the tray and Terry, and walked back towards the chuckwagon.

Den called after her. "We're leaving in less than five minutes."

She waved back. "Thank you! I should be back before then."

Brand greeted her at the chuckwagon's back door, took her tray, and laughingly provided her with more sausage and bacon. The head cook then tossed a bit of bacon to Terry, and the terror bird caught it happily. "He's a cute one. Though, I swear, he looks much more like a miniature adult than a hatchling."

There was an awkward pause that Brand didn't seem to notice.

After a moment, he shrugged and continued. "But what do I know? It's not like I've ever seen a terror hatchling. See you around lunch."

Tala was almost back to her wagon when someone called out to her.

"Mistress Tala!"

Tala turned, a sausage freshly stuffed into her mouth. "Mmm?"

Rane came walking up behind her, his hand still wrapped in a wet towel. "Mistress Tala?"

She pushed the food into one cheek. "Yes?"

"Could I...?" He scratched the back of his head with his left hand, looking a little uncertain. "You see, my assignment for the day is to watch the front of the caravan. Would it be possible for me to...?" He looked at her expectantly.

She blinked back at him for a long moment, chewing, then swallowing. Finally, his words clicked. "Oh! Oh, ummm... Sure? Yes." She turned back towards Den's wagon, but Rane cleared his throat.

"So… I can ride on your wagon with you, today?"

She glanced back. *I suppose I wasn't clear?* "Sure? It does have a good view of the front of the caravan, after all."

*   *   *

Tala felt surprisingly awkward about performing her physical exercises with Rane present. So, instead, she decided to begin with her spiritual training.

Den had just flicked the oxen into movement when she set her knife near the front of the wagon and walked towards the rear.

Rane, for his part, had sat off to one side and was giving her a quizzical look. "Aren't you afraid that'll fall off? I believe I've sensed magic from that. It must be valuable."

Tala quirked a smile. "That's actually a really good point, Master Rane." She held up her hand, willed the knife to come, and it did, zipping through the air to stop perfectly in her hand.

Rane's eyes widened. "I didn't detect any air or movement power in that. How? Is it bound to you…?" He frowned, scratching the outside of his left eye with his right hand. "No… magic-bound items don't gain new abilities, just more means of expressing the power they already have…" He looked back to her, narrowing his eyes. "Do you have a 'come hither' inscription?"

She barked a laugh at that. "'Come hither?'" She laughed, again.

He grumbled slightly and muttered under his breath, clearly not intending her to hear. "It would explain a lot…"

Tala didn't react to the muttering, nor did she remember it for later pondering. That would have been silly.

He sighed, then looked back up. "Secret for secret then?"

She shrugged, then nodded. "You first."

He rolled his eyes but nodded in turn. "Fair enough. I've six magic-bound items. I would have seven, but one is currently with someone else…" He let out a discontented sigh.

He must be thinking about his bag-for-bodies that he left with Brand.

"My clothing is woven from the silk of a retribution spider. The fibers are insanely strong, and they pull back together when severed. I'm told it's rusting hard to work with, but they managed." He smiled. "So, that's four of my items—"

Tala cut him off. "Four?"

He shifted. "Well, yeah. My robe, pants, sandals, and… undergarment."

She blinked at him. "Sandals, too?"

He shrugged. "Well, the sandals are immortal elk leather. New, too. Those are insanely hard to kill."

She frowned. "Where'd you get the leather?" *Grediv knew what my clothes were made of.*

"Master Grediv bought the hide off of a hunter. He said there was only enough left for the sandals, so that's what I got." He smiled sadly, tapping his shoes. "This stuff's tougher than the silk, though not by too much. Even so, I'd love to not look so much like a rich fop."

She grinned at that. "You do look a bit like you're going to a ball." *Well, that explained why his clothing is always so clean and seemingly perfectly pressed.*

"So, each piece is an individual item?"

He sighed dejectedly, nodding. "Yeah. Master Grediv explained that once I become an Archon, I can meld them into one, but that's a ways away, isn't it? The books I've found agree, it seems." He smiled sadly. "Until then, I get to start each day feeding my outfit."

Her grin widened. "Ahh, a true slave to fashion."

He snorted. "Fair, fair."

"And the last two?"

He patted the wooden handle poking up from his belt. "Force, my sword, is one."

She cocked an eyebrow. "Force?"

He shrugged. "Objects only change velocity with an applied force." He patted his sword's hilt, again. "So, when I want something to change, I apply Force."

She rolled her eyes but kept smiling. "That's pretty funny."

He shrugged. "I was bored and fifteen when I named it. Seems to fit, though."

"Will you tell me what it does?"

He shook his head. "We're at first level secrets, here." His eyes twinkled a little. "That's at least…" He faked pondering. "Fifteenth level?"

She blinked at him for a moment. "Fifteenth?"

"Meh." He shrugged. "Something like that."

She shook her head. "So, the last?"

"Dimensional storage."

She looked to the sword. "Where you keep most of the sword?"

"Yeah, but that's just the smallest the opening gets."

"So… is it a pouch? Or…?"

"It's a leather cord, but more information than that is like… eighty levels of secrecy from where we are now."

She rolled her eyes again. "You're a bit of a child, aren't you." But there was mirth in her tone.

"You are what you eat?"

She gave him a perplexed look. "Say again?"

He put a hand to his face. "I'm sorry… That sounded funnier in my head."

"How?"

Rane just shook his head. "I have no idea, honestly."

Den was laughing very quietly, barely in range of Tala's hearing, and he was doing a masterful job of not letting his attention be known. Even so, Tala couldn't tell if he was laughing at the pitiful excuse for a joke or at something else. *Probably something else.*

Rane cleared his throat, clearly hoping to change the subject. "So… Those are my opening secrets. Your turn."

Tala sat. "So, funny that you mention immortal elk leather." She gestured at her outfit.

He nodded. "I thought it seemed familiar. Isn't it amazing how much it looks like fabric to the casual eye?"

She nodded. "Yeah, and it's so comfortable! It fits perfectly, stays clean, and doesn't stay torn to shreds."

"Yeah, I've never owned better shoes." He tapped one sole with the back of his knuckle. "So, that's what? Three items?"

Three? Oh… Right. She had a choice to make. She could likely lie, and he would never know, or she could be honest when it didn't cost her anything. *Truth is better.* "It's one item for me."

He frowned. "Are they joined under the tunic?"

"No… they're joined spiritually. They're one item, but not physically."

He blinked at her for a long moment, then leaned forward. "You know how to bond items together?"

"It's *very* similar to a complex spell-form that I've been working on, so yes. Master Grediv does too, so I'm not sure I should be the one to tell you…"

He nodded, leaning back. "Yeah, the Archon Star. The rusting books on bound items always seem to describe the combining of those items in reference to that spell-form. Master Grediv wrote me a description and sealed it in an envelope."

"Warded against you until when? That's just mean."

He shook his head. "No, not warded. He just said, 'Be sure you're ready before you read this.' I've never heard him so serious, before, so I decided to train more before reading it."

"That's why you're on this journey?"

He hesitated a moment, then let out a long breath. "No... Master Grediv is irritated that I haven't opened the letter, so he sent me on this as an 'eye-opening quest' to get me to take some responsibility and read the 'rust-cursed letter already.'"

She quirked a smile. "So, how long have you had it?"

He shrugged. "A few years."

She blinked. *Master Grediv thought he was ready to learn the Archon Star a few years ago?* "Huh…"

He glanced at her. "You think I should read it, too… Don't you." It wasn't really a question.

"Well… yeah. You're being offered power and a means to advance. Why not take it?"

He sighed and looked away. "I don't know if I want to have the Archon Star form given to me. I'm told that the greatest Mages discover it on their own."

She opened her mouth at that but then closed it, feeling an unexpected blush of happiness from the unwitting compliment.

"But that's not what we're talking about now, is it? You've changed the subject."

She cleared her throat. "Fair enough…" She gestured to her belt pouch. "This is my dimensional storage, Kit. And—"

"Wait, wait, wait… You named your dimensional storage?"

"Seemed reasonable."

"But… it's a bag."

"Don't listen to him, Kit. You're awesome."

The pouch did not respond.

"Mistress Tala…"

"You named your sword. Why can't I name my belt pouch?"

He opened his mouth to respond, then seemed to think better of it, shrugging and sighing. "Very well."

She then pulled out her hammer and knife. "Knife and hammer, each bound."

He looked closely. "A repeating hammer? Let me guess: Mister Taps."

She glared. "No. I haven't named it... yet." She shrugged. "I wasn't even planning on keeping it, but it was starved of magic, and I thought it was better to keep it than let it become just another hammer." *Wait, if he doesn't know about the hammer, that means Trent didn't tell the other Mages the specifics of my accident.* She felt an odd sense of gratitude for that.

Rane was still regarding the hammer. "...couldn't you have put it in an iron box?"

She gave him a long look. "Well... yes. If I'd thought of that." *Oh... I'm an idiot.* True, that assumed that most of its power loss wasn't from using its power, but even so.

He grinned at her. "You do seem to be an odd combination of 'new to this' and strangely 'in the know.'"

"That's what I do. Search out esoteric knowledge, while forgetting the basics." She shrugged. "But those are my bound items."

Terry piped up from where he was curled, squarely in the center of the padded square in the wagon's roof.

"No, Terry, I've not bonded you. Not in the way he means. And you're not an item."

Terry shimmied down a little farther, letting out a small, irritated squawk.

"He's an interesting one, isn't he?"

Tala gave him a guilty smile. "Yeah."

"How'd you find him again?"

"He tried to kill me, failed, then wouldn't go away."

Terry gave her a truly offended look, and Tala tossed him a hunk of jerky.

"Sorry, Terry, I didn't mean it like that."

The bird snapped the meat from the air and settled back into his restful pose, somewhat mollified.

"Yeah... That's not a standard hatchling."

Tala glanced to Rane and saw the inscriptions around the man's eyes already filled with power.

He looked to her. "Not my business, but don't let it kill anyone, please?"

"I'll do my best."

His face suddenly turned serious. "No, Mistress Tala. I'm serious. That bird kills *no one*. If you can't promise me that, I'll kill it now."

Terry's head came up, eyes locked onto Rane.

Tala raised a placating hand towards the bird but kept her eyes on Rane. "He won't kill anyone who doesn't need killing."

Rane hesitated, clearly hearing the gold in her tone. After a long moment, he nodded. "Very well." He looked to Terry and gave a slight bow of his head. "I apologize for any offense given."

Terry continued to regard Rane for a long moment before glancing to Tala.

Tala sighed and handed a piece of jerky to Rane.

Rane barked a short laugh, rolled his eyes, took the meat, then tossed it to Terry. Terry caught it happily and curled up once more.

"As I said, not a standard hatchling." He turned back to Tala. "I do hope you know what you're doing."

If hopes were gilded, I'd be rich. "Of course." She smiled in what she hoped was a convincing manner.

"So... you haven't explained how you can call the knife to you."

"Oh! Right." She dropped the knife over the side and waited a few moments before calling it back to her. It was more difficult calling it up and back but still within her abilities. *Don't wait so long next time...* "It's a function of the bond, to the best of my knowledge."

"The magic-bond? That shouldn't give any additional categories of ability."

She hesitated, then sighed. *In for a copper...* "A soul-bond."

He gave her a long look. "You aren't an Archon."

"No."

"Then, you shouldn't be able to work with souls, let alone form bonds."

"I'm odd like that."

He blinked at her a few times, then shook his head. "No, Mistress Tala. That's not how this works. This isn't 'I'm a Mage and fight with my fists' odd. This isn't even 'I'm an assassin, but I love to bake' odd. This is 'I'm a fish that can fly' levels of odd."

She cocked her head. "Are there flying fish—"

He raised a hand. "I'm terrible at metaphors, okay, but you get my meaning."

He is Grediv's student. "Not really?"

He groaned, scratching both of his cheeks at once as he frowned in concentration. "It's like meeting a toddler who can speak a foreign language fluently, without speaking his own, and there's no one around who speaks the other language to have taught him."

"That's... odd, I'll grant you. But an Archon Star is hardly as complex as a whole language."

"Not conceptually, but it is for your soul. Souls talk to their bodies. That's their native language."

"My soul talks to me? Wait... no. Now, I'm getting confused."

He groaned. "See? Bad at metaphors... An Archon Star is supposed to be as complex as a language for your soul, that's what makes you an Archon. But you can do soul bonds without being an Archon." He snapped his fingers, seeming excited. "It's like writing a masterwork piece of music, then claiming you can't read notes."

"That sounds... implausible."

"Exactly."

"Huh... Maybe my soul just has a nice sound to it, regardless of the skill of the composer?"

"That... that actually makes sense..." He seemed to ponder. "Is that really it, or did my metaphor mess us over?"

She shrugged. "What I'm doing works. I'm getting better at it. It seems to be good. Why gainsay it?" When his skepticism persisted, she added, "Master Grediv knows what I'm doing and gave me guidelines." After another moment, she added, "Which I am following."

He rolled his eyes but still seemed deep in thought. "You're an Immaterial Guide... Is that it?" He was muttering to himself, again. When he spoke more loudly, he seemed uncertain. "A soul is immaterial. Is your ability with guiding immaterial things allowing this to be easier for you?"

"No idea."

He grunted irritably. "Fine... fine."

She quirked a smile. "You know... if you read the letter..."

He gave her a weary half-glare. "Really?"

"Fine. Can I read it, then?"

"No!"

"Well, someone should."

He sighed, looking down at his still-bandaged hand. "I don't suppose you have any water you'd spare for this? The evaporation helps keep it cool."

She winced, remembering how she'd hurt him. "Yeah…" She pulled out her incorporator and gave it a moderate amount of power, sending a dribbling stream to re-wet the wrap.

"Those are really inefficient."

"As inefficient as carrying around barrels of water?"

He tilted his head, considering. "Huh… fair enough, I suppose. You aren't a Material Creator, after all."

That done, she had a thought. "Hey! You're an Immaterial Creator."

"Yeah…? So?"

"You changed the forces of my attack, earlier. That's a guide spell-working." She hesitated, then belatedly added, "Sorry for the low blow, by the way."

He smiled ruefully. "It was a bit of a cheap shot, but mine was hardly much better." He pulled his hand, and the re-wetted bandage, back. "As to your implied question, Master Grediv has been pushing me to bridge the quadrants for a long time. That was the first working I understood enough to add it to my inscriptions. Pretty useful, yeah?"

She snorted. "Kept you off the ground, so I'd say so."

They fell into a bit of awkward silence before Rane cleared his throat. "Do you mind if I stretch a bit? I didn't really have much of a chance to after our fight."

She shrugged. "Sure. I probably should do some physical work myself."

With that established between them, they each began working through their own sets, Tala at the front of the wagon, Rane near the back.

Tala, for her part, went through her spiritual and magical strength training as well. As breaks between groups of sets, Rane read, and Tala continued her in-depth review. They occasionally filled the silence with talk about various small things.

All in all, it was a pleasant, safe, and wise way to spend the morning, and Tala found herself smiling more and more as the time wore on, content.

Chapter: 22
A Silly Accusation

As Tala and Rane sat atop the front wagon's roof, Rane finally asked a question that caused Tala to hesitate.

"So, are you from Bandfast, then? I don't think you ever really answered that."

I could lie... but what would be the point? She sighed, sitting back down. "No... I'm not."

"Where, then?"

"Marliweather."

"Will you be heading home after we arrive in Bandfast, then?"

"Bandfast is my home, now."

"Ahh..." He looked like he wanted to ask but didn't press. Instead, he shifted to a different if related topic. "So, youngest?"

"Oldest. You?"

"Middle. Dead middle. Five above and five below."

"Ahhh. Got lost there?"

"A bit, until Master Grediv picked me." He gained a bit of a mischievous smile. "My eldest brother had been campaigning for *months* to get Master Grediv to come to our home and evaluate him. He was basically ready to be certified as a full Mage. Even so, he hoped to be a mageling under Master Grediv." His smile widened. "After testing my brother, Grediv said, and I'll never forget his words, 'Why would I want to paint on a used canvas?' He rejected him on the spot. My brother was so startled that he never actually responded." Rane let out a small laugh. "That knocked him from his high horse. It mortified Mother and Father, too. Then, Grediv looked around, muttering about a wasted trip before seeing me. He pointed me out and said, and I'm not joking, 'You! Blank canvas. Get over here. We're leaving.' And that was that."

"He's a colorful one, isn't he?"

"Oh, you've no idea. So, what about you? Eldests usually have a lot of responsibility."

She huffed a mirthless laugh. "You could say that. I wasn't born the eldest, but I was when I left. Eldest of twelve. My elder brother, may his soul be gilt in gold, was really a half-brother. His mother died in childbirth, as did mine. I guess my father got better at picking a woman after that, because the other rascals all came from his third wife."

"Not kind to you?"

"Oh, she was fine. Treated me like her own, then helped give me the family debts and send me off to repay them." She froze. She'd not told anyone that. *Why are you blathering, Tala?*

Rane smiled consolingly. "Ahh, indentured into the craft, then... even more than most. I'm sorry to hear it. I've heard of such, but I can't say I've met any, what with not going to the academy."

She hesitated, then sighed. *Already talking about it, I suppose.* "Not many at the academy, either. It takes a union of large debts and magical aptitude for such to happen, usually."

"Well, I'm sorry. That's a pretty bad hand to be dealt."

"I'll admit, I considered just dying and leaving the rusting people with nothing, but I think I'm mainly over that." She snorted a laugh. "I honestly think I tilted so far towards defense as a reaction to that way of thinking." She found herself smiling, just a bit, despite the topic. "Many have it worse, and things are looking up." She shrugged.

"I'll pay off my debt and then be better off than I ever hoped."

"Good way to look at it, I suppose. Glad you took countermeasures, I suppose. You do seem a bit carefree about danger."

"Yeah, I'm working on that." She glanced away.

There was a short lull before Rane refocused the conversation. "So, how did they justify it? Sending you off to a better life?"

"Don't know. Refused to talk to them after I heard, and I haven't spoken to them since I left."

He seemed stunned by the revelation. "Tala… I…" He closed his mouth, frowning. After a long moment, he nodded then spoke. "Losing your family like that… I'm sorry, Mistress Tala."

She gave a sad smile. "I appreciate that." And, strangely, she found that she actually did.

"Do you… Do you think you'll ever see them again?"

She snorted. "I used to have these grand plans. Pay off the debt, get a mountain of gold, and go throw a handful at their feet. 'How do you like that? I'm just gold to you, right?' But it seems really childish, now."

He gave her a half-grin. "Just a bit. Would probably be cathartic, though."

She grinned in return. "It would, at that." She sighed. "Let's talk about something else, yeah?" She scratched the side of her neck. "We'll be in Bandfast tomorrow, right?" The days had flown by on this return trip.

"Tomorrow evening, that's right."

"It will be good to be home. And, it seems we have a place to train, right?"

"Yeah, Guardsman Adam seemed *quite* interested in seeing you hurt me again."

She rolled her eyes. "I don't think that was it."

"Fair, fair. But it should be fun."

She just smiled in response. *Yeah. It should be.*

The morning passed amicably, and Brand brought lunch for Tala and Terry almost perfectly at high noon.

When he saw Rane, he gave Tala an odd look but didn't otherwise comment. Shortly after the cook left, however, the servant for Rane's wagon clumsily climbed up the ladder, bearing Rane's lunch.

"Oh! Thank you, Manth."

The servant nodded. "Will you be needing anything else, good Master?"

"No, thank you."

The servant gave a slight bow and left, climbing back down and hopping free of the still-moving wagon.

Rane seemed a bit embarrassed. "I forgot to let him know where I was going to be for lunch… I'll apologize to him this evening."

Tala shrugged, not feeling the need to comment.

They ate, chatting about various small things. When Terry vanished after finishing what Brand had brought, Rane paused, mid-sentence, and gave Tala a flat look.

"He's fine. He won't hurt anyone from the caravan, and we're the only people out here."

Rane didn't press further.

After lunch, Tala continued her note-taking review of anatomy, and Rane read while their stomachs settled. At nearly the exact right time, Adam arrived. In lieu of sparring, he first worked with Tala on her basic techniques.

After that, it was decided that Adam should see Rane move through his own attack and defensive patterns.

His sword was two handed and as tall as he was, a true greatsword.

The cross-guard, it seemed, was sequestered within Rane's dimensional storage, along with half the handle, thus only a single hand's worth of the hilt was exposed for easy drawing of the weapon.

As he pulled it free, Tala had found herself gawking.

It was entirely wood in appearance. Its grain was tight but clear, and the red tone of the material made it look almost dipped in blood, then left to dry. The color had not been at all clear from the small portion of the hilt that had been poking out, though that didn't make much sense to Tala.

The power flowing through the weapon was two-fold. First, the obviously required strength and sharpness magics were readily apparent. Second, there were hints of kinetic energy redirection that seemed similar to her hammer but more refined and tailored to the martial applications of a sword.

When Rane pulled the blade free, a little clumsily because of his still-bandaged hand, Tala got a good look at the magics. She shook her head. "No."

Adam gave her a puzzled look, and Rane cocked his head. "What?"

"You heard me. No. That looks like an item, perfectly inscribed for your needs, but it's an artifact. There is *no* way that's a coincidence."

Rane gave a sheepish half-smile. "I'm really lucky?"

She sighed. "You'll tell me later."

He sighed in turn. "Maybe…"

She narrowed her eyes, giving him a searching look.

"Hey, it isn't a 'no,' alright?"

"Fine…"

Adam didn't understand magic item variations, exactly, and he seemed content with his ignorance. He ignored their exchange and instructed Rane to walk him through his fighting style.

That took more than an hour, and Rane just covered the basics, while Adam was asking *extensive* questions. Most demonstrations were short, due to Rane's hand, but they cleared up questions that would have been hard to answer with words alone. Finally, Adam had to depart, and Rane and Tala went back to their alternations of training and chatting.

Terry returned sometime during Rane's demonstration for Adam, but no one commented on his arrival.

Other than the oddly tailored artifact, the day passed without incident.

More than a couple dozen small, arcanous encounters came and went, though Rane wasn't needed to repel any of them, and Tala restrained herself from interfering. The guards handled most, and the other Mages were in better position for the others, so their pattern was uninterrupted.

It was actually a pleasant way to spend the day, if Tala was being honest.

Ashin came by and sparred with Tala, while Rane continued to read. The guardsman was a bit hesitant, given her earlier damaging of Rane, but Ashin got past it quick enough. Tala, for her part, kept to the basics that Adam had been teaching her. *No more damaging partners, Tala.*

The wagon train pulled into formation for the night, and dinner came and went. Trent finally asked Tala about her endingberry harvesting, and she gave the barest of answers possible without lying. She felt a bit bad, but she didn't intend on telling him, or anyone, that she had gallons of endingberry juice on hand. Also, as much as she trusted Trent, she was *not* going to share about the men Terry had killed to protect her. *Nope, nothing good down that road.*

The only thing of true note that evening was Tang.

As Tala headed back towards her wagon, finally alone for the night, Tang called out to her, hurrying across the larger circle of wagons. "Mistress Tala! A moment, please."

Tala turned, Terry on her shoulder, and waited for the older Mage. She frowned as she saw something in his hand. *Is that...?*

He held the item out in question. "I found one! I had a whole host of collars to search through, but I did, indeed, have one for a young creature with dimensional magics."

Tala cocked an eyebrow. "You just happened to have the exact collar we need?"

"Hmmm? No, of course not. I have at least one of almost every variation."

She blinked at him in confusion. "What?" *Wait... Tang was the buyer?* That made a sort of sense now that she thought about it.

He smiled. "The foremost artisan of arcane domestic collars lives in Alefast. I bought out her supply and then some. I bought up every available collar in the city!" He gave her a self-satisfied smile. "I'm carrying them to Bandfast, then on to other cities, to sell." He was nodding happily as he spoke. "It's a side venture. I get all my funds in hard currency, travel to Alefast, transfer the money to my account with the bonus, then spend the increased amount on goods to travel back with. Once a year, I do so with collars. In the spring, it's…" He hesitated, giving her a sidelong look, then waved the topic away. "Never mind that. I've an exclusive deal with her, so I don't mind telling you about the collars. I buy out all that she can make in a year, virtually every year. Have for half a decade."

Tala blinked. *That is surprisingly reasonable… still a bit fortuitous.* "And this particular collar costs…?"

Tang's eyes held a glint of greed. "Well, this particular collar has three features that make it more expensive than most. First, it is a growth collar, meaning it's designed to remain perfectly sized for the arcane creature as it changes size, growing with it. It's dynamic, so it doesn't require fiddling with buckles or the like. Second, it is designed to connect with its wearer, becoming integrated, so that it moves with them. My understanding is it alters the collar so that the creature's magic sees it as a part of it. I'm not privy to the 'how,' unfortunately. Now that would be a valuable bit of information..." He seemed to lose himself for a moment before snapping his focus back to their conversation. "Where was I? Right! This feature is specific to dimensional arcanous creatures, so they can't jump out of it. Without that, the collar will be left behind, and the creature killed, if it's within the city."

Tala gave Terry a glance. The bird looked a bit wide-eyed. "Yeah... that would not be ideal."

"Finally, it is a training collar. It is two pieces, woven together. For lack of a better description, you magically bond one, the terror hatchling the other. It uses the magic of any city you are in to ensure that the creature stays within a hundred yards of you. It won't do anything outside of cities, but it shouldn't need to, yes?"

She frowned. "I really can't get over how convenient it is that you have exactly what we need."

Tang sighed. "Dimensional rabbits and cats are very popular pets, and arcanous dogs are often used as guard animals. This is actually one of the more common collars, after the generic. The only really stand-out feature is the growth component, but as most pets, and guard animals, are acquired very young, this is, again, not a rare feature."

"What about the fact that you have collars at all?"

He lifted his hands in frustration. "Would you prefer I have barrels of ale and not be able to help you?"

Tala frowned. *No...* "I'm sorry, Master Tang. I'm just suspicious of things that seem too good to be true." She sighed. *That has been happening a lot the last three weeks or so...* "I apologize. Thank you."

He smiled, seeming at least somewhat mollified. "I suppose I can understand that... If it makes you feel better, the collars are only one of about eight different types of artisan goods I'm taking with me."

"What else?"

He gave her a flat look.

She smiled at that. "Fair enough." She looked to Terry. The bird hesitated, seeming to examine the collar. "So, it doesn't do anything outside of cities?"

"That's right. Except stay on."

"How often will it need to be recharged or re-inscribed?"

"It won't."

Tala cocked an eyebrow.

"It is more like an incorporator, for its basic functions. From what I'm told, it alters how the creature's powers are perceived by city defenses. The resizing comes from the wearer's own dimensional power once the item is worn and bonded. And the tether, for lack of a better word, works similarly." He shrugged. "Most standard collars don't need to be reinscribed or recharged, because they only have that basic lens-like function. If this was a growth collar for a non-dimensional animal, that would be a different thing entirely."

In truth, Tala had never studied such things, but it seemed plausible. "Alright... What happens if he tries to enter a city, and I'm nowhere around?"

"I've never seen that attempted myself, but I would bet that the city's defenses would bar his entry or strike him down, depending on his persistence."

Simple... The lensing effect again? Changing the incoming defenses to a forbidding? She was out of her depth... again. *There are so many fine variations of magic items...* She needed to finish reading the volumes she had available on the subject. *After the anatomy refresher.* "Fine... How much?" She was loath to ask. She looked to Terry, again, as covertly as possible. The bird gave a slight bob.

"For this? At such a time of need? Five ounces gold."

And Tang's earlier change of attitude suddenly made sense. *The rusting...* "Five? That's insane!"

"Supply and demand, Mistress. You've a demand, and I've a supply. An unscrupulous man would charge you double that."

"Three."

He shook his head. "No, Mistress Tala. The price is five."

Her eyes narrowed. "What would it cost in the city?"

"For this?" He held it up. "Honestly, if I sell it in Bandfast, I'll get three or four ounces gold. If I take it to a farther city, I'd get four and a half or five. I can get as much as six, with the right buyer."

He didn't really have a reason to lie as he didn't seem to have any interest in negotiating. She silently grimaced. *He also basically admitted that I could buy it from him in Bandfast for three...*

Terry flickered and was suddenly holding the collar. Tala's eyes snapped to him, and Tang gasped as the transport seemed to activate something within the strip of leather.

The collar whipped out and wrapped around Terry's neck, settling into place partially hidden by his feathers, down near his shoulders. The dark color of the leather blended nicely with his plumage.

Tala reached out to touch the collar feeling around the outside. *No seam.* It felt hungry, though, like her bound items, and without thinking, she fed it a trickle of power.

Tang stood there, open-mouthed, as a tendril of power locked onto her, and she knew the dual magic bond was complete, her to the collar, and the collar to Terry.

Tala looked up to Tang. "So, if you want, I can cut it off of him. Otherwise... you said three gold ounces, right?"

Tang's eyes widened further, anger clearly beginning to build within the man. "Now look here. You just stole that from me! You can't steal a pie, wolf it down, and then offer to give it back if the baker doesn't agree to a lower price."

He had a point. *Rust it.* "Fine. Four."

Tang opened his mouth, clearly going to reject her offer, if not call for the guards, but neither of them had noticed Trent approaching. "Master Tang." The Mage placed a hand on the older man's shoulder. "What seems to be the problem?"

Tang turned on the man. "Master Trent, Mistress Tala just stole from me, then willfully bonded the item without purchasing it."

"I heard and saw. The bird snatching a bit of leather you dangled before it is quite expected, as you likely knew."

Tang cleared his throat and glanced away.

"You are right, though, that Tala chose to bond with the item. But that likely simply stole a bargaining chip you'd hoped to employ. How much were you planning to charge her to not bond the collar yourself?" He gave Tang a hard look. "Trying to steal her hatchling, were you?"

Tala frowned. *That makes no sense. Collar or no, Terry wouldn't have gone with him… except, he believes Terry is a hatchling, and he bet that either I'd pay up, or he could take over training Terry, himself.*

Tang shook his head. "That is a silly accusation." *Maybe, he's right… It doesn't seem likely to have worked…*

Trent cocked an eyebrow. "Then, how about we end this in good faith? She pays you four gold ounces, and everyone walks away."

Tang began to object, but Trent gave him a hard look. "That is plenty of profit for you, Master Tang. You know that it is."

The older Mage closed his mouth, clearly still unhappy. "Fine." He pulled out a small stone tablet and made a few alterations before pricking his finger and confirming his side of the transaction. "Here."

He held it out to Tala, and she saw that it was for a transfer from a buyer's account to his, in the amount of four ounces gold.

Tala let out a defeated sigh. "Fine." Then, she confirmed the transaction. The tablet flickered green, then went blank.

Tang grumbled at her for a moment after taking the stone slate back, then stalked off.

Trent was shaking his head. "Well, at least I know, now, why he was being so out of character."

Tala was afraid to ask, but she did anyways. "How much should this have cost?" She lightly touched the collar.

"Hmmm? Oh, three or four gold is a reasonable, if higher-end, price. He was hoping for five, clearly. I don't know if he was actually going to try to extort more if your hatchling had bonded the collar before the sale, but I wouldn't put it past him."

"That's... He didn't seem like that much of..."

Trent shrugged. "Then, maybe not. From what I know of him, he is genuinely fascinated by arcane creatures, so that wasn't an act, but he is also obsessed with building his fortune. He's given up studying or improving magically and simply plays the trader."

"Is it working?"

"Don't know, don't really care."

She smiled. "Fair enough. Thank you, Master Trent."

"Happy to help, Mistress Tala."

She hesitated a moment, then smiled, giving Trent a nod. "Goodnight."

"Goodnight."

Without another word, they each turned towards their respective beds.

*   *   *

Tala woke, late in the night, suppressing her own screams.

She'd learned to scream silently through her years at the academy. Most people were sympathetic the first time you woke from a nightmare screaming, but after a few weeks of near-nightly wails?

No one had patience for that.

Why are you back...? She couldn't even muster the strength to be properly irritated. The nightmare was always the same, always stupid and childish.

Her parents pushing her under a falling ledger.

That was it.

Oh, there was usually variation in the buildup. Sometimes the family, now faceless with years to forget details, would go to a park for a picnic before the falling ledger would appear. She would try to escape with her family, and her father would trip her, leaving her behind.

Or they'd be climbing a tower, and he'd push her out a window as the ledger swept past.

Or she'd be watching her younger siblings, and her mother would rush in to snatch the young ones from her arms before scurrying away just in time for the wall to shatter, the book coming through to crush Tala.

It's the most ridiculous thing I've ever heard of... But she still woke screaming, silent or not.

She wiped a stray strand of hair from her face. *I thought I escaped these...* Perhaps, it was the contemplations of her debt that had returned the dream. *Idiot. I can't plan a way out from under the debt if I can't think about it...*

With a groan, she stood and moved off the roof, leaving Terry asleep atop her bedroll.

She checked the sky, verifying that it was sometime after midnight. *Good enough.*

She charged the twenty cargo-slots with ease, her work and practice obviously paying off, even given her tired mind.

After the short bit of work, she still wasn't quite far enough removed from the dream to ensure she wouldn't return to it if she fell back asleep. Returning to the dream was worse by far.

She would be trapped, unable to move, barely able to breathe under the suffocating weight of the ledger book.

Even so, she would hear her family going about their lives, out of sight, ignoring her whimpers, her pleas, for help.

She never woke from this part screaming. She felt lucky to wake at all. The dream would continue uninterrupted, forcing her to live every minute of it, crushed by the weight of their indifference until dawn woke her.

I hate them. She drew her knife and strained against her gate, rage and hate and hope and desperation fueling her.

The blade of the knife liquified, slowly flowing outward to form the hair thin outline of a sword blade. *Almost... there...!*

But that was as far as she could push it. There was no satisfying *click* as she passed the threshold to ignite the aura within the blade, though she suspected it would still cut.

In anger, she strode towards a nearby rock formation and swung an enraged horizontal slash.

The sword passed the rock, and nothing happened. She felt no resistance; she felt nothing at all.

Her anger sputtered, and her gate closed marginally, removing the flowrate required. The knife shrank back into its resting form.

Useless.

She sheathed the knife and kicked the base of the stone. Nothing happened.

Well, there goes that hope. Some part of her had imagined the rock sliding apart, her cut having been so perfect that the stone didn't move until disturbed. *That's what you get from hoping...*

Still, she was focused on the rock, causing her magesight to activate.

As it did, she blinked in shock. *What?*

She could see power flowing through the stone, as it did in all things in the wilds.

That flow was broken.

In the rock, where she had cut, the flows of magic no longer connected. The tendrils of power had been routed around the line, stretching deep within the stone, and new patterns had developed.

It cut the magic? That made no sense. If you actually broke a flow of magic, power would burst forth, doing who knew what. *So, what then?*

She looked closer and saw a hair thin line in the rock, only visible to her enhanced senses because her magesight told her precisely where to look. *It did cut the rock?* No, no material had been removed...

Her eyes widened. A blade with no appreciable width. Her blade hadn't been long enough to cut all the way through the rock formation, so there was no way for the stone to move, but she *had* cut it perfectly. The upper piece was now resting on the lower.

Well, rust me through. She looked at the knife at her hip and smiled. "Nicely done." She patted the handle. "I think we'll get good use out of you, soon enough."

She pulled herself back to the present and looked around at the night landscape. "But not now... Now, I need to rest."

It had been long enough.

She crawled back into her bedroll and gazed at the stars through the light cloud cover overhead.

Her last thoughts weren't promising as she drifted off to sleep, *I feel like I'm forgetting something important...*

Even so, blessedly, the dream did not return.

Chapter: 23
Crush

Tala didn't know if she'd been asleep for a moment or hours, but when Terry jumped up, she suddenly found herself fully awake, throwing off her coverings.

"What's going on?" She looked around frantically, her vision slightly blurry but clearing fast.

Her sleep-addled mind, while awake, was not focused yet, even as she tried to take in their surroundings.

No one else was awake, but Terry was staring up at the cloudy sky, crouched and wary.

Tala looked up as power flickered around the terror bird, taking him away.

She had just enough time to blearily wonder why a large portion of the sky was so much darker than the rest when an arcanous avian slammed into her, its massive talons closing around her torso.

She didn't have time to fight as it snatched her from the roof of the wagon, bearing her off into the cloud-shrouded sky.

Tala's first reaction was to yell for help, but the nearly crushing grip of the great bird kept her from drawing a full breath, and the initial impact had driven the air from her lungs in a soundless *whoosh.*

Unable to scream, she tried to turn and bring her magic to bear, but she had been snatched in a way to force her to be face down, and so all she could see was the ground rushing past below.

In theory, she could lock onto the creature by targeting the talons wrapped around her, but she was iffy on the result, which might just be the claws opening to drop her.

Now that she thought about it, even if she could target the beast, best case would be the bird dropping from the air like a super heavy rock to land directly on top of her.

Not a great plan, Tala. Could she use Restrain? *That wasn't designed to affect anything this high up... What would it even do?* It was probably not a good idea to test that spell-working with her life on the line.

What else did she have at her disposal?

Her knife. *Yeah, that would work.*

The caravan was already lost to her sight in the blackness, and if her eyes weren't deceiving her, snow was beginning to fall. *Just my luck.* She almost laughed at that. She knew she'd been lucky of late. *Just my fate?* She hoped to the stars that this wasn't reality balancing the scales…

Flickers of dimensional energy zig-zagged across the landscape below her, but if she was right in her guess, she was moving much faster than a galloping horse… or a teleporting terror bird.

Right, knife! She scrabbled at her side, trying to get to the weapon that she had hanging there, but she couldn't reach it as it was pinned to her side by one of the massive taloned toes.

She panted, trying to draw in enough breath for her continued efforts. *Where is it taking me?*

She craned her neck, looking in the direction they were flying, allowing herself to focus and her magesight to activate despite the range.

Mountains loomed before and below her. The largest were not close, but they were coming closer far faster than she'd have wished. Hanging her head down, she actually thought she could see the lights of cities in the distance in varying directions. *How high are we?*

That prompted her to check her endingberry power reserves. *Not bad.* She wished she had more, and she wasn't sure if it would protect her from such a fall…

Wait until we land? It was likely taking her back to its nest to eat her… *Why not kill me and eat me closer?*

The obvious answer came to her mind immediately. *Babies… She's going to feed me to her babies.*

Tala had no issues killing baby monsters, though she doubted it would be that easy. *If I'm even right… Maybe just back to the flock?*

Her arms were free, but the strength of the grip around her middle left no doubt as to the power of the bird holding her aloft, so she didn't even try to pry the talons open. *Not worth the effort.*

She briefly considered trying to pull the knife to her hand, spiritually, but dismissed the idea. If she tried to pull it out, it would have to overcome the strength of the talon holding it in place. *I'll have to wait until we land to fight.*

This was a new experience. Most of her violent encounters had been sudden, save her slaying of the thunder bull for which she had a plan, however dubious. Now, she knew that she would be in a fight for her life very soon, but not now.

I can pull magic to fuel the sword, and that is likely my best weapon, beyond gravitation magic, which may or may not easily work… The midnight fox was still fresh in her mind, and if anything, she felt more stressed about this fight than that.

Okay. Focus, Tala. Don't think about then, think about now.

She took a deep breath… well, she tried.

She took several slow, shallow breaths. *I need as much magic as I can get.*

Tala threw her gate wide, pulling magic into herself and keeping it close around her gate, not allowing it to pour through her inscriptions. As Holly had demonstrated some weeks before, Tala already had a *very* high magic density. Under duress, Mages could usually hold beyond their capacity for a short time, but it was only a fraction more than normal.

For Tala, a fraction more was still an ocean of power to most new Mages. *Probably not Archons, but still...*

She drew deeply, doing her utmost to increase the flow, which would also help sustain the sword when she invoked it.

Scant minutes later, she was truly full, near to bursting, and the mountains only appeared a bit nearer. *Huh, I started too early...* She examined the mountains, seeing that the tallest were farther than she'd originally thought and much bigger.

Her focus also highlighted close to a dozen more flying, arcanous creatures, lower down.

Tala's abductor seemed to be losing altitude, heading for those other birds. If her guess was right, it hadn't even been half an hour since she'd been snatched up. *And... can't wait. Here's hoping!*

She was belly down, so her first two fingers were extended towards the ground, rather than the sky. The second two bent down. All four fingers and thumb were tucked close together. She then slapped the clawed foot holding her, and the avian blossomed white to her vision, even the wing tips, which occasionally came into view lit up. *Yes!*

She was not startled that the color of her targeting had changed. It simply made sense. Blue, now, meant something different to her, especially after the distant conflict she'd so recently witnessed.

Focus, Tala. Mind on the fight.

She extended the two bent, outer fingers, altering the configuration of the spell-forms. *Crush.*

Power leapt through her already wide-open gate and down the spell-lines for her one lethal attack spell.

The gravitational constant was altered for the large bird, and they suddenly began to drop.

Yes! Now, I just need to survive... Could I get into Kit if it lets me go? That might actually work...

Power exploded from the bird as its reservoirs of power began to drain at a markedly increased rate, granting greater lift to the creature, and they leveled off.

Oh, come on!

Her spell-forms were still active, the target still intact. A second golden circle burned away. The exception her magic had created for the target within the gravitational constant was amended, the beast's weight quadrupling again.

They began dropping once more, much faster this time. Tala *pushed* downward. It was an odd sensation.

Again, the beast pulsed with power. It reacted more quickly this time, and it began gaining altitude instead of just leveling off.

Not good... It's now an endurance game. But she had seventeen rings to throw at this stupid bird. It was laughable in the extreme to think the beast could resist what would end up being billions of times the normal force of gravity...

Yeah... I'll die from any impact far weaker than that.

The other arcanous avians were getting closer.

A third golden ring was burned away, and it was too much for the bird that was carrying her. It streaked for the ground.

In the animal's panic, it began flailing. Tala was tossed out into open sky with a slight upward arc, relative to the plummeting bird. *Huh, that worked out well.*

Another avian snatched her as she began to arc back down. *Or not. Are you rusting kidding me!*

She targeted the new avian, even as a fourth ring burned away, activating just before her original kidnapper slammed into the ground with a thunderous boom, the sickening snapping of bones a subtle background to the greater cacophony of the general impact.

The new bird didn't seem content to just carry her, and it began pecking at her even as it tightened its grip. They were probing jabs that didn't even pierce her elk leather, yet.

Rust you, too! It was already targeted. *Crush.*

It immediately began to plummet, flinging her aside. The new bird was clearly weaker than the first because it never recovered, though its struggling did prolong its plummet towards the ground and death long enough that a second golden ring was burned to increase the pull.

Six down... not good. Her spell-forms were not designed for aerial combat.

She began laughing a bit manically as she fell. *Humans aren't designed for aerial combat!*

Another bird struck at her as she fell, and she lashed out. Despite her now spinning perspective, the rushing wind, and the quickly approaching ground, she got a lock. *Crush!* The third one dropped towards its death.

A fourth swooped up, catching her and carrying her up quickly. The sudden switch of direction whipped her neck painfully, or it should have, but the endingberry power came through. By the sensation, and the amount of power lost, small though it was, she should have just broken her neck and spine in at least four places.

This just gets better and better.

To her surprise, her knife was now uncovered, though she couldn't reach it.

She called it from her belt, and it whipped into her waiting hand. Flush with power, she dumped it into the knife, and it flowed outward into the shape of a sword, even as she swept it behind her back. The great bird—she still couldn't tell what species it was—screamed in abject agony, and Tala fell free, still clutched in the now-severed claws.

She stopped the flow of power to her sword, and it returned to the form of a knife. She kept her gate thrown wide, taking the brief space of time to begin refilling her body's reserves.

Another bird dove for her as she began to pick up speed. It was diving beak first. *So, not to catch me.*

Her right hand came up in a perfect, practiced gesture, her knife tossed to her left on pure instinct. Only a small tug with her spirit guided the knife into her left grip. *Huh, I can call it to my other hand, too? Why didn't I ever try that before?*

The bird was highlighted in a glowing white. *Crush.*

Two gold rings were burned away at once. A second ring for the third bird, just before it impacted, and a new ring for this new bird.

The jerk downward on her most recent attempted attacker caused it to mostly miss.

Blessedly, as it fought the influence of her magic and tried to pull upward, it bumped her from below, even as it streaked past.

This had two effects, one good, one bad. Good: it slowed her quite a bit, the much greater mass of the bird easily stealing much of her momentum, though it felt like landing from a great height even so, making her joints ache. Bad: it started her spinning, end over end.

Even with her enhanced senses, she was unable to focus or right herself.

One.

Two.

Millennial Mage, Book 2 - Mage

Three birds struck her in quick succession, increasing the spin, driving in unpredictable directions, and wearing away at her reserves.

Then, she struck the ground.

* * *

A pulse of power exploded from the base of Tala's skull, and she returned to consciousness, violently.

She was lying in the bottom of a crater, staring up at a cloudy sky, snow gently settling around her.

A shiver ran through her from head to toe, and a sense akin to her magesight picked up the signature of what had awoken her. It was the inscription, set to watch for any loss of consciousness not due to falling asleep.

Once again, a sound, almost like a bell, hummed through her thoughts. Even knowing it was coming, she jumped at the internal sound. She ground her teeth in a purely voluntary response. *Rust Holly, that note is calming, and now is not a time to be calm.*

Then, a mockery of her own voice came to her, once again.

-Consciousness lost for 0.50 seconds due to unknown, full-body impact. Defensive magics of unknown origin consumed to negate all but a fractional portion of the damage. Severe concussion was imminent. Unknown magics did not seem to protect neural tissue to the same extent as the rest of subject's physicality. Noted for later study.-

-Cranial inscriptions activated to cushion dura-mater.-

-Mild, targeted, electrical shock and hormone cocktail utilized for near instant resuscitation.-

-No lasting effects detected or predicted.-

-Ancillary note: Repeating such activities is ill-advised.-

-Log complete.-

Three times. *I've been rendered unconscious three times...* That couldn't be good for her. And now the magics were getting uppity with her. *Great.*

She groaned, pushing herself upright. She checked herself over. Her clothing was pulling back together, having suffered from the blunt force of the impact, but its reserves had been full, so she didn't give it another thought.

Worryingly, her endingberry power reserves were all but exhausted. *How hard did I hit?*

The deep depression in the earth, in which she was currently standing, seemed to indicate: hard.

After she'd had a moment to consider, she realized that she was lucky to be standing, let alone have any power in reserve.

Unfortunately, the screeching of arcanous avians overhead told her the fight wasn't over.

She was now where she was used to: on solid ground. *My turn!* As she stood, she noted that she had seven remaining golden rings on the back of her right hand. Apparently, it had taken another to bring down the fourth bird. *May your soul be plucked...*

Quickly, she let her eyes and magesight sweep the sky. She locked on to every bird she could see as they swept lower to get a better look at her.

She took down seven more birds in quick succession, each dropping from the sky into the ground more quickly than they could compensate, each one rendered dead upon impact. *How big is this flock?*

She counted three more birds, still circling overhead, and she was out of offensive magic.

Not bad, Tala. Seven for seven. She ignored the ten to four ratio from her fight in the air. That had been unusual circumstances. Once her feet were on the ground, she was able to be more strategic with her resources. *I wonder if I'll be able to harvest anything from these raven-spawned nightmares.*

Indeed, she'd finally gotten a good enough look to determine that they were some form of arcanous raven. The magics she could discern were entirely for flight, far-sight, strength, and regeneration.

Come on… Are you coming down or not!

As if in response to her thoughts, the first one dove for her.

She held her knife off to the side, building up power just before the sword-path within the weapon.

The war-pick of a beak streaked towards her at unbelievable speeds.

Her perception let her see it coming.

This was not something that she'd practiced, but it was close enough to dodging a punch that it allowed her now quite-practiced muscles to feel the movement as familiar.

She waited as long as she felt was wise, then dove to the side.

She slashed out, pushing the pulse of power outward, forcing the knife to flow into a sword mid-swing.

Her timing was off.

She dodged too early, allowing the bird to track with her, but not perfectly. It dealt her a cutting, glancing blow as it shot past, draining the dregs of endingberry power from her, even as it caused half her body to light with defensive spell-forms.

And… it *hurt*.

She spun away, immediately letting the knife flow back into its resting form.

Blood splattered the ground around her, and she realized that she'd cut the beast, too, though not fatally.

It cried in rage even as it beat great wings, tempests of magic swirling, to regain height.

Not great, but not bad.

She had a new problem now, however.

She was glowing.

The next bird dove, spotting and tracking with her much more ease. *Come on, Tala!*

She delayed a heartbeat longer this time, and she struck, empowering the path of the sword within the knife once more.

She struck true.

The blade, just as for the rock, gave her no resistance as the bird passed.

She failed to duck beneath the wing, and its incredibly resilient flight feathers sliced across her like so many razors, even as she bisected the creature's main body, beak to tail. The lower portion dropped away, sloshing across the ground behind her even as the wings continued for a short way, the magic of their flight maintained ever so briefly.

The slices across her had been as a passing cut, so she didn't *think* she was bruised.

Her clothes pulled back together over her still-glowing flesh, and she wheezed in air, trying to recover her breath. *More endingberries!* She felt like an idiot for not thinking of it sooner.

She pulled out her flask, opened it and tipped it back... empty... She hadn't refilled it after her last drink. *Stupid. Stupid!*

The third bird was coming in for its turn. No more time. *One injured, one down, and one to go.*

She timed her counterstrike perfectly this time... for an attack that didn't come.

She swept her flowing blade through empty air, where the attacker should have been, but the avian had flared its wings at the last instant, stopping so suddenly that Tala had trouble believing it was possible.

Instead of streaking through where she had been, beak used as a lance, the bird seemed to hang in the air before her, talons already striking out.

Her still-moving sword, by chance more than anything else, split one of the great bird's feet, even as the other drove Tala backward, easily slicing through her leathers, hitting previously un-struck flesh and activating her defensive scripts there.

It's smart enough to know the glowing part has some sort of defense... That wasn't great.

They each struck again, Tala wildly, the bird with animalistic instinct and precision.

Tala stumbled back with more of her skin glowing and the certain knowledge that *something* within her was broken.

No time for that now. She was about to strike with the sword, again, when she realized that she was dangerously low on power. She pulled back from the path of the sword, and the knife was once more in her hand.

In desperation, she plunged her hand into Kit, pulled out the hammer, and flung it in one motion.

The bird was still beating its wings and tried to twist away, the full exchange having taken less than a handful of heartbeats.

The hammer struck the bird in the head, and for a moment, Tala despaired. *I'm not wielding it! Will it activate?* She screamed out with her will: *Kill it!*

The hammer's power blossomed outward, hitting the bird again, and again, and again in a single continuous impact. The sound of cracking bone was sweeter than any she'd ever heard.

What remained of the bird went instantly limp, dropping to the ground with a *whump* in the snow.

Snow? Snow was, indeed, gathering about her. Her impact and the beating of her attackers' wings had mostly cleared the nearby space, but even so, there were drifts of the stuff all around her.

How high up in the mountains did it take me?

But now wasn't the time.

The final arcanous ravenine dropped silently from the sky, directly overhead. *I already injured that one.*

She had no tricks left. Her only hope was that it didn't crush her, or otherwise break through her defenses, before she could stab it sufficiently with the knife to kill it or drive it away.

A flicker of dimensional energy was the herald of glory as Terry appeared, now larger than the attacking bird, his powerful claws seizing the final opponent around the neck and jerking it off-course.

The two birds tumbled to the ground, Terry immediately vanishing and appearing behind the flier.

He struck, again, and again, and again. Each time from a different direction. Each time evoking a fountain of blood and a screech of enraged pain.

The flier tried to beat its wings and retreat to the sky.

Terry forbade such a retreat.

The fight was so laughably one-sided, that Tala, indeed, began to laugh despite the pain in her sides that screamed of broken bones.

Her stress, fear, anger, horror... All her emotions came crashing down upon her in an uncontrollable laugh. *I'm going to live.*

In the snow, as her companion eviscerated and then began to consume her final attacker, Tala laughed and laughed and laughed, tears flowing freely down her ashen face.

Chapter: 24
One Thousand Ounces Gold

Tala slowly got her emotions under control but was left shaking as much from the physical backlash of fading terror as from the cold wind whipping snow about her. *Ahh, adrenaline; how I wish I didn't need you.*

"Thank you, Terry." Her voice was steadier than she'd expected it to be. "Any interest in some jerky?"

The terror bird wearily lifted his blood-painted beak from the downed arcane bird and regarded her for a long moment. Finally, he shook himself to indicate a negative. He then returned to gorging on his fallen prey. Terry's movements were slower than she was used to seeing. *How hard did he have to push to stay so close?*

Tala, for her part, took out her incorporator, painstakingly funneling power from her gate into the device, and took long, careful drinks. Jerky followed, and she chewed and swallowed at a measured pace. Some leftover, heavy bread was next.

As she ate, she trudged through the snow towards the closest downed enemy not currently being eaten by Terry. It turned out to be the one that had flared its wings, almost stopping mid-air to strike at her, near the end. She'd moved away from it as she'd been seeking the final bird without realizing she was doing so.

She quickly found her hammer in the snow nearby. Thankfully, her magesight picked it out with ease, and she dropped it into Kit. Then, using her knife, she began to work on the fallen bird.

Keep moving and the cold won't take you. Her inscriptions should prevent frostbite, but they didn't block the pain of the cold. *Shoes would be nice to have about now...*

She paused her work to pull out her jug of endingberry juice, carefully refilling her flask, drinking a cup of the sweet, power-filled liquid, and topping the flask off once more. *I should never have let this remain empty.*

She was taking all sorts of lessons from this insane night.

As she felt the cold settle in, her leathers responded. That reminded her of just how much the garments had done this night, so she slapped her hand onto the confluence near her right thigh and gave them a healthy amount of power... slowly. She was exhausted.

The leather felt much thicker than she was used to but also had much more give. *What under the stars?*

She looked at the bottom of the tunic, focusing to activate her magesight. What she saw surprised her, even given how adaptive the outfit had been up until now.

The leather had thickened, the fibers spreading apart within the increased depth. Then, the leather had joined together in a lattice, creating uncountable, isolated microbubbles of air. There were so many, that she would guess at least twenty isolated bubbles were in a direct line from the outer surface to the inner at any given point. *This should be a fantastic insulator, now.* And, in fact, she immediately began to feel warmer, from her wrists to her ankles, though her neck, head, hands, and feet only received peripheral benefits.

With that improved, she turned back to the kill before her.

What to harvest, what to harvest. She worked on the most obvious thing first: the talons. The amazingly strong, sharp finger-feathers were next. Her still-active inscriptions kept her hands from being cut on the vicious edges and needle-like barbs of the vanes.

Her book on bound items had implied that a Mage could increase the power of soul-bound items through the incorporation of other items of magic. *These should qualify.* If not, she could always sell them. Sadly, she couldn't take everything, and these seemed the most useful and, therefore, valuable.

As she could only read volume one on bound items, there was little more than implication, but even so, she wanted to be prepared. Her knife had been part of what tipped the scales for her between life and death. She wanted that tool to be as potent as possible going forwards.

Now that she wasn't fighting for her life, she was able to appreciate the scale of the creature before her. From beak to tail-feather, it was nearly twenty-six feet. *That's close to ten times a mundane raven!* Well, if she was remembering correctly.

The magic of the arcanous ravens was entirely bent around flight and the regular functions of the beast itself. No special or elemental abilities at all. *Huh, they're almost mundane.*

The bird she was harvesting had a total of eight talons and eight finger feathers. *Seems standard, I suppose.* The other feathers were more flexible and suffused with power for flight. *Not that useful.* She'd never even heard rumors of magic flying constructions. *Doesn't mean they don't exist, though…*

She'd easily placed the talons into Kit, but now she stared down at the finger feathers. Each was nearly fifteen feet in length, also surprising light, all things considered. "Kit… you can't carry these, can you?"

The pouch did not respond.

Now free from the bird's body, the feathers looked like some eccentric piece of art; plumage wrought from a dark, impossibly light metal. *With the bird seeming to weigh close to four-hundred-fifty pounds, the feathers are much lighter than I'd expect.*

Even so, the feathers were fairly unwieldy. They were much longer than they were wide, being less than a foot across at the widest part. *Let's try it.*

She set Kit on the ground, wide open, and dropped a feather down into it, doing her best to center it so as to not brush the sides. To her surprise, the entire feather disappeared down inside. *Nice!*

Curiosity nagged at her, so she knelt and looked down in.

Kit had rearranged, with most of her items neatly crammed to one side of an extremely tall, narrow pit. The pit was barely larger than the hole opening into it. *So, no going in there until I get these out it seems.* Still, they fit.

The endingberries' power was blunting the cold but being steadily drained in doing so. The diminishing wasn't something that would run her power dry, even if she decided to sleep naked in the snow. Still, given her recent desperate reliance on the power, she didn't like the slow drain. *And it doesn't stop the discomfort... or the pain. And it's getting harder to move my cold muscles...*

Keep moving. Keep your muscles warm.

More to the point, her moving, flexing, and straining to harvest from the great bird had highlighted to her that she had not come away from the fight cleanly. If she had to guess, she had at least one broken rib and likely some internal bruising.

The now-refreshed endingberry power within her would prevent further damage from occurring, even if the already present bruising caused massive swelling. *Huh, I'd not really considered the power as an effective wound isolation technique.* Infection should also not be able to take hold, not that she had any open wounds.

The first bird harvested, she fought through the pain to return to Terry.

Terry was just finishing his meal, which seemingly consisted of the entire carcass, bones and all. Tala arrived to find a wide splash of bloody snow and a small pile. *So, not quite everything.*

As she walked up, Terry was swallowing the last bit of broken bone. He regarded her, feathers matted with thick, congealing blood. Finally, he gestured to the pile with his beak.

"For me?"

He bobbed a nod.

She grinned, striding over and picking up the eight talons, one at a time. She took a moment to pare away what little flesh remained attached to each, tossing the bits to Terry as she worked.

By the time she finished, her fingers were growing numb. *Gloves. I have gloves.* She felt foolish for not considering it earlier. She cleaned her hands with rags and cool water. Interestingly, the water felt warm to the flesh of her fingers. *Probably not a good sign.*

After her hands were dry, she pulled on her gloves. They weren't thick, but they would help.

Terry had settled down into the snow, resting his head, eyes closed.

When she moved, Terry's eyes snapped open. "Over there, there's another. Still hungry?"

He slowly pushed himself to his feet. He didn't stagger, but he definitely lacked some of his usual pep. *And he didn't teleport to come to his feet.* It was possible that he'd exhausted his magic, following her, then fighting. *I hope he recovers soon.*

She returned her focus to the next task, even as Terry began wolfing down the body she'd already harvested, tearing it into manageable chunks, then swallowing them whole. *There were fourteen total, in the flock.* Assuming they'd been from the same flock. *What's a flock of ravens called again?* She thought back through her studies, and her enhanced mind brought forth the result.

She began laughing again, and now that her adrenaline was fading, the pain that laughing evoked in her cracked rib made her gasp.

"I was almost killed by the unkindness of ravens." She wheezed. "By the stars, that would have been embarrassing."

Keep moving. She was able to find ten of the birds, not including Terry's dinner, from which she got a total of eighty talons and half as many finger feathers. Sadly, many of the feathers had been destroyed or damaged to the point that their magic was leaking away too fast to be useful. *I suppose hurtling into the ground isn't the best for physical integrity.* If she was honest, she was surprised that she'd found as many intact as she had.

Terry moved behind her, resting while she worked, then quickly rending and eating what she left behind.

He didn't so much as slightly bloat despite consuming what seemed to be *many* times his own volume of food. *Maybe, he doesn't need a cow a day because he has some means of having insane reserves?*

She would likely never know.

As they moved across the sparsely wooded mountainside, they also encountered other carcasses, or evidence of blood, layered within the snow. *This was the killing ground for this group. They brought their prey here and either dropped it from great heights or worked together to tear it apart.* She was *very* lucky to be alive.

The last bird they found was the one who'd grabbed her in the beginning. It was beyond salvaging.

By the half-liquified slurry, at the bottom of a deep crater in the rocky ground, this bird had been bigger than the others—maybe by a lot. *Likely why it went so far afield?*

She did not watch Terry consume the… bowl of sustenance, but the sound of it made her gag.

When he was done, she contemplated continuing to hunt. There should be at least three more birds. *No, Tala. You've already been harvesting for close to two hours, if not longer. We need to get back.*

"So, Terry. Back to the caravan?"

He cocked his head, then glanced towards the southeast, the direction she believed the caravan to be. Then, he looked back to her, seeming contemplative, his head drooping a bit.

She frowned. "We came a long way… didn't we?"

Terry bobbed his agreement.

"And you're really tired…"

He bobbed a yes.

She sighed. "I am, too…"

She groaned, pulling out a blanket and wrapping it around her shoulders. "Can you teleport with anyone or anything else?"

As an answer, Terry blipped away, instantly appearing on her other side, perfectly clean. The blood, gore, and viscera that had been splattered across him rained wetly down in the spot he'd left. Even his half-hidden collar was clean.

"So… no…" She sighed. *That would have been too easy.*

Terry walked up beside her, pressing close and hunkering down as she considered. His warmth radiated through her painfully. Even so, she snuggled more deeply into his feathers, even as the terror bird laid his head down, closing his eyes.

"Thank you, Terry."

Terry crooned softly, seeming pleased.

After a moment of stillness, the world around Tala blazed yellow-green, and she had the fleeting assumption that she'd somehow fallen asleep, and the sun was breaking through the surrounding trees.

No. She turned, straightening and keeping one hand on Terry. A being whose aura radiated yellow-green power landed a dozen yards away with a *whump*, which sent a cascading wave of snow flowing outward.

It was a woman of such surpassing beauty that Tala considered that she, herself, might have died. *Is this one of the gods?*

No, that didn't make sense either.

The woman walked forward, the details of her magic unreadable to Tala save the undercurrent which blatantly signified just how outmatched Tala was. *She's letting that through, showing that aspect of herself to me on purpose.*

Belatedly, Tala realized that, even aside from her magesight, there was a pressure from the woman, one that spoke of power and dominance.

For her part, the woman walked casually towards Tala, the snow melting away from her delicately sandalled feet as she came. Her simple, one-piece dress swayed pleasingly around her. There was a slight cream color to the material, which appeared to be silk of some kind. The woman carried nothing else that Tala could see.

"Mage." The woman's voice was somehow more like silk than the dress appeared, and while it was softspoken, the force behind it shook snow from some nearby trees.

Tala swallowed, knowing that the inscriptions around her ears had likely reduced the impact on her. Terry, for his part, crouched low, seeming both fearful and defiant at the same time. *Yellow-green...* She recalled the books in her pouch and picked what she thought was correct. "Paragon... Or is it Refined?" Only after she spoke did she realize that her words could be taken as an insult.

The woman froze, halting her advance. A small smile tugged at one corner of her lips. "So, you aren't ignorant, and you have backbone." She nodded. "Good. I saw what you did, here." She gestured around them to the bloody forest. "Reasonably handled for a mortal."

That's a bit insulting. Still, this woman could likely kill Tala without a second thought. *And it's very likely that I just insulted her as well...* "I am Tala."

"Tala." She almost purred the As in the name. "You may call me Mistress."

That's not foreboding... Tala swallowed again, steeling her resolve. "What do you wish of me, Mistress?"

The woman tilted her head almost delicately at the question, seeming to consider. "You are no Archon, clearly you aren't even Bonded, but I sense Archon Stars." The way she said Bonded reminded Tala of the other books. *She means the rank.* "You would make an interesting servant."

Tala shook her head, immediately. "I would not. I am contracted with the Caravan Guild and have other debts besides, which I am obliged to fulfill."

Mistress waved the notion away. "I will buy out your contract. And give you an additional thousand ounces gold to become my bonded."

Tala blinked, startled. *A thousand ounces gold?* That was insane. She blessed the stars that a contract couldn't be bought out without the agreement of all parties, and she did *not* like the way the woman had said 'bonded.' "I'm unfamiliar with that term. What do you mean, bonded? You said it as if it were different than the ranking."

"Oh! Silly me." Mistress laughed slightly. "We would exchange Archon Stars, and you would become my bond servant."

"For... how long?"

Mistress blinked at her for a long moment. "Maybe I don't want you, child. Archon Stars create a soul-bond. It would be forever."

Tala remembered what Grediv had said about bonding humans. "Isn't human soul-bonding forbidden?"

The woman waved her hand dismissively, again. "One-way bonds are, yes. But two-way? I could uplift you. Give you power, make you *more*."

But I'd always be subservient to you... And that 'always' would be literal. She also had avoided saying if it was forbidden. "Thank you, but I don't think I am interested."

The woman sighed. "Ahh, well. If that is your decision." She turned to go.

"Wait!"

She paused. "Yes? Did you expect me to force you? You should know better than that. Such a bond can only be entered into willingly."

Well, yeah, I did sort of expect you to. "No, of course not, Mistress. Before you go, could you return me to my caravan?"

She smiled, mischievously. "Of course!"

Tala brightened but was still wary of a trick.

"For the low fee of five hundred ounces, gold."

And there it is. "That is insane."

"My time is valuable." She waited a moment before nodding. "I thought not. Now, if there's nothing else?"

Tala groaned. "You would leave me stranded out here?"

Mistress shrugged. "Mortals die all the time, child. If you're of no use to me, then I've no time for you. If you were a village or city in need, I'd likely help, but..." She shrugged. "I do hope you survive. Maybe, our paths will cross again sometime in the future." She seemed to consider that for a moment. "Yes, I think that we will get along much better if we meet again in the future."

A village? Tala knew the term; it was meant to refer to something like a city but smaller. *Where was this woman from that there were villages?*

She didn't get the chance to ask as Mistress strode forward, resolutely.

Tala flinched backward but found the very air hardening around her.

Terry hissed but seemed similarly locked in place.

Tala almost smiled. *Terry doesn't have to move as I do.*

As if on cue, Terry flickered, appearing behind Mistress, already poised to strike. There, however, he froze once more, locked in place.

Mistress turned to regard him, holding up one hand but stopping herself from touching Terry. "A dimensional terror bird? Fascinating."

Tala saw power thrumming around Terry as he clearly fought to move or teleport. He couldn't do either.

Mistress shrugged. "I'm not going to hurt her, little chick. Quite the opposite, actually. Now, stop wasting my time." She spun and took the last few steps to stand before Tala. "Now, you've something dampening magic around you... no, through you?" She tsked. "How could you possibly function with such an envelope? Unless..."

Tala's arms were moved upward, her palms turned towards Mistress.

"There we are." Mistress placed a finger against each of Tala's hands, and power pulsed between the women.

The endingberry power within Tala was suppressed and compressed, driven aside by Mistress's working. Tala's ribs clicked back together audibly, her bruises disappearing, and she gasped. An instant later, her restraints vanished, and she dropped to the snow. "How?" She took another deep breath, reveling in the lack of pain. "To heal such an injury in the past, I've had to remove my protection against magic."

Mistress quirked an all-too-condescending smile. "The same way you move power through your body, dear. Your blood. The iron content creates wonderfully efficient pathways for the transmission of power to where it's needed. You'll learn to better utilize your body's natural pathways soon enough. You should survive just fine, now." She patted Tala's cheek.

Tala, for her part, was still so stunned that she didn't react.

Mistress took a few steps away from Tala and Terry, crouched down and leapt away, leaving a concussion of sound, a deep depression, and a tempest of swirling snow in her wake.

"That was..." Tala shivered, looking to Terry. "That was deeply disturbing."

Terry's eye watched the departing Mistress from his unmoving head. After a long moment, he suddenly dropped to the snow, then flickered to beside Tala, where he pressed against her more forcefully and firmly than before.

After taking another minute to collect herself, she felt a flicker of doubt. *I could have been done. My debts erased, my contract over. I could have been free. That woman would have given me power and taken me away from here...* But at what cost? *Am I to trade virtual slavery for the real thing?* If she'd understood the offer correctly, she would have been binding her very soul into the woman's service. *That has to have larger implications than I'm capable of understanding right now...*

Tala felt herself hardening with resolve. *It seems that there will always be people who want to rule over me. I need to get stronger.*

She patted Terry. "I've a request, Terry."

Terry, who was settled down to rest once more, craned his neck, twisting his head to fully face her. He seemed to be feeling much better after his meals.

"Can I have a ride back to the caravan?"

Terry gave her a long, searching look.

"I could probably walk or run back, but you would be much faster, and if we want to rejoin the caravan before we reach Bandfast, it's likely the only way to make it in time." She nodded to herself, clarifying. "If we don't arrive with the caravan, there will be a lot of difficulty getting in. Strangers generally don't wander in out of the Wilds on their own."

He hesitated for a moment longer, then bobbed a slow nod, crouching down so she could hop up.

She tucked her feet back in what felt like a natural position, and they fit nicely under Terry's small, flightless wings.

Terry took a hesitant step, shifting beneath her. He paused, then a ripple of power shivered through him, and he grew, just a bit, expanding to be a better size to carry her. He tested a few more times, fine-tuning his size to best manage her on his back.

"Thank you, Terry. I won't forget this." And she wouldn't, not the least because Terry, as it turned out, was *fast*.

Chapter: 25
Smell Like Blood and Death

As Terry took off, Tala held on tightly, finding that the magical collar was a great thing to grasp. He clearly knew where he was going, crouched low to give power to his driving run. Even so, he was having to move slower than on his chase after her, given that he couldn't teleport with her atop his back, lest he leave her behind.

Tala, for her part, was huddled low, head hunched in close to Terry's neck in an attempt to get some shelter from the wind caused by their speed. Her blanket was tucked tight around her, and her feet were quickly warming under Terry's wings, though they were prickling painfully at the returning heat.

Terry's running had a rhythmic cadence that was hard to fight, and Tala felt herself begin to slip several times before she was able to bring her mind back under control and force herself to stay awake.

She did everything she could to maintain her focus.

She moved through mental puzzles and riddles, searching for new solutions or new ways of looking at the problems.

She focused on her breathing and balance. Her posture was shot, but that wasn't a primary concern at the moment.

She attempted the meditative techniques found in Grediv's advice for masters and magelings books.

She reviewed the information she'd been reading and did her best to extrapolate the answers she'd been seeking, as well as construct deeper questions to help expand her knowledge when she again had the ability to read.

When all that failed, she began at her feet, silently naming each facet of her anatomy and describing what purpose it served and how it functioned.

They'd been traveling for what felt like days but was likely closer to an hour, when something caught Tala's eye. A column of power, flaring within her magesight, having just come into passive range.

"Terry? Can you go that way?" She lifted one hand to point, and Terry complied.

Less than a minute later, Terry slowed, and Tala climbed off his back.

They were beneath the snowline, now, so cool grass flexed softly beneath her feet as she shook out her legs and walked to the crest of a hill.

In a valley below, a storm of lightning swirled around a single, discrete point. The column that she'd seen was hidden to normal sight behind the rise and the trees covering this portion of the landscape. *That probably means it is hidden to most people's magesight, too.*

Most magesight inscriptions didn't allow for the penetration of mundane matter, after all.

To Tala's magesight, it looked like nothing so much as a gate, ripped out of a Mage and fixed in place. There even seemed to be something like inscriptions drifting around the gate, drawing power and enacting their purposes. *Material Creator scripts, focused on lightning?* They actually reminded her of Renix's spell-forms, to an almost disturbing degree, though they were twisted and changed as necessary given their change in medium and construction.

Thankfully, for the small part of her that had immediately begun to worry about Renix, these seemed to have come from a smaller person. *Maybe a woman?* But she was assuming that it had come from a Mage, somehow, and that was probably wrong.

Tala stood, examining the anomaly for a long moment. *What is it?*

If it was a gate, the keystone was clearly gone, and the inbuilt restrictions with it. *Is this what happens to a Mage if their keystone fails?* No, that couldn't be right, or early Mages would all have ended up like this. *Maybe this is what* can *happen without that protection.* Even so, she still wasn't sure her guess was correct.

Whatever it was, it had clearly affected everything around it. Rather than scorched earth, grass grew right up to the fount of magic, electricity jumping between the slightly metallic blades.

Trees grew nearby, subtly glowing with their own internal magics. When she examined them with her magesight, every bit of power below was some variation of the source in the center of the little valley.

The air *thrummed* with power, and the ground did, too. If it hadn't been so clearly elementally bound, it would have put Alefast's magic density to shame. As it was, the power seemed restricted, somehow, the concentration falling off precipitously with distance from the source.

As she examined that decline more closely, she thought she understood what was happening. *Most of the power is being lost as it loses its bent towards lightning. It is increasing the power density in the land all around, but not nearly as much as if it were non-elemental power to begin with.*

As she watched, an arcane rabbit with obviously similar magics zipped in from the edge of the valley and to the source. It seemed to draw on the power there, briefly diminishing the surrounding storms by a minute fraction.

Instead of refilling the rabbit, like topping of a water-skin, it seemed to twist something within the tiny creature, and when the rabbit vanished out of the far side of the valley, Tala would have sworn that it had a new form of lightning magic coursing through its previously mundane ears.

Arcane creatures get their power, here? She looked around and realized that the surrounding vegetation was soaking up the power. *We just happened to come close enough to notice it...* How many such founts were there in the wilds?

Did all arcanous creatures receive their abilities here, or places like this? Why ever leave? *Why not just cover yourself with more and more random inscriptions, Tala?*

It was dangerous. Some probably died, and they likely could only return a few times.

She glanced towards Terry. "Do you have to go to something like this? To renew your power?"

He hesitated where he crouched down, curling up to wait for her. Finally, he shook himself, indicating the negative. Now that she thought about it, she'd never taken the time to deeply examine Terry.

She focused, allowing her magesight to delve into the terror bird. She immediately had to turn away, blinking her eyes to clear her vision.

She returned her gaze to him more carefully, allowing her inscription-granted-sight to adjust.

Terry was a *deep* reservoir of power, and that power coursed through him like a force of nature.

Even so, it didn't have an underlying color behind the power. *He's not of an Archon rank, somehow.* So, the progression wasn't just about a quantity of power, then...

She looked through the maelstrom within Terry. She couldn't see a source for that raw power; like all arcanous creatures, he lacked a gate. *He'll run out, eventually.* She gave him a long look. "You have to refill your power, somehow... You said you don't need to come to a place like this... Are you capable of converting food into power?"

After another moment, Terry bobbed a hesitant nod.

She gestured towards the spring of lightning power, below. "But the magics, themselves, were granted to you by a place like that?"

Another bob, firmer this time.

"What would a dimensional well even look like?"

He laid his head down back on his own back, closing his eyes.

"Fair enough. You can't really describe it, can you." She felt herself grin tiredly. "This probably isn't the best place to rest." She looked again, frowning. "There are a lot of these, throughout the wilds, aren't there."

Even though it hadn't been a question, Terry bobbed a nod, standing and moving over beside her.

"Well, that helps explain why I've never seen a gate within arcanous creatures." The beasts could draw on their own strength to power the workings, but these wells were likely the source of what amounted to natural, internal inscriptions. *With no need for re-inscription...*

She had a passing desire to walk down there and get the natural inscriptions herself, but she squashed that as the foolishness it was.

"The ancients *must* have known about these." She sighed. "They must not work on people."

She gave another long look at the glowing valley, unable to shake how closely the fount resembled a Mage's gate to her magesight. *What are you?* She'd have to ask Trent... or Holly. *Someone will know.*

She climbed back up onto Terry and settled in, deep in thought.

In this way, she passed what remained of the night.

With her weight, and their down-sloping path, Terry could not go at top speed. So, as dawn broke across the wilds just more than an hour later, Tala and Terry were only about half-way back to the caravan's campsite, assuming Tala's estimates were correct.

How far did those stupid raven things carry me? Seems like it was more distance than from Bandfast to Alefast...

She was no longer able to focus well enough to keep fully awake, and Terry seemed to have sensed that.

I wonder why the caravans are so slow... She yawned. She remembered something about how increased mass, or increased speed, drew attention? *Something like that.* She shook her head. It was hardly important at the moment.

Thus, as the first light of a new day bathed the autumn landscape, Terry stopped beside a short cliff. Above them, a tree arched out over the drop, and below the tree, a small alcove was visible among the roots.

Terry vanished from beneath Tala, and she barely caught herself, stumbling in her exhaustion.

Terry had appeared instantly on her shoulder, in his much smaller state.

Barely conscious, Tala staggered to the alcove, laying her blanket out and collapsing upon it. She was asleep even before Terry had curled up between her and the outside world.

* * *

Tala woke suddenly to a low, rumbling shriek.

She rolled backward, away from the noise, coming up in a crouch, her back pressed hard against a wall of packed dirt.

Soil rained down around her, and she lifted a hand to protect her eyes as she took in the situation.

Terry was crouched low, now about as tall as herself. He was facing away from her, head sweeping from side to side, keeping constant watch on their opponent.

Six terror birds were arranged in a loose arc in front of their little alcove.

Tala shook her head, brushing away the dirt and clearing her mind. *Six.* She focused her intent, and her magesight blossomed. Each bird held lightning magics. *Not unexpected, given the region.* She passingly wondered if these had received their power from the well that she and Terry had found or another.

Hardly relevant.

Six were in front of her. *If it were me, I'd have at least one on the cliff above.*

Why hasn't Terry slaughtered them? She took another look. Terry was positioned between her and them. *Protecting me until I woke?* Until she was ready.

She threw her blanket into Kit and pulled out her knife and hammer, holding the hammer in her offhand. *Punches won't really do much.*

She began drawing as deeply as she could through her gate, saturating herself in power.

"Terry."

His head flicked slightly to one side, allowing one eye to see her easily.

"Ready."

Terry vanished, and the storm began.

Tala lunged to one side, out from under the cliff, as soon as she saw Terry appear behind one of the birds in the other direction.

Their attackers had a mix of reactions.

Three looked around in confusion, clearly uncertain where Terry had gone. *That explains why he's not bigger. He'd be easier to spot.*

Two threw their mouths wide, sending trees of lightning scouring towards her. *...and easier to target.*

One died as Terry took its head off with a viciously precise swipe of his claws. *Nicely done, Terry.*

Two more dropped down towards Tala from where they'd been perched on the short cliff, above and behind them. *I knew it.*

So, there were eight... well, seven now.

Tala cursed her lack of ranged spells, even as the uncountable branches of power threw dirt, rock, and clumps of sod in all directions, the lightning itself falling short of her position.

She felt strangely detached as she analyzed the magics before her. *This isn't an attack technique. It's meant to herd, directing prey into a trap.* It still might seriously hurt her, but it wasn't intended to kill. *Just like an elemental barking or howling, then.*

She quirked a smile and flung the hammer straight at one of the confused birds, between the two sending forth lightning.

The hammer, being entirely metal, drew the lightning like a magnet draws iron. Thus, the target of her throw was hit, first by the handle of the hammer—hammers like that were *not* meant for throwing—and second by lightning from two directions.

The electricity had no discernable effect, the nature of the bird's feathers easily shunting the power into the ground, though it did squawk awkwardly as the hammer's handle struck its throat.

Terry had not been idle, and another terror bird was falling, spraying sparking blood across the grass. *There is no way that isn't ridiculously valuable...* As Tala sprinted after her hammer, she shook her head. *Focus, Tala!*

She tripped as one of the previously confused birds lunged forward, slashing at her legs and opening a long gash through her pants, if not her skin.

Tala turned the fall into a roll, coming up and taking the last step to pick up the hammer. Her leg was poorly positioned and almost buckled beneath her, even as she crouched at the feet of the now thoroughly enraged lightning terror bird.

It struck. Tala jerked the hammer upward, falling backward.

The hammer made a hollow *thunk* against the underside of the creature's beak, rolling immediately into a series of wet squelching sounds, the avian's lower beak turning to pulp.

Tala was already acting, striking out to take advantage of the situation.

She threw some of her gathered power through her knife's second path, causing it to flow outward into a hair-thin outline of a blade, filled with blazing heat.

She struck upward again, this time with the blade, while her current attacker continued its forward movement despite the injury.

Her blade hit the bottom of the beast and passed cleanly upward, bisecting the terror bird before Tala cut off the flow of power and the knife returned to its inert state.

She nearly staggered in weariness at the sudden expulsion of power but managed to keep herself from falling.

That might have been a mistake.

The bird hit her shoulder with a glancing blow, even as it fell into two sizzling pieces. The hit imparted lightning, and Tala found her entire body locking up.

Unfortunately, the attack had not been a direct working of magic, so her iron salve had done nothing to prevent it, and while the iron had directed most of the power across her skin, instead of through her organs, it hadn't diverted all of it.

All over her body, her defensive inscriptions activated despite the endingberry power within her already working to protect her from internal burning or damage.

At the activation, she felt a sinking feeling. Several sections didn't activate at all. They were depleted to the point of ineffectiveness. *I was too tired to notice that last night.*

None of her defenses kept her muscles under her control, however, and she found herself temporarily unable to act.

Much too close for comfort, another terror bird released a screech of utter fury and rage. The near-deafening sound was undercut by the continued deaths around her as Terry maintained his grisly rampage.

She internally thanked Holly for the ear-protecting inscriptions yet again, even as she regained a small amount of control over herself, allowing her to turn and face the bird who was, by its strong reaction, her previous victim's mate.

Great…

It stalked towards her, head down, eyes alight with malice.

"Bad birdy." She held up both her weapons before her, protectively.

The bird crouched lower, then seemed to turn *into* lightning, streaking past her faster than she could track.

Tala gasped as the impact twisted her, even as it eviscerated her clothing on her right side from halfway up her ribcage down nearly to her knee.

The immortal elk leathers immediately began to reform, growing across her faster than rushing water.

Having spun with the blow, Tala was facing the creature when it reformed out of the lightning, turning slowly as if in triumph to survey its defeated foe.

It froze in obviously shocked confusion when it saw Tala standing, apparently unharmed.

She smiled. "Yeah, I seem to have that effect on your kind." *That would have been viciously effective against almost anyone I've seen fight. Glad it's me, here…* Her eyes flicked to where the last other opponent was beginning to drop, already dead. "Thank you, Terry. You're welcome to this one."

Terry manifested behind this last enemy, towering over their foe, now much larger than before. His talons were already around his victim. With a slight flex of the muscles in his leg, he created five clean pieces, letting them fall, squelching across the newly turned earth.

Lightning flickered out of the mutilated body, but like with the others, Terry barely twitched, seeming able to resist the cavalcade of power. "Thank you, Terry."

Terry bobbed, quickly blipping around the area, devouring the often still-twitching remains. *That's still a bit terrifying…*

She looked up at the sky. It was nearly noon. *No time to harvest anyways.* "Eat up, my friend. We need to depart."

He complied with alacrity, soon crouching next to her, the perfect size to carry her once more.

Tala, for her part, had used the brief minute to drink deeply from her incorporator and to wash herself from the little blood that had reached her skin, mostly on her face.

The sword killed surprisingly cleanly, leaving cooked meat and sealed off blood-flow in its wake. *Good little knife.*

As she climbed into place on Terry's back, she considered the weapon. "You need a name, little knife."

Terry gave her an odd look but simply shimmied slightly, shifting her weight to what must have been a more comfortable location. He then crouched down and took off at a run.

*   *   *

They arrived at the caravan's campsite from the night before and found it predicably vacant. Even if they had looked for her, when they hadn't found her, they would have departed for Bandfast, hoping to reach the city quickly enough that the cargo could be unloaded before the scripts ran out.

Standard procedure. Still, it was a bit irritating. *They're six, maybe eight, hours ahead of us?* She grinned widely. "I think we can catch them in half an hour or so."

Terry looked back at her, and she could feel his accusation.

"Right, sorry. *You* are capable of catching them in about half an hour. Thank you, again, for allowing me to ride."

Terry bobbed, seeming mollified.

"Shall we?"

He leaned his head forward once more, launching back into a ground-eating pace as he followed the tracks left by the recently passed wagon train.

*   *   *

Tala peeked over a hill, looking at the back of the last wagon in the caravan, retreating away from them, Terry perched on her shoulder.

"How should I even do this?" She'd already considered riding up on Terry's back, but had dismissed that as foolish, even if Terry had been willing, which he didn't seem to be.

She could simply walk up behind the wagon, allowing the guards to see her catching up.

They shouldn't attack me. At the very least, a guard or a Mage would be sent back to see what the humanoid-shaped thing following them was.

"Mistress Tala?"

Tala turned her head in a startled jerk to see Rane just coming out from behind a nearby outcropping of rock.

"Is that really you?" His nose crinkled as he cautiously drew closer. "You smell like blood and death and…" He hesitated. "Well, you smell really bad."

She found herself grinning in relief. *Well, that's one decision made.* "Hello, Master Rane. Permission to rejoin the caravan?"

He gave her a searching look, and she could tell that he was examining her with his magesight. *How can he look at Terry so easily? I guess that much of Terry's power is below the surface, so not viewable by most…*

"You do seem to be you, strange and alien as always."

"You just say the nicest things."

Rane smiled, having the good grace to look slightly abashed. His hand was still wrapped, but he seemed to be using it with a fair degree of ease. *Good.*

"So… can I rejoin the wagons? I'd love to get a nap. It's been a long night and morning…"

After a long moment, Rane nodded. "Let's get you to the chuckwagon. They likely will have a means of getting you bathed."

She gave him a hard look. "You're joking… right?"

"No. You smell horrific. You might even scare the oxen."

That's hardly fair. They don't shy from anything. Tala glanced to Terry, but the little bird was seemingly asleep, curled happily on her shoulder. "Fine…" She sighed. "Take me to a bath."

Rane smiled genuinely at that. "I truly am glad to see you, Mistress Tala. We had no idea where you'd gone." His smile lost a bit of its happiness. "What did happen? Did you go off to find something? You promised not to do that, you know. No one could find you this morning. Den said you'd never leave your bedroll behind willingly, but we couldn't find any evidence of an attack, and none of the guards saw or heard anything."

After she'd taken a moment to process the flood of words, Tala smiled. "That, Master Rane, is an interesting story."

Chapter: 26
A Foolish Form of Immortality

As Tala and Rane walked to catch up with the caravan, several mounted guards came by to check in with Rane, to ensure that all was well.

He sent them off quickly to report Tala's return and to confirm there were no threats approaching from the rear before returning his attention to Tala's abbreviated tale.

As word traveled through the caravan, the wagons slowed just slightly, the need for haste seemingly negated by her return.

I'll have to apologize to Den for the trouble. Rane, for his part, kept a bit of distance, clearly still affected by the smell. *I guess it's grown gradually, so I've gotten used to it?* As she focused on the possibility of a smell, she was suddenly hit with it, her mind allowing the sense through the dampening that it had been providing. She gagged. "Oh, that's foul."

Rane rolled his eyes. "Oh, now you smell it."

Where could the smell be coming from? Where is it coming from? A moment's thought provided the only logical explanation. "It's my hair."

Rane gave her an odd look. "What?"

"My hair is likely what smells." She pulled out her knife, stopping her forward movement to carefully run the razor-sharp blade over her scalp in several quick strokes.

She felt a drain on the endingberry power within her as the action should have left her bleeding, but her skin was protected and the knife was sharp, so the hair fell away quickly.

Before she allowed the vanity inscriptions to activate, she pulled out her water incorporator and fed it a large stream of power to gently rinse the residue from her scalp and down her back.

Terry grumbled indignantly, flickering away and back so quickly Tala barely caught it, but he was then clean.

That complete, she put the knife and incorporator away and dried her head with a handful of rags, then stepped away from the hair she'd left on the ground. "Better?"

Rane leaned closer, sniffing. After a moment, he smiled. "Yes! You don't smell like a careless mortician, now."

She allowed her power to move across her scalp, and new hair blossomed outward, reaching its proper length in moments. She shook her head and ran her fingers through the hair, helping it settle naturally into place. She smiled. "You know, that does feel better. Thank you."

Rane shrugged, and they started walking again. "It's sounding like you had quite the night." He snorted a laugh. "Morning, too, it seems."

"Too true." She continued her retelling, then, shortly reaching the end of her story. She left Terry out of it, mostly, simply stating that he helped without giving specifics. After a moment, she nodded to herself. "Let's still go to the chuckwagon. I'm positively starving!"

Brand greeted her at the back of the chuckwagon with a surprisingly fervent embrace.

"Brand?"

He released her, pulling back to arm's length but maintaining his hands on her shoulders. "Mistress Tala. I'm so glad that you are alright. What possessed you to run off like that?"

"I didn't run off. I was snatched from the top of the wagon by a massive bird."

He stared at her for a long moment before clearing his throat. "You're joking." He glanced to Rane, and the big man shook his head. Brand looked back to her. "You're not joking?"

"Nope."

A confused expression stole across his features, and he turned to more fully face Rane. "How did no one hear her get taken?"

Rane looked a bit abashed. "Well, while we do watch the skies, it isn't our only task, and anyone high enough, during the hours of darkness, is tied to a wagon in some form or other to prevent things exactly like this."

Brand turned back to Tala. "That's right. I thought you slept under a shield or something. How did this happen?"

It was Tala's turn to feel a bit embarrassed, and she scratched the back of her neck absently. "Well… I sort of fell out of the habit…"

Brand shook his head and gave a great sigh. "Then, I am even more grateful that you are alive." After a moment, he narrowed his eyes at her. "You didn't bring in some insane amount of meat for processing, did you?"

Rane made a quiet choking sound but otherwise didn't comment.

Tala laughed. "No, no. I wasn't exactly in a place to properly harvest." She felt Terry stir on her shoulder, but she didn't look at him. "No consumables. I'm sorry, Brand."

He waved that away. "We couldn't have done much with it in any case. I've another project that is filling all our spare time." His eyes flicked to Rane once more before returning to Tala. "So, I imagine you're hungry?" He began moving about the chuckwagon, even while Tala and Rane waited on the back step. "Coffee too, yes?"

Tala nodded gratefully. "I would appreciate anything you can spare."

"Absolutely! I'll bring the food to your wagon." He paused long enough to turn towards them and make a shooing gesture. "Go! I've work to do."

Tala grinned before closing the door and hopping down with Rane. "Well, I've got to go talk with Den."

"Want company?"

She gave him a perplexed look. "Aren't you on rearguard?"

He shrugged. "I can get it changed."

"Would Master Tang approve?"

He grinned. "I'm technically head Mage Protector for the guard on this expedition. The only one to outrank me, under specific circumstances, would be you." He hesitated. "Well, you or the head driver, but he's not a Mage."

She frowned for a moment. "Right…"

He shrugged. "If you didn't have cause to think of it, then it likely wouldn't have applied."

"Fair enough. Isn't it only in cases pertaining to the integrity of the cargo?"

"Generally, yeah. Many baggage Mages use that to leverage a say in the route, or so I was warned." They were walking towards the lead wagon, and Rane grabbed the attention of a passing guard, sending her to inform the other Mages of the change in roster.

"So, how'd you get first chair?"

"First… Oh! Orchestra metaphor?"

Tala frowned, again. "Wait, really?"

Rane chuckled. "Yeah. Didn't you know?"

"No. It was a common saying at the academy. Never really thought about where it came from."

"Huh. Kind of stupid to say things when you don't know what they mean."

She cocked an eyebrow, giving him a level look. "Pretty stupid to say insulting things when you are trying to get on someone's good side."

He hesitated, then slumped slightly. "Apologies, Mistress Tala. I often don't... feather my opinions."

"I've noticed." But she was smiling, and that seemed to lighten the admonishment.

He sighed. "Still want an answer?"

She shrugged. "I'm curious, yeah."

"Part of it is Master Grediv, but mostly I think it was due to my much greater combat experience." He shrugged in turn. "Around a decade of fighting to stay alive will do that, I suppose."

"So... did Master Grediv just... throw you to the wolves?"

Rane snorted a laugh. "Sort of. Once I was 'passingly competent for a child,' he began dropping me beside people in danger and leaving me to fight in order to save them."

Tala's eyes widened. "That's horrible! How could he leave innocents under the protection of a child?"

He grinned. "I'll try not to be insulted, but he didn't. He always stepped in if things got out of hand, or if I was in danger of losing someone." His grin slipped. "Well... until I became stubborn."

"What do you mean?"

Rane took a long breath and sighed. "I became frustrated with what I saw as my lack of progress. So, I stopped trying, and he had to step in more and more. Eventually, I would just sit down and wait for him to arrive." He sighed again. "Finally, he got sick of it and swore that he'd never help me again. I called his bluff... but he wasn't bluffing." The last had come out barely above a whisper.

Tala could see deep sadness in Rane. "Rane?"

He shrugged. "It was a young family. I still don't know why they were outside the walls. A blaze wolf had come through the pass and was starving because it was suddenly near the bottom of the food-chain. A single, starving wolf… It ripped out the child's throat and charred the parents before I realized that Master Grediv wasn't coming…" He fell silent then, and they walked on, slowly drawing closer to the head of the wagon.

Tala didn't speak, but she laid her hand on his shoulder.

Eventually, Rane took an especially deep breath and exhaled. "Master Grediv returned to find me covered in the wolf's blood, the splattering scorching through me." He gestured to his face. "I don't even remember killing it, but I must have. I only remember horror, blood, and pain."

The scars. She realized with surprise. *I'd almost forgotten them.* That was an almost humorous thought because they were absurdly obvious, but it was hardly a humorous moment.

"He kept the wounds, or the pain, from killing me, but no more. He did something to preserve the family's bodies. Once I had healed enough to walk, we returned, and he forced me to look at 'what foolishness has done.'" Rane's voice had taken on a deeper tone for the last, and he kept the clear imitation of Grediv's voice as he continued. "'This is the price of laziness, boy. This is the price of failure. I was clear that their defense was up to you. My hands are clean. You, and you alone, are responsible for the loss of more than a century of human-life-years, at the least.'" His voice returned to normal. "And he was right. I never shirked the duties, or the training, again." A small smile crept back onto his face. "And I've never lost another person." He straightened a bit, looking to her. "Until you." His smile became a bit sad. "I cannot express how glad I am that you are back, but I must confess that much of that is selfish." He gave a little self-conscious laugh.

She squeezed his shoulder before letting go. "I think I can forgive you for that." After a moment, she worked up the nerve to ask. "How old were you when…?"

"Fourteen."

Silence fell between them once more, and they finally closed the last of the distance to the ladder on the foremost cargo wagon. Tala pulled herself up, Rane close behind.

When she reached the top, Den was facing her, face painted with a broad, exuberant smile. "Mistress! I could kiss you, then slap you across that pretty face."

Tala tilted her head in confusion but found herself smiling, nonetheless. "Den, good to see you, too."

"I thought you'd gone and gotten yourself killed."

"It was a near thing, a couple of times."

Den's gaze shifted to one screaming of accusation. "You aren't careful enough, Mistress. You promised me you would be more careful this trip."

Rane reached the top of the wagon but moved towards the back to allow Tala and Den to talk. Tala thought she could still see lingering sadness in the big man.

"Now, what happened? Why weren't you here this morning, and how are you back?"

Den doesn't want or need the full story. "An arcanous raven snatched me from the wagon-top in the night. I fought, I won, and I came back as quickly as I was able."

"Hmmm…" He gave her a searching look. "That sounds true, but you must be leaving things out."

"Yes, Den. That was a five-second recounting of… twelve hours?"

He cocked an eyebrow at her. "Don't get sassy with me, young lady."

"Not Mistress?"

He hesitated, clearly torn.

Tala grinned, waving him off. "You are fine, Den. I don't need propriety. I am grateful for your concern, but I'm fine. While I didn't choose the encounter, I did make mistakes, and I will take better precautions in the future."

Den grunted. "Very well..." He then shook himself and smiled. "I am glad to have you back in one piece." He reached down and pulled up a rolled bundle. "It was obvious that you hadn't left on purpose when I found this."

"My bedroll! Thank you, Den." She took it, then gave him a quick, slightly awkward hug. "I appreciate you taking care of it."

He waved her away, while clearly smiling happily. "It was nothing. Enjoy the rest of the day, Mistress. We'll be arriving back in Bandfast in a few hours." Den turned back to his task, hands returning to his reins, eyes to the rolling plains ahead.

Brand brought a truly impressive tray of food less than an hour later, and she found herself devouring it with abandon.

Around that time, Rane and she fell back into the routine of the day before. *I got a reasonable amount of sleep. I can sleep more, tonight.* Her body and mind protested, but she didn't really feel like sleeping. Even so, she found both her magic and her spirit had been greatly stretched by her night's stresses. Once she got a good night's sleep, she thought she'd almost be ready for her next steps. *Ever onward, towards Archon-hood!* She shook her head. *Or a break might be nice...*

It was mid-afternoon when Trent climbed up the ladder and regarded her from a distance. "You don't look like an undead."

"Well, I'd have to die first." She smirked back at him.

"Ahh, the worst ones don't die first."

She blinked at Trent, not understanding. "Okay. Explain."

"If you don't know, you don't get to."

"That seems needlessly"—she groaned, rubbing her face in irritation—"exactly like everything else I've encountered."

Rane cleared his throat. "He's talking about liches."

Tala frowned. *Like the children's stories? Dark castles, undead armies, evil incarnate?*

Trent gave Rane a deeply frustrated glance. "Master Rane, has Master Grediv taught you nothing about containment of information?"

Rane shrugged. "Mistress Tala's more likely to become one by accident, due to ignorance, than choose into it."

Trent hesitated for a long moment. "…You make a good point."

Tala felt vaguely insulted but decided not to make a case of it. *He's probably right…* "So…?"

Trent sighed, walking to sit beside the two of them, out of easy hearing of Den. "So. A lich is made when someone binds their soul to an item, in order to seek a rusting foolish form of immortality."

Tala blinked, blood draining from her face as she glanced down at her knife.

Trent was on his feet instantly, power blazing across his face as he stared at her knife. Immediately, he let out a rushed breath. "Mistress Tala. Don't. Don't do that to me." He had his hand on his chest, and he returned to his seat.

Tala felt relieved but also confused. "So… not like this?"

Trent shook his head. "No… No. While you have soul-bound that knife… somehow." He rubbed his forehead. "Your oddities aside… You bound that knife to your soul. If you were to die, the knife would lose its magics, and your soul would depart the world of the living. A lich is one who has bound their soul to an item. Thus, if their body dies, the soul goes to that item, instead. Usually, it is done in such a way that a new body is then created, and the lich continues on as if they haven't just died."

Rane cleared his throat. "To be clear, this is different than an Archon choosing a vessel for their physical form that is not their original body."

Tala frowned, deeply confused. "I don't know that I understood any part of what you just said." She looked to Trent. "Well, I understood what *you* said." She looked back to Rane. "What?"

Rane glanced to Trent, who was glaring, again. "Some Archons choose to bind themselves into constructs, leaving their human bodies behind. It is rare, and usually only done in cases of irreparably damaged bodies."

"And that's different from a lich because...?"

"Because a lich's soul is tied to an object, which is not their soul's vessel. The object is an anchor for their soul in this world, not a body in which to live. That's why there's a different name for it."

"Which is?"

"Phylactery."

Trent grunted. "Usually, only Mages who are sent to kill a lich, when they're discovered, are told these details." He gave Rane a significant look. "That said, I agree with Master Rane. It is possible you might create a phylactery by accident..." He frowned. "You really shouldn't have bound something to your soul before..." He hesitated. "But you wouldn't know to do that..." He scratched feverishly between his own eyes, growling in irritation. "I'm not supposed to know about that..." He groaned. "Please, don't do any other soul-bonds until you become an Archon? There are too many ways it can go wrong."

Tala thought for a long moment. "I think I can do that."

Trent looked up in surprise. "Really?"

Rane cocked his head, seeming curious. "Really?"

She glared at both of them. "I'm not in the habit of doing things that I *know* are stupid." She continued before either could argue, "And enough sources have given me similar warnings that I'd be a fool not to listen."

"Well, I agree but..." Rane began, but he tapered off as her glare renewed. "Fine, fine."

Tala straightened. "Why do you know all this, Master Trent?"

He smiled. "I've been given the information by Master Grediv, mostly. He thinks I'm ready to advance, so I now also have the spell-form for an Archon Star." He gave her a grateful look. "Actually, I had a head start, after examining yours. I knew what to look for to identify one, but I'd never had enough explained to create one. Seeing yours in person helped jumpstart my own process."

"So, you've made one?"

Trent laughed. "Oh, by the stars, no. I hope to, sometime this winter, but I'm still at the start of that quest."

Rane was frowning. "Didn't you want to discover how on your own?"

Trent shrugged. "Why let pride slow me down?"

Rane reddened, clearly with embarrassment, and Trent frowned, "Master Rane?"

Tala was grinning. "Read the letter, Master Rane."

Rane grunted. "Fine. You people are infuriating."

Trent gave Tala a confused look, so she explained, "Master Grediv apparently gave Master Rane, there, a letter, which I believe explains exactly what we are discussing. He's refused to read it."

Trent turned on Rane. "Don't be an idiot. You can't advance with that level of pride, and your master says you're ready."

Rane had hunkered in on himself. "Fine. I'll read it. Just leave me alone."

Trent rolled his eyes, turning back to Tala. "But, that *massive* tangent aside. I'm glad you are alive and back with us." His eyes were sparkling mischievously. "After all, losing a baggage Mage would have hurt our payout considerably."

Tala laughed. "I'll try to be more considerate next time."

"You know, you've said that before…"

She hesitated. "That's fair… I really don't mean to keep getting into dangerous situations…"

Trent gave her a sad smile. "Oh, I know that. Even so, you've much to learn."

"True enough."

Rane, for his part, begrudgingly pulled out a sealed envelope, broke the wax seal, drew forth a heavy stack of pages, and began to read.

Trent bid them goodbye and moved to climb down, heading back to his assigned post.

Tala realized that she'd forgotten to ask something. *And Trent's right here.* "Oh! What's with the magic wells in the Wilds?"

Trent's body froze, but his head swiveled, his eyes checking for anyone else who might be nearby. "Rust, girl. You don't make anything easy."

Chapter: 27
I Might Need to Be Attacked More Often

Tala was surprised by the weight of emotion in Trent's response, but she didn't comment. *Let's see what he'll be willing to tell me about the wells of power in the wilds.*

Den, for his part, turned to look at Trent. "Master Trent, you might as well tell her."

Tala blinked, looking between the driver and the Mage. "Den? You know?"

He gave her a curious expression. "Of course, I know. I have to steer us around them, don't I?"

She hadn't considered that. "Are there that many?"

Den shrugged. "I'm not really sure. One or two for every ten square miles?"

Trent grunted. "At least." He sighed, pulling himself back up onto the wagon's roof. "Seems we'll need to discuss this, too."

Den helpfully held up something that looked like a compass but with half a dozen needles pointing in various directions. "These point to nearby, non-mobile sources of power. The biggest needle points to the closest, and so on."

Tala found herself nodding. "That's how you avoid so many dangers."

"Precisely. Though, sometimes I wish that it would point out the mobile ones, too." Den gave a meaningful look towards Terry. After a moment, Den shrugged, then waved absently towards Trent. "You can take it from here, Master Trent."

Trent shook his head but was smiling even so. "Thank you, First Driver."

The three Mages sat near the back of the wagon once again.

"So, what do you know?"

Tala shook her head. "Oh, no. If I tell you that, you'll refuse to tell me more. Explain the wells of power."

Trent grunted irritably, rubbing his forehead.

Rane leaned back and gave Trent a serious look. "If you don't tell her, I will."

Trent's gaze back at Rane was weary, more than anything else. "You know? Of course, you do. You spent years in the Wilds."

Rane shrugged. "They're hard to miss if you spend any time out here, undirected."

Trent sighed, nodding. "That's true enough." He straightened, looking at Tala. "The wells are magical springs, which grant ingrained magic to any creature that touches them. I don't know how the various magics are selected, nor why creatures get the same effects or different, seemingly at random. Some wells always grant the same, and some never seem to give the same ability twice, according to what's been shared with me."

Tala was frowning. "But… that's fantastic. Wouldn't that remove the need for inscriptions? What are we doing avoiding them?"

Trent shook his head, dampening her enthusiasm. "They can't attach to anything with a soul, anything with *true* sapience."

Tala looked to where Terry lay. "Then, how do you explain the more intelligent creatures?"

Trent shrugged. "Most seem to develop such intelligence either after receiving their gifts or as a result. Again, I don't know which. That intelligence, once acquired, however acquired, does mean that they cannot gain more."

That made sense. If Terry could have been collecting various powers from these wells for hundreds of years, he should have a much broader power-set. *Well, what Grediv said strongly implies that the magics can override one another.* "Huh…"

"In addition, this is virtually only true for arcane creatures. Magical entities either get their power from elsewhere or gain enough power from elsewhere to advance. These wells only grant abilities that seem to closely mirror inscriptions, if not exactly."

"And humans are sapient, so they can't get…" Tala's eyes widened. "Babies."

"Babies." Trent nodded. "Their soul isn't fully established, they aren't fully sapient, or something else, I don't know, but occasionally, a baby would be able to gain power from such as these."

She swallowed. "You say occasionally…"

"Maybe one in a thousand. The others die horribly, or so I was taught."

Tala felt sick. "Some would see that as acceptable."

He nodded, again. "For permanent power? Unfortunately, yes. And that's why the powers that be don't give the option."

"You know, the more I learn about this world, the less I like it… What other horrors await me over the next hurdle?"

Trent shrugged, but Rane cleared his throat, deciding to answer himself, "The evils of this world are too much for average citizens to grapple with. They aren't directly affected, so they needn't have the burden. Archons, and to a lesser extent Mages, are the bulwark of the common man's defense, but even we can't bear everything."

Tala grimaced. "So, we're left to stumble around blindly until someone with the right knowledge notices that we should be told."

Rane shrugged this time. "It isn't a perfect system, but it has served to shepherd humanity for more than two thousand years. This policy has grown our species from around ten thousand hiding, scared savages to right around thirteen million, living in comfort and security." He sighed. "I hate it, too, but the world is such that one evil person, with the wrong information, could undo a lot of that progress. People just don't need to know everything that's out there."

Tala was not happy, but she supposed she understood. *If I'd known, as a child, that the right pattern of metal in my skin would let me throw fire, what would I have done, trying to gain that power?* She shuddered. "'We are but children, searching in a darkness full of knives.'"

Rane nodded, finishing the quote. "'What good father would not remove the blades, that our fingers may be safe.'"

She shook her head. "Pruning the tree of knowledge still seems foolish."

Trent interjected. "But it isn't pruned. What teacher starts with calculus when his five-year-old student begins to learn math?"

"But what good teacher says calculus does not exist when an inquisitive student asks?"

Trent cocked an eyebrow. "Any who know to ask are told... generally."

"So... what makes an Archon an Archon?"

He didn't answer directly. "You have an alchemist background. What would you say to a child who asks how to make an acid that can dissolve anything?"

"I wouldn't say, 'Go mix things and see what happens.'"

Trent grinned. "Have you not been told what to avoid? Even without a proper master?"

Rane frowned at that but didn't comment.

Tala grumbled a bit but had to concede. "Fair, I suppose." She let out an irritated sigh. "So… we really are still children."

Trent and Rane spoke at the same time, both clearly quoting Grediv. "'Archon is but the beginning.'" They then glanced to each other and grinned.

Tala nodded. "Well then. I suppose we need to reach Archon."

The expression on the two other Mages became solemn, and the men nodded.

"Well then, gents. It seems we've work to do." She nodded to Trent. "Thank you, Master Trent. I wish you luck on your quest towards Archon."

"And you yours." He nodded to both of them, in turn, and departed.

Tala stood, moving through her stretches. *If I'm going to spend the rest of the day making a star, I need to prevent cramps.*

Rane, for his part, returned his attention to his letter from Grediv. As he read, he occasionally nodded or shook his head. At a few points, he barked out laughs, followed by mutters to himself, which even Tala couldn't hear.

As Tala finished her stretches and moved to a comfortable, seated position in the center of the wagon's roof, she saw Rane upend the envelope.

A sapphire fell out.

It was the largest gem she'd ever seen, and her magesight provided details beyond what even her enhanced senses could distinguish. It was completely magically inert. It was a shaped gem, but she couldn't discern any facets. Even so, she *knew* it was a sapphire, though it was smooth and rounded. *I thought gems had to be facetted...*

Rane held it up, eyes wide. "It's huge!"

Tala cleared her throat. "So... how'd that fit in the envelope?"

He grunted. "Dimensional storage, only accessible twice."

She gave him a deeply skeptical look. "Master Grediv found a one-use, envelope-shaped, dimensional storage item."

"...Yes?"

"And he's wasting it on you."

"Hey..."

She rolled her eyes. "You know what I mean."

"Fine..." He huffed. "It's highly temporary. It will only last another couple minutes or so, now that I've opened it."

Tala stood, striding over and snatching the envelope.

"Hey!"

She examined it. "By the rusting stars..." There were minute inscriptions embedded in the paper, with a more complex set woven through the wax seal. She couldn't determine the metal or the specifics of the spell-forms. They were simply too minute and too complex. "How would you even go about making something like this?"

Rane took it back from her, pulling it from her hands. "With great difficulty and expense."

"Obviously, but you said you'd had that for *years*."

He shrugged. "It would have lasted a lot longer if I hadn't opened it."

She gave him an irritated stare. "So... how?" *It clearly doesn't have an ingrained power source or reservoir.*

"How was your outfit made?"

"What? I've no idea."

"But you're wearing it. How can you not know every detail of its construction?"

She grunted, unhappily. "Fine. I'll concede that you probably don't know." She growled in frustration. "More things I don't understand." She glanced back to the envelope. "Well, I understand some, but not..." *Does it only use power to access a space elsewhere? That would allow for the longevity...* She huffed a breath. "It doesn't matter. So, are you going to become an Archon, now?"

"Hmmm? Oh! No. I have to do quite a bit of practice, first, and I can't be on assignment. There can be no chance of interruption after I begin. I could not replace this if I failed." He held up the gem. "This is a kindness, compared to a normal gem."

"Why?"

"Well, because..." He hesitated. "You know what? I'll tell you after you craft an Archon Star as powerful as you need. Master Grediv told you what that threshold was, right?"

She nodded, dejectedly. "Yes..."

Rane tucked the gem away. "Well, I, for one, am going to practice. What about you?"

"Yeah... I am, too." She returned to her seat. *Last time I reached almost ten percent of my goal with four hours and a mistake.* She nodded to herself. "I need a baseline." She centered herself and began to shape her power. *Let's see what I can do with an hour.*

* * *

An hour later, her exhaustion had become manifest. *I'm glad I wasn't planning on doing this for longer.*

She pulled back her defensive powers, pricked her finger with a non-magical knife, and caught the drop of blood containing the Archon Star in an empty iron vial. *I suppose I could use glass vials... might be cheaper?* She actually had no idea if it would be less expensive.

She maintained her focus, letting the power of her regenerative inscriptions activate to heal the small cut. Then, and only then, did she allow herself to relax.

Nicely done, Tala. No slips, no mistakes, just good, solid work. She focused on the drop within. She had dedicated her entire flow of power into the spell-form for an hour, doing her utmost to open her gate as wide as possible. This was the result.

A drop of power spun furiously without seeming to move. Her magesight locked onto it easily, partially because it was 'new' to her.

Her jaw dropped. *There is no way.*

The Archon Star before her was half as strong as the one she'd made most recently, despite taking only a quarter of the time.

She looked up to see Rane sending thin streams of his power out between his hands. He obviously couldn't control the power once it was out, but he seemed to be doing *something* to cause the magic to twist and curl around itself, between his hands, after he released it.

"Rane?"

Something in her voice must have come across strangely because he was up and standing over her with surprising speed, the power he'd been working with harmlessly distributed into the air. *I guess he was using little enough to not be easily detectable.* "Mistress Tala?"

Tala cleared her throat. *Right... decorum, and focus.* "Master Rane, how quickly should a Mage's flowrate increase?"

He seemed to relax, moving a bit away and settling back down, sitting and facing her. "You got a boost, eh?"

She nodded. "Much more than I really should have. My power accumulation seems nearly double the last time I tested in this way."

"Well, you have been practicing more dynamically. That can help." He held up a hand to forestall her. "That said, life or death battles push Mages farther than anything else... assuming they survive. I'm guessing there were a few times that you had to utilize your magic-flow to stay alive?"

She nodded. "To use my weapon, yes. Every bit of increased flow through my gate allowed me to use it longer without exhaustion."

He nodded in turn. "That kind of thing changes you at a deep level." He quirked a smile. "That's why Master Grediv had me in almost constant battle for most of my training."

"So... your gate is a city gate beside most Mages' trap doors?"

He laughed. "Not quite." After a moment's hesitation, though, he nodded. "If you exclude Archons? I suppose that's accurate enough. I can refill my reserves from empty in... two minutes?" He seemed to consider. "Yeah, that seems about right."

"That doesn't tell me much..."

"Oh! Well, my current power density is gold, by the inscriber's scale, and I'm quite a bit bigger than you. So..."

She laughed in turn. "I hadn't actually considered body size."

"I'd guess you were tested for density, given your type of inscriptions. Assuming I understand them. It's pretty irritating not being able to *see* them working."

"Yeah. Mistress Holly tested my density."

After an expectant moment, Rane prodded. "And?"

"Off the scale. She said it was in Archon ranges."

Rane's eyes widened. "That shouldn't be possible."

Tala shrugged. "It's nothing more than a deeper lake, right?"

"Yes, Tala, it is. The human body shouldn't be able to handle that level of power. There's a cap. How are you still alive?"

She found herself smiling. "You know, now that I think about it, the inscriber asked a similar question."

"So... what? Does it take you ages to refill from empty?"

She shrugged. "Something like that. I think around three or four hours, last time I was foolish enough to let it happen." *When I made the star before this one...*

Rane seemed shell-shocked, and he took a moment or gather himself. "Tala..." Then, he caught himself. "Mistress Tala."

"Hmmm?"

"An untrained child should be able to refill my reserves in less than an hour if such a thing were possible."

"So?"

"You are hardly untrained."

"Again, I ask: So?"

"You have a terrifying amount of power within you if what you say is even halfway correct. I'm even accounting for the fact that most of your inflow is likely being siphoned away by your body's currently-active inscriptions."

She shrugged. "Hasn't done me too much good."

He cocked an eyebrow. "Have your spells ever failed?"

"No. Why does that...?"

"Whether a spell grabs hold can be a function of the amount of power behind the working. That's why Mages use secondary effects to attack anything of unknown power or of a tier higher than they are."

She thought back to the midnight fox. *Trent, Atrexia, and Renix threw attacks but hadn't tried to affect the beast directly.* She had. She had locked onto the beast, if poorly, and had directly affected it. "Huh..."

"You're remembering something."

"I think I know what you mean. I altered a fundamental property of a red-auraed creature." She shook her head. "A Bound entity, though that ranking still seems odd…"

"That's… That's impressive, Mistress Tala."

She let out a long breath. "So it would seem." She frowned. "It didn't seem like it took more power than usual."

Rane shook his head. "It wouldn't unless it was actively defended against the particular magics you used. It's more about the weight of power behind the working." He grunted irritably. "I'm not explaining it well."

She shrugged. "So, my power density is high. I knew that. My flowrate is growing quickly and does so even more quickly when I'm fighting for my life?"

"That's the gist of it." After a moment's hesitation, he added, "Expect your gate to shrink, again, in the coming days. You will still have an increase, when it's all said and done, but not this great." He smiled. "It's only been, what? Eighteen hours or so?"

"Yeah. Hmmm… I might need to be attacked more often…" Tala smiled and winked at Rane. *I need to competently defend myself more often is more like it.*

Rane opened his mouth to answer, frowning, but at that moment, a call came from beside the wagon. "Mistress Tala?"

"Guardsman Ashin?"

Ashin climbed up the ladder, a wide grin on his face. "You are alive! I knew we'd slowed, but I couldn't get a straight answer while I was on duty." He pointed a thumb over his shoulder. "I just got off and thought I'd come check."

She smiled. "Yep. Still in one piece."

"So… what happened?"

"Short version? An evil, black, flying chicken snatched me up in the middle of the night—"

Rane muttered under his breath, "Nightwing raven."

She ignored him. "Brought me back to some other evil chickens."

"More nightwings."

"I killed them and came back." She hesitated. "Some electric chickens ambushed me when I was almost back. Killed them, too."

Ashin, it seemed, had heard Rane because he glanced to the large Mage, waiting for an explanation.

"Lightning terror birds, I think. Mistress Tala, are all birds chickens to you?"

She shrugged. "Not Terry… Well, I did think of him that way at first… so, only those I don't like or don't know?"

Ashin was smiling, still. "Well, I'm glad you're alive. It sounds like you aren't really up for sparring today, though. I can't blame you." That seemed to trigger a memory. "Oh! Adam asked me to give this to you." He searched for a moment, then pulled out a folded piece of paper, holding it out to her.

Tala took it, unfolding it to reveal a map of a portion of Bandfast. A red arrow had been drawn, pointing at the guardsmen's main compound, and 'Please arrive as soon after dawn as your duties allow.' was written across the bottom.

Tala looked up, eyebrow cocked, and Ashin explained, "We've several training grounds throughout the city, and he wanted to be sure the two of you would show up to the right one." He gestured to include Rane. Then, he returned his attention to her. "He said he's glad you're alive, by the way."

She grunted. "Well, thank you, I suppose?"

Ashin smiled, turning to go. "I've got to gather my gear, and it seems that I've time to win back some pay tokens before we arrive in Bandfast. I suppose I'll see you tomorrow, if not before."

"Seems so. Take care, Ashin."

"And you as well, Mistress."

He had just departed, and Tala had just picked her book back up, not up for another Archon Star, when she heard another voice. "She's alive!?"

Tala glanced at Rane, who shrugged. "Mageling Renix was acting as forward scout."

Renix practically flew up the ladder, stopping at the top to stare.

"Hello, Renix." She smiled.

"Mistress Tala…" He froze there for a long moment.

"Can I help you?" She hadn't closed the book.

"You're alive."

"Regrettably, no. I'm simply the result of a collective hallucination. Brand really should learn not to add strange mushrooms to his meals."

Tala saw Rane shift and glanced his way. She grinned when she saw his face.

Renix was frowning.

She stood, stowing the notebook and walking over to give Renix a platonic hug. "Yes, Renix. I'm alive."

He returned the hug, the frown never leaving his face. "You know, we looked for you, as long as they would let us." He glared at Rane.

Rane held up his hands. "We had a time limit. I'd planned on coming back out to search, once the caravan arrived, but"—he shrugged—"I didn't give you good odds."

Tala looked back and forth. "Did you two have a fight?"

Den snorted a quiet laugh from the driver's seat but didn't turn around.

Rane grunted. "No. I gave an instruction, and he threw a tantrum."

Renix reddened. "Excuse me?!" She saw power building within the younger man, seemingly subconsciously.

Tala held up her hands. "Woah there, Renix." She waved her hands, drawing Renix's eyes back to her. "Renix, thank you for your concern. Master Rane is in charge of getting the caravan safely to Bandfast. He had to prioritize that."

"And if you'd been dying nearby? Just beyond our last quick sweep?"

She hesitated, then sighed. "Then, I'd be dead. But that isn't a justification, either way. The person you're searching for could always be just one rise over, or they could be fine, already heading to meet up with you farther down the trail." She gestured to herself. "Like I was."

She then glanced to Rane. "As for you. You don't need to be so condescending."

Rane opened his mouth to object but hesitated, shrugged, and turned his attention back to his book with a nod. "Fair enough." He did not apologize.

Renix glared at the top of Rane's head for a long moment before turning his attention back to Tala. "Well… I'm glad you're okay."

"Me too." She smiled. "Truly, thank you for the concern."

Renix smiled at that, then shrugged and glanced away. "We have to take care of our own, right? Humanity needs all of us." He glanced at Rane and sighed. "I do need to get back to my position. I'm to sweep the left side of the caravan until we reach Bandfast."

"Good luck."

He waved and climbed back down, out of sight.

There. Now, hopefully, everyone knows I'm back.

Chapter: 28
More Dangerous Than We Realize

Tala whiled the rest of the afternoon away in what had become the usual fashion.

There were quite a few arcanous encounters scattered around the wagon train, but Rane wasn't needed, let alone Tala. She was sorely tempted to investigate, whether for harvest or just to get involved, but wisdom won out. *My defensive inscriptions are mostly shot, after all.*

So, pragmatism won out.

It was a surprisingly peaceful afternoon, all things considered, and Tala felt tensions that she hadn't noticed slowly releasing as her body seemed to finally realize that the danger of the previous night was over.

Finally, as sunset was approaching, the lead wagon crested a slight rise, and Tala looked up to see Bandfast laid out below them.

While they had initially departed towards the south when she'd left Bandfast, they were now arriving from almost due east.

From her vantage among the outlying, now-abandoned mining districts, Tala looked upon the concentric rings of defense, keeping the humans within safe from the dangers of the wilds. She had to shake her head at her own thoughts. *The mining districts are gone.* Though the Wilds lacked the power of those around Alefast, they had still reclaimed the territory once held by the mining areas so thoroughly that Tala couldn't see any indication of the previous operations.

Though, now that she thought about it, her magesight was detecting… something. It was far too faint for even her enhanced sight to truly 'see,' but she still felt a pull. As she concentrated, she was able to detect that the pull wasn't on her, per se, it was on her inscriptions and the metal they contained. *Something is drawing precious metals down into the ground around the city?*

She tried to look deeper, to sense more, but didn't get anything further. *Why didn't I sense anything like this when leaving? Or around Alefast?*

Had she just been too otherwise preoccupied? It was a *very* minute feeling. *Maybe, I'm just imagining it.* But that seemed wholly unsatisfying.

She sighed, returning her focus to the inhabited part of Bandfast as a whole.

It was an interesting contrast, having just come from Alefast. Where Alefast was a single ring, with high walls and powerfully active defenses, Bandfast was a many-tiered, defensive structure with sprawling agricultural development, stretching for more than a mile past the outermost wall. The land was lush, even now in autumn. The surrounding defensive towers ensured that it wasn't really the countryside, but it was far from urban.

Alefast had had what appeared to be old-growth forests pressed hard against the walls. Bandfast faded almost seamlessly into the surrounding, rolling plains.

To her magesight, Alefast had blazed with power, seeming under constant assault by the magic-dense environment around it. Bandfast looked almost undefended, with tendrils of relatively weak magic lazily flowing in, towards the city, and being absorbed by the city's spell-form networks.

If I didn't know better, I would assume that Bandfast was the ancient city and Alefast the new outpost for humanity. We build up in small ways, but the world is constantly trying to break us down.

The young city had a vibrancy, an expectancy, a sense of hope and life. *Incredible.*

Even though it made no sense, it also felt like home.

I've spent more time with Trent than with Lyn or Holly. But she found herself excited to see them, nonetheless. The inn in Alefast had accommodations more comfortable than her room in Lyn's house, but she was looking forward to sleeping there tonight, even so.

We are a strange lot, humans. She found herself smiling, contentedly.

The wagon started down the far side of the hill, approaching the outer defensive towers.

Rane walked up to stand beside her. "So, this is home?"

"It is." *It really is.*

He nodded. "It's big."

She glanced his way. "Is Alefast the only city you've been to?"

"Yeah." He shifted a bit. "The air here feels… weak."

"Low magic density."

He grunted. "Feels strange…"

"It's been this way since we came through the pass."

"But it's worse here."

She thought about it, examining the area around her. He was right, of course. With all the area's power being drawn into the city's spell-workings, it left very little free-floating. None within the city. That made Tala frown. "Aren't you used to being within the city proper?"

"Yeah, of course. I wasn't in Alefast often, but it wasn't that rare."

"There's no power there."

He grinned. "None in the air, but the deeper layer, that's still power-laden. That's what artifacts feed on, within the city."

She frowned. "Is that enough?"

He shrugged. "I'm not an item expert. All I know is the feel of Alefast is not one of starvation... It's like a beach as compared to a desert. Similar if you look closely, but the wider view gives context and reveals how different they really are."

Tala found herself nodding. "I think that makes sense." It certainly lined up with how it had felt to her. *Great... I'm going to have to feed my items more often.* With that in mind, she went through the process of doing just that, filling the reservoirs of each item bound to her. The knife didn't need a top off, but she poured into it, nonetheless, increasing its capacity by a fraction.

She'd been tending to her items off and on, but it was good to top them off before they entered the city proper.

Terry appeared on her shoulder, shifting nervously as they came abreast with the outer towers. That reminded her of his collar, and she placed her hand on that, filling the reserves in her portion of the strange, dual-bonded item. *Let's not forget that.* The other half didn't need power. *Tang said even my half wouldn't need re-inscribing...* Might be worth asking the Constructionist about that.

Tala felt the hard line of distinction as they passed the outermost ring.

Terry, for his part, shivered slightly, and his collar began glowing subtly to her magesight.

Tala had been watching closely, and no attacks came their way, no nearby towers triggered to drive Terry back, and he continued, unmolested, atop her shoulder.

She grinned. "Well, Terry, it seems that you're welcome here."

The terror bird stood up taller, stretching his flightless wings and reaching his head towards the sky.

Then, he vanished. The sudden loss of weight caused Tala to sway, almost losing her balance. She had been able to track Terry, and he stood some hundred feet away, stalking alongside the caravan.

She could feel a pull towards him. It wasn't a physical thing, so much as a certain knowledge of exactly where Terry was. It also wasn't like her sense about where her knife rested, not a knowledge of 'self.' *Interesting.* Thinking of the knife reminded her that she needed to name it, but other things were more pressing at the moment.

Terry's collar was now glowing to normal vision, clearly a warning yellow in color. Terry was looking down, obviously trying to observe the glow as he prowled farther away.

The color moved through the spectrum to red, and it seemed to begin vibrating slightly. Though how she knew that she couldn't have guessed.

As he moved, Tala felt the sense of his location grow stronger, though not with proximity. It was more like a different type of warning, delivered directly through her magic-bond to the collar. Terry bobbed, as if to himself, and vanished, reappearing on Tala's shoulder.

The collar lost its visible glow, stopped vibrating, and seemed to calm once more. Though, it still had a power to it in Tala's magesight.

"Done testing your tether?"

He paused for a moment, then shook himself.

"Fair enough, I suppose." She looked away from Terry and saw Rane regarding them. "Yes?"

"It will be interesting to see how that works out." He gestured to her and Terry. "I wouldn't want to fight him, and I suspect I don't fully understand all he can do. Terror birds are *powerful*, Mistress, and that's before they become arcanous. Be careful. The fact that he was able to go through a well, or more than one, so young?" He shook his head slowly. "He is more dangerous than we realize."

Oh, you have no idea. "Thank you for the warning. I'll keep it in mind."

Farmers were closing out the day in the fields as the wagon train passed, now on a clear, well-maintained road. The caravan guards and farmers exchanged greetings, both via waves and with words. Some of the farmers seemed to know some guards personally, and a few longer exchanges took place around them as they continued.

Everyone had relaxed, now that they were within city defenses, though not all wagons had made the transition, yet.

Tala turned to look back, and again, she noticed how the human-made road ended in an almost crisp line at the edge of the tower's defensive formation. *That used to continue, connecting the mines to the rest of the city.* It had been reclaimed.

As she surveyed the caravan, she was reminded of the battle she'd witnessed two nights previous, even if just at a distance. *Or was it three nights ago?* She sighed. *Doesn't matter.* If the Reforged entity attacked Bandfast, would the defenses hold? She had no idea if the spell-forms were capable of resisting anything in the Archon power range, and she hoped to never find out.

Rane cleared his throat, resting a hand on her shoulder. "Tala—" He seemed to catch himself. "Mistress Tala?"

"Hmm?" She turned to face him.

"Are you alright?" He didn't remove his hand.

"I was just wondering if this city would survive an attack from a Reforged beast..."

Rane's hand tightened, slightly, before releasing. "There are Archons within the city who would rise up to face such a threat, but"—he looked away, out over the fields, letting his hand fall from her shoulder—"these outer defenses were not designed to repel such a danger. Master Grediv hammered that point home, clearly. 'City defenses can only defend against the expected level of threat for the given ring.'" He shook his head. "If that happened, the outer rings would burn, and only the innermost would put up any form of resistance. If it happened at night, most of the populace would survive, to be rescued when possible. During the day?" He gestured.

"It would be a slaughter."

Rane shook his head, solemnly. "No, a slaughter implies violence. These outer defenses would do nothing against such a being. The people would simply cease to exist, instantly. Unless the attacker had other plans for them."

"Other plans?"

Rane shook his head. "That isn't for me to share." He smiled ruefully. "You really need to be raised to Archon."

She grinned. "Yeah. I'm going to be getting the remainder of my inscriptions, soon. After that, I'll have time to train and, hopefully, advance." She turned to him, only to find the other Mage open-mouthed and staring. "What?"

"You aren't fully inscribed?"

She shrugged. "No." She frowned. "I thought you knew that." *I'm pretty sure I told him… Right? Maybe that was Renix and Trent…*

"No. No, I did not know. How are you this incredibly… still alive, while being unfinished?"

She laughed. "I'll try not to be insulted." She shrugged, again. "My inscriptions are bent almost entirely to defense; surviving is half the battle." She grinned.

"More than half, honestly…" He was nodding. "But, why not? Why aren't you fully inscribed?"

"I didn't have the funds for a full set of inscriptions. Now, I do."

"Not have the… What? That's ridiculous. How can you not have enough to properly equip yourself?" His face was the picture of consternated confusion.

"By being poor, Master Rane."

He opened his mouth, then closed it. A moment later, he opened it again, then closed it.

"I've rendered you speechless? Maybe my powers are complete."

He snorted a short laugh, a small smile returning. "But you have the funds now?"

Something in his tone made her wary, but she didn't want to lie. "I do. I mean, I'm not flush or anything, but I can pay for what I need."

He shrugged. "I could give you some."

She blinked at him. "Master Rane. I don't really think…" She didn't really know what to say. "I appreciate it, but any reasonable amount wouldn't change my finances very much."

"A thousand ounces of gold?"

She stiffened. *Mistress's offer to become a soul-bound servant.* She had no reason to believe he was asking for such from her, but the amount was too much of a coincidence.

Den, who had apparently been quietly listening to their conversation, barked a laugh. "Take it! Take it and run, Mistress."

Den's interjection allowed Tala to refocus, and she shook her head. "No, Master Rane. That wouldn't be right. I'd be all but a slave to you. I can't easily repay that kind of money."

He shrugged. "I have very little use for it right now, and it isn't that much in the scale of cities."

How wealthy is his family? "No. Thank you." She felt the fleeting relaxation bleeding away from her, and she pulled inward, hugging her arms to her chest. *Even if I didn't sign a contract, I would be in his debt forever.* She almost laughed. It might be worse without a formal obligation. She'd simply owe him, forever. She shook her head. *I can't. No. That... That isn't right.*

Rane was giving her a quizzical look. "Is it too much? I probably don't actually have that much, in truth. I've not really had to do many purchases... ever, I suppose. Something just reminded me of the tale of Heraza, so the amount came to mind."

Den groaned from his perch at the front of the wagon. "Master Rane, with all due respect, referencing the slave price of a famously indentured wife was *not*..." He stopped himself, shaking his head. "Nope. No. I'm already interjecting too much. Not my business." He turned to fully face forward, beginning to whistle.

Tala had gone rigid at the name. *I forgot that part of the story...*

Rane turned to her, a look of humored exasperation melting into panic when he saw her stance and face. He held up his hands quickly. "I didn't mean to imply that! Oh... rust. I'm an idiot." He shook his head. "Mistress Tala. I... I was pulling a number out of the air, that's all."

She felt herself straighten, and when she spoke, her tone was cool and poised. "Thank you, Master Rane, for the offer. I will make do on my own. I neither need nor want your charity." Without another word, she turned and strode to sit near the back of the wagon.

Rane looked from her to Den, then back to her, then groaned, moving to sit where he had been positioned all afternoon, near the mid-point of the wagon top.

She pulled out her notebook and pointedly opened it, continuing her anatomy review and preventing further discussion.

Should I be flattered? Heraza is a famously beautiful character. Or should I be insulted because she was only rescued from folly and ruin by the attentions of a king...? What she truly felt was weary, frustrated, and irritated.

The last of the ride into the city proper was silent and awkward.

They passed through the gates without incident and entered the workyard with light still in the sky. The half-day of expedited pace had allowed the caravan to arrive a bit ahead of schedule, though Den seemed to have slowed sufficiently that they had lost some of that time, likely in order to not push the oxen too hard.

As Tala closed her notebook and tucked it into Kit, she stood, surveying the yard. To her surprise, she saw both Lyn and Holly waiting near the paymaster's table.

Rane stood and moved to intercept her before she got off the wagon, but she turned and hopped off the side, allowing the endingberry power within her to absorb the impact to her legs.

Huh, I'd have broken both ankles. She had tried to land in a crouch, but she'd apparently not absorbed the impact sufficiently. Her growing experience with the power allowed her to determine the extent of the injuries that had been prevented. *Glad I'm full of the stuff.*

Rane, for his part, growled in irritation. "Mistress Tala." He didn't shout, but she heard him clearly.

So, he's been paying attention. He thinks he knows I can hear him. No need to confirm.

"I know you can hear me."

Well... fine then.

She turned, giving him her best disinterested look. "What." She spoke softly, trusting him to hear her as well. It seemed that he could. *I wonder what abilities he has to allow that?*

"I am sorry. I truly didn't mean anything by it. I don't even have a thousand ounces of gold; I was trying to be whimsical..." He reddened a bit. "I have a habit of saying things as they come into my head." He scratched his left shoulder absently. "I... I'm sorry."

She shrugged, feeling some of her irritation leak away. *This isn't worth it...* "It's in the past, Master Rane. I will see you tomorrow, in the training yard."

He hesitated, then seemed to hunch slightly, even as some deep tension seemed to melt away. He nodded and waved goodbye.

She simply turned and strode through the already growing swirl of people as the wagons disgorged their passengers. It didn't take her long to reach where Lyn and Holly waited. As Tala came close, she pulled out the gloves, which had been a gift from Lyn, and pulled them on.

Lyn, for her part, almost tackled Tala in a careful hug. "You're alive! Bless my stars, woman! What's wrong with you?"

Tala's emotions went through a whirlwind, even as she fought to maintain balance. "What are you talking about?"

Lyn pulled back. "You! I was notified that you were lost and that the caravan was proceeding with all haste. We needed to prepare for emergency unloading procedures, and that doesn't factor in the less-than-ideal reports of your... more dangerous actions."

"Why were you notified?" Tala interrupted.

"Because I'm your handler for the guild—or near enough." She lightly tapped Tala's forehead. "Remember?"

It was then that Tala noticed the gloves on Lyn's own hands. *So she doesn't have to be concerned about touching me.* It was almost a sweet gesture.

"We've lost a few incoming caravans, and we thought whatever had taken you might have been the same." She let out a small huff. "But as I was saying, I was told you were gone early this morning. Then, after hours of panic and planning, I got another message. 'Dimensional Mage recovered, resuming standard schedule.' That's it."

"Well, if it is the same thing, it won't be an issue, now, but I seriously doubt that my problem could have taken a whole caravan." Tala looked to Holly, who was standing politely to one side. "Why are you here?"

"I have an invention I'm going to try on you, and it is time to do the next portion of your inscriptions."

Lyn spun on Holly, but the other woman raised a hand placatingly. "I know she has duties, and I know she just got back, but there is no reason to wait, and it won't interfere with her duties." Holly glanced Tala over, her gaze clearly stopping on Kit, Tala's knife, and on her outfit more generally. "We can discuss your... alterations in my workshop."

Lyn pursed her lips. "Fine." She turned back to Tala. "Well?"

Tala was grinning. "Let me settle up with the paymaster, and I'll tell you the story on the way to Holly's workshop. Okay?"

Lyn nodded. "I suppose that makes sense; we should get dinner on the way, too."

"Gretel's?"

"Of course."

Holly shook her head resignedly, but she had a small smile, nonetheless.

Lyn suddenly seemed a bit awkward as she sighed and cleared her throat. "Also, I am obligated to inform you that you'll have to have a *lengthy* meeting with a senior guild official before you can sign up for any other contracts."

Tala hesitated. "That doesn't sound too good."

"It's not great." After a moment, she shook her head. "I'd have been told if they were planning on nullifying your contract, but don't expect an easy meeting." She gave a pitying smile. "Oh... and your disappearance caused a whole host of expenses, from the messages to a scramble to gather workers to unload the cargo-slots more quickly...

Most of that was mitigated, but you're still on the hook for what can't be recuperated."

"What? I was snatched! It's not like I wanted to leave the caravan."

"You were only snatched because you weren't sleeping in a wagon—a wagon which you rejected." Lyn grimaced in sympathy. "I'm sorry. It's not a lot, but it's still about an ounce gold."

"Great..." *Could have been worse...* Tala sighed in resignation.

Then, Lyn seemed to take Tala in, fully, for the first time, and she used the opportunity to change the subject. "Are those new clothes?" When Tala nodded, Lyn smiled. "Nicely done."

Tala rolled her eyes, pushing away the sinking feeling that was trying to settle into the pit of her stomach. *More money I owe...* Still, she would at least pay this obligation immediately. She turned to approach the paymaster behind his table, waving over her shoulder. "I'll be right back. Don't steal any wayward children while I'm gone."

As she walked, she felt a blip of power, and Terry was suddenly on her shoulder. Behind her, she heard both women inhale sharply. *Where were you hiding, Terry?*

Lyn didn't otherwise react, but Holly muttered under her breath, "Seems that it will be an even more interesting tale than expected."

Chapter: 29
Not Nice

Tala found herself telling an abridged, and only slightly redacted, version of her trip. She didn't feel like her secrets were really needed, here, and the two women had a lot more knowledge than she, herself. That said, she didn't feel it was time to discuss her Archon Stars.

She tried not to focus on the fact that she'd had her pay docked by one gold and twenty silver ounces for expenses incurred due to her disappearance. It didn't seem fair… *No, Tala, focus on the story. You can argue with the official later.*

They didn't interrupt, only asking minimal questions as they walked through the city to the lively square and Gretel's meat pies. While the other two each grabbed a few to eat on the way, Tala bought five for herself.

Gretel was excited to see them all, but she was busy, as were they, so they only exchanged brief greetings after the cook gushed over Tala's new clothing. All in all, Tala was a bit sad to leave the boisterous woman behind them so quickly, but they really did need to get to Holly's workshop.

They ate as they walked, and as she renewed her retelling, Tala found herself pacing the tale to finish about when they arrived. She more or less succeeded.

The only reactions she noted came at the mentions of the endingberries, Grediv, the battle she'd witnessed, and of… 'Mistress.'

With regard to the powerful battle she had witnessed, Lyn had been aghast, but Holly had seemed contemplative. As to the endingberries, Tala had almost skirted around the issue, but she realized that Holly would need to know as it would definitely be important with regard to her inscriptions.

The endingberries had rendered Lyn speechless for large sections of the story.

Grediv got a grunting, snorted laugh from Holly, and the inscriber had seemed to pay special attention to Tala's descriptions of Mistress and their interactions.

"And then, I rejoined the caravan, thanks in large part to Terry, here." She patted the terror bird on the head, where he lay, curled up in her lap.

The three women sat in a back room of Holly's complex, having just recently arrived.

"You know the rest."

An attendant arrived, bringing tea for the three.

"So... thoughts?"

Lyn took a deep breath and let it out. "Well, I'm a bit speechless. It was supposed to be a quick out-and-back run. A nice, easy assignment for your first contract. The route to Alefast is famously the safest, quickest route from Bandfast..." She shook her head.

So much for being speechless. Tala grinned at the woman's contradiction. *I missed you, Lyn.*

"You are just a bucket of trouble, aren't you?" It was said with affection. "I'm so glad that you survived all that. I'm also glad that no one was seriously hurt." Lyn gave her a hard look.

Tala nodded, smiling a bit guiltily. She had neglected to mention Terry's butchering of the men outside of Alefast or his likely incredible age. "Yup." In fact, she'd skimmed over much of her interactions with the bird, only explaining enough to justify his presence and hint at his role in getting her back safely.

Holly sighed. "Well, I'm going to have to do some tweaks to your spell-forms, but I expected to have to. You left out a few things that we will discuss. Your... bond to the knife, for example." She gave Tala a meaningful look.

Tala smiled back. "When there's time."

Holly shrugged. "Very well." She stood and pinched Tala's arm.

"Hey! Ow." Tala rubbed the offended flesh, glaring at the inscriber.

Holly shook her head. "You changed your workout routine. I'm going to have to do a thousand little tweaks to make your spell-forms work properly." She was frowning. "If I wasn't planning on a vastly different set-up, this would be *most* inconvenient."

"Wait... what?"

Holy waved her off. "You clearly aren't suited to dormant defenses. I'd expected this at some point, and you seem to have been working on your accumulation rate, so we'll transition to always active defenses."

Tala frowned. "That sounds not only expensive but like it will run out much more quickly."

Holly smiled with a malicious glee. "With previous techniques, it would be, but you gave me an idea. I will be able to make your inscriptions small enough, and numerous enough, that the power distribution and inscription erosion should be kept to a manageable level."

Tala opened her mouth to argue, then sighed. "I don't have a choice, do I...?"

Holly just grinned.

"Great... how long will this take?"

Holly waved that off. "It won't be an issue."

I guess I'll see? Holly was likely going to have some of her apprentices do a portion of the work to speed it up. That made her surprisingly nervous. *Huh, I really don't want anyone else working on me.*

"I was going to have us remove the silver activation scripts before we reworked the core functions, but you seem to have used them up already."

Lyn scoffed a laugh. "You heard her story. Are you surprised?"

"Not at all." Holly cleared her throat. "Now, let's get you scrubbed down and ready for the work. Yes?" She stood, drink in hand. "Grab your tea and follow me."

Tala shrugged, taking up her cup and following the inscriber, Terry flickering to her shoulder.

Lyn followed as well.

They came to a waiting bath, in a private chamber, and Holly closed the door behind them. Terry immediately blipped over to the edge of the tub, tested the water with a taloned toe, then settled down on the edge to watch the three women, no further interest taken in the tub.

"First, scrub the iron from the back of your neck. I need to collect the records stored there if I'm going to be efficient with our time. Then, while you scrub the rest off, I can be modifying as appropriate."

That's right! Tala felt indignation rise up within her. "I almost forgot!" She raised a finger, glaring at Holly. "You put a voice in my head and gave it power over my hormones? I didn't know you were going to do that!"

Holly blinked at her, a bit owlishly. "Mistress Tala… dear."

Tala drew up short, hesitating. *Did I miss something?*

Holly continued, after a short breath. "Did the spell-form work?"

"Yes…?"

"Then, you must have known."

Tala opened her mouth to object, then hesitated. *Oh… huh…*

"I am surprised that you heard a voice, however. Your magesight must have detected the activation and functions, and a voice was the easiest way for it to convey what it picked up." She clicked her tongue, tapping her chin in thought. "Yes, that is fascinating. I'll have to keep that in mind. Maybe, we could use that..." She stopped her contemplations. "Well?" She gestured at the bathtub. "Get your neck clean. I need that information."

Tala sighed, much of her indignation spent. "Fine, fine." There was a stack of pumice stones, and Tala picked one up, wetting it and running it over the back of her neck. It wasn't very pleasant.

As she scrubbed, she felt a mild drain on her endingberry power. Thankfully, it only protected her skin, not the salve atop it. *I should probably let that run dry while in the city... I don't have an infinite supply.*

In another burst of furious scrubbing, she finished. "There." Her skin felt raw, though she knew it was largely undamaged. The endingberry power would prevent any true damage. Still, it felt quite uncomfortable. *Yes, woe is me, I suffer so for my power!* She snorted, and Lyn and Holly gave her odd looks. She waved them away. "Is that good enough?"

Holly stepped forward and took out a stone, clearly inscribed with intricate spell-lines in a complex three-dimensional pattern, woven through its whole structure. Holly funneled a bit of power into it, and it burst to life.

The inscriber placed the stone on the back of Tala's neck, and she felt a strange tingle like a dog was slobbering on the back of her neck, then licking it clean.

"Aaaah, that feels *weird!*"

Holly stepped backward, bringing the stone with her. "All done. I'll get this analyzed."

Lyn cleared her throat. "Do you need me?" She looked to both women.

Tala shrugged. "It might be nice. Who knows what she has planned for me…"

Holly grinned in a very 'I'm a mad researcher' kind of way. "You should at least stay to see my newest invention. If it works as expected, it could revolutionize inscribing."

Lyn cocked an eyebrow. "Oh?" She seemed to contemplate. "Your last success was those needles…" She nodded. "I can spare a few hours." She looked to Tala. "Welcome home, by the way." She winked and walked from the room.

Holly waved absently as she left, as well. "Be quick, please. This won't take long after you're done."

As the door closed behind the two women, Tala sighed and began stripping off her clothing, setting it, and her gear, off to the side. Lowering herself into the tub, she basked in the warmth for a good minute before getting to work. The familiar feeling of raw skin soon pervaded her senses. The removal of the dead skin exposed the living, and the endingberry power didn't prevent that.

Holly had been thorough, providing both mirrors and pumice stones on sticks to allow her to get every inch of herself clean. It was a familiar process but not a pleasant one. *Nothing for it, though.*

Twenty minutes later, she was done. She likely could have made the process more pleasant by going slower, but she was tired, and she still had whatever Holly had in store before she could sleep.

Her artifact comb dried and detangled her hair with a few strokes, and she pulled her clothing back on, reveling in the now-familiar feel.

Do I even need the other sets of clothes? She could find a use for them, she was sure, but that was for later.

*   *   *

Tala stared at the contraption hanging before her. It looked like nothing so much as a full arm gauntlet, without visible seams or joints. *From the abyss.*

Hundreds of Holly's special needles were attached to the thing, on various tracks, and the entire contraption radiated magic. The surface was as intricately worked as the needles themselves, and Tala found herself gaping from the doorway.

A secondary difference was that all of the needles were almost comically small.

"Come in, dear." Holly's voice floated from a corner that Tala couldn't quite see.

She stepped in, seeing Lyn and Holly to her right. "What is it?" She had a guess, probably a good guess, but she still wanted to know.

"Well, child, it is an automated inscriber. We already have every Mage's inscriptions in the archive, why manually take that out and apply it?"

Tala nodded, hesitantly. "It looks… painful." Terry had come in on her shoulder, but he was now walking around, below the device, examining it critically from beneath.

"Don't be silly. It still won't have to pierce your skin."

Tala gave her a flat look. "Yes, and the simultaneous injection of metal all through my… arm?"

Holly nodded.

"Through my arm will feel like a warm breeze."

"Ahh, yes. I suppose that's true." She shrugged, disinterestedly. "You've suffered worse."

Tala shook her head in a mix of bafflement, confusion, and amazement. *Did she really not think of how much it could hurt?* "Why are the needles so much smaller?"

"Because this system will allow for a much more complex, minute, interwoven mesh of inscriptions. This will be laying down spell-forms with as little gold as possible, to make them as small as possible."

"Won't that cause them to run out sooner?" *Is this what she meant, earlier?*

"Yes and no. Each individual part *would* run down sooner, but they bear a much smaller amount of the overall load. Like I hinted at before, you could see them as each only handling a very small percentage of the overall spell-working, so the same amount of material will be used up but much more slowly for each individual portion of overall spell-form."

"And this isn't normally done because…?"

"Because it would be impossibly tedious for an inscriber to do this by hand, even if they were precise enough to do it accurately, which even I wouldn't be. This is only possible because of this invention."

I suppose that makes sense…

"Well… if you aren't willing, it will take us three to four days to get the work done, solid. No breaks. Does that sound better?" After a moment's pause, she added, "Also, it won't be as good, because we can't do as minute workings and layering. I'd have to rework the spell-forms from scratch."

"That… sounds like too much? Why so much…?"

"We're adding innumerable layers to you, dear. You will be inscribed throughout your bone and soft tissue, and we're refreshing your enhancement and skin inscriptions." After a moment, she shook her head. "No, we're overwriting them, incorporating the lines that are still there."

Tala groaned. "How long will that take?"

Holly shrugged. "I estimate it will take about five minutes per limb? I eventually want to make a whole-body version, but I wanted to prototype, first, and this seemed a reasonable size. We won't have to wait for integration, like before, because we're working with much smaller amounts of metal per injection."

Tala gave her a highly skeptical look. "Why me?"

"Hmmm? Oh. A few reasons, actually. First, it really isn't worth my time to inscribe you at so many levels. I was considering having several apprentices work on you alongside me, but that isn't ideal." She was scratching at her chin. "Then, this occurred to me. Seems reasonable."

"Okay... so why me? I inspired the idea, but I've been gone?"

"Oh, your fortitude, child, and the complexity of the spell-forms you can sustain. Much about your self-imposed training and powers requires you to endure... much."

"You just said you thought it wouldn't be painful."

"Of course, dear. You'll be fine."

Tala narrowed her eyes. *Is she trying to be funny?* After a long moment, she grunted in irritation. "Fine. What about my torso?"

"It can expand to do that as well. Though it will take a bit longer. We won't do your organ-specific inscriptions today. I want you to read some information I've put together on the exact function of the organs and how the inscriptions will augment them. I know you've a good deal of anatomy training, but I want it to be better. No need to put the work in place until you understand it well enough to activate the inscriptions." She pointed towards a side table, where a stack of books waited. "Those have a section on each organ or system, what it does naturally, and how the inscriptions will interface with those functions. They are customized to your physiology, based on my initial scans of you before you left."

On second inspection, Tala realized that 'stack' did not do justice to the massive number of volumes awaiting Tala's inspection. *I can find the pieces I'm missing and brush up on what I need to review.* "Did you write these yourself? By hand?"

"Don't be silly, dear. I used this." She gestured to the device. "I wanted to test its precision, so I placed the stack of blank books within it and supplied it with mundane ink." She smiled self-satisfactorily. "It performed flawlessly." After a moment, she nodded. "You will, of course, have to pay for the tomes."

"But I didn't ask for them."

"But you need them."

Tala grimaced. "…How much?"

Holly seemed to be taking her in. "An ounce gold. They cost more to make, but I used them as a test case, thus reducing my overall expenses. One gold ounce seems fair."

Tala growled. *First, I have to pay more than an ounce for being abducted, now another ounce for these books?* She sighed. "Fine…"

"And, while we're discussing prices, you used up all your golden rings."

"I did."

"I didn't factor that into the price of this inscribing."

Tala sank into a chair. *Why fight it? She won't let me win…* "How much?"

"Hmmm? Oh, let me see." Holly pulled out a slate and looked over the text on its surface. "Four and a half ounces gold to fully refresh the thirty rings."

"Oh, rust that! You didn't assume that I'd use *any* of them?"

"No, I didn't. You were specifically sent on an easy, safe mission. Your danger-mongering isn't on me."

Tala grumbled, but again, she didn't really have a choice. "Fine… So, what do I owe you, then?"

Holly showed her the slate. "Thirteen and a half ounces gold."

Tala's eye twitched. *That's more than half of what I have…*

"My math is good."

"I can see that. You seem… chipper about all this."

Holly was grinning. "Of course, I am, dear. You are a *wonderful* specimen to work on."

Tala's eye twitched again, for entirely different reasons. *Great… I'm her experiment.* Tala supposed it could be worse… somehow.

"Now, as this will take a few sessions, please do not replace your iron, or you'll have to scrub before every session, and that's a waste of everyone's time and resources. Also, the endingberry power within you is unideal. We'll make it work, today, but don't renew it until after we're done."

Tala grunted. *Great. So, I need to walk around with no defense against magic and without one of my physical defenses as well.* She didn't let the fact that she'd already decided not to use her endingberries within the city get in the way of her irritation. "Fair, I suppose."

She did smile as she glanced to the stack of books. She'd planned on visiting a library and eventually purchasing a set of reference volumes for anatomy, physiology, and the like. These were custom to her, along with details on the specific magical inscriptions and alterations she would bear.

And, I'll actually be complete, as a Mage, soon. It was a relieving feeling.

"I do like your ideas for your throat and lungs. Though, again, we'll need to discuss them later."

Tala grinned at that. *Right! So much has been happening that I forgot about making spell-forms within my lungs…* She shook her head. *My lists need better organization. That's a pretty big thing to fall by the wayside.* She walked forward, sitting in the chair beside the new device and slipping her arm inside.

Holly walked over and held out the tablet once more. It now contained both the agreed to transaction, thirteen and a half ounces gold, and authorization for Holly to access, alter, and implement her inscriptions.

"Looks good, I suppose. Let's do this." She pricked her left ring finger, after withdrawing her defensive powers, and allowed a drop of blood to confirm the agreement.

Holly nodded. "Very well, let's get to work. Please pull the endingberry power back from that arm."

The device responded, whether to Holly's words or the signed contract, Tala didn't know. An inner sleeve tightened around her arm, all the way up, past her shoulder and around each individual finger.

The needles began soundlessly moving into position.

"Now, I've made a couple of changes. Mainly, I wanted you to be able to activate your Crush and Restraint magics with either hand." She held up her own hand to stop Tala's objections. "This will not negate other spell-forms being available to your left hand. In fact, I intend to make your right hand able to use those as well, once we decide which to use. I have several ideas that we should discuss. One, in particular, seems perfect, but not now. We will do your left-hand workings after your internals. So... in a week?"

The needles seemed to have gotten into position because they all plunged inward simultaneously.

Tala jerked despite herself, but her arm was held quite immobile, and there wasn't any pain. Still, the visual of seeing them all jab inward had startled her.

I shouldn't have watched...

Then, the pain came.

She remembered the feeling of her bones breaking; dozens of times in the academy training grounds and many times since. This felt like that, throughout every bone from her shoulder to her fingertips.

She screamed, feeling something try to tear in her throat, only prevented by the endingberry power within her. It took all her willpower to keep that power away from her arm, though she wasn't sure how much it would have helped.

Before her scream had even started, the needles had retracted, moved ever so slightly, and jammed in again. And again. And again. It seemed that there would be dozens of jabs, per needle, per second. *How can they work that fast?* If she had been in a better place, she might have laughed at the silly question. *Magic, of course.*

Holly helpfully put a leather tube in Tala's mouth for her to bite down on. Tala glared at the woman but bit down.

Terry, for his part, flickered to Tala's lap, staring up at Holly, then glancing to Tala with an obvious question.

Between excruciating pulses, the needles now looking more like waves as each moved independently, Tala seriously considered unleashing the terror bird on Holly, but finally, she thought better of it, giving an almost imperceptible shake of her head.

Terry let out a breath that could only be considered a disappointed, confused sigh and curled up on her lap.

Inscriptions formed remarkably quickly, taking less than a minute before those in her bones were complete.

Her power immediately rushed through them, and the bone reknit itself around the inscriptions, locking the precious gold into place.

Only gold. Always active.

The needles didn't stop, however, as they slowly moved outward, meticulously inscribing every layer.

The torture device worked its way outward, moving through her muscles, tendons, and other mid-level tissue. Her arm remained locked in place, completely unable to shift or in any way ruin the precision of the inscribing.

The needles finished with the muscle and other mid-layers of the inscriptions, but those didn't activate. Apparently, Holly had left off the connection scripts for some reason.

Tala growled, mumbling around the leather tube she was still biting down upon. "Why didn't the mid-layer activate?" Since she couldn't move her right arm, she gestured towards the constantly moving device with her head. *Sewing machine! It looks like nearly two hundred sewing machines...* The thought didn't help.

Holly shook her own head, hair bobbing. "We have to wait until the inscriptions around your shoulder are complete, or when the muscle inscriptions activate, you might tear your own arm off."

That... sounded unpleasant. Tala stopped complaining, though tears had begun to leak from her eyes, and she couldn't control the occasional whimper. *The endingberry power would likely prevent my arm from damaging itself... but I'm pulling that back, out of the way.* Much better to avoid that possibility.

The needles continued their methodical action, quickly refreshing, altering, and augmenting her highest levels of inscriptions, including her enhancements, defenses, regenerative scripts, and her active offensive magics. Everything she could feel was gold, except the connections for her offensive spell-forms. *Don't want those powered all the time.*

Less than five minutes after the process had started, it was over. Her arm was released from the sleeve, and Tala ripped it free, cradling it against her chest.

Holly examined Tala's arm, even going so far as to slap Tala's left hand to get her to let go, so Holly could stretch out Tala's right arm for full inspection. "Yes. Good. It perfectly modified for the indicated increase in muscle tone. Very nicely done." She glanced up, momentarily meeting Tala's gaze. "Nicely done, Mistress Tala. We can move to the next limb whenever you're ready. Your body's use of endingberries has primed it to receive these specific inscriptions wonderfully."

Tala found herself shaking her head, feeling a little dizzy. "No. That was *not* nice... You aren't a very nice person..." The leather tube had fallen away from her mouth at some point.

"But I am an effective one." Holly smiled as she continued to examine Tala's arm, poking and examining it from every angle.

Tala just groaned in response. She closed her eyes, bracing against the continued throbbing in her arm. *Oh, right.* She had been holding back her own power from the deeper layers, along with the endingberries'. Now, she allowed power to flow through her uppermost regenerative scripts, and the pain from that top layer vanished, her flesh tightening around, and integrating with, the inscriptions. The skin across her entire arm began glowing, if subtly. It almost looked like she had gone out to get a tan and had brought back some of the sun with her. *Great, the joys of always active surface inscriptions.*

There were three more limbs to do, then her torso.

Tala took deep breaths. This was far from over.

Chapter: 30
Understatement

As Tala did her best to mentally prepare for the next steps, she found the continued pain distracting. "Can I activate the mid-layers?"

Holly was maneuvering the torturous contraption but glanced towards her face while answering. "Hmmm? Sure. The work on your shoulder is fully finished, after all. I thought you already had."

Tala decided it was best to not comment. Power blossomed through Tala's arm, and the pain was washed away as her flesh knit together around the inscriptions. She looked down at her own arm, marveling at how strong it felt, while still being under her control. The glow from her skin had lessened, the excess power now being pulled deeper.

I wonder if the glow means a lack of efficiency? If so, this full set was almost perfectly efficient, only the barest hints of illumination still visible. If anything, it looked like the glow was directed inward.

I'll be visible in the dark, but I don't think I'll illuminate anything around me.

All parts of her arm's biology were increased in perfect proportion, so there wasn't any change in how it responded or how it moved. Even so, she felt like there was more force behind each gesture.

Her head snapped up as something slid over her left arm, locking in place before she could react. "What!? Now? I thought you said we could wait until I was ready."

"Now is best, dear. You're ready." She stuck the leather tube between Tala's teeth, cleared her throat, and addressed the machine. "Begin."

The process of pain and delayed relief repeated itself on her left side, though Tala was able to activate the mid-layer of regenerative scripts more quickly this second time.

Then, hesitantly, Tala agreed to have her legs done. The device of madness was slipped over the first leg, covering from her toes to the top of her hip.

Lyn cleared her throat. "This is fascinating, but I think I've seen enough... I'll... I'll wait in the outer room?"

Tala nodded weakly, taking in the woman's pale complexion. "Not fun to watch; I understand."

Lyn smiled with shame-faced regret before fleeing.

Holly cleared her throat. "I want to add some things to your legs as well, though not at this time. I want you to be more anchored when you need to be, and I want to discuss ideas. I need to grasp what you will be able to enact, and I don't have a full understanding of your limitations, yet."

Tala grunted and didn't really have anything else to add. *Eloquent, Tala.*

Holly smiled, patting her non-encapsulated hip. "Begin." The inscription machine tightened, locking her leg, even her individual toes, into perfect immobility as the needles began their work.

Five minutes later, Tala was barely aware of Holly switching legs. Terry was sitting on a chair in the corner, clearly no longer enjoying her lap. "Sorry, Terry... I'll be done... soon."

"Begin."

And agony began anew.

This time, the pain left immediately as the needles finished each layer, the interconnecting scripts activating as soon as they were complete. Even so, echoes of pain sent twitches through her enhanced nervous system.

Holly moved the contraption after it finished with Tala's last leg, manipulating it to open wide enough for Tala to slip it up, over both her legs and higher, further over her torso. Tala stood, lifting her arms above her head, so it could come high enough.

"Bind."

The device locked the inner lining around Tala but didn't begin. Its encapsulation went around each shoulder, closing around the base of her neck but leaving it and her head bare. It also wrapped around her upper legs, holding her up and allowing no room for escape. "Holly?" Tala's voice was a bit raw, even with the earlier protection of her throat. Tala had pulled the endingberry power into her right hand, what little of it was left.

"There are two things special about this portion. First, I have increased the inscriptions for... support, both muscular and elsewise, around your chest. You will never need a corset. That's for sure." Holly laughed a bit to herself. "I wish I had the fortitude for these inscriptions myself." She smiled and winked.

Tala grunted. *Yeah... why do I feel like that was intended to distract me?* "Second?"

"Hmmm?"

"What is the second thing?" Tala forced out.

"Oh! Yes. Well, we've been doing inscriptions in all your soft tissue, fat, vessels, arteries, capillaries, et cetera, but in your torso, there is quite a bit of movement from your involuntary muscles that I just can't be sure we'll account for accurately."

Tala found herself frowning. "What does that mean?"

Holly smiled, placing a cool object against the back of Tala's neck. "Sleep, child."

Tala immediately lost all sensation below her neck, but before panic could set in, a deep, dreamless sleep took her from the world of the conscious.

* * *

Tala woke to a soothing hand, brushing her hair off her forehead.

"Time to wake up, Mistress Tala." The voice was soft, welcoming, comforting.

Tala groaned and tried to get up, but she couldn't move. Her eyes snapped open in a panic, and she looked up at Holly's workshop ceiling, her head hanging backward. "Gah!" She felt herself beginning to panic.

"Mistress Tala. Please, control yourself. Before I release the block at your neck, I need you fully conscious."

Tala growled, glaring in the general direction the woman's voice had come from. "I'm not very happy about being paralyzed, *Mistress* Holly."

"You will recover. As I think you would care to know this: I had to stop your heart, briefly, for the inscriptions on that muscle group, and your diaphragm, to be done. No damage resulted from the arrest, and as you can see, you are quite alive."

Tala's eye twitched. *You have to be rusting kidding me...* "So, why am I still paralyzed?" After a moment, she growled again. "And why couldn't you have knocked me out like this for my limbs?"

"You see, the nature of most of your inscriptions required *very* specific integrations with your keystone as well as your mind."

She decided to reword her second question. "You just knocked me out for my torso. Why couldn't you have done that for my limbs?"

Holly sighed. "For many Mages, for other inscriptions, I could do just that. In fact, that is likely how this might be worth using. For you, though"—she clucked her tongue—"your power density *rises* when you are unconscious. It is to the point that I don't trust fragments of spell-forms won't be activated if you are so infused. In addition, we needed the spell-forms to be seamlessly accepted by your mind. Once your limbs were complete, they served as both an outlet for that excess power and a platform for connection to your mind."

Tala grunted. She didn't really grasp what the issue would have been, but arguing now seemed pointless. "So… why was my torso different?"

Holly gave her a flat look. "You will understand in a moment, dear. When this comes off, you will feel much, which your body will interpret as pain. Your body is too robust to be deceived about the alterations."

Sounds like a fake reason… But Tala was tired. *I just want to go home, go to bed.* "Fine… let's just get it over—"

Holly pulled the stone away from the back of Tala's neck, and an avalanche of pain tore through Tala's torso. It wasn't pain in the traditional sense; Holly had been right about that. More than anything, it felt like her entire torso was trying to tell her, all at once, that *something* had been done to her. Someone had fundamentally altered her being.

And her 'self' hated it.

She involuntarily threw her head back and let out a single pulse of a scream that shredded her vocal cords, utterly. The endingberry power was still sequestered so was of no help.

The regenerative scripts in her neck activated, and her voice was restored in time to vocalize her first whimpers before she slid out from inside the automatic inscriber and vomited towards the hard floor.

It was long minutes before Tala became aware of her surroundings again, but Holly was kneeling beside her, holding Tala's hair and a bucket. The hair was to one side, and the bucket was directly below Tala's mouth. It had even caught her first retch.

Terry was pressed firmly against Tala's other side, and somehow, Tala knew he was glaring at Holly over her back.

"There, there, Mistress Tala. You'll be alright, now. The first time is always the worst for inscriptions."

Tala's whole body shuddered, and she felt a coldness settle into her core. She began to shiver.

Holly wiped Tala's mouth with a cloth, helping her stand and stagger over to a nearby chair, where a waiting warm blanket was draped over her. A large mug of mint tea settled into her hands.

Tala glared. *She knew. She* knew *it would be like this.* But Tala couldn't gather the energy to accuse the inscriber, at least not at the moment.

Instead, she glared.

As she glared, the focus was intent enough to activate her magesight. Power swirled around Holly, just as before, but now, Tala was used to the sight. She was ready for the influx of information, and she knew what the underlying yellow aura meant.

She croaked out one word. "Refined."

Holly paused momentarily, then sighed and continued her work. "Yes, dear. I am an Archon."

Tala glowered. "Why hide it?"

"I didn't, but there is also no reason to overwhelm others' magesight with one's power. It is polite to veil oneself. My workshop contains my aura, so I let it flow more freely. This is a sanctuary. A place I can let my hair down, so to speak."

Tala was feeling better by the moment, and she looked around, seeing Kit on the chair beside her. She reached in, grabbed the iron vial, which she felt a slight connection to, and tossed it to Holly. Holly, seeming bemused, caught it. Tala felt herself smile, if only slightly. "Open it. Liquid inside."

Holly sighed but nodded, righting the vial and carefully opening it. She looked inside and froze, shock clearly evident across her features. Power rippled across the woman's face, activating her magesight. "Child... That cannot be..." She blinked, moving the vial closer to her face. "But it is... is it in blood?" She glanced up at Tala, then back into the vial. "Mistress Tala, who taught you this?" She held up the vial, demanding an explanation.

"I stumbled across it."

"In what book? The curators will be hearing from me if—"

Tala was shaking her head. "No, not a book. I was experimenting, and the form just felt *right*."

Holly stopped her tirade and looked back into the vial. "No one suggested it? Implied it? Nudged you along? You didn't encounter an oddly friendly stranger in the wilds and began doing unusual things thereafter?"

"No?" *That last one was oddly specific...*

Holly grunted, looking back into the vial. "Well, rust my biscuits."

Tala snorted a laugh. "What does that even mean?"

"Hush. Do you know what *this* means?" She lifted the contained Archon Star.

Tala shrugged. "What you just said? No. That's why I asked."

Holly gave her an unamused look.

"Fine." Tala grunted. "It will mean I can be considered for Archon, once I make a stronger one."

Holly opened her mouth, then closed it. "Well... good. Some things are as they should be."

So, not quite correct, then? Interesting.

Holly's eyes moved to the knife lying beside Kit. "But clearly, you know some."

Tala nodded. "I know some. Master Grediv advised I not soul-bond with anything else until I reached certain thresholds."

Holly snorted this time, shaking her head. "Fool of a man. I would bet you've almost met his meager thresholds?" She gave Tala a rather intense look. "You're almost to them, right?"

Tala hesitated, then nodded. "I am." *She's going to try to stop me.* Tala had already agreed to wait, but she still wanted to rebel against even the implied restrictions. *That's not a wise reaction, Tala. Listen to the wisdom of the Archons.*

"You would be wise to put your energy into making a properly powered star." She looked into the vial, again. "This shouldn't be possible, and I know some elders would be in a *fit* if you came up for consideration based on this." She clicked her tongue a few times. "How long did it take you to make this?"

Why lie? That was the stronger of the two she had with her. "Four hours." The other, which she'd made in one hour, still rested inside Kit.

Holly's head snapped up. "You've been improving your flowrate?" She nodded to herself. "Right. My mind has been thrown by all this. We increased your continually active scripts precisely because of your improved flowrate." She shook her head. "I must be getting old. I recalculated your scripts based on the new measurements, myself." She continued to mutter, but Tala was having trouble focusing.

Her head felt stuffed with cotton, and her whole body tingled with something akin to after-images of pain. "Can I go?"

Holly stopped her pacing and glanced Tala's way. "Can you?"

Tala frowned, then sighed. She pushed herself upright, using more effort than usual because of the expected weight of the blanket. She vaulted up, her head tapping into the ceiling.

She came crashing down, arms pin-wheeling to try to regain balance.

She didn't succeed, falling flat on her face.

A groan issued from her lips as she lay on the floor. It didn't hurt, not really, but it did make her feel quite disoriented. *Yeah, I'm glad that this wasn't coupled with the sense enhancements...*

With careful effort, Tala pushed herself up. Even so, she moved from horizontal to standing in one motion, her feet acting as a pivot point.

"Mistress Holly...?"

"Yes, dear?"

"This seems... more powerful than I expected."

"Of course, we were just discussing your increased power density and flowrate. All your inscriptions were adjusted as allowed for by your new levels." She fell back into the tone of a lecturer. "Remember, the muscle enhancements, including those for regeneration and development, will not allow bulking, though you will still grow in strength with proper exercise." She shook her head, a frown painting her features. "I've never understood why some people try to grow in such... odd proportions. Such a radical change in your shape would force a redesign of your scripts and be altogether too much work." She gave

Tala a meaningful look. "You were heading that way already before we stopped it here."

Well, there is that, at least. She'd forgotten that detail, though she did remember discussing it with Holly, and the particulars made sense. "Gold scripts, right?"

"Yes. As it stands, we should refresh you every six months, just to be safe. Doing so will also remove almost all of the pain and discomfort as it won't be introducing new points of inscription, simply reinforcing the existing lines."

Tala grunted. She turned her concentration to her own body, slowly, carefully, going through some basic movements, getting her body used to its new strength. In less than a quarter hour, she had it mostly acclimated. She placed the books Holly had prepared for her into Kit and sighed. "Mistress Lyn is waiting for me."

Holly looked up from the slate she'd been examining. "Hmm?"

Did… did she forget I was here?

"Quite right. Run along, now. We can do a few organs a day." She clicked her tongue. "Come by each evening around sunset. Yes? Don't forget to read up."

Tala groaned, moving towards the door.

Holly cleared her throat, and Tala glanced back, freezing in place at what she saw. Holly was standing perfectly still, her aura *visible* to Tala's unaided vision. "That was not a suggestion, Mistress Tala. You will be here each evening if I have to come and retrieve you myself."

Tala's eyes widened, and she swallowed involuntarily. "Yes… Yes. I will be here."

Holly smiled, returning her eyes to her slate, the palpable power around the woman vanishing as if it had never been. "Good. See you tomorrow. Be sure to eat. Your body is essentially rebuilding and reinforcing itself with a new blueprint. No skimping!"

Tala rushed from the room, only tripping a few times as her body continued to adjust, Terry already back on her shoulder.

Lyn was waiting for Tala in the outermost room of the workshop. "You smell... Did you vomit? Was that you I heard scream?" Lyn was a bit pale as she quickly came to Tala's side.

An assistant came forward with a wet cloth and some water.

Tala wiped her face once again and drank the water, thanking the young man.

Turning to Lyn, Tala sighed, leaning against the woman a bit. "Let's get out of here... I have to come back tomorrow, and I already feel like I've been here too often and too long."

Lyn simply nodded, walking with her out into the early evening.

After they were a few blocks from the inscriber's workshop, Lyn nudged Tala. "Want dinner? I know we already had some of Gretel's pies, but..."

Tala did, but she really didn't feel like going anywhere, right now. "Yes? But I just want to go home... Is that okay? I'm really, really hungry, though..."

Lyn smiled comfortingly. "Sure thing. It seemed like that wasn't... great."

"Understatement."

Lyn smiled wanly, guiding them towards home.

Lyn and Tala walked in near silence through the streets, making only a single stop to grab a few meat and veggie skewers for Tala as they walked. Tala ate them with ravenous speed. Shortly thereafter, they arrived at Lyn's house.

Tala produced her own iron key, stuck it into the lock, and twisted. The metal groaned, and Tala let up on the pressure before she distorted anything.

"Heh, sorry about that." Tala moved more carefully and unlocked the door, causing Lyn to smile broadly, even as she shook her head.

"Welcome home, Mistress Tala."

Inside, Tala wiped her feet on the mat and walked in to find six large packages sitting in the middle of the living room floor. The outside of each was waxed cloth, clearly meant to protect and preserve whatever was inside. Heavy cord bound each parcel tightly.

Lyn was frowning at the small pile, clearly confused as well, and Tala noticed a note on the top, so she walked forward and took it up.

> 'Mistress Tala,
> It seems that you departed before I could pass into your care the jerky from Master Rane's harvests. I have sent it along to your residence with good Guardsman Ashin. I hope to see you again, soon. If the good master asks, his dimensional duffel was sent with Guardsman Adam, who indicated a pre-arranged meeting with Master Rane.
> -Brand'

A second hand had written another note, below:

> 'Mistress Tala,
> Who in their right mind needs twelve *hundred* pounds of jerky? This was not easy to deliver. I would appreciate being able to compensate the workers who helped me move it—for their time and the use of their carts.
> -Ashin'

Tala snorted. The packages were large, but thankfully, they looked like they would fit through Kit's opening.

Terry appeared next to the large bundles. "Hey, none of that. We need to be sparing, and that isn't yours until I give it to you."

Terry gave her a contemplative look. Finally, he squawked out a low huff and blinked back to her shoulder.

Shaking her head, Tala took off the belt pouch, opening it on the ground... and looked down at the tops of nearly four dozen massive feathers. "Right... I need to deal with these." *What can I do with the jerky, then?*

"Is that a dimensional storage?" Lyn came closer and looked. "Fascinating. I don't see any spell-lines. It is an artifact, right?"

Of course, she would know about artifacts. We have discussed them before, right? "Yes..."

"How much power does it take each day?"

Tala shrugged. "Not much? I just have to remember." With the thought in her mind, she topped off all her items quickly. She'd fed them before arriving in Bandfast, while in the farmland, but thought it wise to keep them as full as possible.

Lyn was nodding. "Those look like arcanous harvests in there. Did you need to sell them?"

"Actually, I was thinking of doing a merging spell-working, to draw their power and potential into another item."

Lyn looked at her, a bit confused. "That's not a cheap or simple spell-form, Mistress Tala."

Tala groaned. "Do we have to 'Mistress' each other?"

A smile tugged at Lyn's lips. "No. I suppose not."

"You aren't wrong, you know. I was considering doing the spell-form myself, but I *really* don't want to get it wrong. It's likely worth going through the Constructionist Guild..."

"Do you need a connection? Or do you want to just approach their offices yourself?"

Tala perked up. "I'd love an introduction." She smiled. "Thank you."

Lyn smiled. "I am happy to help."

Tala stretched, feeling the kinks in her back. "Oh..." She groaned. Then, she had a realization. "Oh!"

Lyn looked around in alarm, trying to find what Tala was reacting to, but she didn't find anything.

"Lyn. Lyn! Do you know a place for body work?"

"Body... work? Do you mean massage?"

"Yes. I have *terrible* knots in my muscles... everywhere."

Lyn cocked an eyebrow. "You're going to need someone with inscribed hands, now, I'd wager."

Tala thought for a moment and groaned. "You're probably right."

"Or... a hammer and chisel?"

Tala snorted a laugh. "At this point, either way."

"You know, I'm not really your manager..."

"Aren't you, though?"

Lyn pursed her lips. "No? Well... I guess sort of." She grunted. "Fine. I'll help you, but as a friend. Not because it's my job."

"Fair enough. Thank you."

"Early afternoon? To finish before you return to Mistress Holly's shop?"

Tala felt an involuntary shudder at the name. *Odd...* "I suppose that would be best, yeah."

Without thinking, Tala grabbed one of the packages and hoisted it up onto her shoulder. Lyn stepped forward and grabbed one of the cords binding together another package. "Oh, let me help you." She pulled upward, but the thing barely moved. "What the rust?" She glanced at Tala, easily holding it on her shoulder. "How heavy is that?"

Tala frowned, shifting under the weight. It *was* heavy but still perfectly manageable. "No idea? Thirty or forty pounds?" She shifted again. *I have been training...* "Maybe fifty?"

Lyn shook her head. "Didn't you just have your strength augmented?"

Tala blinked back at her. *Right.* "Yes... I did. What I meant is that it feels like that much. No idea what it actually weighs." *Twelve hundred pounds, six packages.* "Two hundred pounds?"

Lyn tried to budge a parcel, again. "I think you're right; that has to be around two hundred pounds." She looked towards her door. "How *did* they get it in here?"

"Well, Ashin has a key, but for the load... teamwork?"

Lyn grunted.

Tala took six trips. *How tightly did they bind this?* Each parcel practically felt like a solid block, but she could feel some individuality within, meaning it had likely been cured in small pieces before being compacted into these monstrosities.

Once the final one was stacked in the front corner of her room, she stood up and stretched once more. *I'm really going to get my money's worth out of that massage...*

She looked around herself, taking in the simple room.

Terry was curled up on her bed. *My bed.*

There was a shelf against the wall to the left of the door and a writing desk under the window that she didn't really remember, but she hadn't truly spent much time in here. Smiling, she walked in, taking a notebook and pencil out of Kit and setting them in the center of the writing desk.

She looked around. *It's so bare in here...*

Lyn had likely not wanted to put anything personal in here as it was to be someone else's room. She took out a hatchet and knife, setting each on the desk, attempting to make them look intentional.

She shifted them a few times, stepping back to look.

After a short time, she rolled her eyes, laughing at her own attempts. "They're tools, not decorations, Tala." *And they are reminders of Terry's murder spree on my behalf...* Was that a good memory or bad? She didn't know.

Only time would tell.

I don't need to think about that now. Now, I just need to make a properly powered Archon Star. That shouldn't be too difficult. She rolled her eyes again at her own optimism even as she smiled at the challenge ahead.

Author's Note

Thank you for taking your time to read my quirky magical tale.

If you have the time, a review of the book can help share this world with others, and I would greatly appreciate it.

To listen to this or other books in this series, please find them on mountaindalepress.store or Audible. Release dates vary.

To continue reading for yourself, check out Kindle Unlimited for additional titles. If this is the last one released for the moment, you can find the story available on RoyalRoad.com for free. Simply search for Millennial Mage. You can also find a direct link from my Author's page on Amazon.

There are quite a few other fantastic works by great authors available on RoyalRoad as well, so take a look around while you're there!

Thank you, again, for sharing in this strange and beautiful magical world with Tala. I sincerely hope that you enjoyed it.

Regards,
J.L. Mullins